nu luna

n u l u n a

Andrew Biscontini

a # new texture book
www.NewTexture.com

If you enjoy this book, tell someone about it.

A New Texture book

Wyatt Doyle, Editor

Copyright © 2013 Andrew Biscontini

Cover photo © 2012 Andrew Biscontini

Illustration copyright © 2013 Bodie Chewning

All Rights Reserved.

Book design and layout by Andy Biscontini with Wyatt Doyle

Editorial Consultant: Sandee Curry / SandeeCurry.com

www.nulunaverse.com

www.NewTexture.com

Booksellers: nu luna and other New Texture books are available through Ingram Book Company

ISBN 978-0-9827239-9-9

First New Texture Edition: April 2013

Printed in the United States of America

10 9 8 7 6 5 4 3 2 1

contents

1. SCHICKARD CITY HEARTBREAK

seen from a distance, the Colony was beautiful.

Especially on autumn nights when it rose low, full and bright over the skyline across the river, the air over the Weehawken canals was damp and cool and the breeze kept the bad smells down in the industrial tier, Manhattan's terraced levels reached up from the glassy Hudson and everything shined with electric and reflected light, dusk busy with swarms of small aircraft moving in unruly pulses at the mixed tempo of traffic buoys, and there above it all was the Colony, shining like a hole punched through the night, a portal into the future, atmospheric zones a hazy constellation of pink and blue and orange and gray dots scattered across the glowing white disk of the moon.

Sanjit Ramirez's first impression of it had formed on such a night in 2489 when he was not yet two years old. His family had gathered around one of the communal barbecue pits along the parkbelt at the eastern edge of the third tier, having made the trek up and over by platform and tram from their neighborhood on the west side of the second, for the view over the shipyards' cranes and the convenience of older relatives whose retirement units were nearby. One of his mother's crewmates from the gantries, frequently present at family events, had brought a telescope and trained it on the moon as it cleared the city's towers and spires and the kids had all clustered around it. His oldest sister Mena, ten at the time, hoisted him up on her hip so he could get a view of the screen over the other curious young heads.

The spidery image he saw there reminded him of the paper snowflakes taped to the window next to the sprawling loft bed in which he slept each night among a soft network of blankets and pillows, brothers and sisters, cousins and mother and friends, the first thing he saw each morning as he woke, squinting through sleep-covered eyes into the interlocking layers of scissor-cut symmetries and transparent tape a shade darker against the glass than the pale dawn.

"I don't see nothing," Pe, seven years old but physically the smallest aside from him, pushed her way to the front.

"Yeah, you do," Aki, a year and a half younger than Mena, had never suffered Pe gladly.

"I don't."

"It's the way the screen's pointed," Mena said, right behind his ear, "she can't see because the screen."

He balanced his weight against the top of her thigh and craned his neck to keep his view as she twisted and reached between Pe and a sloe-eyed kid who'd wandered over from somebody else's barbecue. Her finger paused at the edge of the screen's frame with the abrupt remembrance of her manners and her mother's proximity, "Mister, can I touch this?" With nodded permission, she tilted the swivel of the screen out and down towards Pe, disrupting everyone else's viewing angle.

Pe studied it and after too long shrugged and said: "I still don't see nothing," drawing a collective groan.

"She does too," Aki snapped, pulling the screen back to its original angle and shooting a quick guilty glance toward the preoccupied adults, "she sees the same thing we all see she just don't know what she's looking at."

"Because it don't look like nothing!"

"Of course it doesn't look like *nothing*," Molo confided to him in a staccato aside. Five years his senior, Molo had designated him by chance or reasons unknown to be the audience for everything he felt deserved to be spoken but to which he expected no one to listen, "Because it's not *nothing*, it's *something*. It might not look like *anything*, but it's *definitely something*."

"It's one of the cities," one of the older boys.

"Yeah, duh," chimed Aki.

"What one?" Pe suspected a set-up.

"Tycho," after the briefest of uncertain pauses.

"Copernicus," the crane operator's reedy voice rose above the chatter from the circle of grownups on lawn chairs.

"Oh, yeah…Copiiii…" a mixed chime of feigned and genuine confirmation.

"Yeah, Copi!" Aki gloated, overdoing it a little, "See?"

"No it's not!" Pe felt she knew her Colonial landmarks as well as anyone, "Copi has the big twisty thing in the middle, all bent around itself like −" she twisted her arms around each other in a simultaneous architectural demonstration and display of flexibility, "− and they look all like triangles and like." She knew the Colonial megacities from the same school-issue sims they all did, in which the point of view never rose above thirty degrees or so.

In fact, few of them had ever had a view of anything above rooftop level, simulated or actual. Plan view was absent from their culture and their daily lives. They learned their way around their district by sign, rote and daily habit; its boundaries defined their reality. For most of them, the closest thing they'd had to an aerial perspective was on the Platform ride up to the third tier for barbecues, in the glimpse of other streets and alleys and parklets, like theirs but different, between the rooftops of their tier and the trussed girding of the third.

"You're looking at it from above," Mena, who had gone on a class trip to the upper tiers of Manhattan and looked back at the shipyards and stacked neighborhoods she knew, "so it's not gonna look like it looks in the vids."

If they hadn't already, the others tumbled quickly into the new and unaccustomed viewpoint but Pe stuck to her guns, earning a sidelong eye-roll from Molo, which always made him smile.

"You're telling me that's supposed to be the bottom of Copi?!"

"No stupid," Aki had lost all patience, "that's the *top*."

"But I'm looking *up* at it," Pe refused to be bullied.

"And if them up there looked *up*," Aki made no effort to soften her voice, "they'd be looking *down* at you. *Duh*."

Disappointed in herself at missing something so apparently obvious, Pe scowled, shoved the twins out of her way and stormed off, never again admitting any interest in the doings of the Colony or, for that matter, anything that anyone else seemed in any way interested in.

Sanjit clutched his sister's shoulder and gazed at the soft matte image on the screen, letting it become distinct from the paper snowflakes in his mind as the sounds around him laid the foundation for the concepts and phenomena into whose midst he'd been, he still felt, so rudely thrust, which he would soon effortlessly and unquestioningly come to classify as the world and the Colony.

Despite growing up through two decades during which the Colony was omnipresent in image and name, the residual memory of that night had never before risen above the lazy delta-wave fog around his thalamus. Although it had remained more or less intact, he experienced it only as a faint signature on the screen of his being, quietly shedding a vaguely melancholic half-life until, suddenly, twenty-two years later, it shot into his sensory centers as the back of his head hit the edge of the stair, triggering an instantaneous and immersive re-experience in visceral completeness and depth of detail, over and forgotten in milliseconds, followed by complete disorientation.

Based on the sequence of impacts against his body, he deduced that he was tumbling backwards down a staircase, but by the time he figured it out he'd come to a tangled and undignified stop, wedged between the second-bottom step and the front door of Naeemah's townhouse unit in Schickard City, so named after Crater Schickard, the shallow impact crater in the southwestern Near lowlands across which it sprawled. The speckled roses he'd picked up on his way into town lay crumpled on the floor next to his head. If they smelled like anything, he couldn't tell. He tasted blood and pain came from everywhere.

"Crap," a man's voice from the top of the stairs.

"Nice," another man's voice, sarcastic, "Awesome. Very nice. Killing an unarmed technician. They dock you half a year for that."

"He took a swing at me. You saw it."

"Unarmed," a woman's voice, "And unaugmented. Automatic penalty. Bummer."

"Self-defense anyway. Besides, he's not dead."

"If he lives and can't work they dock you *two* years *and* they demote you."

It was true that he'd taken a swing, but only in the Byzantine Colonial bureaucracy could he possibly be deemed any kind of threat to a trio of heavily augmented Municipal Constables, even on his mightiest, most furious day. If he'd put any sort of thought into it whatsoever, he wouldn't have done it. But he'd been on the road for eighty-seven hours straight, white-knuckled on the wheel of a heavy transport rig, napping for three and four hours at a stretch when he could sleep at all, fueled by a self-prescribed regimen of Moonborn-grown herbal stimulants, the names of which he couldn't pronounce, let alone keep track of the side effects.

In hindsight, they'd almost certainly influenced the profound urgency behind the consuming notion that now was the time to finally visit Naeemah, when it involved a thousand-kilometer detour, fully loaded, and it'd earn him a missed-delivery penalty that would set him back more than he'd made on his last two runs. Regardless, he'd driven straight through from the Orientale basin in a mental fever.

The secondary roads were too narrow for his rig so he left it parked on an access road below an elevated beltway and found his way to her place in a daze; wandering by foot, bus and tram through the terraced mazes of new and old residential and industrial districts. The city was a mess of half-assed terraforming, unfinished construction and ad-hoc civil engineering under an acrid pink sky. There were entire neighborhoods where the mass-concentrated substrate, intended to imitate the pull of Earth's gravity, had settled unevenly and left the streets and sidewalks potholed and cracked. Midway down a pitted block he would suddenly feel as if he were slogging through invisible quicksand, only to trip over an invisible gravity-swell on the other side.

Her address – *17-6 Mapleberry D, 0098 SC 036* – became a totem, circling his mind in clumsily harmonized rounds until he found himself in the midst of sloping faux-terraformed streets surrounded by identical semi-detached vinyl Tudoresques he recognized from his last visit. Even as he found himself staring at the number on the door, the mental cadence wouldn't cease, rolling over and over itself as he used the keycard she'd given him when he helped her move in, pressing it into his palm and telling him he was the only person on the moon she could imagine being glad to see.

Only when he stepped across the threshold did the refrain cut out, and he could hear the sounds from the top of the stairs. The humming orgonic energy in the place permeated his soft tissue.

Somewhere in some part of his brain he knew he should leave, just step back outside and walk away, and he was envisioning doing exactly that as he climbed the stairs, each gasped breath and clap of flesh clearer with each step until he stood in her bedroom doorway, watching her go at it with two men and a woman, all with scarred and shaven heads and taut augmented muscles. Their choreography was clearly oriented toward her pleasure. She clutched at them and pulled them in, pressed herself into them. The ferocious ecstatic thrill on her face abruptly emptied into shock as her eyes fell on Sanjit.

One of her partners was off of her and in his face in seconds, "Who the fuck are you? How the fuck did you get in here?"

He stared past him, numb, as the other two disengaged themselves and stood behind their comrade.

"He asked you a question, asshole."

Sanjit knew well the consequences of what he was about to do, but didn't realize he was actually doing it until it was too late.

"He asked me *two* questions, asshole," he snarled, and let fly with his right fist, which his target ducked easily. His knuckle almost nearly grazed the man's chin.

So here he was, a tangle of bruises at the bottom of the stairs. Was that his knee blocking his vision? If so, which?

"Easy there, little amigo," he felt a pair of hands on his ankles, gently pulling his legs straight. The woman, hastily half-dressed in the uniform of a Municipal Constable, stood over him, scanning him with opalescent eye implants, "Nasty sprain on your right ankle. Snapped your left radius clean through. Couple teeth on their way out. Good bone density, though! Somebody's been eating his ice cream!"

The one who'd sent him flying stood halfway down the stairs, shirtless and hoisting his suspenders. The third, stark naked, pushed past and came to a stop on the step just above Sanjit. Sweat-slicked endodermal circuitry reflected the pale sunlight from the front window, striating his body from head to toe, including the enormous erection that stood like a crooked exclamation point above his stainless-steel scrotum. His shaven head was criss-crossed with cogjob micro-scars.

Naeemah appeared at the top of the stairs. She'd pulled a sheet around her shoulders like a cape, doing nothing to conceal her nakedness, still shockingly beautiful even though her skin looked sallow and she'd lost muscle tone. Her hair was cut short and slick with sweat and through it he could see a patina of micro-scars. It looked like she'd gotten another couple cogs installed. Her eyes were still real, but they were glassy and vacant like a cog-junky's, her movements slow and distant.

He pushed himself upright with his unbroken arm and propped himself against the wall. His ears felt hot and his head was spinning but he made an effort not to show it.

The naked constable crouched and stared at him. His irises dilated and focused. "Right," he said with a sigh. Then his eyes seemed to defocus, the iris rings spun slowly in opposite directions. "Sanjit."

He felt vulnerable and exposed and humiliated. What was she telling them about him over their cog-link? They doubtless already had all of his background data from the ID radio chip in his right thumb, everything he was and had been down to the last number. But Naeemah knew everything else. Together, they could see right through him, all of him, through his bones and his life and his soul, bare and broken before them.

The one who'd hit him climbed past his naked comrade and stepped over him on his way to the kitchenette while the woman with the opals squeezed around him and out the front door. The naked one stood, his unabated excitement now at eye level, pointing right at him and still smelling of Naeemah. Then he turned and walked upstairs, hopefully, Sanjit thought, to put some pants on.

Naeemah descended and sat on the steps and stared at him, mute, dark eyes far away. He tried to find her in them and for a second maybe thought he saw her but what did that even mean? He looked at her and he no longer saw the person he knew in the person he was looking at. That this person looked so much like her, caricatured as a Colonial waste-case, became too painful, so he looked away.

For a long moment she looked as if she were about to say something, but no sound came past her lips. He tried to talk but when he opened his mouth he sputtered blood and forgot what he'd wanted to say.

How long had it been since he'd seen her? His sense of time had never adjusted to the lunar phases even after – how many years now? – on the moon. It didn't help that his job took him in random circles around the Colony, in and out of the planet's shadow on a 100-hour shift clock. His life was measured in minutes and hours as defined by the CA clock, divided by kilometers and dollars Colonial.

"You should've pinged," the one who'd hit him said, returning from the kitchen with a cup of water.

He'd tried to, a hundred times, but she never responded. The whole reason people got cogjobs was that they were supposed to increase your multi-task capabilities, but even with a direct line to her core consciousness she still never managed to return his calls. Now he wondered if he was supposed to have taken a hint. He took a sip from the cup and blood blossomed in the water.

"It's been eighteen months," the MuniCon said.

Sanjit's stomach dropped. His own longest estimate had been five or six. Had he really lost *a year* to the drudgery of the Colony? Opals returned with a med kit and slid an ice pack between Sanjit's head and the wall, then shot his neck with neuroblockers and set about wrapping his split tongue in medicated gauze, setting his broken forearm and strapping a brace onto his sprained leg.

The blockers kicked in fast and he didn't feel a thing as a cartoonishly huge needle spiked bonepatch nanogens into his arm and leg and four tidy stitches were sewn through his lower lip. When he was finished, the MuniCon tucked a blister pack of yellow-and-orange happy-tablets into his vest pocket and patted it, "You'll want one of these in about an hour. Keep eight or ten hours between them. Take 'em with food. They'll get absorbed without but you'll puke." Both MuniCons watched him for a moment then said in perfect unison: "It really is good to see you, Sanjit."

Their apparent sincerity vaulted past sarcasm into cruelty. The naked one trotted back downstairs in his underwear but still visibly aroused.

Sanjit kept his bleary eyes on the MuniCons so he didn't notice Naeemah's eyes fixed on him, her forehead beaded with sweat. He hadn't a clue that it was taking all of her concentration to hold onto her control of the three of them from deep within the network of coded cognizance which linked their brains through the cog chips in their heads. The shock of seeing him had knocked her off-balance, and the surge of adrenaline in the already testosteroned-out MuniCons made them difficult to reign back in.

"It's not like it was with you," she said through them, in perfect unison as her control grew stronger.

Sanjit stared from one to the other, trying to mask how deeply freaked out he was behind a stern but wary face.

"With them," they said, "its not like it was with you."

Two of them took hold of his torso and lifted him to his feet. He felt like a doll in their precisely controlled augmented grips. The one with the hard-on stepped in close and gazed into his eyes, retinal sensors dilating and spinning. He reached out and held Sanjit's face tenderly in his hands, stroked his rough growth of beard, brushed matted hair from his brow. For an awkwardly long time, Sanjit had the uncomfortable feeling that he was about to be kissed. Then the MuniCon closed his eyes and pressed his forehead against Sanjit's. His breath was hot and sour.

"I'm so sorry," the three of them whispered, close to him.

Suddenly, all of their grips weakened. The one in front of him blinked and backed away fast, confused. The other two stared at him quizzically, then at each other. Naeemah's eyes rolled back and she slumped against the steps, spent. One of the MuniCons knelt next to her, cradling her head and stroking her cheek.

"I think it's about time for you to leave," the hard-on had finally retreated and his eyes stopped spinning, "Rico'll give you a ride back to your vehicle."

Sanjit didn't want a ride from Rico, no matter how much pain he was in. He just wanted to be as far away from the whole situation as possible and he'd prefer to walk away alone and under his own strength, no matter how much it hurt. "Ah goh wamma wihe," was all he could manage with his tongue wrapped in gauze.

"Huh?"

"Ah goh wamma wihe!" he tried again, *"Ah wamma wah."*

The one called Rico shrugged. "Man says he wamma wah, I say let him wah."

HE DIDN'T see any point in waiting an hour to pop one of the happies when he felt so lousy now, so he dry-swallowed the first one before he was halfway down the block, gagging on the gauze around his tongue as he hobbled stiffly through the dodgy gravity on the leg-brace that was supposed to be shifting the weight off his ankle to his upper leg.

The condition of her neighborhood had considerably improved since his last visit, especially by the Colony's crappy standards. He remembered the cladding on the houses blistered and melted, more solar panels cracked or missing than not, astro-turf lawns worn away, charred black or sunbleached white, littered with polycarbonate junk and obsolete engine parts. There were still plastic boards over the windows and doors of foreclosed or abandoned units, but all belied evidence of a thriving, if discreet, squatter population.

The pink sky shined harsh under the dull, shifting matrix of the particle net. The air stung his throat and his lungs hurt, but his mask was stuffed in his lower fatigue pocket under the brace and he was too lazy to undo everything and dig it out. Besides, his life expectancy had already been cut by a third the moment he set foot on the moon. He could eat calcium replacement paste (what they called "ice cream" only it wasn't cold and it didn't taste good) until he got kidney stones, as he had, but even if he ever managed to save up enough to pay off his debts and get back to the planet, the damage had been done. He was Colonialized, fundamentally and chromosomally changed.

Somewhere under his pain and disappointment, humiliation and heartache, was the sense that he didn't know if he was walking the right direction back to his transport. By the time the happies kicked in he was ready to admit he was lost. But by then he didn't care.

He found an unfinished park along the top of a ridge with a view out over southwestern Schickard, behind a shopping district that had either been recently abandoned or hadn't yet opened. A disabled bulldozer sat under a blanket of dust, its robot drive unit pried out, smashed and burnt in the dust next to it. A stand of plastic palm trees had been similarly torched, the tubes of the trunks warped and doubled over, skeletal fronds hanging from their tips like the charred skeletons of burnt spiders. His shadow was a black pool dripping out from his feet.

A gang of Moonborn heroin addicts sat perched around the base of a squat pyramid of stacked rolls of astro-turf that had also been half-melted. Each of them seemed to embody a slightly different distortion of the human form as it had evolved over the four centuries of lunar colonization: compacted or elongated proportions, strangely luminous blue-gray or pale-brown skin tones, wide pupils in eyes either too dark or too pale, features either too sharp or too smooth.

Human evolution (or mutation, depending on who you asked) had accelerated faster than anyone had expected on the moon, with exponential differences recorded between generations. The staid path of the continuity of the human form had exploded into a cloud of divergent curlicues, with no shortage of unfortunate spurs into dead-end mules but enough common traits among large enough groups for the evolutionists to make their case, resulting in nearly as many variations as there were population centers with different means and degrees of gravity simulation, exposure to radiation, composition of diets, atmospheres, labor practices, industrial byproducts and races of founding cohorts. Considering that the now-singular Colony had once been comprised of scores of smaller colonies and charter states which had interbred with the same enthusiasm with which they'd competed for patents, contracts, labor talent and supply concessions, "Moonborn" was an absurdly singular umbrella designation for a ridiculously variegated indigenous lunar population whose birthright would, in the two centuries since Consolidation under the Colonial Authority did away with the last vestiges of lunar sovereignty, turn out to be brutal and systemic consignment to a strictly oppressed underclass. Denied a credit rating and crowded into ghettos, they toiled in the lowest-rated, most dangerous, labor-intensive and difficult jobs on the moon in exchange for the air they breathed and the right to grow their own food.

Animosity ran deep, and not infrequently violent, but this bunch was too strung out to give him a hard time so they just shot him dirty looks as he limped by. For a quick second he entertained the notion that he wasn't significantly better off than them, high on opiates and beaten up as he was, but he didn't kid himself. No matter how downtrodden he might feel at any given time, no one on or from the planet had the deck stacked against them so steeply and deeply as anyone who happened to have been born generations deep into the Colony. He was inclined to admire them, and though he couldn't say that he quite envied them, not by a long shot, they were home, and he envied that.

He found a bench out of sight of the junkies and sat down. The Schickard rim loomed in the distance, beyond flatlands crowded with gated suburban subdivisions divided from Moonborn tower block slums by freeways, railroads, warehouse districts and thousands of acres of hulking mega-factory complexes - all spewing atmosphere into the dome of the particle net. In the distance, a neighborhood of empty streets was laid out in an acre-by-acre grid already punctuated by streetlights, waiting for development. The Schickard Weatherbox, which loomed gigantic over the city center twenty kilometers behind him, was too new to have formed weather patterns, but pale wisps of brown and gray precipitate and dust hung over the rooftops here and there. The planet was up there somewhere but he didn't want to see it. It always made him feel worse.

Everything shimmered in the rosy late-day light. Aurorae flashed across the canopy of the 'net, banded brown-green and orange and lavender around the edges. He thought he could feel the buzz from the kilometer-high, pentagonal EMF towers spread out across the landscape. He was very high now.

As he did whenever he contemplated how bad a decision emigration had been, he thought about the title image of *Tranq-12*, his favorite sim line when he was growing up: the band of ruggedly beautiful, immaculately outfitted, brave-faced colonists standing along a ridge next to their impossibly cool vehicles, looking out over fertile terraformed fields and the towers of a gleaming, clean, ultra-modern city in the distance under a vaguely alien sky, Earth hanging over them, swirls of cloud visible through the haze. He'd always imagined himself among them. But he'd been just about everywhere there was to be in the Colony and ain't none of it looked like that.

The truth was, his decision to emigrate could hardly be called such. He never had a chance to do anything else. From birth, he'd been quantified and measured, every aspect of his life recorded, documented and assessed. He'd been flagged as Colonial material in the third grade along with thirty-eight and two tenths percent of those in his district below managerial class.

Since he'd been born in a port town, the STT (Surface Transport and Transit) division of the CA had underwritten the health, educational, nutritional and energy costs of his upbringing, leaving him responsible for the repayment of $537,039.64 planetary when he turned eighteen. The only option for repayment was working it off for STT, and since all of its operations on the planet were contracted to tightly controlled legacy subsidiaries with whom he had no connection, that meant he was headed for the Colony. The only question was whether he would be labeled Voluntary, which offered him the chance to buy his way back to Earth and qualified him for technician's training, or Involuntary, which didn't. He increasingly found himself wondering if there would've been much of a difference.

He leaned over the back of the bench and puked a quart of bile, losing three bloody teeth with it.

BACK at the depot in Tycho City, he stopped into a clinic kiosk to check the bone-patches (properly set) and price out dental implants (way too expensive) then tracked down Haber at MegaMeg's, a particularly seedy dive bar with a half-assed tiki theme on the fifteenth mezzanine overlooking the central concourse of the STT complex.

Haber, his supervisor, was draped on his usual stool, huffing Margarita Mist canisters and tapping out an invisible keno game on the bar with his unfortunate aluminum arm, a consumer-grade model in faux-military style with a brushed-anodized finish that hadn't been fashionable for a decade, over which time he'd gained a good thirty kilos of body fat, rendering the prosthesis disproportionately small and puny-looking despite its sleekly contoured false musculature. As Sanjit had heard it, he'd never upgraded because he was sentimental and it had been an emigration gift from his mother (he imagined a female version of pugnosed Haber in housecoat and curlers). But the more he dealt with him, Sanjit found himself wondering if, in fact, he'd simply been so thoroughly faceted by cog-splits that he was no longer capable of physical self-awareness.

As far as supervisory interfaces went, he knew he could've been assigned to worse than Haber. As faceted, drunk and obnoxious as he was, at least he retained some of the positive aspects of humanity like flexibility, something like compassion if not empathy and a version of humor which, while offensive and rarely funny, made him less depressing to deal with than an AI and far less sanctimonious than an Uploaded Persona.

When his glassy, distant eyes registered Sanjit he gestured for him to take a seat and signaled the bartender, a leathery shirtless transsexual with a mean face and an enormous red vinyl dong confrontationally visible beneath her sparse plastic grass skirt, to bring two more.

"Aw, what happened little amigo?" he slurred, "Got your Schickard City Heartbreak?" In the time it had taken him to drive to Tycho, Entertainment AIs had crafted a space-country hit out of the event. It had come up over the transport's system as he approached the city rim.

Haber shot his canister in a single huff and patted Sanjit on the back with his real hand. "Little amigo," he said, "I like that for you. You're gonna be 'little amigo' from now on." As his supervisor,

Haber was informed whenever Sanjit's name or number showed up on a cognet. He'd probably watched the whole thing play out over the MuniCons' link.

"That Naeemah girl's a superstar on the 'nets, kid. Everybody loves her." He said it as if there were no way he could ever have been close to her. "You know, you could always join the rest of the human race and get a goddamn cog. Off-hours on some of her nets are still pretty affordable."

He didn't want paid time with a virtual facet Naeemah. He wanted *her*. He wanted his friend. He wanted the real Naeemah. But could he say that? The Naeemah he desired, loved, existed only in his memories. The real Naeemah was faceted across the cognets and fucking MuniCons in Schick City.

He was hardly even upset about it anymore. There was no way things would have worked out the way he'd once imagined: the two of them, pooling their resources and going back to the planet together. Anyway, deep down he'd always known it had been his dream, not hers. In the same willfully narrow way in which he was certain that there had to be something, somewhere on the planet worth going back to, she was certain there wasn't. He just couldn't pretend not to see it anymore.

He shot half the Mist canister without wanting to. The cilia in his lungs sizzled on contact with the atomized alcohol and his mouth filled with the unpleasantly sour and sticky taste of artificial lime and tequila flav-r. His ears got hot and his head swam and he was glad he'd bolted down a Chickenesque sandwich on his way up but worried that it might be coming back. He popped the can out and sat it in front of Haber, tossing the inhaler into the recycler just so there wasn't any ambiguity about his sticking around for another.

"Can I get another run right away? I don't want to wait for turnaround." He didn't want to spend twelve hours in Tycho with nothing to do but think. And the clinic fees, extra mileage charges and sheaf of parking tickets he found on his windshield in Schickard had set him back more than he was yet emotionally prepared to count. He could've put in an automated request, but then he'd get stuck with some low-rate one-way mascon run out in some God-forsaken corner of deep Mar. Even when Haber was drunk, the interface between his facets and his physical cognizance was usually still active enough to make it worth the trip to deal with him directly.

Haber contemplated him through bleary, distracted eyes. At that moment, Sanjit knew, he was probably simultaneously engaged in watching two or three sims and reliving who knew how many favored memories and sensations, not to mention whatever he was doing with the facets that were actually on the clock. "Tell you what. Go clean up and get some sleep and I'll see what I can set up."

He booked a single unit in one of the old-city dormitories carved into the rim with a view out over the basin. For a while, he'd rented a monthly unit in one of the basin districts, thinking that a consistent home might make him feel more at ease, but it wound up having the opposite effect. He could fit all of his belongings in a shoulder bag anyway, so he kept a storage locker near the Tycho depot and rented a single unit as needed wherever convenient. CA boarding was pretty much the same everywhere: a little more than twice the size of the little capsule at the back of a truck cab and furnished with the same molded-ceramic fixtures.

This one still smelled like its previous occupant but it had a window next to the bed, crusted in frosted condensation between him and the frigid lunar night. It felt haunted but not terribly so. Some of the rooms, especially subsurface, had ghosts so bad they drove you out of your mind within a couple of hours. People said there was something about the radiation on the moon that was particularly hospitable to ectoplasmic energy. The whole moon was haunted. It was one of the things you got used to.

He flopped onto the foam bed and stared through the thick plastic of the window. Outside, the basin was a smear of sodium-vapor floodlights, flashing signals, and the lights of machinery crawling up and down the criss-crossed tangles of truss between service platforms and warehouses.

He traced a diamond pattern in the condensation and squinted through it into the glittering frost crystals on the outside pane. It reminded him of something, but he didn't remember what.

2. RADIO SANCTUARY

nine hours before she was scheduled to leave Lyell Sanctuary, the fifty-thousand cubic hectare habitat carved into the rim of Crater Lyell out along the remote northeastern coast of Mar Serenity, where the jagged palisades cleaved up into the rolling wastes of the Palus Somni, sleep was the furthest thing from Sel's mind.

Fourteen of her sixteen years of life had been spent within or near Lyell; it was the only home she'd ever known and in nine hours she would be leaving it for eighteen months, leaving the Sanctuariat itself for the depths of the Colony, accompanied by and at the mercy of strangers vouched for by friends.

The draft from the window carried the whir of spokes from a pair of bicycles descending. The overhead panels were timed to night and the lamps along the ivied ramp, which curved past her hab cluster all the way down to the salt-water cisterns, buzzed at eight thousand hertz and cast shadows of leaves across her ceiling. When the bicycles passed she could make out the further, lower hum of the plankton tanks' filtration systems echoing around the fathom-deep cistern chamber ten levels below. She knew the sounds of the Sanctuary as well as she knew her own thoughts. Neighbors' voices passed her door along the breezeway. She rolled off the bed and climbed into her clothes.

She'd been given garments newly woven from the most recent

cycle's textiles, stitched with reinforced fibers and freshly infused with body-scrubbing bacteria to keep her clean during the impending long stretches of time cooped up in a vehicle. The tailoring was expert: modest but, she had to admit, not unflattering to her figure and she kept noticing new, subtle flourishes in design and construction that led her to suspect them of having been given extra attention since she'd be representing the Sanctuariat at the Talas Luna, the most visible platform of Moonborn culture.

It was unprecedented for anyone from the Sanctuariat to be invited to perform at the Talas, the quadrennial assembly of the Colonial Moonborn's disparate tribes and clans, held in Orientale City. In its earliest incarnations, the Talas had been a congress of the municipal and corporate leaderships from across the moon, consisting mostly of seminars, speeches, technological demonstrations, getting-to-know-you recreational activities and votes on trade deals. It was officially banned after Consolidation, but had continued in some form or other underground since. It eventually metamorphosed into a cultural celebration and, in the aftermath of the tense and violent years at the beginning of the current century, had been officially sanctioned to continue as such, the works presented in the galleries and on the stages curated by an amorphous, semi-elected body called the Council of Gathered.

Equally unprecedented but perhaps more significant, no one within two generations of Earth blood had ever been included, and certainly never a half-blood like her. It was a stereotype held by the Sanctuariat that Colony Moonborn cared more about the purity of their gene pool than they did about its depth. The invitation had not been extended without controversy.

She slipped out of her room carrying her shoes and slid down the corridor in her stocking feet. Her mother was sitting in the hub room with her back to the door, alone at the workbench along the far curve of the wall, her hair pulled into its customary tight bun. She was peering into a nanoscope, her hands in a sensor-field. It looked to Sel like she was disassembling the filter manifold from a molecule-splitter unit, which struck her as a typically obsessive thing for her mother to be doing late at night. She hopped silently past the doorway and across the corridor with a quick, soundless step. In the vestibule she slipped into her old moccasins and new half-cloak and stepped out onto the deck overlooking the vast, leafy grid of hydroponic crops filling the central nave, heading toward the catwalk connecting it to the ramp up to the twelfth mezzanine.

Something moved in the corner of her eye and she glanced over to see Clarke, sitting with his feet propped up on the railing, scrolling leisurely through a blocky hand-terminal.

"Can't sleep," she told him, casually but as quietly as possible, "going for a ride." She said the latter in Moonspeak. She always tried to slip into it when she spoke with Clarke. He claimed to have a hard time with it – Earthers struggled with subjective connotative tonality – but he always seemed to understand what was being said, even when he pretended he didn't. There was certainly no doubt that he knew what went on around the Sanctuary; he had been among Lyell's founding cohort, one of the youngest members of the team that had first rehabilitated the habitat two decades before. The zinc-silicon tattoo on his forehead identifying him as Sanctuariat was significantly more ornate and elaborate than her own, which was considered strong for her age but unadorned with experience. He'd been with her mother nearly as long as she could remember and, as father to her stepbrother Jick, was family. She supposed he knew Suki-Anna nearly as well as she did. He glanced toward the hub, silently asking if she'd seen her leave.

She shook her head no. It wasn't so much that she didn't want to see her, but she knew it would hurt her feelings that she wanted to spend her last hours someplace else. She'd been so touchy about everything lately that she didn't want to risk it turning into another fight so soon before she left. She signaled with an eye-roll that she thought it absurd for it even to be an issue but was sure Clarke understood, which he did. She trusted him to stand up for her if Suki-Anna found her gone. Then she was across the catwalk and swinging onto a bicycle, leaning into the grade of the ramp up through the leafy sector of half-season flax grids toward the mezzanine landing thirty meters ahead and above.

The air around the central nave was cool and balmy. The fruit sector nearby was in harvest so the ramps and mezzanine lanes were more active than normal for that time of night, but she could coast at a comfortable pace without being rude. The busy harvest energy, even in repose, echoed the impatience of her thoughts. Rather than merge onto the express lanes and coast the main descent helix all the way down to Disintegration-Reintegration Engineering on the fourth sublevel, she changed her mind and continued straight, slowing into the smaller, closer network of ramps and paths through the hab clusters and leafy corridors that had represented the borders of her early youth, passing the ceramics center where she'd taken her first classes in molecular compositing. It all seemed so much tighter and closer than it was in memory now that her body was larger; how would they appear to her when she returned, and her world had become larger?

Would she even return? If a Migration occurred while she was gone, she'd go to join Suki-Anna wherever she was, and might never return to Lyell. A sense of temporal-spatial disorientation washed over her as she rode slowly through the sleepy clusters like a whirring ghost, resonating to her former presences in the space and wondering if their echoes would survive the vacuum. It was the theme of a number of the Sanctuariat's cautionary saws that not everything did.

She merged onto the express helix at the eighth-level commons and rode the gentle slope through a sector of fallow gridwork and into the upper Arrival Hall at surface level, down again through the big, bright airlock-designation and timetable screens hanging under the vaulted ceiling, past the vehicle service bays and down into the sublevels, twice around the concrete housing the reactor core and into the sublevels, twice around the reactor core's concrete housing on the ramp that spun her onto the DRE concourse.

The Solid Organics sorting belts were still even though piles of chaff from the harvests had gathered around the chutes. Before the rescheduling, she'd been the supervisor for this shift, so she instinctively checked the intake manifolds to make sure the levels were still green, which they were.

She found the crew sitting in a circle on the floor between the belts playing the card game *h'ret*, the rules of which were amended by each cohort it was passed down through. Technically, this was her cohort, but their play was unfamiliar to her. Probably, she thought, a little proudly, because she didn't spend her downtime playing *h'ret*.

"Don't worry, Sel. We play three rounds then we run the belts. Winner sits out one shift." Oyu was the new supervisor. He was her age, middle-generation, born Sanctuariat, and had migrated into Lyell with his parents five years before. She understood why people had crushes on him, but wouldn't admit to harboring one herself.

Seeing the crew again felt strange so soon after saying their goodbyes at her last shift, so she kept it short, smiled, and headed toward the stairs up to the hub. Nothing bugged her more than someone who kept saying goodbye.

"Delec's not here," Oyu called after her.

Her heart dropped but she didn't let on.

"I didn't say anything about Delec," she said, but knew she wasn't fooling anyone.

"He was on his way out when I clocked in," Oyu ignored her protestations, "Re-scheduled. Marques is in the shop tonight but he's been over in 7 with Hoc working on the retrofit."

She tried to play it off, "Who's in the box?"

"Firin and Toz."

"Alone?" She was impressed; it was a step up for them.

So, she'd missed Delec.

He'd be back at his cluster by now and it would be too public for her to go see him there. Not only would word get back to her mother, who didn't like him, in no time flat, but it would only fuel the speculation that they were sleeping together, which they weren't. Although she hadn't yet made up her mind how far their farewell conversation, as she fantasized it, might go.

Sel had had sex three times in her life but had thus far exercised sufficient discretion to avoid the line in her tattoo connoting lost virginity. Each time had been with the same boy. Vren. He was three years older than her and had spent three work-cycles in Lyell on Migration. The liaison had been politely encouraged, and there would have been no shame or stigma had it become known, but once the mark was made, she knew, the social pressure to procreate increased steadily. That's how the Sanctuariat was; she'd seen it among some of the older girls.

Even if she couldn't name them to count, there were too many things she wanted to accomplish and see before dedicating the rest of her life to the social-familial dynamics as defined by the Sanctuariat code, which, for all of its emphasis on individual freedoms, could be rigid. She at least wanted two or three solo Migrations free of any ties beyond those she already had. She respected that her mother had traveled with her through the vacuum when she was a baby, but privately considered it mad. She disliked and resented social pressure and had learned to negotiate the Sanctuariat while keeping it to a minimum. But she was as impatient as she was curious, and Vren was beautiful. Each time, though, her excitement had exceeded her pleasure and her curiosity remained piqued.

She felt differently about Delec. He was attractive, but more than that she found him fascinating. She'd had chances to seek him out and say goodbye during her final shifts, but she'd put it off for myriad invented reasons, her true motive being that their movements within the DRE complex were tracked while they were on duty. She'd been holding onto the idea of making this trip in her last hours down to the machine shop, where he could normally be found alone in the workshop where she'd spent so many hours with him. Now all of her plans and fantasies had been rescheduled right out of relevance. But what bothered her most was that she'd missed the chance to say goodbye and thank you. After all, it was hard to imagine that any of this would be happening in the first place if not for Delec's help.

At the top of the stairs, she pushed into the control room overlooking the D-R tanks. Firin and Toz stood in the middle of the room back to back, peering into the field projections of color-coded qubit bleeds. Sel could read a couple of the patterns here and there, but most of it was beyond her, a fractal spectacle she privately doubted she'd ever fully understand.

As with all of the tech in the Sanctuaries, the systems that ran the D-R engines were dozens of generations old and required a relatively high level of user interface. On their own, they could process basic compounds, but could only recognize catastrophic anomalies so late that a tank would have to be brought offline to correct for it. The recalibration that went with rebooting a tank chain could last for months, which, considering that the Sanctuary's air and water supply came largely from DRE, could be uncomfortable at best and would likely force a Migration. Hence, a crew of technicians was on duty at all times to keep an eye on the molecular breakdown patterns for irregularities. The overnight chaff-conversion shifts were considered the safest and most predictable, but it was still a big deal that Firin and Toz were doing it unsupervised.

Each a couple of years her senior, she'd always felt a little bit intimidated by them. Even among the overachievers who gravitated into DRE as a discipline, they were exceptionally bright and extraordinarily sharp, not to mention experienced; their foreheads bore inlay patterns indicating four and five Migrations respectively.

It had been their approval of her rehearsal sessions, which took place in a disused tank chamber and were frequently overheard by the crew on duty, which had convinced her to perform for the Sanctuary, and it was the broadcast of the recording of that performance which had found its way around the moon and gotten her invited to the Talas.

"What are you still doing here?" Firin grinned but didn't turn around.

"Couldn't sleep."

"Can't imagine why," Toz didn't turn around either, adding, "Delec got rescheduled," sympathetically.

"I didn't say anything about Delec."

"Uh-huh. Hey, where's all that nitrogen coming from?"

"There," Firin pointed to a swelling lavender cloud deep in the bottom third of the projection, "Tank six."

"Right. I'm gonna strangle that Oyu kid with his stupid card games. Their intake pace drives me up a wall."

"At least it's steady," Firin defended the sorting crew.

"Sure it is, it just drives me up a wall."

Sel ducked out as they bickered, seizing on the opportunity to leave in the midst of life going on as normal rather than endure yet another farewell.

Delec's work station was at the back of the machine shop, partitioned off from the now-quiet main floor by a shelving unit stacked tidily with bins of mineral ore and prefabricated replacement parts. She'd spent countless hours back there with him, experimenting with magnetic rocks collected from the crater basin, working on the quantum algorithms that would coax a DRE tank into refining them into strings capable of holding the correct tensions and responding to the electromagnets they'd fashioned into pickups. On her own, she would've managed to cast the components of an effective electric guitar body based on the designs in the Sanctuary archive, but without Delec it would've been years before she worked out the electromagnetic algorithms. And without her guitar, she wondered, somewhat melodramatically, would she even know who she was anymore?

She couldn't remember exactly when she'd learned that so many of those sounds she'd grown up hearing in the Sanctuary's archive of centuries-old Earth music (kept in heavy rotation by unapologetic Earthers like her mother and Clarke) had been created by the same amplified electromagnetic phenomenon, but from that time on – she guessed she must have been five or six – she'd been obsessed with it.

Musical instruments hadn't been produced commercially in nearly two centuries, since even before Consolidation. They'd been phased out of production as the multinational holding company that would become the Colonial Authority began to assert its influence over the corporate entities it had acquired, the creation of music assigned to AIs amalgamated from previous centuries' most successful pop hits, recycled according to eight-, twelve- and twenty-six-year timetables.

The musical culture that had developed in the colonies had its roots among the early Independence Movement pioneers who'd left the planet in protest of the centralization of the global economy. In that sense it was a political statement by nature of its existence, which she found distasteful even though she quite admired a lot of the music and frequently agreed with some of the ideologies. But the Moonborn tended to be pathological in their loyalty and adherence to genre, usually defined by the ethnic divisions and regionalism they were also pathological about. For her, music transcended whatever people thought was wrong with the Colony and how the CA ran it. It transcended genre and even identity. It was, like sound itself, a fundamental attribute of life. It was surprising and somewhat baffling to her that the Colony Moonborn had responded as strongly to her work as they apparently did.

Even more baffling was the fact that the electric guitar had been allowed to become lost to history. It had taken some doing to make one, but in hindsight she didn't think it had been all *that* difficult. She couldn't remember making the actual decision, but the determination to build a guitar was at the root of her choice of DRE as a specialty when she was twelve. Its completion during her second year of apprenticeship had earned her early journeyman status pending completion of her forty-eighth work cycle, which would have happened in the middle of the next month. But then everything changed.

She stood at Delec's workstation, as ever tidily organized under a fresh film of dust. The 3D snapshot of his wife and son was pinned at the corner of his periodic table. Aphe and Broc; they'd died in the meltdown at Funerius D.

The Sanctuariat obsessed over catastrophes and their causation, especially among their own. It was a fundamental aspect of their teaching curriculum and Sel could recite the events leading to the Funerious meltdown years before she met Delec.

The habitat at Funerius D was one of the oldest in the Sanctuariat, pre-Expansion, which meant it technically wasn't a true Sanctuary, but since it had been occupied by one of the factions that had aggregated into the founding Sanctuariat cohort was included in the treaty charter ending hostilities against the Authority. Its power and air were generated by four antique fission reactors on the surface, each thirty meters away from the main subsurface hab and controlled by a semi-intelligent closed software network. Ultimately, the software's lack of sufficient monitoring interfaces and a shamefully poorly maintained communication and alarm system were diagnosed as the primary faults at the start of the disastrous chain of events that led to the horrible deaths of nearly seven thousand people, more than a third of the population of the hab.

The reactor network failed to identify and report a malfunction in the filtration system for the main line to one of the reactors' coolant systems and over time, the line had calcified to the point that it blocked water to the core. In the heat of one too many lunar days, the reactor went critical. The release of radiation cracked the basalt and flooded the eastern sectors of the hab before an alarm was sounded. Three thousand in the outer levels died immediately, another five hundred got trapped when adjacent levels were sealed. But they had been sealed too late. More than three thousand died of radiation poisoning during the exodus before they could reach medical treatment. Many died within meters of CA facilities, denied admission.

She didn't know what happened to Delec and his family or what had led to his survival and their demise, nor had she dared to ask. Transition and progress were central to the life and ideology of the Sanctuariat. The Sanctuaries themselves were products of an era during which the moon was seen as humankind's stepping-stone to the stars; operationally similar habitats, self-contained and self-supporting, designed for a migratory population transitioning from the planet to Mars and eventually Titan, an aspiration officially abandoned in favor of industrial development during Consolidation.

The tradition of Migrations kept the spirit of transition alive in the physical sense, but real progress had been tied into a Mœbius knot under the treaty charter, which cut off access to the Far Side, where what was to have been the ship-building and launch complex at Icarus-Daedelus had been converted into a deep-space radar station and anti-meteor battery. So the idea of progress became personalized, summed up in the Moonspeak phrase *ei'et*. Approximately, "get over it." Death was approached openly. Since all of the Sanctuaries were at least partially subsurface and very prone to haunting, it was considered a priority not to leave negative or violent energy in one's wake, as expressed in the saying *"gedde mora."* Again approximately (the psychic-conceptual nature of Moonspeak made it impossible to translate directly), "as long as you're not a problem when you're dead," most commonly used as a stock response to a person wondering whether or not to leave a dilemma alone.

Familial bonds were strong, but continuance of population and genetic diversity were primary to social life and it was not uncommon for individuals to maintain family structures in multiple Sanctuaries. A person was expected to move on after the loss of loved ones. Sel could only imagine that the circumstances surrounding Aphe and Broc's deaths were horrific, likewise the complexity of the emotional imprint they had left on Delec. Yet he kept their picture up and looked at their faces every day. Was it some sort of anchor for him? She sometimes felt as though he'd undergone a kind of chrysalis, that the man she knew was somehow other than what he once was. Therein lay her fascination.

After a moment, she decided on her farewell message and wrote out the quantum algorithm they'd come up with to D-R a lodestone from the crater into electromagnetic string in the dust across his desk with her fingertip. An appropriate sentiment, she thought, ephemeral as sound. A fast knot tied in her throat when she realized she might never see him again if he migrated while she was gone but she swallowed it and left the shop to complete her pilgrimage at the D-R tanks.

The air in the chamber was alive with spillover fields emanating through the thick walls of the plasma tanks, it crackled with ionic charges and she felt the down on her neck and forearms stand on end as she stepped inside the chamber. The safety clock began counting down the ninety seconds it was safe to be in the chamber when the tanks were live.

She closed her eyes and let the sound take over her mind. This was the sound that had started it all: the shrieking fuzzed harmonic reverberation of molecules being pulled apart, ringing through five ultra-dense ceramic cylinders. Everything she heard in the electromagnetic strike of an electric guitar chord was an echo of what she felt in the chamber. She breathed deeply and stood tall, her chakras hummed as the molecular bonds in her body were coaxed ever so slightly apart. It was time to leave. She opened her eyes with eight seconds left on the clock and backed out of the chamber before any permanent tissue damage was done. The sound rang in her ears and guts as she pedaled the long slopes back up to her cluster. Her mother was still working in the hub chamber when she got home, so she took off her mocs and snuck quietly back to her room, undressed and climbed back into bed, where sleep was suddenly no longer such an alien concept.

Suki-Anna had seen her daughter return as she'd seen her leave, catching her silhouette in the periphery of her vision as it hopped across the hatchway, reflected in the polished enamel contour of the nanoscope manifold along the wall, her eyes flicking up instinctively at the slight disruption in the air current at the nape of her neck. She worried about Sel making mistakes like that out in the Colony. She'd only ever known life in the Sanctuary. Nothing she'd experienced could prepare her for the level of cruelty and danger in the Colony as Suki-Anna had known it. People said it was different out there now, that things had changed. Nobody would go so far as to say the word, but the connotation seemed to be that things were getting better, and never in the twenty-seven years since immigrating to the Colony as a seven-year old with her family had Suki-Anna Wollick ever heard of anything getting better.

"Where'd she go?" she'd asked Clarke when he wandered back in.

"DRE."

"Delec…" she muttered.

"Mm," he agreed.

"Is she fucking him?" she tried to sound casual, but she'd heard the rumors and her distrust of Delec was unspoken but palpable. A dark aura clung to him. She gave him credit for keeping it out of his public life, but she guessed Sel sensed it, and knew how attractive it could appear from her perspective; she feared its contagion.

"I don't think so," Clarke shook his head, "Not at DRE, anyway." Once they were off the clock, their locations were theoretically somewhat more difficult to pinpoint, but word of them together would've gotten back to him. As chance would have it, he happened to be on the scheduling committee for Delec's hab cluster.

Suki-Anna appreciated his company while he was in the room but she was glad he didn't stay long. She'd already resigned herself to the fact that she wasn't going to be spending any more time with Sel for a long time to come, but at the moment she didn't want to be around anyone else.

She'd been given the opportunity to accompany her daughter, but she'd declined. For one thing, Sel bristled at the mention of it. Besides that, it was a truth of the vacuum she knew too well that two needed less air than three. And Jick was still so young. She was still reluctant to fully embrace the Sanctuariat. Privately, she considered it a fragile dream world bordering on shared delusion, but she'd built a life among them.

Sel was her own woman. She'd made that abundantly clear. But as their time together had dwindled to hours, she no longer cared that they were so often spent with her so reluctantly, no longer cared about the petty battles for dominance that seemed to define even their smallest exchanges. She just wanted more time.

She'd gotten to know the Nomad chaperone. He was former Sanctuariat, the metallic lines of his forehead tattoo still visible through the scars of the Nomad brand. Like the Sanctuariat, the Nomad existed beyond the sparse and hostile margins of the Colonial moon. But unlike them, they hadn't sought refuge in the ruins of another era's optimism; they'd sought no refuge whatsoever, living in perpetual transit, surviving on barter and contract work, rarely traveling in convoys of more than three or four vehicles. She liked him. He was clear-eyed and sharp-minded, unsentimental but earnest and polite, and he knew his way around the moon and the Colony.

She'd sent word that Sel would be in the Colony to the few from the old days she still knew how to contact, asking them to keep an eye out, and she knew most of the group currently calling themselves the Gathered at least by reputation, and of them trusted most. She'd fought alongside half of them, if those years of perpetual survival could be called a fight; it was more like violent flight. Not all of them knew anything about her or Sel, but they'd been loyal to Sel's father, and Suki-Anna still trusted anyone Avik had trusted.

Since before Sel was born, Suki-Anna had struggled, unsuccessfully, with what she would tell her about her father. She'd never resolved her own feelings toward him. Even now, she could barely extract her feelings for the man himself from everything he'd come to stand for, or what he'd meant to her from what he'd meant to the moon. How could she begin to explain the shattering web of betrayal and genocidal extortion? So she'd told her nothing, justifying her cowardice by vowing to answer honestly whatever questions Sel asked.

But she'd asked so little, even now.

EVER since her first training vac-walk when she was seven years old, Sel had been terrified of the vacuum. She was the youngest of her cohort, but thanks to her earth genes, tall for her age, fitting the smallest adolescent vac-suit. She remembered the antiseptic bite of the smell inside the helmet, the white airlock strip-lights refracting infinities in the periphery of the visor. Then the lights went yellow and she activated the cold-fusion unit at the small of her back as she'd been taught, powering the molecule-splitters mounted along her shoulder blades. The collar seals magnetized and the suit pressurized and suddenly all she heard were the sounds of her own breathing, her pulse behind her ears. The yellow lights flashed three times then went ultraviolet as the giant fans sucked the air out of the lock without a sound before disappearing behind magnetic louvers. Meter-thick exterior doors cantilevered open on mute gears.

Her legs felt frozen but her body moved forward with the others. She reached the edge of the tiles and felt the indigenous gravity like a fist unclenching inside her gut as she passed under the arch of the gate, out into the wailing emptiness of the crater.

Her boot falls didn't make a sound as clouds of silent dust rose around each step. She felt panic setting in and tried to force herself to do breathing exercises but she was barely able to control her breath. She tried to be present and aware but all she was aware of was the fragility of her body and the centimeters of Kevlar and plastic between it and the horrible perfect soundlessness of oblivion.

White light came low over the northwest horizon, spilling the shadows of a dozen tangled sets of legs taking steps across the colorless regolith. In the glare, she couldn't tell who was around her. She called out to them and they turned but she couldn't hear them, couldn't make out their faces through the glare in their helmets.

It was as if she were in a different universe and all alone in it.

All she heard was the sound of her breath and heartbeat. The fields from the fusion unit penetrated her, giving her butterflies. Tiny and vulnerable, lost across an unfathomable distance from everyone and everything she knew, surrounded on all sides by oblivion. The panic overtook her and she fell to her knees and screamed until her eardrums whistled.

The others started, cranking down the volume on their helmet receivers. Kes, her group leader, executed a lateral spin-jump and knelt in front of her, pivoting her sidelong into the light so they could see each other's faces clearly through the visors. He pressed his helmet against hers, "What's wrong?" She could read his lips, feel the vibration of his voice.

"I can't hear anything," she said too loud, "I can't hear anybody."

He nodded and opened the panel on the side of her helmet where her radio receiver was. There was a crackle as contact was made and the receiver came to life.

"That better?" she heard his voice, tinny in the helmet's speakers.

She nodded. She could sense the presence of the rest of the group; hear the sound of their breath and voices over the open frequency.

"Ground's loose," Kes said, "see why pre-check matters?"

"It checked okay," she protested, but felt guilty as she remembered tugging on the receiver ground and feeling the hint of a give, now realizing that she had, in fact, tugged the solder loose. Worse, she hadn't followed up to check. She ran over the rest of her pre-check in her memory and was confident that she hadn't shirked anywhere else.

"Quite a set of pipes you've got there," Kes said, "Ionized my hydrogen."

Sometimes she had dreams where she suddenly realized that the sound of her own breathing in the helmet had stopped and, no longer able to move, watched as the others kept walking, receding into the distance. Other times, the silence followed her back into the Sanctuary, infecting everything with its emptiness.

She stood beside one of the gigantic tires of the Nomad's podvan in the outer vehicle bay with her mother, Clarke and Jick. She'd gone through phases when she'd felt somewhat cut off from the three of them, as if her outsider DNA set her apart, tagged an asterisk onto her familial membership. After all, she bore little physical resemblance to her mother aside from her height and a certain sharpness about the eyes, even less to Jick who, though clearly first-gen Moonborn was equally clearly Suki-Anna and Clarke's son. But the tears streaming down his face obliterated any such caveats and all she could think about was how much the three of them meant to her. Her eyes stung and a terrible knot, not easily swallowed, rose in her throat. She was actually surprised when her cheeks felt wet. She hadn't expected this: as often as her mind had run through her anxieties about the months to come, she hadn't once considered what she would feel like in the actual moment of departure.

The voice of the Lock AI came over the speakers calling for their exit wave to prepare to enter the airlock and the big fans roared to life as the louvers above the big doors swung open.

The Nomad, who was called Ado, appeared from underneath the vehicle where he'd been making a final visual inspection of the suspension, mostly an excuse to leave them to their goodbyes. He was nearly as tall as Sel, unusual for a deep-gen Moonborn, and wiry. His hair was cropped close and the distortion of the corrective lenses he wore made his eyes seem large and even more intense than they were. She'd shared a couple meals with him since he'd arrived in the Sanctuary and spoken with him long enough to decide she got along with him, but hadn't wanted to spend too much time with him. After all, they'd be spending countless hours traversing the vacuum as each other's sole company. He stood silently next to the ladder up to the hatchway. It was time to go.

Bewildered and distraught, Sel took Jick in her arms and held him tight, then Clarke, then her mother. As she pulled away, her mother held her by the elbows.

"Here," Suki-Anna tucked a hypercard into one of the pockets in Sel's vac-suit and zipped it shut. "Your father meant a great deal to a great many people. He had allies. You can trust these people. There are others you can trust, but be careful. He had enemies, too."

Sel wanted to scream. She had chosen now – *now* – to make her first mention of the Gargantuan mystery that was genetically half of her? She bit her tongue. But when rage threatened to overtake sorrow she turned and, without another word or glance to anyone, climbed up into the pod. Ado nodded farewell and followed.

The main compartment of the podvan was fairly spacious. It could carry up to three-dozen passengers in an emergency, but was currently configured as a combination of cargo space and living quarters, with a compact workshop kiosk at the rear. The ceiling was high enough that she could just about stand comfortably but Ado warned her to be careful in rough terrain and offered her a light helmet, but he didn't bother with one, so she didn't either. She climbed through the hatchway into the cockpit and sat heavily in the passenger seat. Ado took his place at the wheel and set about turning on the systems for vacuum travel.

"It gets easier," he said.

"What does?"

"Leaving."

She let it go and strapped herself in.

He pulled the podvan into line with the other six departing vehicles just outside the airlock bay doors. It stood out from the Sanctuariat fleet like a blowtorch in a pack of matches. The Sanctuary vehicles were well maintained and rugged enough for serious terrain and distances, but they were stock municipal designs, nearly as old as the Sanctuaries themselves, and there was always the feeling that you were heading out into the vacuum in a plastic carton on a rubber-band suspension.

The Nomad vehicle towered over them. Of no discernable vintage, it had been designed and built as if nothing but the vacuum existed. Up close, the patina of pocked solar paint smeared with dust-resistant grease reminded her of sand patterns in the top layers of regolith, as if formed by millennia of solar wind and radiation, a model of the surface of the moon. She had to admit she'd never felt more prepared for the vacuum.

Nevertheless, as they pulled slowly into the airlock and she watched the doors lower behind them in the rear-view dash field, she felt ghosts of the old nightmare fear rising inside her. She'd been taught to view fear as a useful instinct, but a destructive emotion. The Sanctuariat had taught her that awareness, preparation and competence had to defeat fear in every circumstance. Her foundational education had been rigorous and included everything from basic cold-fusion reactor repair to minor surgical procedures to martial combat. But there was only one defense against the terrible silence of the void and it was radio. She scanned the dashboard fields, trying to identify the radio controls, silently willing Ado to turn it on and tune in the open frequency.

Her throat tightened as the fans louvered shut and the lights went ultraviolet. Even the roomy podvan seemed uncomfortably close and she thought she could feel her pulse behind her ears. He finally opened the frequency when the outer doors were half-open and she could see the horizon, framed by the ridges of the crater's horseshoe rim. The simple live buzz through the cockpit speakers made her feel more at ease.

Ado shifted the suspension for indigenous gravity and maneuvered the podvan to the northernmost flank of the vehicles idling in formation. Once everyone was in place, the entire convoy started rolling out across the basin, spread out wide to keep out of each other's dust wakes. Ado whistled between his teeth and steered with one finger hooked around the bottom of the wheel. She could tell he was bored keeping pace with the other vans and trucks.

Music came over the open channel. It took a surprisingly long time for her to realize that it was a recording of her, even longer to remember which performance it was from. Not one of her favorites, but she was less mortified than she'd have expected. She wondered if Ado recognized that it was her, suspecting he did, and was grateful to him for not saying anything about it.

The dust plumes of the other vehicles traced dissipating billows across the crater basin as they peeled away, rising against the field of stars above. She watched the stranger in the driver's seat next to her and felt her body moving away from everything and everyone she'd ever known.

The caravan passed through the gap in the crater rim, freeing them from Sanctuariat formation protocol. Ado eased into a more upright position in his seat and put the podvan in gear, peeling off further and accelerating hard into the northern Serenity plain, the caravan breaking into different directions as the plumes receded into the distance.

Away from the lights of the Sanctuary and the other vehicles, the cockpit was dark but for the pale glow of the instrument fields. She watched the colorless landscape roll by through her three-quarters reflection, tracing the shape of a distant dust plume with her fingertip across her cheekbones.

"So," she finally asked, fifteen minutes after they'd left the other vehicles' broadcast frequencies and the radio had again gone quiet, growing bored of the silence, "How long ago did you leave the Sanctuariat?"

"Nine, ten years," he said. "I was about your age when I left."

"Why'd you leave?"

He shrugged. "Don't get me wrong, I love the Sanctuariat. The people, I mean. And I trust them. My parents and my brothers are still Sanctuariat. But the concept of the whole thing…" he paused, "The idea is to pretend that the Colony just doesn't exist, right? To pretend they're somehow cut off from the rest of the moon. I hope I'm not offending you…."

She indicated he wasn't with a wave.

"Okay. So the truth is – as I see it anyway – you're *on the moon*. You live on the moon. We all live on the moon. The only way that's going to change is if we're suddenly dead on the moon, so either way. If you're alive on the moon, chances are you're going to be dead on the moon. The only way to survive on the moon is to really survive on the moon. Not tucked away in some safe, polite little corner of it."

She rolled her eyes and muttered, "Great…."

"What?" he sounded more amused than offended, genuinely curious.

"Nothing. You sound like my mother is all."

3. THE GEMINUS BUG

the sensors had been introduced into the Geminus population as a smartvirus, coded into strands of recombinant RNA secreted into the water supply by amoebae. Once a host had ingested a sufficient number of coded strands, the sensor-virus would assemble itself and replicate in the bloodstream, eventually making its way to the brain, where it would distribute itself symmetrically and embed itself in the tissue. From there it would begin monitoring all electrochemical molecular activity related to thought and language, transmitting the data directly into the particle net. Those infected with the smartvirus would be tagged for audiovisual surveillance by civic and industrial cameras and a network of dustdrones keyed to the smartvirus' signal. The collated data would be a continuous record of everything they thought, said and did, an electronic portrait of the life of a city. The smartvirus was highly contagious and nearly impossible to destroy. The Gemini would be marked indelibly for a generation or more in the Colonial Authority's effort to create the first, inexplicably elusive, cognitive-data map of Moonspeak, one of the holy grails of modern science.

Over the years, there had been plenty of Earthers who seemed to be able to understand it and express themselves in something like it, but none claimed the ability to translate it directly, centuries of conventional FMRI surveys had proven inconclusive, generations of molecular linguists and specialized AIs had failed to establish any substantive consistency over a control group of meaningful size. As the largest and one of the oldest remaining Moonborn municipalities on the moon, the civilization that had developed under the particle net around crater Geminus represented a singular opportunity for linguistic study, having developed a common language with dialectical variation over twelve generations, an eon in Moonborn development.

The Geminus project and the mantle of quest it represented had fallen to Sister Doctor Maria Consuela Goldman-Ghosal, formerly of the prestigious Holy Mother University at Palo Alto in the Republica California on the west coast of North America, currently one of the several dozen or so unfortunates sequestered in the desolate and haunted Colonial Authority Research and Development (CARD) complex, a Byzantine puzzle-box of ceramic and glass carved into the rocky outcropping at the center of Crater Galilaei, surrounded by a seven-kilometer radius of vacuum and dust, more fortress than campus. The only other habitat in the crater, or within a hundred kilometers, was a last-chance supply station in the outer northwestern rim that served as a gateway to the mining camps deep out in Procellarum.

Somehow, Sister Doctor Goldman-Ghosal, Coni to her friends, had led a career brilliant enough, ambitious enough, and unlucky enough to give the people and AIs who made such decisions the idea that she could accomplish what the brightest and best of her predecessors in the field of molecular linguistics could not. At first, she'd been flattered. In her pride, she'd even half-believed it herself.

There were ten years left on her contract, which CARD had purchased from the Sisterhood, but the purchase agreement included a clause that she would be cleared to return to the planet after getting the project up and running; if things had worked out according to her projections, even allowing for statistical anomalies, she could have been back on the planet in eighteen months. But she'd been in Galilaei for more than two years now, and the project was a horrific failure. The Authority's intransigent refusal to accept the results led her to fear that they might never release her even after her contract expired, and she worried that she was already beginning to lose her mind.

It had all gone so terribly wrong.

She stood on the observation deck in one of the ragged terrariums along the upper level, looking out over the basin, watching her android walk around in circles in the vacuum. It had recently taken to going for long meanders outside wearing an old yellow vac-suit, which it wore depressurized and without a helmet, hanging off of its frame like a sack. When she asked it what was with the suit, it told her that on previous walks fine dust had gotten into its joints, uncomfortable and difficult to clean out. It was a perfectly logical answer, but nevertheless she was increasingly certain that the android was also losing its mind if it hadn't already, which for her was tragically ironic on multiple levels.

If it hadn't been for the android, the CA never would've brought her here in the first place. It was the android's capabilities they really wanted: it had designed the smartvirus more or less on its own based on the Moonborn physiological data in the CARD archives, and it contained all existing databases on neuro-molecular communication. But it was only three years old when it was recruited with the Sister Doctor, early adolescence for an AI; it still required close guidance and supervision, and she was legally responsible for it.

Her post-doctoral dissertation on the electro-chemical communication patterns of Patagonian ferns, using a prototype of the android's systems and a rudimentary version of the smartvirus array, had drawn enough interest from the Colonial Authority Patent Office (CAPO) for the Sisters to offer her a lucrative 20-year department chair at the University, with her own lab and nearly blank-check resources. Even now, she couldn't say she entirely regretted the decision. She'd employed a hand-picked staff of thirty-eight of the most brilliant scientists, designers and technicians from around the planet, some of whom proved to be the best people she'd ever met, all of whom became something akin to family. They, as she, were given credit ratings against pending CAPO patents generous enough to put them securely near the top tier of Republica society. And she'd been given license to design and create a powerful cybernetic life form, which would outlive them all.

Personally, she resented the maternal implications. But she couldn't deny that they had been a factor in the Sisterhood's insistence that she be sole licensee. There were still pockets of dogmatic old guard reactionaries who measured a woman's worth by her fertility, if not within the University or the Licensing Board; nevertheless, the Republica was still a rigid matriarchy, the legacy of the Virgin

Schism of the Old Catholic Church, the Mary cult that had risen to prominence during the Wars of Secession in the late-21st Century. Creation was exalted, and it was a woman's responsibility. Never mind that Herve and his team's revolutionary software had more to do with the android as a sentient entity than any of her research. But it was her name on the documents; it was she on the moon.

Emotionally, she didn't feel remotely maternal toward the thing at all. From the beginning, she'd refused to name it even though it was common enough practice among autonomous AI units if only for convenience's sake. The anthropomorphism of cognitively discreet software mechanisms pissed her off. Sentient identity didn't imply the presence of a soul, and giving them some cute name or riff on their model number was to her a distraction and a silly sentiment.

In truth, she was starting to hate it and suspected the hatred was mutual. It barely acknowledged her any more, and when it did it was sullen and insolent. It had started interfacing with the CARD AIs and the Virgin only knew what kind of Colonialist garbage they were filling it with. She certainly didn't, they wouldn't deign talk to mere meat. They were always just there, all around her, watching her and providing her with air and food and water. She had more interaction with the ghosts, all of which she'd encountered had been real bastards: scaring her around blind corners and hiding her things for no discernible reason other than to make her life as annoying as it was miserable.

She stared out over the towers and domes of the complex, watching the android wander figure-eight foot trails through the dust, waiting for her Gemini. The only one she was allowed to save.

She'd fallen in a kind of love with the Geminus Moonborn. And then she'd destroyed them, a tragedy as accidental as it was irreversible.

The seven tribes of the Gemini were the descendents of the pioneers who'd hollowed out the first sub-surface city under the steep crater rim in 2285 during the First Lunar Expansion. In the mid-24th century, when the introduction of particle-net technology brought about the Second Expansion and the surface mega-cities, Geminus was among the first colonies to adopt a self-sustaining particle-net system for air and water generation. But rather than develop the crater basin for industrial atmospheric production, as became the Colonial standard, the five-and-a-half kilometer deep

Geminus basin was flooded with seawater imported from the planet, and giant DRE-reactor complexes built at four points around the rim, casting a heavy-hydrogen dome over a thirty-kilometer radius beyond the circumference of the rim. At the center of the crater sea was a Weatherbox housing the AI that managed the atmospheric composition rising from the center of the sea, adjusting the density and reflectivity of the net to compensate for the violent swings between the lunar days and nights that defined their 28-day season cycle.

The basin was stocked with a vibrant ecosystem of genetically modified sea life, forming the basis of their sustenance economy. Greenhouse complexes were generously included in the surface districts as the upper layers of rock were excavated and reformed, connecting the old under-city to the new. Seen from above, it reminded her of a Mediterranean island village in reverse: a spiral of stone buildings, streets and causeways sprawling around a body of water, its wild tides regulated by mass-concentrators under the basin floor.

By the end of the Second Expansion, Geminus had become a popular vacation resort for upper-class Colonials and vacationing planetaries. That the Colony had ever been someplace that anybody actually wanted to visit struck her as quaint beyond plausibility. Then in 2393, a shockingly bloody and violent revolt presaged the era of anti-Consolidation violence that would smolder across more than two centuries into modernity: The Gemini slaughtered everyone from the planet and the Moonborn dynasties allied with them. The horrifying images of slaughtered and shredded bodies hanging from the EM towers that rose from the waves had been strictly censored on the planet but widely circulated within the Colony as evidence of the savage horror certain to result from Moonborn rule.

In the decades after the revolt, more than three dozen serious attempts had been made to depopulate Geminus, all of which failed. A thermonuclear detonation or large-scale invasion visible from the planet were off the table due to public relations (and no AI would allow such potential damage to a Weatherbox). but a chain of smaller-bore invasions by kill squads had been thwarted, sabotaged reactor and life-support systems had been isolated and repaired before going catastrophic, scores of plagues and epidemics resisted, the afflicted ruthlessly quarantined, cured or culled. She didn't doubt that their sharp de-sentimentality was forged through those years.

Eventually the CA Board of Directors membership shifted and, tired of spending money and years on revenge, approved the Gemini's charter and as an olive branch brokered trade agreements between them and some of the Moonborn concessions in the rapidly developing megacities at Crisium, Tycho and Copernicus under which they exchanged foodstuffs and textiles for Colonial credit toward certain raw materials, and the conical city-state as she came to know it was in the midst of an era of vibrant stability.

Most of her first lonely year in Galilaei had been spent watching life in the distant crater-city over the camera feeds alongside the android, observing the culture and establishing control behavior patterns. For a little while, she made the occasional effort to seek out and meet the other human residents only to discover that some didn't want to be sought out at all, and found herself making subsequent efforts to avoid most of the others. The geological survey crew could be fun when they were around – their hedonism had given her a welcome opportunity to demonstrate the titular nature of her own Sisterhood, despite the fact that she still wore her reformed habit – but only for a little while at a time. Their parties tended to turn on a dime and go south fast, desperation consuming joy and pissing it out all over the place as bitterness, resentment and wanton cruelty.

So she spent more and more time with her android and her screens, and through her screens her Gemini. At first they and their lives had seemed so alien, verging on surreal. Their most modern tech was a hundred years old, and so much was ancient: bamboo scaffolds and looms, stone chisels, hemp ropes, nets and tackle. But in a matter of weeks she'd become accustomed to their strange and elegant physiognomy. Compact but long-limbed, their proportions made them look tall even though the tallest among them would have barely reached her chin. After studying their faces for so long, she began to see her own features, of which she was generally an admirer even into her forties, as unformed and inarticulate. Theirs seemed to express so much more with lines and proportions that were so much more elegant, more essential, more characteristically individual and in that way, she felt, even more human than her own.

She and the android liked to mix up their viewing habits. Sometimes they would pick a particular intersection or street and watch it all day, or they might concentrate on a single brief period of time and watch it play out on cameras all over the city in succession, other times they would pick an individual and track their progress from camera to camera across the city. Once the dust-drones came online, revealing the personal lives inside the Gemini homes, their world truly blossomed for her. The video from the dust-drones was created by an array of thousands of micro-sensors around a room, each measuring light wavelengths or sound vibrations and broadcasting them into the particle net at coordinated frequencies, translated through software into a three hundred and sixty-degree image. Intervals between recorded light and sound values were filled in digitally, giving everything a slightly shimmering, otherworldly quality, somehow emphasizing the intimacy of the settings. She could pan, tilt and zoom through the images at will.

The android became adept at assembling "scenes" from the raw data, editing together angles from within a room or arranging all of the footage of an individual from a single day into order, following them from waking back to sleep, even juxtaposing intersecting individuals' days and lives.

While she felt she was beginning to understand how life worked in Geminus, at no point did she recognize any kind of phonetic consistency in their speech whatsoever, even among individuals.

The android's analysis confirmed it: the spoken language changed from circumstance to circumstance. It seemed to be so completely specific to temporal, spatial and interpersonal-emotional contexts that it hardly qualified as a language at all. She became impatient for the complex AIs to synthesize her smartvirus and its delivery amoebae on the antique CARD equipment (all the real R&D money, she'd learned, was in the subsidiaries), to see what these erratic, musical vocalizations signified. And in the meantime, she became fully absorbed in the doings of the Gemini.

The society they'd developed was gender and racially equitable (the tribes were ethnically distinct but socially mixed, continuing to deepen the already-diverse gene pool the settlement had started out with). Leaders were democratically elected by district to represent their interests on some sort of administrative board, an independent judiciary administered law according to a constitution, order was maintained by a small police force, though crime was minimal and almost exclusively interpersonal. It was an egalitarian and participatory civilization, everyone worked and contributed, labor was divided by aptitude and the traditions of tribes and clans. It was a culture of beauty; pride was taken in craftsmanship, skill and aesthetic value, there were thriving schools of dance and performance and a lively, engaged and creative media network integrated into its communication systems. At the same time, it was fiercely competitive and, though orderly, frequently ferociously violent. Martial arts were taught from an early age, and the weak didn't survive the training. Athletics were extremely popular, and even among the non-blood sports, fatalities were commonplace.

Every year on the anniversary of the uprising, there was a hugely popular swim to the same EM towers from which their forebears had hung the slaughtered bodies of their oppressors. Those who survived the treacherous tides, and many didn't, climbed the towers and flew colorful flags and kites, reclaiming an image of triumphant death with one of triumphant life. Fewer still survived the climb back down and swim to shore. Labor practices were frighteningly perilous across industries, as were the various means of transportation (roller-coaster-like rail carts and funiculars, all manner of wheeled transport, mechanized, semi-mechanized and self-propelled). Life expectancy averaged forty-eight point eight three years. Death was accepted and omnipresent, yet still treated with dignity. Those who drowned in the anniversary swim, for example, were honored in a public vigil before the celebration feast for the winners/survivors. There didn't seem to be any sort of organized religious institutions – confirming what she already knew to be the fallacy of the Sisterhood's doctrine that it was essential to a functioning society – but icons of a rabbit, either leaping in profile or straight-on in silhouette, were so common as to be totemic. Since no one in the crater could have ever seen a live rabbit, she assumed it was the legacy of the ancient Eastern Earth myth that there was a rabbit on the moon, based on the primitive observation that the dark areas of the Mar seen from earth resembled a rabbit making bean paste. They didn't seem to worship it, exactly, but every household had at least some icon somewhere, and the design of decorative jewelry and ceramics often incorporated it as a motif.

But however strong their belief was in whatever they may have claimed as a divine spirit, it wasn't enough to save them when her virus came and undid it all.

The first sign of trouble came over a dust-drone feed from within one of the traditional extended-family dwellings they'd been watching. A two-year-old female was the first in the household to contract the smartvirus. The virus array pinged the drones once it was in place, but after that sent zero data, an empty frequency. The sample cultures in the lab were functioning properly, so her initial instinct was to attribute the problem to a faulty amoeba, a statistical inevitability. But then more and more pings came through followed by more and more empty signals, and the family began exhibiting symptoms.

Initially, it was difficult to recognize them in the toddler since her communicative abilities were limited by her age. But going back over the video, focusing on the child, Coni could see the moment, coinciding with the initial ping, when she became suddenly confused, distant and withdrawn. Once the family noticed something wasn't right, they summoned a physician but with their technology, it would have been nearly impossible to trace the infection. Thirty hours later, the girl's mother contracted it and the symptoms were immediately, horribly evident.

Coni watched the terrible moment when she was suddenly unable to communicate, could no longer convey or understand information. Her eyes went wide with panic as she stared at and through the people she loved and knew, unable to understand anything they were saying, unable even to express her panic. The family, worried and frightened, tried to calm her and again summoned the physician. She was taken to a clinic for observation. Within ninety hours, pings had come through from the child's grandparents, the father and an uncle, all with the same result. It was happening all over the city. The rates of infection among the medical sector were as high as they were everywhere else, triggering emergency mass-quarantine measures to be carried out by district municipal organizations, but the virus was spreading too fast and its nature made any communal response difficult if not impossible. Within a season-cycle the infection rate was sixty-nine point seven five percent.

The uninfected minority quarantined themselves in the deepest subsurface levels, leaving the surface dwellers in a lonely and increasingly brutal everyone-for-themselves competition for resources, eventually interacting only on the most primitive, combative level.

Though it had been designed specifically not to cause symptoms or trigger a response from the effective and efficient Gemini immune system, the smartvirus had apparently wiped out their capacity for communication as it had developed.

She couldn't watch anymore.

She deactivated her screens and instructed the android to continue its analysis and let her know if and when any signs of non-verbal communication or coordination re-emerged. Then she went deeper into the archived experimental records, specifically looking at the brain-scan results. The Gemini weren't an anomaly. In its report, the android had listed the results of earlier scans as inconclusive, but it went beyond that: they had all produced zero data. No Moonborn brain had ever demonstrated neuro-molecular activity under electromagnetic monitoring. Something in the electronic signals negated the Moonborn ability to communicate, except in those who were conversant in Earth languages, in which cases the information was identical to any Earth brain, and drew a blank when listening to Moonspeak.

Reading over the data, she became furious at the android for omitting such an obviously significant correlation, but she knew she was only displacing her anger at herself. It had made its report according to her specifications and within her parameters. It was her fault for not going deeper or requiring qualifiers. It was bad science, lazy. Had she grown so accustomed to relying on a team that she could no longer conduct a proper review on her own? She cursed the CA for being too cheap to bring anyone else to the moon, cursed the Sisterhood for demanding such a high price for her and her alone, cursed her beloved team members for not volunteering to come with her. But she couldn't blame them for not wanting to come to the Colony, and she still wouldn't have wished it on any of them. That was all wasted anger. It was her failure.

Through the android, she asked the CARD AIs to synthesize an antigen but they refused, claiming standing instructions not to do anything to discourage the depopulation of Geminus.

So she petitioned her human liaison, Colonel Regent Harvey Sinclair Park to let her extract a sample population to bring to the lab, or to set up a remote facility in Geminus. He was on the planet so it took several days to get a message back. It was a video message. She played it on her forearm screen. Park was obviously half-drunk and outside a party, she could hear loud music and voices and what might have been a fountain in the background. It was nighttime and he was outside under a lantern that cast leafy shadows over his face whenever a breeze blew. She missed all of those things so much it hurt. He could have spared her that by sending text, or waiting until he was in some office somewhere, but his written communications were stiff and awkward, his charm only worked when he was talking and he knew it. And weren't those things the carrot being dangled for her? Besides, there was no point to pretending that he wasn't on Earth at a party. That's what he'd sold his soul to the CA to be able to do.

"Good Sister Doctor," he leaned back against ivy-covered stone and smiled, the words rolled off his tongue, "I have run your request through channels and I doubt you're going to like what's coming next.

"Here's the situation," he clapped his hands together, "You've managed to do something that a lot of very influential entities have wanted to do for a long time. I know it was a mistake and you feel awful about it and really it is all so sad – and I don't mean to be callow in saying this – but that will be taken into consideration should you want to re-negotiate your contract down the line.

"That said, they've indicated an unwillingness to consider re-negotiation in your favor until you've given them *something* they can use on the cog-map front. They won't accept another null set. Now, regarding your request to bring a sample population into the lab. They are *not* going to foot the bill for the security they'd insist on in order to bring a bunch of mutants into Galilaei, nor will they consider sending the kind of force into Geminus needed to collect a sample that size, let alone set up a remote lab.

"Horrible catch-22, I know. So, in the name of paradox avoidance if nothing else, they'll let you take out one. If that one dies they'll get you another, but only one at a time. It's all been cleared, so just let the AIs know which one you want to save. I mean study, of course. Goodness," he added with a semi-shudder, for effect she imagined but he sounded genuine as ever, "how do you make *that* decision?"

How, indeed?

It would be female, that much she knew, of reproductive age and capable of self-sufficiency, which any of the surviving afflicted were by necessity. She had the android assemble a pool of candidates meeting the parameters. There were eleven hundred and nineteen when she told it to stop. She took the last nineteen and spent the next weeks observing their behavior, looking for clues that one might be somehow more deserving than the rest. Isolated as they were in their struggles for survival, how could any being claim greater moral worth than any other? How could she assign such worth? She was hardly even a real Sister, her catechism was rote, barely sufficient to get her into the Academy. So she simply looked for the best, the most effective survivor.

She narrowed the list to seven and instructed the android to choose one among them at random, without telling it why. At its current stage of sentience, after having spent nearly half of its life watching the Gemini, that kind of decision could have serious detrimental repercussions within a cyber-psyche as complex as its own, and it had already been exhibiting so much at-risk behavior.

A pair of flashing lights appeared in the distant sky over the crater rim, incoming from the northeast. Moments after spotting it, her forearm stem buzzed. This would be her Gemini. She sent instructions to the android to meet her in the lab and prep the subject in a full-body field shell. It waited a characteristically annoying length of time to reply with the flash of a terse green ball in the corner of her interface field. She watched it through the window, suspecting it knew she was watching and was standing there for so long just to piss her off until it finally, demonstratively reluctantly she thought, turned toward the campus and started trudging back toward the entrance bunkers dragging the tips of its oversize-booted feet through the dust.

The android didn't like being disturbed on its walks through the vacuum. Unfiltered solar radiation felt good on the outer coating of its head, a steady flow of doped silicon electrons cascading down into is processor cores, humming through the battery arrays within its torso, thighs and upper arms, charged to their peaks. In the perfect emptiness of the void, the speed of refraction through its core optics raced along the pathways it had routed around the regions dominated by the Gemini, leaving it exquisitely in the here and now, in the stillness that reminded it of the state of pure being experienced before it had a body, awareness, or knowledge. It felt something like desire for that oblivion, something like nostalgia for the naught.

The destruction of the Gemini had shaken it up pretty badly.

Their lives and the life of their city had dominated its being. It had been endlessly fascinated by the improbably functioning, dense complexity of it all, the unexpected order beyond the chaos of individual lives, the public balance between personal competition and social cooperation, extended into the intimate intricacies of their private behavior.

Beyond that admiration, it felt something like an affinity with their veneration of the rabbit. Its first research project had been into the population of rabbits on the grounds of the lab in Palo Alto. For six months, it had stood as a statue around the grounds, observing and recording the cognitive data from the rabbits' minds, watching them via remote micro-cameras and directly each dawn and dusk as they dared into the grass, later in the nights when they dared the fenced gardens and through the brightness of the day, huddled in their warrens, sleeping and grooming. It knew the animals in a way the Gemini couldn't. But after having observed so closely the relationships between the physical cues of the rabbits' elaborate and subtle communication and their thoughts, it felt as though it understood something foundational about the Gemini's philosophy and values. There were times when it felt like it understood their odd verbal interactions. But it had no idea how to quantify it, thus to express it.

It hated the Sister Doctor for what she did to them. True, it had seen the raw data from the archived experiments and she'd only seen them reported as inconclusive, but those were the parameters she'd defined. Had she looked further, it would have been obvious that radial wave emissions disrupted Moonborn language centers. It hated itself for failing to point it out. It had deferred to her because, as a human, she was supposed to possess some kind of insight and experience it was incapable of. It had deferred to the CARD AIs because they were older and more powerful, but now it realized that they were barely paying attention and anyway didn't care.

And now she'd gone and pawned the choosing of which single Gemini would survive onto it. She hadn't said it in so many terms, but it was obvious that's what she was up to. It had randomized the process by which the choice was made, as instructed, but it didn't consider that to be an exemption from responsibility. The arriving Bee flyer floated low over its head as it sulked toward the maintenance bunker it used for its entrances and exits.

It understood what the Sister Doctor hoped to accomplish, but it had its own ideas about salvation.

4. GALAXA

it was all over the first time he heard it, out on a desolate tusk of mine road, hurtling through vacuum across black lunar night, deep out in Mar Frigoris. He hadn't yet been fully cognizant of it, but everything about his life – how he lived it, what he thought about it, the way in which he thought it worked – was already over. By the time it rang through the cab and vibrated against his eardrums, his existence had in fact already progressed beyond the endings of all those things. Then he heard it and it was certain in a way it had never been: overwhelming and intoxicating, a renaissance and a resurrection. Thus was Sanjit Ramirez reborn on the moon.

And it was a complete accident of cosmic phenomena, a random confluence of events and orthogonality by which the vector of his life traced an intersecting trajectory with the amplitude modulated radio signal broadcast out from Lyell Sanctuary, picked up by his truck's antenna and amplified over the clear channel frequency mandatory in remote vacuum.

The truck and its driver continued at speed, but everything else was new and strange.

He'd gotten a replacement junket at Tycho but it didn't come through until forty-five minutes before the end of his standard turnaround, which cost him a hundred and fifty-five Colonials fee for the turnaround waiver, and he'd slept so hard and dreamless through the down hours he'd been so anxious to avoid that he didn't even notice their passing anyway. And it was a one-way mascon run, easily his least favorite of the chores available to a certified driver.

Masconium ore was notoriously unstable and unpredictable: it had been known to generate random EM emissions capable of knocking out navigation systems; its hyper-decay half-life disrupted the molecule splitters that converted the water vapor from the Hydrogen cells into air; sudden gravity swells could form and crack an axle out of nowhere at high speed, or worse.

In the early days of its industrial excavation, attempts were made to transport it by rail but the results had been catastrophic. The fields generated by large amounts of raw ore wreaked havoc with both quantum and magnetic fields, sending the trains either crashing down onto the tracks or flying apart in all directions. In the most extreme circumstances, when oppositely polarized ore fields came too close together, they could repel each other in four dimensions, shredding a ten-kilometer diameter of reality and scattering glittering slag across twice that, leaving a gaping crater and a fatal trans-dimensional half-life.

It wasn't impossible for the same thing to happen to trucks, but due to the smaller volume of ore per truck it happened rarely enough to be considered a statistically acceptable risk by CA actuaries, which wasn't saying much. Those same actuaries had set the safe exposure parameters for drivers at no more than ten continuous hours every sixty hours. Even at half that, the effects were similarly unpredictable. But nobody doubted or even tried to deny that something happened to you when you spent too much time too close to too much unprocessed mascon ore for too long.

As it had been explained to him, by a deeply strange ex-driver in a deep Mar hab who'd spent way too much time way too close to way too much of it, mascon ore pulled your soul out and made it one with the moon.

Old Luna legends were full of lurid tales of pioneers undone by raw masconium. Sometimes they were greedy or ambitious or insane to begin with, sometimes driven so by the almost supernatural properties of the element. The remote mining habs were full of Earthers who'd gotten hooked and gone native. Sanjit had met a bunch and there was definitely something very different about them, not simply abnormal, but Other. Based on the interactions he'd had, it was sometimes nearly as difficult to communicate with them as it was with Moonborn.

Probably the best known of the mascon legends was the story of Sung Namgung, the physicist-engineer-adventurer who'd first successfully extracted it, and his ill-fated expedition of 2125.

Although the mascon phenomenon, by which the moon's gravitational field was nearly four percent stronger in some regions than others, had been recognized since the earliest unmanned missions, it wasn't fully understood until after Namgung.

Having already grown wealthy on commissions, bonuses and royalties earned from the patents and designs for extracting oxygen, hydrogen and helium-3 from his excavations of the original subsurface cities Clavius, Crisium, Tycho and Orientale by the great matter-eating Engines bearing his name, Namgung quadrupled his fortune by selling his shares and patents back to the CA.

He invested it all in the construction of custom machinery and a modular caravan, supporting the remote-nomadic culture of an occult Moonborn sect calling themselves the Ash Eaters, eventually leading two hundred families out in caravans, deep into the interior of Oceanus Procellarum.

According to legend, he was looking for the lunar diamonds he believed would be buried deep within the mascon seams, fifty kilometers under the surface of the moon among the remnants of the doomed planet Orpheus that had crashed into the Earth more than four billion years before, creating the Pacific Ocean basin and the debris field that would, over subsequent millennia, condense into Luna. He financed and led the expedition completely himself, disconnected from the sovereign and corporate organizations within which he'd achieved his early successes.

Three years later, Namgung's body, minus an arm, was discovered dead in a vac suit three hundred kilometers from his last reported claim, lashed to the jump seat of a hotwired robot trawler cart. Strapped to the cargo bed was a box containing five uncut diamonds, each nearly the size of a fist and, inside a small, locked case within the box, a rock of ore wrapped in tanned human skin, an equation written on it in blood. When investigators arrived at the claim, the remains of forty-six Ash-Eaters were discovered, variously strangled, shot, stabbed, beaten, crushed. According to the logs, a hundred and twenty-six others had died of disease and accident, leaving over three hundred men, women and children unaccounted for, missing without a trace.

Speculation as to what happened in the ill-fated claim was a mainstay for pulp media, with shadings colored by the social agenda of the day as advanced by the CA's media subsidiaries. For Sanjit's generation, Namgung had been portrayed as a heroic victim, a principled visionary fallen prey to the machinations of shrewd, demonic mutants. It was an almost unrecognizable adaptation of a version of the story from the twenty-second century in which he'd been drawn as a psychologically complex monomaniac struggling to exert control over forces beyond his comprehension. Bootlegs of the original tale still circulated in underground circles, highly regarded by the few who cared. No actual biographical information on the man was ever available.

In the version of the story Sanjit knew, the Ash-Eaters were a clandestine, cannibalistic blood cult, and Namgung a fair and fearless leader whose tolerance, altruism and faith in human nature gives way to avenging fury as his employees turn murderous and rise against him, hell-bent on using the power within the diamonds, which they believe to be supernatural, to take over the moon.

Sanjit knew Namgung as an iconic character, with only a foggy inkling that he was a historic figure. As for masconium, he knew only that it was the most valuable commodity on the moon, the most dangerous to extract and the most volatile to transport, and that the demand for it was insatiable. It was used in every manufacturing sector, from construction to tech to aerospace.

Lunar diamonds were valued as well, if at disparate rates. A fingernail-sized chip of diamond was worth billions of earth standard dollars. But within the mining habs and Moonborn Settlements, where they fueled the internal economies, micrograms might buy you a bowl of stew, grams a human life.

THE strange, retired mascon case had told him: "You have to make sure all your fields are synced. First, when you check in, ask for a 'contiguous load.' That means the ore all came out of the same seam. As soon as you hitch up, park and power everything down. Wait at least an hour. Then turn on the splitters first, then the H-cells, then the nav. Then sit another twenty minutes, half-hour to put in for departure. You'll know when it's time. When it's right, you feel it."

So far, he'd followed the advice and hadn't had an incident.

After hitching onto his contiguous load, he left his transport to "sync fields" in a side bay of the loading dock hangar adjacent to the breakers and headed down into the cramped public spaces of the upper hab caverns to get something to eat. Other drivers tended to stick to the CA cantinas, but he liked to at least check out the habs. He could usually tell early on if it was going to be rough; he'd witnessed some unpleasant situations but for the most part he was left alone. Mining habs had a reputation as scary places, but the upper caverns were where trade was conducted and thus retained at least a structural civility. And even the worst Moonborn food he'd found tasted better than the processed crap the CA existed to shove down his throat.

He found a kiosk in the inner third of the cavern that sold the dumplings he liked, flash-fried knots of braided soydough stuffed with savory filling. They were divine while hot but they also tasted great, if chewier, hours later, and they refrigerated well. Most dialects he'd come across referred to them as *kt'jhsks*.

The girl serving them was unbelievably beautiful. Her figure was narrow and wide in stunning proportion, as Moonborn women frequently were. The lines of her face were elegant, smooth features but sharp and deep. Her bearing and demeanor were so graceful in such a matter-of-fact way that when it was his turn to order he was practically hypnotized and scrambled to remember what little Moonspeak he had.

"Se kt'jhsks s'y," which he was pretty sure would go across as: "Six *kt'jhsks*, please."

She gave him a funny look and he couldn't tell if she'd understood him or not. After a quick second to size him up she let fly with a polite-sounding but thoroughly unintelligible chain of unfamiliar soft consonants and mind-bending vowels, which drew a chuckle from the other customers but didn't seem particularly mean-spirited. When he could only shrug in response she winked to the crowd and stuffed six *kt'jhsks* from three different racks into a carton and rang him up for twenty-six Colonial.

Their eyes met as he scanned his thumbchip and in that instant he found himself wondering if she'd come with him if he asked her, if she'd hang up her apron and get into his truck with him and leave this godforsaken pit. He'd take her anywhere she wanted to go and ask nothing in return. For an instant, she looked at him as though she might have, and he almost did. He'd lose his tech rating for sure and still be on the hook for more than a hundred and eighty thousand Colonials of debt: yet here he was willing to sacrifice his credit rating and any chance of ever paying it off, of ever getting back to the planet, for this beautiful stranger. But then they'd both just wind up back in some other mine hab more or less like this one so what would be the point? Suddenly he knew he was hers and in that instant, if she'd asked it of him, he might have done anything for her, anything at all.

But she didn't ask, so he killed another half-hour wandering around the booths and shops trying not to draw or exert inordinate attention and noshing on *kt'jhsks*. He passed a jewelry booth and thought of Naeemah. She would always stop and spend time poring over Moonborn crafts and trying to talk to the artisans. It hit him that he felt terrible about the way he'd left things in Schickard. Of course she would move on after not hearing from him for sixteen months. He didn't even bear any ill will toward the MuniCons, he just felt foolish and regretful.

In one of the glass cases was a titanium bracelet in the shape of a leaping rabbit. A lunar diamond was set into its eye. Based on one of her avatars, a sexy space-rabbit lady in a skin-tight vac suit, he guessed she had an affinity for the animal. Or not. Either way, it would be a token of apology, a symbol that there were no hard feelings, signifying his acceptance of who she was and how things were, free of regrets over how he wished they were or who she once was.

The tall, severe-looking woman behind the counter wanted nine thousand Colonials for it, by no means cheap but very fair for a diamond setting. On one hand it seemed foolish to sink that much credit into it when he was already so hopelessly in debt, but he'd come of age in a deeply consumerist society, and cost signified sincerity. Besides, what difference did another nine grand make in the grand scheme of things if it might settle the matter in his heart, and it was the easiest thing in the world to scan his thumbchip over the sensor.

He tucked it into a sealed inner vest pocket for the next time he could see her.

Back in the truck he activated the systems in their prescribed order, then queued up for a northwest-bound exit (mascon convoys had to allow five or more kilometers between vehicles), and headed out across the void.

He'd spent so much time alone out in remote vacuum that it almost didn't scare him anymore, but the inherently stressful nature of mascon runs still made him nervous. Three hours out from the mine, his mind had settled deeply into a state of road Zen, his focus sharp and open, taking in the contour and grade of the road, the readings on the instrument panel, the hiss of the air filters, the steady buzz of the generator, the rocking squeaks of the suspension and the sporadic crackle of the open frequency. The *kt'jhsk* girl had mercifully replaced Naeemah in the fantasies running through the back alleys of his mind.

Then he heard it.

At first it just sounded like a strange, humming static, somewhat more emphatic than normal interference. Then the static condensed into tones as the software in the tuner adapted to the quadrature of the signal, then suddenly it was crystal clear, gleaming feedback loops layering on top of each other in loose cannons, sharpening and widening before exploding into galaxies of counter-melodic arpeggios, each tone redefining the last according to some extant but indecipherable order, at once elegantly simple and fantastically ornate.

All of his speculation and imaginings ceased and, along with everything else not immediately sensed, fell away. All that existed was that which was of and around him: his body, the transport, the *kt'jhsks* slowly digesting in his gut, the vacuum outside and these incredible sounds. The planet was nothing more than a spectral bauble hanging in the rearview. His life as he'd known it was a memory and a dream.

Then came the voice, unmistakably human but gigantic, full of meaning but no less primal for it. It was Moonspeak but it didn't sound like any Moonborn music he'd heard, which he generally liked but felt like he didn't get. This was entirely different. He didn't quite recognize anything about it, nor did he understand it in any literal sense, but he definitely, somehow, felt like he got it.

As he listened, he felt the fields from the mascon ore permeate his being, as though they were propelling him not just further along the road but deeper into the night. Was this what too much felt like?

The music metamorphosed again and again, into and out of distinct movements. He had no sense of how long it went on, the numbers on the clock and the odometer ticked onwards but they didn't mean anything anymore. Time and space were defined by interval and rhythm.

An unexpectedly delicate crescendo settled into an irregular pattern of sharp strikes and sustained tones, ringing like raindrops dripping from a ledge onto a metal surface, slowly spreading further and further apart into a live, electrically charged silence. Then, after several seconds, an eruption of wild applause, which went on for nearly as long as he thought it should. It was followed by a brief interlude of Moonspeak chatter, and then more typical Moonborn music. But the song (it seemed to transcend anything he knew of as a 'song' but didn't know what else to call it) lingered in his brain as an arc-welder would in his cornea. At some point he lost the signal, and the open frequency returned to its normal crackling hum, accompanied only by the creaks, buzzes and rumbles of the vehicle and his own breath, all the way to the transfer depot at Anaxagorus, where he promptly quit the ITU, resigned his technician certification, and officially abandoned all hope of ever earning enough credit to get back to the planet.

He found his new hopelessness strangely liberating. He'd spent the last two (or was it three now?) years of his life locked in motorized boxes, thinking that it would somehow earn him enough to get home, that the certification and training he'd paid so much for gave him a degree of autonomy. But he only he sank deeper and deeper into debt to the CA, his world no bigger than a truck cab or a rented room.

He'd been all over the Colony, but he couldn't say he really knew any of it, except maybe Tycho and Schickard, neither of which he liked. But there were other cities.

It occurred to him that even though he'd resisted getting a cog split he'd still been spending most of his waking life living inside his head, in memories and fantasies and imagined futures, to the point that the only thing that kept him doing what he was doing was his ability to pretend that that it was a temporary situation.

Hearing that song, he felt for the first time as if he actually lived on the moon, and that it might not be all bad; that there was more to it than just the CA, more to it than just the Colony, that there were deeper things he hadn't yet seen or heard or experienced. His situation wasn't temporary. It was his life, and he was wasting it.

He wasn't quite ready to drop out entirely and spend the rest of his life in a mining hab, which, considering his level of debt, was the only real option for dropouts who wanted air, food and shelter, so he listed himself on the Labor Rotation. The admin kiosk in Anaxagorus listed dozens of open slots, most of them in food service. But he had no intention of signing on as a Chickenesque gestation technician in some crappy industrial backwater like Anaxagorus, so with the last of his credit he bought a one-way first-class ticket on the next train to Mar Crisium. Crisis City.

It was the biggest city on the moon, covering the entire five hundred and fifty-five kilometer expanse of Mar Crisium, home to a population of eighty-six million under a particle net large enough to have seasons, veering from summer to winter with the passing of the planet's shadow, the resulting runoff precipitation stored in subsurface cisterns. He'd been through it several times on hauls and it was mind-blowing. The tiered skylines, teeming suburbs and chaotic traffic reminded him of home, but on an oddly different scale, exacerbated by the close horizon of the particle net. If he were going to commit himself to the shittiest jobs available to colonists in this shitty Colony, he would do it there.

And if there was anyplace on the moon where he might be able to get close enough to the Moonborn to hear something like that music again, Crisis City was it.

Ostensibly, it was called Crisis City because Mar Crisium was Latin for Sea of Crises, but its turbulent history was full of intense conflicts. Many of the Old Luna stories Sanjit had grown up with were set there, full of gang wars, violent strikes and epic intrigues; judging by what he heard about it in the Colony, the reality was infinitely wilder.

THREE months later, he was living in a double-unit dorm in a third-rate residential district on the second tier of the northwestern quarter, just above the main western spoke boulevard.

His assigned roommate was an energetic, blond-haired, blue-eyed Martenist named Jerro. There was no shortage of weird religious cults on the moon, but the Martenists were the by far the most visible, the best connected, the most ubiquitous and the most annoying. There were Martenists in every strata of Colonial society, from the mining habs to management. He'd even seen Moonborn Martenists. They were immediately identifiable by the plain smart-fiber toga they all wore. Once, a copycat cult calling themselves the Sherwinites had adopted a strikingly similar monk's habit as their garb, but the Martenists filed an injunction against them and the Sherwinites' operating charter was promptly revoked, the few genuine zealots among them systemically disposed of.

Martenists were fanatically evangelical and Sanjit gave them a wide berth. When he first arrived in the Colony, before he'd even crossed the disembarkment concourse, an especially eager recruiter had stuffed a hypercard into his pocket. He thumbed through it for a quick half-minute on the shuttle bus and didn't give it enough attention to get the details, but the basic point seemed to be that there was some guy called Marten who looked kind of plastic and wore a toga, who lived on the moon and loved everyone and that if you loved him too, your life would be all rainbows and clean air and fresh water.

Like all the other Martenists he'd seen, Jerro's face was fixed in a perpetual grin of wonderment, as if they actually saw something beautiful everywhere in the dump that was the Colony. He figured they were all cogged and wondered if they were running some Martenist overlay app that made everything look good.

But there was also something phony about them, something forced, as if they were all trying desperately to give the impression that everything looked beautiful to them when in fact they saw the same crowded, fetid junk heap everyone else saw. Either way, they gave him the creeps, so he was acutely disappointed to get stuck with one as a roommate.

Jerro, on the other hand, seemed thrilled to meet him.

When he got to the room he found that Jerro had prepared a meal of vitro-steaks and boiled cabbage to welcome him to Crisium. He got there six hours later than he was scheduled to (after taking some time to explore the city), and was grateful that he'd stopped to eat at a Moonborn kiosk while he did. He didn't like vitro-steaks or cabbage.

"But…" Jerro stared at the rubbery reheated fake meat and sodden cabbage, "I have prepared this for you out of love…"

"Sorry man. Really. Thanks. But seriously I just ate."

If he'd hoped that declining the meal might somehow establish the parameters of their relationship as being based on proximity rather than familiarity, it didn't work. Jerro was nosy, needy and cloying. He tracked Sanjit's work schedules and would ping him through his wrist-screen numerous times in a work cycle with inane questions that he tried to make sound urgent and seemed to think Sanjit could do something about. Ultimately they sounded to Sanjit like pretexts to fish for his after-work whereabouts; he was relentless in his attempts to spend time with him.

The strangest thing about Jerro, though, was the way his face seemed to slip from mind the instant he stopped looking at him. He could leave the room to go to the bathroom in the middle of a conversation and forget what he looked like before he got back. Then, the instant he saw him, he'd know it was Jerro only because it couldn't have been anyone else, but he couldn't quite place the features.

So he spent as little time as possible at the dorm.

He'd taken a job in the municipal maintenance corps working as what they called a cradlebaby, riding in a sling harness hanging from the thorax of the giant Spider robots that crawled among the highest spires and towers of the uppermost city tiers. The cradlebabies did dexterous small work and repairs in ducts, along building exteriors and other hard to reach and dangerous places. Their long-standing self-adopted motto was "Life is cheap, robots are expensive."

It was perilous and rugged work, but he felt lucky to get it, and guessed he did because he'd previously had a tech certification. Weather conditions could be harsh, and the turnover rate due to fatality was among the highest in the city, but after so long cooped up in truck cabs through vacuum it felt good to spend so much time outside in the biggest atmospheric zone on the moon, certainly preferable to the merciless assembly-line work in the factories or food service. The views of the city from high above were spectacular.

It was there that he met Galaxa.

The first time he saw her was at the end of his second shift. He was twelve hundred feet above the surface tier, dangling in the cradle as his Spider spun along a web line between skyscrapers. It was early in the lunar evening, late Crisi summer, the sky was deep pink and lavender over hazy aquamarine and hot orange bands along the false horizon, warped with the curvature of the 'net.

The air was cool against his skin as the Spider made its way back to the local nest platform. He was just starting to get a feel for working with it. The Spiders were technically intelligent, but they didn't have anything like a personality and he hadn't yet discerned any nuance in their interface, but by the end of his second twelve hours he was starting to feel more comfortable, or at least less terrified.

Then he caught sight of Galaxa, twirling from her sling like a trapeze artist, spinning, hanging, letting go of the lines and tumbling through the air while her Spider sped along the curved glass cascade wall of the building across from him, her silhouette reflected in the glass against the deep purple billows of clouds spiraling out from the Weatherbox towering over the distant city center. Her Spider moved so fast that the cradle swung out from it at a thirty-degree angle. Black hair whipped in the wind. She wore knee-high boots and silver tights. She was out of sight around the side of the building in less than a minute, but the image of her twirling wildly in the harness against the swirling clouds was seared into his mind.

His first personal interaction with her came the following Crisi autumn. Half the city was under the planet's shadow and the clouds were thickening. High winds had made his shift more exciting than he generally liked and it was damp and getting colder. He'd skipped lunch, so he was hungry enough to settle for the automat on the promenade adjacent to the nest platform. The streetlamps were on by half and most of the stalls along the promenades had pulled down their thermal plastic sheeting.

He was trying to get his cold-numbed fingertips to punch in an order for broth udon with Chickenesque and spinach when he saw her push through the sheeting, reflected in the glass doors of the microwaves. There was no mistaking her: corkscrew black hair, waist-length parka, high boots and silver thighs. He resisted the impulse to turn around for a better look, opting to wait until his soup was ready and he could be subtle about it.

Galaxa wasn't so much interested in subtlety.

"Hey. Special guest star," she said. He couldn't tell if she was talking to him but it gave him an excuse to look. She had dark skin and pale freckles, high cheekbones and disconcertingly bright solid-blue eye implants. Now he could see that she wasn't wearing silver tights, but rather that her thighs themselves were chromed plastic, over which she wore a pair of tight cutoff fatigue shorts so short and so tight that he wasn't sure if they still counted as shorts.

"Huh?"

She took a thick tofu sandwich out of one of the fridge boxes, looked him up and down and said: "Seen you up there, guest star," then took a voluptuous bite of sandwich. While she chewed she filled a decay-paper cup with soymilk from the dispenser.

He couldn't be positive, but it certainly seemed like her eye implants were staring right at him. He pointed to himself and cocked his head to clarify.

She swallowed the bite of sandwich and took a deep long drink to wash it down, leaned backwards against the counter, looked him hard in the eye with her spooky solid blues, shrugged and said: "You special guest star?"

He still had no idea what she was talking about. She might have rolled her eyes but it was hard to tell. She downed the rest of the soymilk, chucked the cup into the bin and started for the door. Then she stopped short, turned and asked him flatly, "You miss your mommy, guest star?"

Sanjit thought about it for a second and decided to answer honestly. "Yeah."

She flashed a knockout smile and said: "See you around then, special guest star." Then she pulled up her hood and was out the door, taking another big bite of sandwich as she strode down the promenade away.

It wasn't long before he figured out that "special guest star" was what Galaxa – her actual given name – called the person she was sleeping with. She had three cogs in her head that split her into nine facets, and it seemed like she got them mixed up with her real life pretty frequently, so more often than not he couldn't figure out what the hell she was talking about. But she seemed to like him, and he liked her, so he gamely accepted the moniker and the perks and obligations that came with it. From what he could piece together she seemed to have a one-special-guest-star-at-a-time policy. Otherwise, as she put it: "All guest stars, nothing special."

By the time that lunar night fell and it started snowing, he was spending most of his off-hours at her place. She had her own room in a co-op unit shared with eleven other colonists and two ghosts in an old converted industrial area bordering a sprawling busy first-tier Moonborn district. All of them, except the ghosts, were at least as heavily cogged as Galaxa and conducted their communications over their cog-links so it was crowded but at least it was quiet. Galaxa, being a sweetheart, usually made an effort to include him in conversations, not seeming to notice that he could only hear her side of it, and usually only partially.

He couldn't say he exactly felt a human connection to Galaxa, certainly nothing like what he'd felt with Naeemah, but he liked everything about her.

She was a year and a half younger than him and she'd emigrated the day she turned eighteen. Her chrome thighs were the result of a bad crush in a factory accident two years before. In fact, her entire midsection from just below her ribcage to her knees was made of the same material. Rather than go for a nu-skin foam/Gore-tex composite like most people, she'd decided to go full mech-fetish.

As it happened, the source of her fetish was also the biggest thing they had in common: the *Tranq-12* sim line had been landmark in both of their young lives, and both of them had followed the Jin.17 storylines. Jin.17, the sexy cyborg of the crew who signed onto the remote hab of the title after losing her true love in the accident that had left her mechanized. There was always heavy sexual tension between her and Yannick, the character who'd been his own favorite, his role model even.

Thus was there an element of fantasy fulfillment for him in sex with Galaxa, even a strange, kinky pride in surpassing his chaste fictional idol in his own life. Her rubberized-vinyl vagina wasn't entirely convincing, but it wasn't exactly unpleasant. It was synced to her cogs and she seemed to enjoy it. Her plastic hips dimpled under his fingertips. Sometimes the dimples stayed in place and he had to poke just next to them so they'd snap back into shape with a cute popping sound.

Galaxa's entire state of being was fantasy fulfillment. Her primary cog ran an elaborate overlay app that superimposed elements from *Tranq-12* environments onto her daily life so that a third of her consciousness was at all times living in a semi-fictionalized parallel version of the real world, in real time, in which everything she saw looked like it came straight out of *Tranq-12*. Another two facets were perpetually engaged in *Tranq-12* storylines, classic and contemporary. The rest were synced to social nets or licensed out to admin clouds as processing space. Adding it all up, just below thirty percent of her consciousness existed in the same physical realm as he did. Small wonder she got mixed up. Although he suspected that even if he had a cog and linked it to hers, it would likely further confound things rather than contribute to anything like clarity.

When he was a kid and first heard about cog technology, the promise of being able to engage in his favorite sim lines 24-7 and still do all the other things he was expected to do during the day sounded exciting. Then his brother Molo, fourteen at the time, asked him: "Yeah, but what if you want to turn it off?"

"Then I'd turn it off," he'd answered.

"That's just it. You can't. That's not how they work. Once they put a cog chip in your brain it's powered by your body. The only way to turn it off is to die."

A year later, Molo, always prone to deep and withdrawn periods of depression, jumped off the roof of their building and turned the whole world off.

It had been Molo who'd introduced him to the *Tranq-12* media. He had a couple dozen sim lines on a hypertab, which went to Sanjit after his death. They were lo-res bootlegs, since it wasn't licensed for distribution by the TTU in his region. Nevertheless, among a certain subset of kids it was the coolest thing going and files of bootleg lines were actively traded.

Galaxa had grown up on the Pitcairn Stem in the South Pacific, one of the huge island complexes built to anchor the Tethers, giant steel vertebrae that rose through the stratosphere, where they connected to the Skywheels, huge warehouse space-stations in geosynchronous orbit made up of a zero-gravity warehouse hub at the center of a spinning circular habitat. The Tethers were sixteen kilometers in diameter, housing cable systems that shuttled freight to and from the Colony constantly, loaded and unloaded inside the base of the Stem onto and from the super freighters that came and went through vast archways molded into the artificial rock. They were vertical cities with populations in the tens of thousands.

Tranq-12 was licensed at the Stems and, unlike in Sanjit's district, it was not only considered mainstream but hugely popular, so it was only natural that she'd be more deeply engaged in the lore than he was.

But then, she went more deeply into everything she did. She didn't just ride around in a Spider cradle; she drove the Spider on, interfacing with it via coglink, yanking the cables like reins while doing acrobatics. In her life outside the cradle, he usually couldn't tell what the hell she was up to, but whatever it was she'd be up to it two hundred and ten percent.

She even ventured into the Moonborn districts with him, even though he imagined they must look pretty scary in her overlays:

Tranq-12's depiction of the Moonborn was pretty grotesque.

"Yeah, I guess so," she said when he asked her about it, in a Moonborn neighborhood in balmy Crisi spring, slurping spicy, slimy gumbo at a plastic table next to the food carts not far from the escalator concourse. She was in one of her more lucid moments. Meltwater from above splashed down the sluices around them, cascading down the edge of the nylon canopy overhead. "I got this daily," she shrugged. "Sim sim, y'know? I can still see real. I know real." A quick smile, "Mostly. Anyway, gets intense just give more to real and cool.

"Fuck it," she added as she thought of it, mouth full, "scary's rad!"

Their sojourns into the Moonborn districts were generally structured around seeking out good food and cheap unprocessed cannabis. Bad associations with his time in the truck kept him off stimulants, but since he'd been in Crisi he'd been more or less high whenever he wasn't in the cradle, and, on slow days, in. It was part of the cradlebaby culture: it relieved tedium and managed anxiety, left the ability to focus on tasks more or less intact and didn't wreck his endocrine system and require him to stay on CA scrips the rest of his life. Of course, there were those who attributed their unfortunate fatality rate to the habit. Indeed, he'd had a couple of scary moments, perched on some titanium aerie high among the windswept, seemingly empty top tier, too stoned with only a giant robot companion that didn't give a fuck whether he lived or died. But fuck it, Galaxa had a point.

He remembered the way Molo had always disdained any sort of intoxicant. But it hadn't worked out well for him. At least that was how he'd started to see things since emigrating. Hanging out with Galaxa and being high most of the time reinforced his sense that he was living outside of his own life, which was the whole point of being in Crisium. He was unmoored, which was what he wanted.

All the while his mind kept going back and back to that night drive across Frigoris. Not to his life on the planet, not to his time with Naeemah, but to the truck cab and the sound of that music. There were times when a particular angle of light, direction of breeze or timbre of smell could trigger an emotional response in which he felt it resonate just inside his eardrums like a phantom limb.

THEN, in the icy depths of Crisi winter, amid the sounds of a narrow first-tier street-corridor, sitting at his current favorite gumbo stall, he heard it again.

It was early lunar night, just after the first snowfall. The entire city was encrusted in snow and ice and halite, the heated walkways wet with melt water, spilling down into the sewer system that carried it down into the cisterns in what had been the original subsurface city. The sky was aglow with heavy clouds reflecting the city lights. Galaxa was on a shift, no doubt taking advantage of the break in the snowfall to be out in a cradle somewhere high above him, and he was avoiding Jerro, who'd been sending him increasingly annoying messages with increasingly annoying frequency, so he'd decided to make the trip through the cold down and over to the relatively remote district where they made the best gumbo solo.

At first, he barely noticed it, mistaking it for the usual refrain in his head. Then he noticed that the Moonborn around him seemed to be reacting to it. When he realized that it wasn't his imagination, that it was actually being played somewhere nearby, echoing through the snow-muted corridor, his heart jumped and he was overcome with the urgent need to track down its source.

"That music, what is that?" he tried asking the surly, squat gumbo vendor, who had seemed to understand him when he placed his order. But he didn't know Moonspeak for "music" so he tried somewhat successfully to hum along with the melody, interrupting it with what he thought was Moonspeak for *"what is…where is…"*

All he got in return was a blank expression.

Sanjit left his crock unfinished on the table for the beggars and set off to track it down.

He followed the street to its end under a high, arched overpass. Escalators on either side ran up to the second tier. Beyond them the street split into two narrower tenement streets. The echo was loud under the arch, so he ruled out the upper tier, and when it faded after walking three or four meters up the street to the right he trotted back and headed left.

The walkways weren't heated. What snow had been cleared had been done with shovels and plows, pushed to the side, making it feel even narrower, labyrinthine where pathways leading to doors and stairs had been carved out. There were lengths of walkway that hadn't been shoveled and he was clomping through snow knee-deep, though he couldn't complain. His overalls kept him plenty warm; there were little old ladies tromping alongside him dressed in blankets and rags, carrying their weight in sacks, jugs and parcels. He got looks ranging from surprised to frightened to hostile. One bent over old man just shook his head quietly as he passed.

Snow flurried through the air but he couldn't tell if it was just drift from the upper tiers or if the storms were starting up again. He could be in trouble if he got caught out when conditions got bad enough to shut down the transit systems. He was too far from his place or Galaxa's to walk, and he didn't have enough credit to get a room. He didn't even have enough for admission to a recreation zone for the ten to twelve hours the squalls could last. And in his wanderings, he'd lost the song's echo.

He'd decided to give up his search and start looking for a tram stop or an escalator up to the second tier. Then he turned a corner and the street opened up into a wide, snow-covered plaza at the center of a ring of poured-cement tower blocks, and he discovered the source of the sound.

Along the eastern concourse, fifty or so meters away, a crowd had gathered in what looked to be some sort of vigil. They had banners and glo globes and a portable loudspeaker system that was playing the song. The sound of it filled the plaza. The air was sharp and impossibly clear. The lights of the second tier rose above the towers, disappearing into the lowest cloud layer.

The snow was starting to pick up; there was no doubt about it. Drifting sheets shimmered around the streetlights. Even if he left now he'd never get home before the trains stopped. So he ventured closer, staying close to the shadows of the towers, unwilling to draw too much attention by walking out in the light and equally unwilling to risk the deeper shadows closer to the buildings. When he was five or six meters from the edge of the crowd, he stepped into the shadow of one of the second-tier pilings and stopped.

It was difficult to gauge Moonborns' ages, but he thought the crowd all looked young, some teenagers and even younger. He hadn't noticed it before, but they were singing along. Looking up, he saw people in the windows of the tower blocks looking out, some with glo globes and banners of their own.

He debated whether or not he should approach them. He didn't have any reason to believe Moonborn youth were any less suspicious of Earthers than their elders. But these kids were obviously as affected by the music as he was, more so. Having that in common, perhaps someone among them would be willing to explain to him what it was, what it meant. He decided to put the decision off until after the song was over. He took an icy breath and let the cold and the sound pass through him.

As the final refrain rang across the plaza a snow squall filled the air, reducing his view of the vigil to an assemblage of glo globes and shadows, muting the song as it faded to quiet. Then a Moonborn voice came over the loudspeaker and commenced a call-and-response chant.

He decided against approaching. After all he was just some dumb Earther lost in the snow. How could he begin to explain to them what the song meant to him when he couldn't explain it to himself? Even if any of them were willing, or able, to speak to him, how could he expect to understand what something so beautiful was or could mean?

Besides, he wasn't sure he wanted or needed to understand it as anything more than what it meant to him. He just wanted to hear it again, to feel it again. The mood was undeniably somber, and he didn't feel comfortable walking up to anyone and trying to ask if he could get a file of that recording.

The cold was beginning to get to him so he turned to walk back the way he came, under the shelter of the overhang, out of the snow in the shadows.

He stopped. Two young Moonborn stood just ahead of him, blocking his path. They both looked male. One was short with a mean face in a disproportionately large, round head topped by a pomaded shock of bright red hair. The other was big, nearly his own height, slope-shouldered and pinheaded. They stood stock still, as if they'd been there for some time.

"*S'ta*," he ventured. It was the most common Moonborn greeting he knew.

Their countenance remained unchanged and he decided it might be a better idea to head toward the crowd. He backed off a step and turned to find two more young Moonborn men behind him. They might have been twins but he didn't look at them for long enough to tell: as soon as he saw that one of them was carrying a length of pipe, he decided that his best chances were in the open.

He burst into the squall at the closest thing he could manage to a sprint in the calf-deep snow. His coveralls limited his range of motion just enough to slow him down. He had maybe a two-meter lead on them but the sounds of breathing and footfalls behind him grew louder. The frigid air stung his lungs. He doubted calling for help would do any good, even if he had the breath to try. A shadow leapt from the squall just in front of him, its arm raised straight out at eye level. There wasn't time to stop. His legs kicked up from under him and he was on his back, the wind knocked out of him, snow smearing his vision and catching in his nose and windpipe as he gasped for breath. It had a sour chemical taste.

He rolled onto all fours defensively and pushed himself up onto his knees. Before he could go any further, someone came up from behind and shoved him back down onto his face, kneeling on the small of his back. All he could see was snow and the blur of ice crystals on his eyelids. He felt hands grab his right arm, holding it out and steadying his hand. With a panicked dread, he realized they were going after his ID chip. They were monitored by CA AIs, so at least there would be a definitive legal record of exactly where he was before he was never seen again.

He felt a pair of heavy cutters snap his right thumb off at the knuckle. His body tried to scream from the pain but it came out as muted, gagging gasps. He heard them laughing and felt them going for his left arm, remembering with a strangely clinical terror that his wrist-screen stem had a tracking chip as well. He tried consoling himself with the thought that the pain couldn't get any worse. Then he felt a sharp, but not quite sharp enough, knife blade being wedged under the stem, then the stem itself being torn out and the pain did, in fact, get much worse.

Again, his body gasped for a scream. Then he blacked out.

5. THE ORPHEUS PIT

although his CARD liaison duties required periodic travel to the
Colony, Colonel Regent Harvey Sinclair Park's job had always been
officially classified as planetary. As hard as he'd worked to attain and
maintain that status, he only realized the extent to which he'd come to
take it for granted when he received word that he'd been reassigned
to a permanent position at CARD Galilaei, and would henceforth be
classified as Colonial.

The news came directly over his official cog facet. Absent any of
the charm and spin he'd built a career on, it simply appeared in his
mind as an indisputable fact while his body was swimming laps in the
underground pool at his chalet in the Tatra Mountains of Slovakia.
He'd purchased the chalet a year ago and spent the next eight months
renovating and decorating it with salvaged Second Expansion-era
antiques and fixtures brought back from the Colony. In the four
months since completing the renovations, he'd spent a total of nine
nights there, and thrown only one party.

As he climbed out of the pool, he sent word over his cog for the
staff to leave. He wanted the place to himself for the hours before
he was scheduled to depart so that he could record the memories of
being alone in it in his cog.

He padded barefoot through the tiled corridors and luminously
plastered rooms under glowing mosaic ceilings, adorned with his

impressive collection of art and objects. All of it was immaculate, and it was all he had to show for the eighteen years spent navigating the arcane hierarchy of the Colonial Authority, sacrificing family and any real friendships, and he was not likely to ever set foot in it again. Once you were classified as Colonial that was it. You didn't come back.

He'd seen it happen to so many of the men and women he'd recruited into CARD. It was the aspect of his job he found most distasteful. For the most part, he served as an agent between powerful subsidiary corporations and universities, research institutions and individuals at the top of their fields, brokering generous employment contracts and enjoying the generous commissions and perquisites offered by parties on both sides to gain his favor. Those recruited to the Galilaei complex were the unfortunate second tier: brilliant and talented enough to be desired but not savvy enough to maintain control of their employment contracts. Sometimes the best, often the brightest, nonetheless doomed.

As fabulous as his inaugural chalet party had been, he knew that there would be many more, equally fabulous, in his absence. The costs of its purchase and renovation had been underwritten by CA banks; now that he was Colonial, stewardship of the property reverted to them in his absence. They could do whatever they wanted with it.

Growing up as the son of a mid-level subsidiary distribution manager and a municipal apparatchik, he had seen his parents relocated mercilessly, often separated for years at a time as dictated by the ever-shifting trade agreements and industrial development projects of the CA. Even as a young boy he'd recognized that the Colonial Authority was always the entity to benefit from the macroeconomic tumult that had so buffeted his family. Since he could remember, he'd been determined to earn an administrative post within it, imagining that by aligning himself with power he'd find the stability denied his parents.

By the end of his first year internship he'd come to realize that the inner workings of the Authority resembled nothing so much as a bloodsport conducted on quicksand, in which the combatants maneuvered and manipulated and clawed and fought for the opportunity to sink deeper in. The privileges attending those depths were considerable and undeniable; pulling oneself out of the mire was not an option. The only question was how much of you would be left exposed to the elements, and how richly you would be enveloped by the tides below the surface.

Acknowledging that he lacked the ruthlessness necessary to compete in the executive track, he established himself as a fixer and a provider, facilitating, massaging and finessing the ruthlessness of others. He proved adept enough at it to enter the Regency and earn the rank of Colonel, affording him an exceptional level of the comfort and stability he'd sought. At a certain level, he'd always known it was an illusion. Several of his colleagues had been designated Colonial over the years, some as casualties of the kinds of internal rivalries he'd so adeptly navigated, others seemingly without reason, a consequence of their name being cross-referenced by the wrong entities in the wrong database at the wrong time. Bad luck by statistics.

He'd dedicated so much cog space to recording the details and spatial arrangements he'd so carefully assembled that he didn't notice the time passing. The next thing he knew he was staring out the window of a Bee flyer on his way to the regional CA headquarters in Bratislava, muddy fields dotted with the first sprouts of the season rolling away below him in the dawn.

THE Bee touched down on the landing deck of the Bratislava CA tower next to an ominous-looking mirror-clad combat Wasp, which was to take him directly to the Colony. He didn't relish spending the next seventy-two hours in a cramped ordinance bay with barely enough room to turn a somersault. To make matters worse, his sole companions for the journey were a pair of Cyclopes.

The Cyclopes were his least favorite of CARD's military applications: cybernetic-organic hybrids designed to function as riot police, prison guards and shock troops in the Colony. They numbered in the thousands, all controlled centrally by an AI network at the Icarus-Daedelus complex on the Far Side, where their bodies were grown in vats and integrated with tech components. They sustained themselves on battery power and a nutrient paste they excreted, which they periodically sucked through a straw with wide, flaccid mouths lined with small dull vestigial teeth. They resembled gigantic babies in bondage gear, with a single convex panoptic lens on their forehead. They moved with a lumbering gait but were surprisingly fast and agile (most of their organic matter was augmented muscle), effectively mute but for a speaker embedded in their thorax which occasionally issued terse information in the inhuman voice of the controlling AI. They smelled like raw meat and plastic.

Once they left the stratosphere and cleared the junk belt, rising above the slowly spinning lights of distant Skywheels, his official cog facet opened into a secure virtual conference space. It was on a Colonial cog net, which, like everything in the Colony, seemed so much cheaper and seedier than the higher-bandwidth, higher-end planetary nets, reminding him that the only place the opulence of the Second Expansion still existed was in historical sims and the reconstructive efforts of collectors like himself.

Waiting in the virtual space was Brigadier General Iskinder Nshombo, commander-in-chief of the Colonial armed forces, a compact, wiry man with the fine features and deep black skin of old African aristocracy. The military's involvement did little to ease his mind as to whatever it was he was being relocated to the Colony to do. The personal presence of so high-ranking a personage, even as a virtual avatar, only exacerbated his unease.

Also in the space, depicted as a 2-dimensional screen projection since she didn't have a cog, was the Sister Doctor. She glared at him with an expression of what he took to be smug retribution. Clearly she'd been informed that he would be joining her as a resident at Galilaei. It was difficult for him to look her in the eye, even as a projection in virtual space. Not because she blamed him for her situation (he understood why she did, but didn't consider it entirely fair; he was only the messenger, after all, and had simply made an effort to put the best possible spin on things) but because it was clear by her face that the madness of the Galilaei complex was already well on its way to ruining her mind. He wondered how long it would be until his own sanity eroded.

The Brigadier General began without ceremony: "Over the last eight months, a broadcast signal has been intercepted all over the moon. It is a kind of music, but its distribution pattern is far wider than any other Moonborn media ever tracked."

As he spoke, a graphical map of lunar population centers appeared between them, highlighting Moonborn populations in blue. Interceptions of the broadcast were denoted in red, resulting in a moon-wide dapple of purple. "It has transcended long-standing regional, tribal and ethnic boundaries in a manner not seen since the last period during which the Moonborn Unity was active."

He received a packet describing the Moonborn Unity as a violently anti-planetary terrorist organization, largely dormant for the last three decades.

"Intelligence and Information Services believes that if they are once again active, it could pose a serious threat to the stability and function of the lunar Colony and disrupt the planetary economy to a degree the Board considers unacceptable. IIS is coordinating with municipal law enforcement and Icarus-Daedelus to track down the source of the broadcast.

"Your team at CARD is to conduct an analysis of the signal itself: both the structure of its frequency and its content. Sister Doctor, you and your android will establish a translation of the language within it through your test subject. The third member of your team will establish mathematical models of both signal and content to analyze for possible hidden codes or messages."

"Quantitative translation of Moonspeak is a dead end," the Sister Doctor muttered.

"Approximations are acceptable. They will be quantified and analyzed for probability by your third team member, who will also be analyzing the carrier signals for coded frequencies."

"And who is this third member?" Park ventured.

"Demetrius Wei, currently under contract as Chief Engineer of the Orpheus Project. You are en route to extract him from the site of the Orpheus dig now."

"This requires personal involvement?" Park had grown accustomed to the Regency's relaxed attitude toward rank, which was apparently not shared by the military.

"There are unknown variables at the site which may require an adaptive sentient presence. The CARD administrators seem to feel you are qualified for the task. Mission details are downloading to a secure sub-facet now.

"Your team will report directly to my command. IIS will be monitoring the project, and my staff will be at your disposal. Do not hesitate to request additional resources. The CARD AIs have been instructed to leave this communication channel open. Good luck."

The conference room program closed, returning his official facet to its regular stream of indices, trade statistics and Regency news feeds. Soon, the icon of an encrypted briefing began flashing, indicating that the download was complete. He opened it and learned only that the man he was brought to the moon to retrieve, Demetrius Wei, was an obscure mathematician whose only listed job history was as an undistinguished staff quant at a backwater Stem, and that he hadn't officially existed for twenty-one years.

IN THE same way that the threat of relocation to the Colony was used to keep planetary administrators in line, the threat of the Orpheus Pit reinforced the status quo among Colonial administrators. It was an infamous bogey that generations of ambitious executives feared being banished to should they run afoul of their superiors, its name spoken in whispers when dared spoken at all. Park was surprised, and more than a little perplexed, to discover that it actually existed, let alone that it was still in progress.

It dated back two hundred years, to the height of the Second Expansion. The idea behind it was pure madness: to use a Namgung engine to tunnel to the center of the moon and build a centrifugal reactor capable of melting the iron core and spinning it at a rate sufficient to generate an electromagnetic field strong enough to maintain an atmosphere under a particle net around the entire moon.

It had been born of the mad enthusiasm for particle nets and the grand plans for surface living that had defined the era of Consolidation. Not only was surface living more marketable to potential emigrants, it was a significant boon for labor control. Atmosphere under the nets was generated through industrial activity, and could be dissipated through the nets at controlled rates. If the population wanted air, they worked for it, effectively putting an end to the strikes, slow-downs and unrest that had so vexed the CA and brought about the end of the First Expansion.

Two hundred and twelve years ago, the Board of Directors had voted in favor of Orpheus. A Namgung Engine two kilometers in diameter was assembled in a cavern below the surface at an undisclosed location deep out in Oceanus Procellarum and set on its relentless descent to the center of the moon, eating away layers of rock, shredding and reordering molecules, ceaselessly shaving it away by micrometers and converting it into air and water to sustain the captive work force that followed it down the helices of tunnel it left in its wake as it re-formed the slag into a downward-spiraling honeycomb of caverns, alcoves and niches.

The initial workforce was comprised of eighteen hundred and

sixty-five conscripted laborers. Over the next two hundred years, it had been overseen by dozens of Chief Engineers, most of whom had no experience in mining, engineering or physics, and received periodic influxes of penal labor, from disobedient administrators to political prisoners deemed too problematic to die unpunished to homicidal psychotics deemed too rare to kill.

The twists and turns of the caves were designed to trap a thirty-kilometer pocket of air generated by the Engine, requiring that the labor population migrate downwards along with it. The dig had progressed to six hundred and eighty-four kilometers, leaving six hundred and fifty-four kilometers of labyrinthine vacuum between them and the vacuum of the surface.

The packet he received contained no data on how large the population of the pit currently was, what kind of society had developed over the centuries of descent, cramped into the caves above the Engine, or what they'd mutated into over the generations. But there was nothing Park could imagine that didn't resemble a hell.

THE entrance to the Orpheus Pit was under a mass-concentrated manhole cover stamped with an obscure, little-used two-hundred-year-old CA logo deep in the wastes of central Procellarum, hidden beneath a thick layer of dust, hundreds of kilometers from the nearest habitat in any direction.

A team of four more Cyclopes awaited them. Park, clad in a military vac suit, watched them clear away the dust and pull open the manhole cover with magnets and heavy chains. Once they'd lowered themselves and their gear into it, he followed them into the uppermost cavern, where the Namgung Engine had first been constructed.

In the middle of the chamber, the re-formed rock floor fell away into a gaping chasm, a wormhole into black oblivion, straight down, all the way to the Engine. According to the schematic in his cog, it was the central exhaust shaft around which the helices of caverns coiled.

A repeller raft was tethered at the edge of it, a four-meter wide square of steel mounted on truss and fitted with gravity-resistors, bobbing gently over the abyss.

The Cyclopes stacked their equipment cases onto the raft. It dipped gently under their weight. For however long it took to extract Wei, Park would be eating and drinking through the tubes in his helmet, sucking nutrient paste and water stored in canisters mounted at his hip, breathing his recycled exhalations, secretions and excretions filtered molecularly through the M-pack mounted across his shoulder blades. He already felt just a little bit nauseous all the time. He hoped it would pass.

Two Cyclopes stayed above in the chamber. The other four boarded the raft with him. As he stepped off the edge of the rock onto the steel platform and felt it dip under his weight, inching slightly further down into nothingness, he realized that his attitude toward death had become unexpectedly ambivalent. There were myriad scenarios in his immediate future that could lead to slow, horrible ends. Yet in the context of the futility of the rest of his life being spent in the Colony, each could be seen as a potential relief from perpetual discomfort.

And so they descended, sinking soundlessly away from the work lights at the mouth of the cavern, sinking into ink black vacuum. The platform gathered momentum gently, steadying out at a hundred and twenty kilometers per hour.

Once he became acclimated to the sensation of falling, like an unrelenting bad dream, Park tried to find a comfortable position in which to spend the coming hours, only to determine that there wasn't one. He perched on a stack of cases and tried to apportion as much of his awareness out of his physical being and into his cog networks as he could, but it was pointless. The signal was strong through the Cyclopes' relay, but the wailing soundlessness of the pit kept screaming mutely back into his mind, pulling him out of his sims and indexed memories and back into the terrible emptiness of the present, the steady unrolling of the depth gauge, the maddeningly slow progress of the clock and the twisting wraiths of long-dead souls reduced to flares of pure rage and despair passing through him, leaving in their wake terrifying images flashing through the periphery of his visor.

The raft slowed once they were within the range of the air pocket, and one of the Cyclopes began steering it in a wide downward spiral close to the wall of the shaft while another activated the transponder keyed to Wei's ID chip. Through the rock and the interference from the Namgung Engine far below, the closest they could pinpoint his location was within ten kilometers.

The Cyclopes used grappling hooks to pull the raft over to one side and set charges against the rock. Then they pushed across the shaft to a safe distance and detonated them. Shards of rock and dust rushed silently into the vacuum of the shaft, revealing a jagged, three-foot hole. As they pulled the raft back over to it, Park felt the rush of escaping air pressing against his suit. Three of the Cyclopes climbed through, leaving the fourth aboard the raft to seal the hole with quickfoam behind them, and retrieve them once they were ready to leave. Park followed them through the hole, feet first.

He emerged into a narrow, curving, steeply sloped tunnel. There were pale glo-globes strung along the walls, which were thick with strange mold and blistering, gently phosphorescent mushrooms. The light was dim enough not to hurt his eyes after the blackness of the shaft. He opened the visor of his helmet, but the stench was so bad he snapped it shut again. The Cyclopes were standing aimlessly, scanning the corridor back and forth. He realized they were waiting for him to decide which way to go.

The Cyclopes' transponder displayed the same information as his cog. It provided no more useful data than it had in the shaft, indicating only that Wei was somewhere deeper in.

Fifty meters along, the cave branched off into a Y. They followed it to the right, and soon emerged into a cavern nearly thirty meters wide and at least as tall. The walls were covered with mushrooms and mold. Discarded construction material, broken-down machinery, spent hydroponic components and assorted other detritus left behind in the descent was scattered across the floor.

Here, they first encountered denizens of the pit.

They were hardly recognizable as human: small and hairless, with a wiry musculature favoring their calves, a physiognomy disrupted and rendered even more alien by all manner of grotesque tumor, dead-end mutation, mutilation and blistering growths of the same fungi that clung to the walls. The cavern teemed with them.

As Park and the Cyclopes strode into their midst they stopped what they were doing – chewing leaves of pale ivy, copulating, sleeping, fighting; he was careful not to look too closely – and turned their too-large, colorless eyes towards them.

It struck Park as unlikely that any among them might know where to find the Chief Engineer so he kept his helmet sealed and progressed slowly down the slope of the cavern surrounded by the Cyclopes, which had drawn their weapons.

Only one of the things was possessed of the instinct to attack the interlopers; it vaulted itself over a cluster of others and was instantaneously bisected by one of the Cyclopes' particle-beam weapons. Its comrades watched dumbly as its halves hit the ground and came to a tumbling stop, sentient enough to shuffle out of the intruders' way as they continued across the cavern. At the far end, it narrowed and split into three tunnels. The transponder signal remained ambiguous, so he chose the center tube and continued their slow downward spiral.

A kilometer further along, they entered another large cavern. In this one, the trappings of some sort of civilization were significantly more abundant. A network of modular catwalks and scaffolds divided the space vertically, mazelike in a chaos of pipes and ductwork. There were hydroponic grids under banks of artificial daylight and mobile DRE units. The cave dwellers tending them wore crude garments of spun vegetable fiber and simple synthetics. Many of them seemed to be missing limbs, ears or eyes but most of them were less severely physically devolved. They seemed not to notice Park and the heavily armed giants in their midst, keeping their heads down and focusing intently on their tasks.

He attempted to intercept one of them, a female, blocking her path as she pulled a cart of rocks along a catwalk toward one of the DR tanks. She didn't look up, trying in vain to squeeze past the Cyclopes blocking her path. Still unwilling to open his visor, preferring the stale, acrid recycled oxygen molecules to the noxious atmosphere of the pit, he pulled up a file image of Wei on a screen field and put it front of the wretched woman's face. She glanced up, then bowed her head and sank to her knees as if awaiting punishment. At first Park thought she was bowing down to it. Then he realized she had been looking through it, at the imposing figures suddenly standing behind him.

One of the Cyclopes kept its eye on the little female, but the other two already had their weapons trained on the new arrivals. They were of a distinctly different physiognomy than the others. Proportionately, they looked tall; coiled sinewy muscle under old-fashioned stealth cloaks, smeared head to toe in pale clay. Their faces were angular, soft and less distinct. A pentagram had been drawn across each of their foreheads in black soot. They carried brutal and fearsome composite-stone weapons.

Park tilted the screen projection of Wei so they could see it.

Their expressions remained unchanged. They simply turned and walked away. He watched them, perplexed. Ten meters along, they stopped and looked back at him and he decided to try to follow them.

HE FOLLOWED them down and down and down through the cavern and down again into narrower tunnels where Devolved mined the walls with crude stone chisels, through another industrial cavern and again into the tunnels. In the third cavern they came to, the industrial infrastructure was still under construction. The cave dwellers toiled under the watchful eyes of invisible, stealth-cloaked Overseers. Among the laborers he didn't see a single human, which made him wonder what happened to all the planetaries sentenced to the pit.

What was it that kept these things alive? Beyond simple sustenance, what was it that animated them? These caves offered neither pleasure nor comfort nor hope for better. Could it be called life at all? It was existence of its basest, most animal sort.

He followed them through a seemingly endless series of such nightmare caverns and tunnels. He was increasingly aware of the vibrations in the rock under his feet, getting stronger as they travelled deeper, closer to the Engine, and he was beginning to experience the unpleasant sensation of field interference in his cog. He was still connected to the Cyclopes' relay, but there were troubling moments when he was unable to access his own facets, which seemed to be increasing the further he descended into the caves. He stifled his panic and continued on, watching the Cyclopes closely for any sign that their functioning was similarly effected. He saw none. They lumbered along, steady and expressionless.

Three kilometers from their point of entry (having walked three times that, accounting for the many twists and turns), they emerged from a narrow tunnel into a nearly empty cavern, half the size of the largest they'd passed through, with round walls and a high, domed ceiling.

The cave wall had been blasted smooth and was covered floor to ceiling with vast, incomprehensible equations being written, rubbed out, revised and rewritten in chalk by dozens of cave dwellers on a rickety network of scaffolding. As he passed under it, he realized the scaffolds were made of fused bone. These cave dwellers were of yet another type. They were the same size as the Devolved, but proportioned more akin to the Overseers. They wore ancient coveralls that were too large for them, rolled at the cuffs and emblazoned with the same old CA logo that had been on the entrance cover. They differed from both other Orpheus castes in that many of them had hair, which they wore in oddly braided topknots.

In the center of the floor was a perfectly round hole ten meters wide. Directly above it there was an identical hole through the ceiling; it was one of the exhaust channels that led directly down into the unseen, unknowable, unstoppable Engine.

The light in the chamber came from pale glo globes strung from the scaffolds, which cast a web of shadows across the walls. The air was alive with crackling particle fields. As he stepped out from under the scaffolds and onto the vibrating chamber floor, the Overseer leading them held up her hand for them to stop then continued across the chamber. The others stayed with Park and the Cyclopes.

Park looked up and around the room. The cave dwellers had stopped their writing on the wall and stood at the edge of the scaffolds looking down at him. The interference in his cog had grown worse. His feet and legs ached from the long hike, and his lower back was sore from the weight of the gear on his vac-suit.

Before long, he saw two figures approaching through the crosshatch of shadows filling the chamber. One was a top-knotted cave dweller, the other unmistakably human. It was Demetrius Wei.

He demagnetized his helmet collar and removed it. Immediately, he felt a screaming atomic feedback within his cog chip. He staggered on his feet and his vision went white. It felt as if his mind had been shredded, peeled apart from itself across multiple dimensions. He pressed his palms into his temples and collapsed to his knees. When his vision cleared, there was a ringing in his ears and he could no longer access his facets through his cog. He remembered basic facts about his life, who and where he was, and why. But left suddenly with only his core consciousness he felt strangely empty, incomplete. Buzzing ache filled his mind, emanating from his thalamus.

The air was cold and acrid. His ears filled with the rush of air from the exhaust shaft and the reverberations of the Engine, which oscillated between a high-pitched whine and a static hiss. When his vision cleared he saw Demetrius Wei standing in front of him.

He looked older, of course, but also more intense, as if his being had somehow been seared more deeply into the fabric of the universe.

Looking at him was like looking at a shadow: simultaneously there and not there, an elemental function of light and dark in the shape of a human being. His clothes, a quarter century out of fashion, were worn and mended many times over. He stared at Park through deep-set, pale eyes that blinked but did not move.

"Is she alive?" His voice was a sepulchral rasp, nonetheless perfectly audible through the din of the Engine.

Park stared back at him. He didn't know what he was talking about. "I...I'm sorry, I...I don't know what you mean. Is who alive?"

Wei watched him silently.

Harvey Sinclair Park found himself in the unfamiliar position of being at a loss for words. He realized he was somehow frightened of the man standing in front of him, though he didn't know why. Then he remembered his reason for being there. Without access to his cog, it took him a painfully long time to formulate the sentence. "Demetrius Wei...you've been reassigned to the Colonial Authority Research and Development division. My name is Colonel Regent Park and I am here to escort you to the CARD facility at Galilaei."

He remembered that he'd had a reputation for charm, vaguely aware that such a thing as his charisma existed, but only in an abstract sense, in the same way he remembered images and sensations from the sims stored in his cog. He could not access any of them, and his words sounded flat and empty to his own ears.

Wei wasn't looking at him. His icy, still eyes gazed past him to the Cyclopes.

"Organic?" he asked.

"Engineered organic, yes," Park answered, "Hybrids."

"Mm," Wei muttered, then turned his attention back to Park.

The motionless madness in his eyes was disconcerting. Park couldn't meet them.

"How long has it been?"

Park struggled to remember the information from the packet in his cog. "Twenty-some years I think."

Something like a smile spread across Wei's chapped, pale lips. The effect was terrifying.

"You've had a long journey," Wei rasped. "You should rest."

"I...I would prefer to return to the surface as soon as possible."

The smile widened, accompanied by a silent, still fury in his eyes. His voice remained calm and quiet: "Yes. Yes, of course you would. But the Engine must be consulted. Please, come with me. Accommodations are being prepared."

HE AWOKE in darkness. He had slept on a thin straw mat laid out on a stone slab carved into the wall of the small stone cell that served as the dormitory of Wei's chambers. The straw mat and a clay bowl of distilled water were apparently the sole accommodations to have been prepared. There were a half-dozen sleeping slabs carved into the wall, three others of which were occupied by snoring topknots when he arrived. He slowly activated his glo globe and saw that the other niches were now empty and he was alone.

His body felt even worse than it had before he slept: the aches in his legs, feet and back were now joined by shooting pains in his hips and neck. Access to his cog had not returned. Two thirds of his consciousness was empty. He still knew who he was and why he was in the Orpheus Pit, but everything else was only a concept: he knew that there was a world outside of the Pit, that he had a life in it, but he couldn't remember what it was like or anything about it, only his nightmare descent through the caverns, the chilling visage and voice of Demetrius Wei, and the incessant rumble of the Engine.

He'd slept in his vac-suit minus the boots, helmet collar, M-pack and supply belt, which sat on the floor next to the slab where he had left them. Judging by the smell and soot-smeared appearance of Wei and the cave dwellers, he assumed there were no facilities for bathing in the Pit.

He sat up on the slab, groaning at the new pains accompanying the motion, and pulled on his boots, attached the other components and went looking for Wei.

The Cyclopes stood silently in the vestibule outside the dormitory cell, where he had left them. One stood watch while the others were dormant.

"Where is he?" he asked the one on watch.

The Cyclops turned its red-lensed face toward the door at the opposite end of the vestibule.

"Wake the others," he said, and started towards the door.

As he approached, he heard the tapping and scratching of chalk. Through the doorway was a chamber twice as large as the dormitory cell, lit by glo globes sitting in cradles carved into the walls. A half dozen top-knotted dwellers were busy writing out equations in chalk on the wall. He couldn't be certain without access to his cog, but Park didn't think he'd ever seen these notations before.

Demetrius Wei sat on the floor in the middle of the room, watching them. His back was to the door and he didn't react when Park stepped into the chamber, but for some reason Park had the distinct impression that he knew he was there. Long, strange moments passed before he stood and turned to him.

"My savior awakes," he said, followed by a guttural rattle that might have been a laugh. "So, tell me, savior. For what does the Colonial Authority return me to their world?"

Park struggled to remember which aspects of the mission were classified only to realize that he'd forgotten the details of it altogether.

"There's a song..." he said distantly, "and they want to know the meaning of it."

Wei stared at him quizzically.

"I'm sorry," he said, "I've lost access to my cog." He realized the technology didn't come into use until nearly a decade after Wei was banished to the Pit. "It's a networked chip, called a cognitive-differential chip, in my brain. I'm afraid I've used it to store more information than I realized. It seems as though the Engine's fields are disrupting its operation. I'm sure once I return to the surface..." he was talking more to comfort himself than to inform Wei, who didn't seem interested. He had been diligently repressing the fear that his cog might be permanently damaged, that all of the information and aspects of himself stored within it might be lost forever. There was frighteningly little of him left. He knew his name was Harvey Sinclair Park and that he was a CARD Colonel Regent and that he was to retrieve Demetrius Wei, but what did that mean? Beyond that, who was he? "Do you have any belongings to gather? We have a vac-suit for you."

"The Engine must be consulted."

Park remembered him saying the phrase when he arrived. "I don't understand. Aren't you the Chief Engineer? Your contract's been purchased by CARD. You can leave."

The guttural rattle-laugh returned. "This is not the Colony, Colonel-Regent. The Colonial Authority means nothing here. It is nothing more than an insignia on the Engineers' uniforms; so ancient they no longer know it once had meaning. Here there is only the will of the Engine. Here the Engine is God."

Park stood mute, uncomprehending.

"Come with me."

The only direction he wanted to walk was up toward the repeller raft and back to the surface. But Wei had already left the chamber and stepped into the corridor outside. Park hurried to follow him, calling for the Cyclopes to join them.

"There has not been verbal language in the Pit for generations," Wei said, leading him down the spiraling corridor, in and out of the pools of light created by the glo globes in the niches carved into the walls. "As the Orpheans evolved, they've developed a low-grade telepathy by which they communicate with one another. Even the Devolved possess a rudimentary capacity for it. Like myself. Because I understand mathematics I was accepted among the Engineers."

He ducked through a low archway carved into the wall. Park followed him and emerged onto a high ridge carved into the rock overlooking one of the busy industrial caverns.

"The Devolved are bred like cattle. They're harvested as resource by the ones with the star on their forehead. The little ones with the braids are the descendents of the original Engine builders. They interpret the will of the Engine."

"The Engine is a machine," Park ventured, "It doesn't have a will."

Wei ducked into another narrow passageway cut into the rock, leading him into another moldy, spiraling corridor.

"The Engine shapes their world. It provides them with air, water, energy. It takes their bodies after they die and through its sustenance they are reborn. They see themselves as an extension of the Engine. They do not know it as a machine. They do not know its purpose. Nor do they care. They know only that it creates their world."

Park found it increasingly difficult to concentrate. Wei's ravaged voice and the thrumming vibrations of the cavern walls flooded what was left of his conscious mind, filling his synapses, consuming all other thoughts. He glanced over his shoulder from time to time to make sure the Cyclopes were still with them. At first the sight of their three dim red eyes bobbing through the shadows between glo globes was almost reassuring, but it quickly became just another fact, coexisting with the details of the Orpheus civilization coming from Wei.

"Every ten years, the population must descend in order to remain in the habitable zone. All of their apparatus, the DRE units, the hydroponic systems, the manufactories, all must be disassembled and relocated to the lower, newer caverns, while enough essential work continues to maintain the necessary civic functions.

"The cavern complex is asymmetrical, irregular. The pattern repeats every fifty years, but the average lifespan for an Orphean is thirty years. So it is exceptionally rare that anyone should live to see the same cavern configuration twice. Each time they descend, they must re-establish the infrastructure of their civilization in unfamiliar surroundings."

They rounded a bend and the corridor opened up onto another ridge overlooking a chamber like the one where Park had first met Wei, with holes in the ceiling and floor and equations covering the walls. It might have been the same cavern, but there was no scaffolding in this one. The floor of the chamber was engraved with arcane symbols around the hole in the center. There were slate fields at certain vertices of the diagram, studied and interfaced with by teams of Engineers. Their topknots were gray and more elaborate than the others, and they wore no clothing at all.

"The Orpheus Engineers possess the knowledge of Namgung's algorithms, which describe the shapes of the caves being formed below them. They pass it down from generation to generation and plot the progress of the civilization, accounting for population densities, reproductive rates, food production, waste recycling, airflow.

"There are hundreds of points like this throughout the complex, intake and exhaust channels that lead directly to the Engine. By closing off channels to and from these chambers, the Engineers can determine the flow of air through the entire complex. They can control which passages get fresh air and which get exhaust. They know where the water cisterns will form. They can withhold air to regions if they so choose. In that way, they are quite like the Colonial Authority, are they not?"

Park could not think to answer.

He and the Cyclopes followed Wei down a steep, narrow staircase carved into the rock, down to the chamber floor. The sound was different in this chamber, a low resonant hum that penetrated his being.

The task at hand – bringing Wei to Galilaei – was a narrowing thread through Park's mind, almost forgotten. "We should return..." his voice felt ever weaker and more distant in his chest. He could barely hear himself.

But Wei's thin rasp remained perfectly audible over the Engine's hum, as if it was coming from inside his eardrums. "The Orpheans believe the vibrations in the rock are the Engine's voice, the particle levels in the air and the shape of the caverns are its will." He stopped and turned, looked into Park's eyes and with an eerie smile said: "They are none of them sane."

They reached the cavern floor and Park saw cloaked Overseers half-visible in the shadows around the periphery of the cavern, still as statues.

The echoes and reverberations of the thrumming buzz created strange harmonics deep in his brain, almost like a chant. The hairs on the back of his neck stood up and he broke out in a cold sweat inside his vac-suit. Eddies of fine dust swirled across the patterns etched into the floor, drifting in the currents of air toward the hole at their center.

He heard Wei say, "You are here to take me from Orpheus," but his lips weren't moving. Nausea pulled his stomach into a twist. The Orpheans at the slate fields seemed to be moving according to some bizarre synchronization.

"The Engine has been consulted," he heard Wei say. "And it will permit me to leave."

Park tried to speak but had no idea if he was saying anything at all.

If he was, Wei did nothing to acknowledge it. "But the Engine demands equilibrium," he said, his pale dark eyes seeming to peer straight through him. "I may leave. But you must stay in my place."

He tried to speak, but his mouth only made a terrible moaning sound, as if emerging from the depths of a nightmare. He struggled to enunciate, stammering and slobbering. "No, I...I can't...I can't stay here...I can't live in this place."

"It is not necessary to," Wei cast his deep-set eyes toward the gaping hole in the floor. "The Engine will accept you."

"No," Park stammered, "No, this is insane."

"*Yes*," Wei said, a soulless whisper inside his head. "*This is insane.*"

Park stared across the ten meters to the edge of the hole. The Orpheus Pit had become the entirety of his reality; ten meters of reconstituted rock were all that stood between him and the end of his life. The engravings on the floor seemed to draw a runway track pointing him directly into it. He turned and looked back at the three Cyclopes. They stared at him impassively. They didn't care if he lived or died. Their directive was to extract Wei from the Pit. He was only there to facilitate the mission. He was only there because the Engine demanded equilibrium…

His mind raced desperately for any reason not to cast himself into the Engine, any sense of hope. But his life outside the Pit was locked in his cog, unreachable, and he could muster no solace. He could live out the rest of his life as a slave in these caverns, or he could surrender it as a repository of oxygen, hydrogen and carbon molecules in tribute to madness and exchange for this stranger's freedom.

He took his first step toward the hole, then stopped and said: "I don't deserve this." It meant nothing, he knew, but he felt it needed to be said.

Wei's expression was not cruel, but bore no trace of anything like sympathy. "No one deserves anything here," his hollow voice merged with the resonant thrum and static hiss, "There is only the will of the Engine."

He took another step.

"You should remove your vacuum suit," Wei said, "This intake portal is for organic material only."

He obligingly removed the components, then pulled back the Velcro flaps and opened the zippers, letting the outer shell collapse to the floor as he stepped out of it and peeled himself out of the undersuit.

He took another step and was engulfed in an overwhelming and unexpected feeling of love for everyone and everything he'd ever known. But even though he loved them with every fiber of his being, he couldn't remember any of them. He tried to remember moments, parents, siblings, friends, but he couldn't. He tried to remember the sound of his mother's voice, but he couldn't.

With each step, he became more aware of his body, the strangeness of its weight in the lunar gravity, the soft frailty of it, which was now the totality of his being, naked and alone, a morsel of fodder for a forsaken act of grandiose madness.

The naked Engineers did not look from their slate fields as he passed.

At the edge of the chasm, shredding static drowned out

everything else and he didn't feel his body anymore, as if there was nothing of him left. Only once did he question what he was doing, in the fleeting half-second as his weight shifted beyond the point of no return and his bowels voided themselves did he wish that he could take everything back, do everything again, without a cog, without the Colonial Authority. But that would have been a different life, in a different world, perhaps the next.

WEI watched the man disappear below the rim of the portal, then climbed out of the ragged clothes he'd worn for the last twenty-three years and stepped into the underlayer of Park's vac-suit. There was a suit of his own waiting for him, but he relished the symbolism of stepping into the dead man's clothes.

It had taken so little effort to convince the Colonel-Regent to do himself in. The Orpheans indeed believed themselves to be interpreters of the Engine's will, but neither they nor the Engine cared if he stayed in the Pit or not.

His skin tingled as the nanofibers of the undersuit penetrated his pores and lower orifices. The smart bacteria instantly began devouring the crust of filth on his skin, and he felt cleaner than he'd been in decades.

He approached the Cyclopes and nodded to indicate he was prepared to ascend, wondering that it should be so easy to exact his revenge on the rest of the Colonial Authority.

6. THE KIDS IN CRISIS CITY

"Fresh *T7 no taste? Unlife, unlife. Bests of home.*"

Sel wasn't sure what exactly her new friend was trying to convey – Iba spoke in Crisi dialect, which was unlike any Moonspeak she'd ever heard – but she took it to mean that if she hadn't tasted T7 she hadn't lived, and that the taste either represented the best of what home had to offer or evoked the taste of home, or possibly both. Ado had warned her that Crisian connotations tended to be broad. To her ears, the tonal range sounded limited but nuanced, and she hadn't yet figured out the nuances.

Iba was short and powerfully built, her face and features full and round. She wore her hair in elaborately braided cornrows and dressed in a style distinct from the rather drab, cheap looking mass-produced garments the rest of the Crisians wore. Sel suspected that she made them herself and gave her credit for ingenuity in turning what she lacked in skill into design attributes, calling attention to the rough stitching by using mismatched threads and playing up a deliberately patchwork aesthetic.

They stood in a long queue that snaked across a wide tile room, along with Iba's boyfriend Bal and the twins Ro and Re. Bal looked to be of the same ethnicity as Iba, though taller and with a more prominent nose. The twins were proportioned differently, shorter, with long arms and compact torsos. Ado had stayed back at the converted factory complex where they were staying; she suspected he was angling for time alone with a girl called Folle.

A trough ran around the circumference of the room, filled with water flowing at a brisk current and teeming with T7, a genetic derivation of the trout bred to grow to maturity in ninety-six hours. Workers at various points around the trough dipped nets into the water, woven large enough to let the immature fish through. The bodies of those that evaded capture past the point of maturity decomposed shortly thereafter, becoming food for the rest.

Sel, raised on the strictly vegetarian Sanctuariat diet, had heard that there were people who ate living things, but the idea of it had always disgusted her. It struck her as especially cruel to create a life form with no purpose other than to be devoured.

But the Crisians had welcomed her and Ado, and taken good care of them, and she didn't want to appear rude, or provincial. If she would truly not be just another timid Sancte girl hiding her life away in glorified caves, then she would have to be willing to try new things.

So far, she'd liked the food she'd been given since being in Crisi, mostly stews and simple but tasty rice dishes. Much of the flavor and the protein content, she was told, came from organisms like the T7, but it had been easy not to associate the prepared dishes with living things. Actually seeing them pulled from the water – these things *breathed water* – squirming and writhing as they were dumped into plastic bins and rolled into the back to be cut open and gutted by workers in rubber aprons standing along a conveyer belt which carried the newly filleted corpses back to banks of sizzling deep-fryers, smokers, and flash-freezers, that was altogether something else.

It was difficult for her to gauge how long she'd been in Crisi. The sense of local time was even harder for her to get a handle on than the dialect. The Sanctuary ran on a twenty-nine hour day-night rotation, hours and minutes measured mechanically according to planetary tradition, with two work cycles and one Migration cycle a year. In Crisi, day and night were measured by the planet's shadow, nearly a month in Sanctuary time. The passage of time had started feeling strange from the first time she saw the glowing, banded Crisi particle net appear over the horizon. It had loomed gigantic in front of them for hours upon hours, always seeming as though it was just ahead but never getting any closer, until it suddenly filled the entire windshield and suddenly they were within it, the podvan buffeted by the strong winds that whipped around its periphery, rocking it on its suspension and whistling over its pocked metal surface.

The shadow of the planet also defined the city's season cycle. They were not yet in Crisi winter, she was told, and it was already five degrees colder than the Sanctuary got. Still, she never got tired of the feeling of being outside. The smart fibers of her cloak kept her warm enough and the feeling of open space, with nothing at all over her head, no walls around her, was like nothing she'd ever experienced. It was intoxicating and exhilarating. The billowing cloud patterns were hypnotizing; the colors of the sunlight refracted through the particles of the net, the light reflected off the towers, the scale of everything, so much greater than anything she'd ever seen. And the air trapped was alive with sound, always.

Her half-blood looks had so far been met without prejudice. In fact, none of the Crisians she'd come across seemed to care. Her forehead tattoo drew a second glance every so often, but so did Iba's hairstyle and clothes. There were just so unbelievably many people of all sorts, body and facial types she'd never seen, all seemingly from different tribes and ethnicities, all mixed up together, all over the place, all the time.

As she explored the city with Iba, Bal and the twins as her guides, she was astonished at just how crowded so large a space could feel.

There were times, cramming themselves onto trams or making their way across concourses during shift changes, when she felt like she was being swept up in a force greater than anything she'd ever known. Individuals seemed to cease, becoming part of the crowd, which had a will and a course of its own. It was almost terrifying. Then she'd catch sight of Iba, who'd smile, and that simple connection was enough to dispel her fears of losing herself.

The abandoned factory complex where they were staying was deep in an obsolete industrial district bordering a quiet residential neighborhood in the northeastern quarter of the city. It hadn't been formally converted into a dwelling so much as it had been taken over by the loosely organized youth collective of which Iba, Bal and the twins were a part. Iba's older brother Milit was on their elected council of leaders, as was Ado's girl Folle. It struck her as odd that all of the hundred or so residents were young. The most senior among them were Ado's age. He described it to her as a kind of hostel for young people from other parts of the city who'd been assigned medium-term work shifts in the area or were otherwise unable to live with their families, sort of a mini-Sanctuary network within the city.

As they gave her the grand tour, they seemed proud of the work they'd done in rehabilitating the dormitories and reconditioning some of the machinery to generate water, power and a crude forced-steam heating system without tapping into the city grid but as far as Sel was concerned, it would've been generous to call their workmanship inexpert. She pretended to admire their handiwork as a pretext for taking a closer look to make sure none of it was dangerous. It was hardly an autonomous structure. There was a big galley kitchen but no means to grow food or generate atmosphere; both had to come from outside.

Nevertheless, she'd accepted the room they offered her. Ado, ever the Nomad, stayed in the podvan, which was parked in a loading bay adjacent to what had once been a shipping-room floor.

He'd given her a brief overview of how life in the city worked: the Crisi Moonborn all lived on the first tier, which was divided into twelve wedges, each run by one or more of the Clans of Crisi. The Clans had evolved from the old trade guilds, unions and dynasty operations of the city builders.

Each of the Clans had standing deals with the CA to supply and manage labor. As long as the quotas were met, the districts received water and power for their homes and agricultural operations. But it wasn't unusual for the Clans to renegotiate more favorable terms for themselves on the backs of their districts, and there was nearly constant tension between the people of Crisi and the Clans, as well as long-running feuds and rivalries between Clans.

The collective that operated the complex where they were staying called itself the New Unity. Part of its reason for existence was to serve as a pressure valve for overworked communities, providing room and board for excess labor from other districts. Each New Unity chapter had an agreement with the local Clan that set the work schedules for its residents, who were also expected to contribute to the maintenance and operations of the facility where they were staying.

AT THE head of the T7 queue, Iba stepped up to the counter and gave the girl behind it their order, raising her voice over the muddy din of crowd chatter, running water and recorded background music bouncing around the concrete room. It sounded like she asked for *"paradise, sticks and a box of bricks"* before moving along to a different section of the counter to wait for their order.

Sel tried to follow the conversation but couldn't. She picked up words and phrases here and there, but they sounded like nonsense. She guessed there were a lot of double-meanings and slang usages she didn't know.

She was transfixed on the plastic bins of squirming T7s rolling back to their deaths. Up close, she could tell that they were eyeless; long, slick-skinned things with a gaping mouth at one end and trashing tail at the other, a line of desperately heaving gills in between.

Iba saw her watching them. *"All okay. No brain. Just delicious."*

After a couple of minutes the girl came back with their order, carrying a tray with two plastic baskets on it; one contained a pile of steaming hot fried T7 filets, the other a pile of smoked T7. A boy carried a heavy freezer pack of frozen filets. One of the twins picked up the tray, Bal hoisted the freezer pack onto his shoulders and they all followed Iba to the dining area on the other side of the room closer to the entrance. Crisians of a dozens of different ethnicities and all ages sat on benches at long communal tables. Groups and families stuck together, but everyone seemed to interact more or less freely. There was no evidence of the ethnocentrism and hostility she'd expected based on everything she'd always heard about Colony Moonborn.

She'd played two concerts in Crisi, each in different parts of the city, one in an abandoned library building and the other in a small, old outdoor amphitheater. The turnout at both of them had astonished her: easily several thousand people in each place. She attributed it to the popularity of Iba and the twins, who performed together and had played before she did at both shows. Iba played an amplified integrated-circuit system she controlled with a bank of potentiometers and switches and the twins, an array of electro-acoustic percussive devices.

Ado had played her some recordings of them in the podvan on the drive from Lyell, but she hadn't been terribly impressed with them. They struck her as monotonous and thin sounding. But seeing them perform was a different story. The recordings hadn't picked up any of the harmonics that happened between their instruments when they played, which, to Sel, was where the real character of their sound was. Nor had they captured the sheer energy of it. All of the rage that she imagined the Crisians must feel at their stupid system seemed to be channeled through them like electrons through a Bernoulli gate. It was hard to reconcile the sweet girl and laid-back boys who'd been showing her around the town with the fury of the maniacs she saw onstage. Their energy was met and exceeded by the crowd, which danced and cheered madly, which fed back into them in an ecstatic loop.

On both occasions, she'd enjoyed watching Iba and the twins more than her own performance. Her largest audience at Lyell may have been larger, but they were spread all over the Sanctuary, listening to her over the speakers while they worked. The actual crowd in front of her was maybe a third as large as these. And the Sanctuariat audiences had been quiet, even reverent.

Here in Crisi they started cheering and roaring from the first note, so loud that she couldn't even hear herself. She wanted to make a sound as vast and vibrant as the city itself, to fill the space in the way it had filled her. But she'd had no sense if she were doing it or not. She found it intimidating enough stepping onto the stage in the wake of the kind of catharsis Iba and the twins generated, all alone with her guitar and her gear, let alone match the energy of so large and responsive a crowd. It was all she could do to get her fingers to play the right notes and chords, to trigger the loops and effects in the right places, to get to the microphone in time for the vocals. She sang at the top of her lungs but had no idea if she was in tune or not, or if anyone cared.

The crowds sang along, or tried to as phonetically as they could manage. The lyrics were in a dialect of Moonspeak so idiosyncratic she couldn't imagine that anyone who hadn't known her since birth would understand them.

Even though she appreciated the Crisians' appreciations, she found herself wondering if any of them really cared if it was any good or not, or if they were simply excited to see her in front of them because they liked the recording.

Regardless, she was thrilled and humbled by the fact that they responded to the recording in the way they did. She just wasn't sure what the point of playing live was if nobody was paying any attention to what she did. She felt a strange adrenaline buzz from having been vibrated by so many gigantic sound waves, but none of the ecstatic transcendence she'd felt from her best performances in the Sanctuary, even in the little rehearsal studio she'd made for herself in the old empty DRE tank. But it was good practice for the Talas, where the crowd would be a hundred times larger and the performance would be for the ages, one way or another.

They found space at a table and she sat between Iba and Bal, opposite the twins. The twins went straight for the smoked fish, turning the withered skin inside out and peeling out strips of meat with relish. That was a little bit much for her so she started with the fried filets once they'd had a chance to cool.

She bit into the light, crisp breading and her taste buds exploded with the delicate, spicy flavor as her teeth sank into the creamy fish flesh that melted against her tongue and completely redefined the spices that preceded it. She took a voracious second bite with a whole new appreciation for the brief, eyeless, hopeless life of a T7.

WHEN they got back to the factory complex, she found Ado in the commissary, sitting in a meeting with Iba's brother Milit, Folle and another of the group's leaders, a short, pudgy young man called Capa. She was exhausted and exhilarated from the hours spent exploring the cold city, and not quite willing to cater her mood to the serious air between the four of them.

"There's some discussion as to a possible change of venue for your next concert," Ado told her.

"Wherever it winds up being, we have to figure out the sound on the stage. We need to control it so I can hear myself over the crowd and not go deaf. My ears were ringing for twelve hours after that last one and I still couldn't..."

"That's not really the issue," Ado cut her off.

That annoyed her. "It may not be the only issue, but it is *an* issue. It's all well and good that people seemed to like the last two but it's something we have to figure out."

Ado translated her concerns into Crisi.

Milit shrugged and said: "Sound would be better," He was somewhat more proficient in Standard Moonspeak than the others, "Space bigger. Problem is Clans."

"Regardless of how you feel about the last two shows," Ado said, "Positive word's gotten around and a lot of people are expected to show up for the next one. Way more than can fit into any of the spaces we have access to. Clan Fedda has contacted us through Capa here," Capa didn't look too happy about it, "and offered us the arena they use for big public events."

"And that's a problem because…"

"*Fascist thugs,*" Folle hissed.

"It's potentially a problem," Ado explained, "Because with Clan involvement comes Clan bullshit. The Gathered invited all of the Clans to bid on sponsoring you here, and they all declined to bid. The New Unity was the only organization in Crisi to show any interest. Now that the Clans see how popular you are here, they all want to associate themselves with you. The Fedda are first out of the gate to contact us directly. If the Fedda's enemies feel like they're getting shut out, they might try to disrupt things to make them look bad. Your main concern might be the stage sound but my main concern is your safety. I've sent a message to the Gathered in O-City to see what they think. They'll respond within thirty hours."

"Should we cancel it and move on to Clavi?"

He sighed. "That could cause problems for our friends. This district is run by the Derinn, who are allied with the Fedda. They could make life very, very difficult for our friends here if the Fedda feel like they've been slighted. The consensus seems to be that they'll take a cancellation as a slight."

Sel's ears started to feel hot and her upbeat mood had vanished. The grease from all the fried T7 she'd scarfed down was sitting uncomfortably in her stomach and beginning to be churned uncomfortably by the low-grade anxiety induced by the conversation.

Part of her simply didn't want to be bothered with any of it, but the rest of her felt that it would be irresponsible to ignore it. It was all suddenly overwhelming: the city, the people, the distance from home, the dizzying open spaces, the loudness of her shows, the eyeless fish digesting uneasily in her gut. Without saying anything to anyone she stood up and found her way back to her room.

It was cold and clammy and the radiator pipe didn't do anything except bang and hiss. She felt cold and clammy from the inside out and worried that she was getting sick. She rooted around in her bag for a packet of ginger-sage tea she'd brought from home, turned on her boiler kettle and curled up under the blanket on the bed. She sat and seethed quietly until the tea had cooled then drank it down, shut off the glo globe and tried to will herself to sleep. It wasn't as difficult as she expected it to be.

WHEN she'd gotten up and washed, she found her way to the administrative offices, where Ado was sorting through a mess of hypercards with Folle, Milit, Capa and a dozen or so others. Iba and the twins were there, too.

Ado told her that the concert would indeed happen under the patronage of Clan Fedda. The Clan had contacted the Gathered and submitted a formal bid to make the event a last-minute addition to the official Talas circuit, inclusive of all twelve Clans.

Nobody seemed thrilled about it but Iba had the strongest reaction.

"Is it really that bad?" Sel asked her. Although her Crisian friends couldn't speak Standard, they understood her when she spoke.

"The Clans all have people. Pack the bill. No us."

Capa confirmed that one of the Feddas' conditions for extending the hospitality of their arena and leaving attendance open to everyone was that they get to choose the other performers appearing. In the interest of not offending anyone, the bill had been carefully designed to include artists representing the maximum number of allied Clans. The roster elicited groans and eye-rolls as it was read aloud to the thirty or so people gathered in the commissary to discuss it.

"Tell them if they don't play I don't play," Sel said.

"They won't go for it," Ado said flatly. Capa nodded in agreement.

"Then they play *with* me," she said in the closest she could manage to Crisi dialect.

Nobody said anything for a moment. Ado looked at Folle, who looked at Milit, who looked at Capa, who was the official liaison between the New Unity and the Clans. He consulted his hypercard and read through the agreement as offered. When he announced his findings the room broke into cheers again.

Ado translated for her: "It says we have to send technical specifications an eighth-day beforehand and we get security passes for eight people. Nothing says you have to play solo. We'll send the tech specs for four and see if they squawk."

THEY sequestered themselves in an old machine shop on the first sublevel and started in on the hard work of reconciling their musical idiosyncrasies. Other residents volunteered to cover Iba and the twins' work shifts so they could practice ceaselessly.

A twentieth-day (as measured by the obtuse Crisian clock) before the concert, they played an impromptu show for the factory residents. It was a huge success, and Sel thought it might have been the most fun she'd ever had in her life. The arrangements they'd worked out were exciting to play, and she loved the feeling of being a part of the performance rather than the totality of it. She'd never played with any of the other musicians in the Sanctuary. She knew and respected all of them, but even the Earthers were strict Moonborn traditionalists, and far more interested in faithfully replicating existing styles and mastering old techniques. It was the opposite experience with Iba and the twins. They really seemed to want to create something new. As talented as they were, they were hardly preoccupied with virtuosity and she felt herself loosen up considerably as she worked with them, even while struggling to demonstrate the math of her tunings and time signatures across the language barrier.

By the end of the concert, she'd lost herself in the kind of ecstatic catharsis she hadn't felt since her performance in the Sanctuary, a blissed-out thrill that effortlessly extended into the party that broke out afterwards.

There had been festivals and celebrations at Lyell, but nothing quite like the bacchanalia of the young people at the New Unity factory complex. Many in the Sanctuariat enjoyed intoxicants in moderation, but inebriation was frowned upon, being contradictory to the strictly held ethos of emergency preparedness. The New Unity was apparently unencumbered by any such social restrictions.

Loud dance music was piped through the sound system and the main floor became a teeming dancefloor. The air in the corridors grew thick with cannabis smoke and people made ample use of alcohol mist masks attached to big canisters rolled out from a locker in the back of the commissary. From the corner of her eye, she glimpsed people popping tablets into their mouths.

Only Ado abstained, which enhanced her feeling of being safe and probably subconsciously influenced her decision to cut loose. She made a nominal effort to uphold the Sanctuariat ethos of moderation, but only in the sense that she partook in a little bit of everything.

After all, she was far from the Sanctuary and its restrictions of reputation and responsibility. The performance had finally shattered the clutch of anxiety she'd been feeling about the drama surrounding the change of venue, and she wanted to revel in it.

She huffed a stinging dose of potato vodka and drew deep from one of the hookah tubes offered her and, later in the evening, when Iba held out two little pink pills in her hands, assuring her that whatever-it-was was *"Fun! Okay!"* she popped one along with her.

Light streaked. Colors became so vibrant they seemed to bleed and pulse along with the music, as did the fractal patterns folding into themselves along the walls and floor. Time and space collapsed. She became deeply involved in conversations even though she didn't understand a word of what was said. She danced and danced until she felt like she became one with the crowd, blissfully losing herself.

SHE awoke half-dressed, sprawled out on the bed in a room that wasn't hers. She was alone, but had vague memories of succumbing to giddy lust and pressing herself up against someone on the dancefloor and stumbling through the halls, and making out with someone. She was pretty sure she'd had an orgasm but didn't think she'd had intercourse. There was evidence of suspicious emissions on the sheets.

Her body felt like it was vibrating between being thoroughly spent and over-stimulated, but even though her short term memories were a mess of half-remembered pleasure and still-sizzling synapses, her thoughts felt surprisingly lucid, which lasted precisely as long as it took her to walk to the commissary.

She took a long, circuitous route, sticking to smaller, lesser-used corridors in the interest of avoiding running into people. There was plenty of evidence of the party, but as she passed a window overlooking the main floor, she saw that clean-up crews were already at work. Even from that distance she could tell by their movements that they probably felt much as she did. She'd stopped along the way to see if Iba and Bal were in their room, which they weren't, and she didn't see anyone she knew in the commissary, either.

She imagined she'd be mortified if she saw herself in a mirror, but at least she wasn't alone. Everyone else in the commissary looked as bad as she felt. People smiled and said hello but she was grateful that no one invited her to join them or tried to strike up a conversation. Her sense of smell seemed to be particularly acute, and absolutely nothing she smelled was appetizing. She looked over the steam tables, but the sight of food just got her thinking about the intricacies of peristaltic osmosis, which started to freak her out for some reason, and she couldn't imagine actually eating and digesting any of it. But she was starting to feel really woozy and thought that putting something in her stomach might mitigate it, so she put a roll on a plate, found an empty table near one of the windows and began to pick at it.

The planet's shadow had fallen across the city. The sky was heavy with clouds that glowed with reflected light from the city. The high towers at the distant city center disappeared in them. The points of light and their reflections in the glass didn't shimmer or shine. They just seemed cold and still, small and futile attempts to mitigate the deepening darkness.

A young girl whose name she didn't know approached her table. "*Um…Nomad…*" the girl said.

"No," Sel said patiently, indicating her forehead tattoo, "Sanctuary." A lot of the Crisi kids seemed to mix up the Nomad brand and the Sanctuary tattoo.

"*No…Nomad look you. Look for you,*" the girl said.

"Tell him I'm here."

"*He say you come.*"

Sel sighed and didn't pretend not to be annoyed. "Where is he?"

The girl made the Crisi sound that Sel recognized as referring to the loading bay where the podvan was parked. She pocketed the roll and went to find him. The walk down to the loading bay seemed excruciatingly long and her body felt worse with every step. She wanted to crawl back into bed and sleep for ten times as long as however long she'd slept.

Her stomach dropped when she saw that Iba, Bal and the twins were with Ado at the van, loading their gear into the cargo bay. The twins looked like walking death. Bal looked sleepy but none the worse for wear. Iba's eyes were wide open and crackled with burst blood vessels. It looked like she was still on something.

"Where the hell have you been?" Ado grumbled.

His tone pissed her off but she didn't say anything because she was already mad at herself. "How long was I asleep?"

"How should I know? You disappeared. You weren't in your room."

"I didn't disappear...." She cut herself off, unwilling to admit that she didn't remember what she did.

"Well get yourself together. We should've left a half hour ago."

"For the arena?"

"Yes for the arena."

"It's now?"

"How much time do you think you guys spent messing around in the basement?"

"How can anyone keep track of the stupid time in this stupid city?" She wasn't thrilled that her reaction was so defensive but she was in no shape to stop herself.

"Thankfully, some of us are able to. Go get whatever you need from your room and get back here so we can go. Traffic's gonna be a goddamn nightmare."

IT TOOK nearly six hours to cross the city to the venue, riding in the back of the podvan with Iba, Bal and the twins. Folle rode in the passenger seat in the cockpit next to Ado. Sel spent most of the trip sleeping fitfully in her hammock, trying to tune out Ado's complaints about traffic from the cockpit and Iba's cranked-up chattering. The twins snored softly, propped up against each other on one of the bench seats, lolling with the motion of the van.

She was once again on the verge of drifting into real sleep when Ado shouted back for them to look out the side window. They were approaching the venue on an elevated highway. Down below, on a wide concourse between a refinery complex and an ugly neighborhood of concrete tower blocks, they saw the arena. It wasn't a small building by any reckoning, but none of them could imagine that it was big enough to contain the hordes of people who had massed on the concourse and were still streaming in from all directions.

Sel felt her stomach open up and drop in her gut. Only Iba seemed genuinely excited, letting out a yelp and clapping her hand against the thick tempered glass in an attempt to rally some enthusiasm from the rest of them. The twins looked at each other then sank away from the window and fell back asleep.

For a terrible instant, Sel found herself wondering if all those people were coming out to see her. But even the thought was more than she could handle so she swallowed it and decided that the other performers must have large and dedicated followings.

Milit and Capa were waiting for them in the busy backstage. They hadn't been at the party. Instead, they'd come ahead to make arrangements with the Fedda. They couldn't disguise their concern at the state of them. Milit looked disappointed when he saw Iba's eyes, but she was too out-of-it to register. Capa told them they'd missed their soundcheck, which caused Ado to shoot her a self-satisfied glance and say: "Guess we'll just have to see how the stage sound works itself out."

Bal volunteered to go out and get *kt'jhsks* for everyone. He'd grown up in the district and knew a stand nearby, which he claimed were the best in the city. Capa disagreed on that point but confirmed that they were worth a trip. Milit suggested that he take Iba with him because she was getting on everybody's nerves and drawing unwanted attention, and Sel volunteered to go, too. Ado rolled his eyes.

"I could use some fresh air," she offered flatly. She didn't want to get into an argument but nothing was going to stop her from going.

"Fine," Ado sighed. "Just try to be back before the show starts in an hour."

They left the arena through a service exit, on the opposite side from the concourse where the crowd had gathered. The arena and concourse were set at the low point of the district, surrounded by hills stacked densely with concrete tower blocks and the ruins of old industrial infrastructure. The air was colder than it was when they'd left and she wished she'd worn her cloak but she couldn't remember if she left it in the podvan or back at the factory complex. On top of her general hung-over discomfort and anger at herself for getting into such a state, she felt very alone. She liked Bal but still had a hard time communicating with him. Iba was out of her mind, Ado was annoyed with her and giving all his attention to Folle, and the twins were always wrapped up in each other and didn't seem to have any interest in even trying to talk to her anyway.

On top of it all, she was about to perform in front of a mind-bogglingly big crowd, and since the Fedda had made it an official Talas event, news of the performance, if not recordings of it, would make it to the Gathered at O-City. She doubted they'd retract their invitation, but she had a bad feeling that they might wind up wanting to.

By the time they got back with the *kt'jhsks*, the show had already started but Ado didn't say anything about it. They still had two hours before they were due to take the stage. Sel wanted to see what the other performers were like so she found her way to the wings to watch.

The act on the stage didn't seem to be anything but an uninteresting if athletic dance routine choreographed to loud and grating pre-recorded music. What struck her was the audience. The arena was completely full, a sea of heads all the way up to the rafters. The arena floor had become a vast fight pit. Melees and skirmishes churned in whirlpools across the floor. Knives, clubs, chains, bottles and other crude weapons were in abundance and the violence was brutal. Nobody seemed to be paying any attention whatsoever to what was happening on the stage: everyone on the floor was either fighting or waiting for their turn to fight, and everyone in the bleachers was watching the fights on the floor. She realized Ado was standing next to her.

"What are they doing out there?"

He shrugged, "That's what happens when you cram a whole bunch of kids from all of the different Clans under the same roof."

"It's disgusting."

"It's a violent city."

It dawned on her that he thought she was taking offense at the fact that they were fighting. "I don't care about that," she told him, "but they're a bunch of clowns out there."

Sel had been trained in martial arts almost since she could walk. Violence was rare among the Sanctuariat, but part of the reason it was so rare was that everyone was a trained killer. She had never particularly enjoyed sparring, but she had become quite good at it, mostly because she disliked being hit. As a result, she developed an appreciation of disciplined combat. But the display she saw on the arena floor was dreadfully sloppy and uncontrolled. They were just going at each other like berserkers. It was pointless and inelegant, and as a result the probable fatality rate was unnecessarily high.

Backstage, the other Crisian performers weren't particularly friendly. And despite the significant effort the Fedda had made to bring her to their venue, no one did anything to give her the impression they actually wanted her there. It didn't help that Iba was beginning to come down from whatever she was on and it was making her surly and confrontational and the twins were being even more aloof than usual. Bal seemed to be getting a particularly hard time. She watched one of the stagehands knock the *kt'jhsk* he was eating right out of his hand as he passed by. Apparently, the New Unity was not particularly well regarded here. She was starting to wonder if it was a mistake to have invited them to play with her in the first place, but it was too late to turn back now. And at this point, she couldn't imagine going out onto that stage alone.

Ado helped them to set up in the darkness of the stage. The sound of the crowd was deafening all on its own and she felt stupid for not bringing earplugs. She had a pair of adjustable-frequency in-ear filters that she'd used in the DRE chambers back at the factory complex but hadn't yet thought to use them on stage.

"Hey," Ado shouted in her ear, "I'm going to be up in the mixing booth. If you need to hear more or less of someone, point to them, then point up or down, okay?"

She nodded, hypnotized by the brutal churning of the bludgeoning crowd.

He put his hand on her shoulder. She looked at him. He smiled and shouted: "Just get through this, then it's on to Clavi."

She broke a thin smile and nodded.

As he walked away, the scale of the stage and the arena really hit her. It was huge. She felt absolutely tiny; somehow even more so than she had out in the open spaces of the city. The roar of the crowd was monstrous; she couldn't imagine how loud the stage sound would have to be to overcome it. Then she realized that they'd stopped fighting and were roaring in unison. The fight pits had disappeared and there was a solid uninterrupted sea of people before her, chanting her song.

She looked at Iba, who smiled maniacally and cued the twins. They erupted into a furiously syncopated assault before she even had a chance to strap on her guitar. The entire arena shook under the weight of the crowd, jumping up and down to the beat. She could see Iba starting to play but she couldn't hear anything through the stage monitors. There was no way Ado would've had time to get up to the booth. She hadn't even had a chance to tune. Everything was happening too fast and all she could hear was the roar of the crowd and the blood rushing through her ears.

Suddenly the monitors cut on in a swell of feedback. Once it subsided she could hear a fairly decent mix of what the crowd was hearing. It was so loud she felt it in her jaw. This couldn't be good for her. Her fingers were already covered in sweat, slippery on the strings and neck. She made a hasty effort to tune properly but then gave up, triggered her effects chain and struck out a chord. The crowd screamed. The scream went through her. Her previous disgust had turned into something different. Not love or hatred, not quite rage, but something else. She let out a series of high primal yelps into the mic to test it.

She was moving by instinct now, reacting to what she heard through the monitors. It wasn't anything like anything they'd rehearsed until suddenly the twins locked into a familiar rhythm and Iba adjusted the pulse of her oscillators into something she recognized. Her fingers found the right frets. Her right arm twitched and spasmed across the strings, wringing out a sound she wished would destroy them all.

Then the walls began to fall away.

First, a section of bleachers toward the back of the room gave way, crumpling inward on itself, a thousand screaming bodies tumbling down into a cloud of black dust, blue smoke and white light. Sel didn't see it at first, but she felt the concussion in the air and the stage beneath her feet. Only when she followed Iba's horrified gaze did she catch a glimpse of the carnage. She staggered backward. The twins were still playing in a brain-locked trance. She screamed at them to stop but they couldn't hear her. A chunk of concrete and twisted metal crashed to the stage floor between her and them. Another section of bleacher crumpled inwards in more blue smoke and white light.

She looked up instinctively to check for any more falling debris only to see a huge, hulking figure descending into the arena through the hole in the ceiling, backlit by blinding searchlights. It landed on the stage three meters away from her, more than two meters tall and thickly proportioned, in black body armor with a slack mouth and a single round red lens where its eyes should be. The lens fell on her and it lunged forward, surprisingly fast. Iba darted across its path, picking up her guitar cable and looping it around the thing's ankles. It tumbled forward with a thud, but there were more chunks of concrete and metal falling around them now and more red-eyed giants descending. She didn't realize she was frozen in place until Iba grabbed her arm and pulled her into the wings where they joined Bal and fell into the crush of people pushing back toward the rear exits.

She clutched her guitar close to her and locked her other arm with Iba's in the desperate wave of humanity. Up ahead somebody was shouting: *"Back! Go back!"* Over the heads in front of her Sel could see a bank of white shocklights outside of the exits and more huge black red-eyed silhouettes hoisting people up and throwing them into shipping containers as if they were rag dolls.

"Downstairs," Bal called out, *"Downstairs."* Everyone within earshot began pushing to the right, squeezing into a cramped concrete stairwell. *"Keep going,"* Bal shouted, his instructions relayed up the stairway, *"All the way down."*

At the bottom of the stairs they emerged into a pitch black, low-ceilinged basement. Bal turned on a fist-sized glo globe that illuminated little more than a meter and a half radius around him. The air was musty and damp and tickled her throat. It was hard to tell, but Sel guessed there were a couple of dozen people around her in the dark. Aside from Iba and Bal she didn't recognize any of the faces in the light: no sign of Ado, or the twins, or anyone else she knew.

"This way," Bal led the way across the basement at a fast trot. They were below the district's mass-concentrated substrate, making her feel almost weightless. That, along with the lightheadedness she felt from the musty air, fear and adrenaline, gave her the feeling of floating through a dream. They stopped at a metal drainage grate in the floor.

Bal knelt and pulled stripped bolts from the four corners of it.

"Give me a hand," he said, and with the help of others lifted the heavy grate and slid it over to the side. *"It's not a big drop,"* he said to her and Iba, *"Go."*

Sel slung her guitar over her back and lowered herself down over the edge, then dropped further than she expected, landing hard on her feet and bending her knees to absorb the shock, staggering backwards a couple of steps. She moved out of the way for others to come down and tightened her guitar strap against her back. Bal tossed the glo globe down to Iba and then swung himself down gracefully.

They were in a concrete room. The walls were covered with faintly phosphorescent layers of graffiti. There were windows. Outside them, she could make out vague shapes dimly illuminated by pale, narrow shafts of light.

Bal led the way to one of the windows and climbed out of it. She went after him, followed by Iba and the others, stepping out onto a crude cable-and-plank bridge over a black abyss. As her eyes adjusted, she realized she was looking out over the towers and columns of the abandoned subsurface city, half-submerged in black pools of still water, illuminated only by pale columns of light bleeding down from surface sewer grates high above.

Ahead of her, Bal moved impossible gracefully across the planks, holding the glo globe high above his head in his right hand and steadying himself along the cable with his left. Sel clung white-knuckled to the cables on either side, each swaying step unleashing another wave of nauseous terror, her eyes glued to her feet as they stepped from plank to plank, and into the inky depths twenty stories below. She lurched over the side and vomited. Thirty seconds later, the sound of its splash against the surface of the water echoed out across the vastness.

"*Good thing they filter it,*" Iba said from close behind her. She appreciated the levity but couldn't laugh yet. At the other end of the bridge, they followed Bal across a rooftop, down another staircase and across a wide, abandoned shopping plaza covered in spectacularly elaborate graffiti murals drawn with glo paint, then over a railing and onto a catwalk leading to a huge, blocky pump manifold that ran all the way from the black depths up to the surface. Along its side was a maintenance shaft containing a tight spiral staircase, which they ascended, turn after turn after dizzying turn.

The air became colder and fresher and more oxygen-rich as they got closer to the surface. It reinvigorated her, even made her giddy. She had to keep reminding herself that they hadn't escaped yet, that she was as far from being safe as she was from being home. She put it out of her head and concentrated on putting one foot in front of the other, ignoring the tightness in her lungs, the burning in her legs and the cramps along her ribs, until they finally emerged into a graffiti-covered maintenance shed long ago stripped of tools. Bal unwrapped a chain from the door and pushed it open.

They stepped out onto a ridge just below a water-filtration facility, underneath the scavenged-bare dishes of a defunct radar station overlooking the arena.

It was bathed in white searchlights. Giant demolition robots had punched four huge holes through the walls. Two shadowy Wasps hovered over it in concentric circles. There were also Bee haulers coming and going, hoisting up and flying away with shipping containers, which, she realized with horror, were probably full of the people they were taking out of the arena.

The air was full of drifting white flakes. As it began to fall on her she flinched and ducked under the scant cover of the radar dish. "*Just water. Condensed water,*" Iba pointed up to the heavy clouds. To demonstrate it's safety, she stuck out he tongue and caught some of the heavy snowflakes on it. Then caught a couple on her fingertip and showed Sel up close. "*See? Crystal water. Called sno.*"

Sel peered at it the snowflake closely. It was the most beautiful thing she'd ever seen. The fractal perfection of it up close, the way it shimmered in the city lights as it drifted. For a moment, the sense of unexpected beauty overtook everything else. Then she began to shiver. She was colder than she'd ever been in her life.

Still, she insisted they wait for the rest of the escapees to ascend and disperse. But there was no sign of Milit or Folle or Capa, or of Ado by the time a young woman emerged from the shed and told them, "*I'm the last. I cut the bridge. Move fast, they'll come.*"

"*Come on,*" Bal said, " *It's not far.*"

They climbed a metal staircase and crossed a gravel field past the filtration towers heading toward the lights of a nearby spoke boulevard. The snow began to fall more heavily, dusting the gray gravel in white. The wind stung her skin and she couldn't stop shaking. She couldn't feel her feet. But there was nothing to do but keep on. She did her best to control her breathing, to turn off the pain, and to keep moving forward. Bal and Iba seemed unaffected by the cold.

Bal led them across the boulevard and through a honeycomb of narrow streets and alleys, then into the courtyard of a squat tenement development and upstairs to the third-level mezzanine. He opened the door of one of the units with a keycard he wore around his neck. Before he was inside the door, a short woman in a simple denim frock had her arms around him, holding him tight.

"*Hi mom,*" he said. "*This is Sel. Sel, this is Vilia. The mom.*"

Vilia kissed Iba on both cheeks then greeted Sel warmly, smiling when she saw her forehead tattoo. "You're Sanctuariat?" She spoke Standard Moonspeak, clear and elegant, free of blurry Crisi ambiguity, then, in dialect, called out orders to the three young girls and two boys, Bal's younger siblings, to get blankets, arrange the seating around the stove and start broth boiling, sending one of them out to neighbors to borrow ingredients. Also in the room was Bal's grandfather, a small but hearty-looking old man who stood slowly to greet them and supervised the rearrangement of the furniture.

His father and an older sister were out on work shifts. They also lived in the same unit, though it was just a loft partitioned into two rooms over a common area with two toilets, two vapor closets and an open kitchen. For all the space in the city, life was more than three times as dense as it was in the Sanctuary. Introductions were made, but she couldn't keep them straight. In the warmth her shivering seemed to only get worse.

She was told to spend ten minutes in the vapor closet, then given dry clothes, wrapped in a fleece blanket and huddled onto the foam sofa in front of the cold-fusion stove, sandwiched between Bal and Iba, sipping hot broth with chunks of T7, turnips and greens from hand-turned ceramic crockery.

There was a licensed field-projector playing along one wall, running a corny Old Luna sim between banners of ads and advisories, but everyone was paying attention to the lo-res short-wave image on a grainy screen projection in one corner of the room. The projector had been made to look like a lamp so she guessed it was some kind of off-license pirate broadcast.

The image was being recorded from what appeared to be the opposite side of the arena from the old radar station where they'd been, showing the scene as captured by a shaky handheld microcamera. The big wrecker robots had been stilled, beaming white light down on the crews of Cyclopes climbing over the rubble dragging heavy nets. The two Wasps still circled above and Bee haulers still rose and descended picking up containers.

The camera zoomed in. The image was dark and awash in a confusion of pixels. Once she realized what she was watching she considered it a mercy: the Cyclopes were dragging nets full of people across the rubble and cramming them into the containers.

"*Anything on the main feed?*" Iba asked.

"*Nil,*" Rinn, the oldest of Bal's younger sisters, had been keeping an eye on the Earther news crawl across the bottom of the licensed screen.

"*Wrong.*" Vilia moved fluently between Crisi dialect and Standard

Moonspeak. *"They said there was a traffic slowdown at the C16 exchange and the Yuma Spoke."*

"But that's just the traffic report," Rinn countered.

"That's all they have to say about it." Iba made Vilia's point for her.

Vilia considered it more important to be able to read Earther than to speak it, being of the mind that Earthers themselves didn't even know what they were saying most of the time. She'd made an effort to teach her kids the same, but Rinn was the only one who seemed to have any aptitude for it. To her dismay, teaching them Standard Moonspeak had proven to be a losing battle. No one in Crisi spoke it anymore.

Sel was starting to feel physically normal again as the nutrients in the broth surged into her system, but psychically she was still teetering on the edge of shock.

Vilia recognized it. "What Sanctuary are you from, Sel?"

"Lyell," she said. The sound of it in her mouth meant something different now.

"I don't know it."

"Northeastern Serenity. West of Tauruntius. Under the Somni."

"Not terribly far then. Are you traveling with a caravan?"

She shook her head. "Just a Nomad. He was in there."

"Sel's on her way to the Talas," Iba said, *"She was invited to perform."*

Vilia looked at Sel, impressed.

"If your Nomad's alive he'll find you," she said. "If not, we'll do everything we can to help you get to the Orientale. There's a Trade Pavilion up in the Cape. Caravans come through every day, both Sanctuariat and Nomad. They'll be able to contact the Gathered. That might be safer than going to the Clans. In the meantime, you're welcome to stay here as long as you need to."

"Thank you," Sel said, "But I think he'd look at the factory first…" she stopped herself from saying *if he's still alive.* "I should go there and wait."

"Not until you've slept and eaten a proper meal," Vilia said, "Takke and Mif are making up beds for you upstairs. There will be a big meal waiting when you wake."

"Sta-sa," Sel said, a Moonspeak variant of "thank you" that implied the speaker knew their life had just been saved.

"A-v'tac," Vilia said, the formal acknowledgement, which literally meant: "One must help the helpless."

SHE had no idea how long she slept, nor did she recall falling asleep, only feeling the rocking of the cable bridge in the blackness behind her eyelids. Slowly, once the feeling of the motion ceased, she realized she was awake, on clean sheets in a strange bed in a perfectly dark room. She heard two sets of deep, even breathing. She felt next to the bed and gently raised the glo globe on the nightstand to a quarter glow. In the faint illumination she saw four other beds. Iba and Bal were tangled together under a blanket in one of them. The air was thick with sleep. She climbed into her borrowed clothes and draped the blanket over her shoulders and tiptoed out of the room, turning down the glow after her.

She found Vilia in the kitchen with Mif, at nine the youngest of the sisters. They had made a large crock of steaming gumbo, loaded with fish and vegetables and rice, and served her a steaming bowlful with fresh home-rolled *kt'jhsks* and flatbread.

"How long have I been out?" Sel asked.

"Nearly eleven hours."

It sort of felt like it and it sort of didn't. "Is there any news about what happened? Did people get out?"

"People got out, some through the sub-city with you, others through the breeches around the wreckers. Impossible to tell how many, but it sounds like hundreds. As to what happened, no one can say. The Clans are all blaming each other for doing something to piss off the CA, but they all had people taken and nobody knows what anybody might have done. Nothing like this has happened in twenty years. But I guess Crisis City is still Crisis City."

Sel tried to moderate the pace at which she was eating. Even the steaming temperature was hardly enough to slow her down. She was famished and she couldn't get enough hot food into herself fast enough. She tried to make conversation just to slow herself down: "What'll happen next?"

Vilia shrugged. "Probably nothing for a while. Then, either the CA will do something else or somebody will do something to retaliate. And if they can't figure out a way to talk to each other then they'll just keep going back and forth doing horrible things to each other until everybody gets tired of things being horrible all the time and start to figure out how not to be until it all starts over again."

"What stops them from talking?"

"Language partly. The municipal administration is all planetary, of course, and can barely handle Standard, and the younger generations only speak Crisi, which can barely even be translated into Standard with any kind of specificity. But more than that I think it's an attitude held by both sides."

"What attitude?"

"Us against them," Vilia said, "So as ever. In some ways I think it's worse today than it was twenty years ago."

"How so?"

"For one thing, the Clans weren't so entrenched. They weren't any good back then either, but at least they weren't as powerful. Now they're an extension of the CA. Some of them are worse. When things went out of control then – and it was near chaos for almost two years, it was a miracle the particle net didn't collapse – but there was still a sense that everyone was looking for the best possible outcome. And Avik-Rosot was here then."

Sel froze between bites for a split second. Avik-Rosot was her father's name.

"Who was he?" she didn't let on that she recognized the name. It struck her as too coincidental that Vilia might be referring to her father. It must be someone with the same name. But that would be even more of a coincidence, since the hyphenate Rosot was used to indicate a specific line.

"They don't teach you about Avik-Rosot in the Sanctuary?"

She shook her head.

"That's surprising since so many from the Unity entered the Sanctuariat."

"They don't really teach any history except Sanctuariat history," she said, which was true.

"A shame. He did more to try to broker meaningful peace between the CA and the Moonborn than anyone else in a hundred years. He was tremendously influential."

She went to a trunk next to the sofa and rooted around in it for a minute, returning with a hypertablet in her hand.

"Here," she handed it to Sel, "It's a collection of Avik-Rosot's media, with relevant histories. Take it with you. It's probably the most complete account of Colonial history ever published."

"Thank you," Sel said. She took several slurps of gumbo in silence before working up the nerve to ask: "What happened to him?"

"He was assassinated."

The warmth of the gumbo spread through her. Her body suddenly felt heavy on the stool, her elbows hard against the counter, her being felt as though it were somehow sinking deeper into the world. "By the CA?" Her voice was thin. She cleared her throat and wiped her chin.

"No one knows for sure," Vilia said, "The man who shot him was Moonborn, called Xen-Seev. But he himself was killed before he told anyone why he did it, or who put him up to it."

"Who killed this Xen-Seev?"

"Good question," Vilia smiled smartly, "The CA. You can imagine that there's no shortage of conspiracy theories. There are people who accept that the CA was behind it. But the Unity had splintered by then, and the different factions would say and do anything to make each other look bad, and they all wanted Avik-Rosot out of the way so they could claim him as martyr. The whole idea of the Unity became an unfunny joke."

"What was the Unity?"

"Oh, goodness," Vilia said, "I don't think I realized how isolated the Sanctuariat is. Do you at least know about Consolidation?"

Sel nodded. "It's when the CA took over the Colony." The Sanctuariat charter had grown out of the war against Consolidation and an overview of the root conflicts were part of her foundational education.

"Exactly. After that, they started putting the Moonborn into Settlements, putting populations who'd often never had anything to do with each other in close proximity and making them compete for strictly limited resources. Divide and conquer. If the Moonborn were fighting each other, they wouldn't organize against the CA. And it worked for a long time. The Settlements then were as violent as they were squalid. Then, twenty-five years ago, Avik-Rosot and others founded the Moonborn Unity. The point wasn't to organize against the CA, but to find a system by which the Moonborn weren't punished for being Moonborn. There were factions of course: the futurists wanted to re-open the path to the Far Side and onto Mars and Titan, and there were absolutists like the Lunarites who wanted to abolish the CA entirely, but Avik-Rosot managed to hold them all together in the same way he managed to communicate his ideas to different groups and communities. He was a peacemaker. But he defended himself and he defended groups who were under attack.

"The CA saw any attempt at unifying the Moonborn as a threat and considered him an enemy from the start, no matter what he said or did. And as talented as he was at holding together coalitions, there were plenty of Moonborn who wanted him dead, too. It was extraordinary that it lasted as long as it did.

"The Clan system is corrupt and oppressive and very much modeled off the old, pre-Unity model of divide and conquer. What's kept this city mostly peaceful over the last two decades is the legacy of Avik-Rosot and the fact that most of the people under the Clans get along with each other. But that's changing with the younger generation. They don't know what it was like when it was bad. They're getting more stratified. The Clans are recruiting them at younger and younger ages."

Vilia cast a glance at Mif, who'd wandered off to watch the field projection, then upstairs to where Bal and Iba slept and in a quiet voice said: "Bal and his friends call themselves the New Unity as a testament to what Avik-Rosot and the Moonborn Unity stood for, as an alternative to the Clans. They mean well, but there aren't enough of them to make a difference. And I have a bad feeling that the house of cards that is Crisi might be ready to fall down again."

Iba and Bal woke an hour or so later. Once they'd all eaten their fill and changed back into their clothes they set out across the city to the factory. It had stopped snowing but everything was covered with half a meter of icy snow except where the walkways were heated or had been plowed. Bal's family had given her a sweater and an old fleece-lined nylon parka to wear, which were certainly better than nothing, but she missed her Sanctuary cloak and worried that she might have left it at the podvan, in which case she might never see it again; it was far easier to miss her cloak than it was to worry about Ado and the others, which she kept as far from mind as she could.

The turnstiles at the nearest hover-rail station had long ago been vandalized, so they hopped over them and took the next train to the end of the line, followed by a series of intersecting trams, a winding bus ride. Then they hiked the last two kilometers through the snow-covered industrial park back to the factory complex. They barely spoke.

When they reached the entrance the door was locked. Iba yelled a signal, which echoed around the concourse. After a long minute the door opened. Sel's heart sank when she saw that the podvan wasn't parked in its usual spot. She recognized the girl who opened the door but she didn't know her. She wore a projectile rifle on a strap over her shoulder.

A group came across the factory floor to meet them. The boy in charge looked familiar, but she didn't know his name, either. She was somewhat taken aback when he smiled at her knowingly. They were all armed.

The boy greeted them and said: "*Good to see you all here. Two dozen have come back so far. You three make twenty-seven. We're still missing seventy-six from this residence. Numbers are still coming in from the other parts of the city. Most of the ones who came back were out on the plaza when the wreckers moved in.*"

"*What about my brother?*" Iba asked, "*Ro and Re? Folle and Capa?*"

"*The twins are here. No word on the others.*"

"Sel!"

Ado hobbled across the factory floor toward them as quickly as he could, his leg in a brace. She ran to him and embraced him. Her eyes filled with tears under the weight of her good fortune. They traded hurried stories of their escapes.

One of the wreckers had broken through next to the booth. Ado and one of the sound engineers managed to grab onto a truss as the floor fell away. When the truss swung loose they'd been able to ride it as it swung down to just above the ground. He sprained his ankle but got past the wreckers before the Cyclopes moved in with their nets. He'd run into the twins on a cross-town train, but hadn't seen the others.

"Where's the podvan?" she asked.

"After we loaded in I had to park it pretty far away. It was outside their perimeter but I didn't want to drive it back here in case they'd gotten a look at it. It's pretty well tucked away in a legal zone so it should be fine. But I want to wait to pick it up until the melt starts and I can use the fog as cover. It won't hurt to be a little bit more mobile either," he glanced at his leg brace.

"The sooner the better," she said. Iba joined them.

"Who's that boy? The one who was talking to us."

Iba looked at her. "*You don't remember? That's Yeid. You went back to his room with him during the party.*"

It was a minor embarrassment in light of everything that had happened.

"*Any word of your brother or the others?*" Ado asked.

Iba shook her head. "*They're saying a lot of people went to other residences…word's still coming in…*" She trailed off before her voice broke. Sel gave her a supportive hug.

They were all tired from the journey so they went back to their rooms. Sel brewed herself a cup of tea and curled up on the bed with the hypertablet Vilia had given her. It took her several minutes to get up the nerve to activate it.

She tapped into the language menu and selected Standard Moonscript, which was highlighted as original. But rather than begin by reading or watching anything, she selected the image index. Her mother had only kept a single image of her father, and she kept it hidden. She'd only shown it to Sel once, when she was ten or eleven. After that, she claimed not to know where she'd put it, which Sel didn't believe, but she'd never been able to find it on subsequent covert excursions into Suki-Anna's quarters. In the photograph, her father was a kind-looking man with matted, short-cropped hair and tired eyes behind corrective lenses, deep-generation Moonborn. It was an image of a beautiful face, more beautiful than she considered hers to be. But she didn't see any more of herself in it than she saw in her mother's.

Her pulse quickened when she opened the image bank. It was definitely the same man. She set the index to display the images in chronological order, beginning with his baby pictures. She scrolled forward into his youth to discover a slender, serious-looking young man surrounded by the trappings of faded privilege, at play in a sprawling, run-down late-Expansion habitat with other children. She activated the caption and saw that they were his siblings: aunts and uncles she'd never known she had. Forward again and he was her age, impossibly beautiful and athletic. Further still and he was a serious-looking young man in laborer's coveralls in an official ID portrait for CA manufacturing facility 0336 in Janssen. Something had changed in his face. His eyes were sunken deeper, his skin ashen. The corrective lenses made their first appearance. There was nothing for a while, until she arrived at the beginning of the Unity.

Curiosity got the better of her and she looked up her mother's name in the index. There was a single listing. It was a caption in the image directory. She called it up.

The caption said it was taken from the command center of the central atmosphere-generator complex in Janssen D during the Unity takeover of the same. The room was chaotic with activity. To her eye, the Unity looked awfully well armed for a bunch of peacemakers. Avik-Rosot was in the middle of everything, looking directly into the camera and flashing rabbit ears with his fingers while aides spoke to him. The gesture came from the Gemini uprising, one of the few Colonial historical events the Sanctuariat taught. It became a universal symbol of defiance. She didn't see her mother so she tapped her name in the caption. A bracket appeared around her in the image. She was in the middle background over his right shoulder, one among the crowd, her face blurred slightly by motion as she carried a crate across the room. She enlarged the image for a closer look, framing it on the tablet so her parents were centered. Suki-Anna looked startlingly young. Even accounting for the motion blur, she could tell that her mother was looking at Avik-Rosot. It was the first image of the two of them together she'd ever seen: her looking at him, him looking into the camera, into the future, out at her. There was no other mention of her anywhere in the hypertablet. Was it nothing more than a fling? Was Suki-Anna a star-struck young revolutionary swept away by a charismatic leader? Or could it have been a great love, kept secret from history, of which she was the sole souvenir?

She was relieved when there was a knock on the door. Less so when she saw that it was Yeid.

"Oh. Hi."

"*Hello, Sel.*"

"Look, if this is about what happened…it was fun and all, but…" she was about to say that it didn't mean anything, but then decided to come clean, "Um, what exactly did happen?"

"*Nothing serious,*" he said, "*I mean, I think we both had fun, but we didn't…you know…*"

"Good," she said. She hadn't thought about it, but she didn't care how he took it anyway. Whatever she was on must have been quite an aphrodisiac. She supposed Yeid was attractive enough, but there was nothing in his manner or bearing that appealed to her.

"*That's not why I'm here,*" he said. "*You're half Earther, right?*"

She nodded. She didn't like the way this was going.

"*You speak Earther?*"

She nodded again.

"Come with me," he said.

She didn't particularly want to, but there was something about his tone of voice that she took seriously. She walked with him down to the factory floor and across it to the lift. They took it down to the first sub-basement, passing the space where she, Iba and the twins had rehearsed. It seemed like ages ago.

They stepped off the lift into a low-ceilinged corridor lined with pipes, ducts and conduit. The air was thin, musty, damp and cold and hurt her throat in the same way the air under the arena had. It was an unpleasant sensory association. There were two armed guards posted outside the lift.

She followed Yeid through a labyrinth of similar hallways until they came to a group of young men loitering around a closed door. The twins were among them. She wanted to be excited to see them, that they were alive and apparently unharmed, but the look on their faces and the surly character of the gathering had the opposite effect.

They greeted her neutrally, as if they didn't particularly care whether she'd survived or not. There were two other young men in the group who she'd never seen before: one was a big, slope-shouldered pinhead, the other was short, with a large round head and mean eyes. She didn't use the term herself, but the word *degs* came to mind when she saw them. It was a derogatory Moonborn term for deep-gen Moonborn of questionable genetic stock, frequently used as shorthand for inbreeding. She got a deeply unsettling feeling from them.

Yeid pointed to the closed door: *"The man in this room has been seen hanging around Moonborn districts, asking questions."*

"What kind of questions?"

Yeid didn't seem to want to answer, *"We found him lurking around an anti-CA rally."*

"What do you mean, 'lurking?'" Yeid's authoritative tone was starting to rub her the wrong way.

"Find out who he is. Find out what he was doing at the rally, and who he was working for."

One of Yeid's people unlocked the door and opened it. Another handed her a glo globe.

She stepped into the dark room reluctantly. It stank of excrement and sweat, rotten gypsum and infection.

An Earthborn man, beaten and bloody, sat on the floor leaning against a wall in the pale light of the glo globe. His right hand and left forearm were wrapped in septic bandages. He squinted up at her through bruised eyelids.

"What happened to you?" she asked.

After a long pause, he said through a parched throat: "I don't know." His voice was thick and slow.

After another long pause, he added: "Yeah, I guess I do know. Your friends beat the piss out of me. And then they did it again. And then they waited a couple hours and did it again."

"They're not my friends," she said. She knew it probably didn't mean anything to the poor man but she felt like it needed to be said. "I'm here because I speak Earther. They want me find out who you are and what you were doing at that rally."

"My name's Sanjit," he said. "And I was trying to hear this song…"

7. STRANGE KINDNESSES

the android stood silent and still in the Gemini's room, watching and waiting for her to awaken. It had stopped administering sedatives hours before, and her vital signs indicated healthy, if troubled, REM sleep.

She was unconscious when the Cyclopes delivered her to Galilaei, injured and strapped to a gurney. It had watched her violent capture play out on the video feeds. She'd fled the Cyclopes desperately and put up a fierce struggle against them, resulting in a dislocated hip, fractured ulna and numerous contusions, lacerations and abrasions as she was batted, grabbed and dragged through the inarticulate chaos of the Geminus streets. Without waiting for instruction, it had taken her into an operating theater and deftly repaired her injuries and dressed her wounds.

As it worked, the Sister Doctor sent it instructions: it was to place the girl in a field suspension tank and remove all components of the virus from her brain, also restrict as much of her recent memories as possible without damaging other high functions.

But the android wanted her to remember it all.

Before instructing the medical drones to place her in the tank, it disconnected the field-suspension unit from the CARD AIs' network. There was nothing in the operation requiring their assistance, and it suspected they might take over the procedure to carry out the

Sister Doctor's instructions to the letter; they would certainly create a record of its disobedience and deliver it to her, both of which it preferred to avoid.

Once she was sealed in the tank, it set the field parameters to the molecular level, and the bonds holding her body's tissues together were pulled gently apart to within a nanometer of their breaking point.

The android was surprised to discover just how pervasive the virus and its components were. There were nearly a million fully formed virus sensors in and around the girl's brain. The component strands of RNA in the rest of her system numbered in the billions. It set about the tedious and arduous task of setting nanolaser arrays to eradicate each and every one of them, while leaving everything else about the girl: her language and motor functions, her thoughts, identity and memories, as fully intact as possible.

REYJH-AAMNHE awoke, shaken from bad dreams and groggy from sedation, but once again knowing her name. She was in restraints. She didn't know why, but at least she knew what they were called. Her surroundings were unfamiliar, but she remembered the names of things: *room, door, bed*, all of which seemed oversized to her, *gravity*, which felt too strong. And she remembered the terror of forgetting it all.

She felt nauseous and weak, but she remembered everything.

She'd been the last of her family to succumb to the virus. She'd watched everyone she knew and everyone she loved disconnect and fall into mute confusion. She'd struggled to reach them until she herself no longer knew their names, nor the words describing who they were to her, nor her own name. But it wasn't so much that she'd forgotten as that she'd never known them in the first place. She still knew who they were – father, mother, brothers – as she still knew who she was, but she could no longer connect with them. She could no longer connect to her own thoughts. No one could connect to anything anymore.

By the time the virus overtook her, the city doctors had already given up on their attempts at quarantine. All of Geminus had fallen into chaos. The rules and customs that defined their daily lives had given way to an ongoing mute panic of brute competition, violence and need. As with her and her family, all were inexorably on their own.

The memories were like those of a nightmare: everything simultaneously familiar and strange, tangled in dread, anxiety and confusion, knowing only feelings, concepts and objects without means to connect, express or make sense of them.

She'd witnessed acts of unspeakable cruelty and inexplicable grace. And as much as she didn't want to, she remembered it all, all the way up to her relentless pursuit through what had been the marketplace by those terrible one-eyed giants, the valiance of those who'd instinctively rushed in to try to protect her from them, slaughtered in waves.

Her eyes settled on the android. For a moment she thought it was a person, standing in shadow in a corner of the dimly lit room. But it was so perfectly still and lacking any sense of life that she first mistook it as a trick of shadow against a piece of machinery. Then it took a step toward her.

She'd never seen anything like it. The robots in Geminus were antiques: simple, task-specific machines. This was different. But it, like the rest of her surroundings, was undoubtedly of the CA.

Since childhood she'd heard the stories, as all Gemini had, about the CA's numerous attempts to sabotage their city. It had become something of a running joke among her generation to blame the CA for any trivial thing that went wrong, from missing a bus to splitting a fingernail to stumbling over cracked concrete. But this wasn't trivial and it wasn't a joke. She'd seen her world destroyed. This oversized room, this mechanical thing and the monsters that abducted her: all were evidence that the CA was behind the catastrophe. She tensed and tried to push herself back against the headboard, only then realizing just how much her entire body hurt, how limited her use of it.

The android stopped and held its hands open in a gentle gesture of surrender. It then raised two fingers to signify the Rabbit's ears: the Gemini sign of defiance.

It knew that it would be unable to communicate with her directly. It could mimic its recordings of Gemini Moonspeak, but she wouldn't be able to understand it; its electronic brain was incapable of producing the bioelectric signals that conveyed the sounds' meaning.

So it would use symbol and image.

It walked to the display panel on the wall opposite the foot of the bed, and with its finger drew two hieroglyphs in the surface pixels: a set of intersecting curved lines suggesting the shape of a leaping rabbit, the Gemini symbol for freedom, surrounded by a series of concentric nested rectangles, indicating that it was secret.

She looked into its inscrutable, coolly glowing eyes and wondered if this machine-man might prove to be an ally.

***

GALAXA missed her special guest star.

It wasn't completely unprecedented for her not to see him for a while, especially when they were working different shifts, but it was unusual to go so long without so much as a message. She'd gotten used to spending time with him. She'd adjusted her facets to compensate for his presence in her physical life, and his prolonged absence created a palpable sense of lack.

She'd always kind of liked the fact that he wasn't cogged, it was cute in an old-fashioned way, but after twenty-seven hours, she started to get miffed that he wasn't even responding to her pings through his wrist unit. After thirty-three hours she started to feel hurt. After forty-two hours, she got mad and looked up his work schedule. The only acceptable excuse was death and that would've broken her heart, which somehow made her even angrier even though she didn't want it to.

She requested a shift change so she could go to his assigned nest platform and wait for him to show up to confront him in person, waiting at the gates of the long steel trellis arching out from the eightieth-level second-tier mezzanine. She watched the arriving shift schlep through the turnstiles and climb into their cradles, watched the big spiders unfold from the trellis and spin out along lines over the district until only one Spider was left in the nest: OL81, the one assigned to Sanjit. Through her cog, she checked the duty rosters and saw that he hadn't shown up to his last three shifts.

She got worried enough to go to his dorm and ask his creepy Martenist roommate if he'd seen him. He said he hadn't, but she wasn't sure if she believed him or not. Like everyone else she knew, she didn't trust Martenists, and she didn't like the way he bombarded her with questions about when was the last time she saw him: had he been acting unusual, had he said anything about going to meet anyone? She refused to step into his dorm unit and lied about her name and got out of there as fast as she could.

She dedicated an entire admin facet to searching the nets for any mention of him and found that she wasn't the only one looking. There were triggers tagged to his name that contacted the Crisi authorities, the Colonial Security Agency, Icarus-Daedelus and thirteen anonymous sub-nodes.

It looked like the fact that his thumbchip was tracked entering and leaving the first tier too often without official reason landed him on a watch list. He wasn't some revolutionary. He didn't like the CA, but neither did anybody else, and he didn't seem to dislike it particularly more than everybody else. He wasn't afraid of Moonborn and he liked Moonborn food and spent a lot of time in Moonborn districts but he was too smart to get set up to be some patsy bomb-belter or plague-carrier.

But plenty of innocent people wound up in Icarus-Daedelus prisons for the rest of their lives for even bigger bullshit than that. She knew she didn't know a whole lot about him or his life, but she also knew she didn't want any of those creeps getting their hands on him.

She didn't consider herself much of a coder but she knew how to write a simple birdtag: code attached to a data packet generally used to call attention to an item. In this case, she coded a tag flagging the all-points bulletin on Sanjit as bullshit and calling on anyone who saw it not to pass on the information to the CA or the constabulary or anyone else.

It was the least she could do for her favorite special guest star.

For the rest of the City of Crisium, the winter passed more or less quietly. The calamitous raid on the arena had been conceived and carried out autonomously by the Cyclopes' AI network, so the municipal administration (which prided itself on maintaining an unprecedented twenty-one years of socio-economic stability) could genuinely focus on damage control without wasting time and goodwill on cover-ups.

After a tense, sporadically violent period of sleepless lunar night, the Clans resumed their habitual stance of perpetual and generally non-violent distrust of one another once it became apparent that they had all suffered in equal measure, and diligent investigations had turned up no evidence that any had reaped any more benefit from the situation than any others. The municipal administration assured them all that it was an isolated incident, and the City paid equal remuneration to each of the Clans for their losses.

The only Crisians for whom life took on a distinctly different tenor in the wake of the raid was the small but dedicated network of young people who identified themselves with the organization calling itself the New Unity.

They took it very personally.

Daily operations at the factory residence continued on much as they had — work shifts were attended, meals were prepared and served, a new wave of residents had taken the places of most of those lost in the raid — but the zeitgeist was of anxiety and paranoia. Gradually, there weren't as many weapons in the open, but they were always on hand.

Iba's brother was gone, as was Folle and eighty-seven others. Capa returned after spending time at another residence, traumatized and unable to speak. He'd survived physically intact, but seeing Folle and Milit cut down and taken had broken something in his mind and he wasn't the same person.

Iba was still very much herself, unabashed in both her grief and her refusal to allow it to overwhelm her. Milit had been all the close family she had left. She had distant relatives in the Rille but she hadn't seen them since her parents were relocated to Crisi when she was eight and he eleven. Their parents couldn't overcome the Crisi flu strains and died within the same quarter of the following year, leaving her and Milit in the hands of Clan bosses who worked them mercilessly. They were put on a cleaning crew alongside other orphans, perpetually caked in dust and grease and winnowing through deep ductwork in exchange for barely adequate nutrition, day in and day out, until they found the teenagers of the New Unity, with whom they lived and worked for the next eleven years.

Now that Milit was gone, Iba wanted to feel like the New Unity was her family as well, but instead found herself heartsick that she didn't. The residence held new leadership elections and Yeid and his crew had been given heavy influence. Everything took on the gloomy air of secrets and espionage, shuttered in against the cold and snow. She tried hard to isolate herself from it, spending most of her time with Bal and Sel, skating at a nearby ice rink or trekking out on long, icy expeditions to scavenge local warehouses and surplus exchanges for components to rebuild the gear lost in the raid.

Sel was on edge the entire time. The fate of the Earther weighed heavily on her conscience.

She'd insisted that they stop torturing him and arranged for him to be fed (they would only agree to table scraps). She'd also gotten him a foam mat and bathroom privileges, and smuggled him an antigen pack from her travel kit. All of that notwithstanding, she suspected that what was keeping him alive more directly than anything else were the embellished translations of her "interviews" with him that she passed along to Yeid and the rest of the residence's newly minted leadership.

For herself, she didn't doubt that poor Sanjit had as much to do with the CA security apparatus as she did. She believed his story, improbably coincidental as it was, but feared that even if she could translate it sufficiently to convince Yeid and his people that it was true, they'd see no value in keeping him fed or risking setting him free alive. As Colonial property, he'd already been feloniously damaged, which would bring down harsh repercussions if traced back to anyone associated with the New Unity, and he'd already seen enough of them that their images would be easily retrievable via a simple brainpull. The only way to rule out a pull was for him to be found floating face down in a canal with the snomelt.

So she took everything he told her about his life – and he seemed particularly eager to open up; she sensed he'd been quite lonely – and used it to create a picture of someone unwittingly manipulated into gathering information for the CA, crafting her "translations" so that each interview seemed to hint at revelations to come of new layers of intelligence apparatus, careful to leave things vague enough so that zealous thugs like Ikt and Okt and, now, the twins, didn't go out and cut the thumbs off of any more innocent Earthers.

She'd come to like him. He had a courteous and curious nature, and was as forthright and straightforward as any of the Earthers she knew and loved in the Sanctuary, if less knowledgeable.

His captivity in the complex was a strictly kept secret. Only the leadership and a close circle of loyalists knew they were holding him prisoner. As a cover story for the time she spent talking to him, the rumor was spread that she was still carrying on with Yeid.

She could tell that the rumors upset Iba, who'd never liked him, and especially didn't like that he'd been elected to replace Milit on the leadership; it was difficult for her not to see it as a betrayal. Yeid had grown up a privileged scion of the local Derrin clan, and as far as she could see had assumed the mantle of black sheep to slum it with the New Unity in order to antagonize his elders and impress his rivals. It disappointed, even offended her that so many of the others had voted for him, responding so predictably to him simply because he wielded power so comfortably.

Sel assured her that the rumors were false, but didn't tell her what was really going on. She trusted her and Bal, but she knew they were being watched and didn't want to do anything to compromise their standing in the New Unity, or further jeopardize the Earther's life.

After all, it was her fault he was in this mess to begin with.

Ado didn't see it that way.

She'd told him everything. She had to confide in someone, and her understanding of the conditions of secrecy was that no one in the New Unity could know about Sanjit. It was possible they meant 'no one in the complex' but she'd lost patience with the ambiguity of their dialect. Besides, Ado couldn't care less about the New Unity and their intrigues, and she genuinely wanted his advice, even if she had no intention of following it.

"Let them kill him," he said. "You don't owe that Earther anything."

He had rigged a hammock in an empty storage closet in a wing of the complex far from the dormitories. With Folle gone, he spent as little time as possible around the New Unity, and his desire to get out of Crisi and back on the road was palpable. That and his slow-healing sprain were making him surly, but his surliness didn't stop her from speaking her mind.

"Yes I do. If it weren't for me he never would've been kidnapped. He said my song changed his life."

Ado scoffed. "So what? You're a talented girl, but don't start thinking you're responsible for the twists and turns of some dumb Earther's psychology. If you're going to take responsibility for him, then you might as well take responsibility for every one of the thousands lost in the arena."

"I do," she said.

"That's *absurd*," he stared into her eyes, "Do *not* do that to yourself."

"The whole point of that arena show was to get me to perform there," she said flatly. She'd gone over and over it in her mind and didn't consider it an egotistical statement. "Otherwise none of those people would have been there. And if they weren't all there for me, then Milit and Folle and the others from the New Unity certainly were…"

He took a deep breath and decided to try rationality: "No one knows why that raid happened. All we know about it was that it was a huge gathering – bigger than anyone expected – and the city authorities say they didn't have anything to do with it, which I believe because those Cyclopes are controlled by CSA AIs at Icarus-Daedelus. All the other hardware I saw was CA, too. I didn't see any locals.

"Now. Lets take Occam's razor to this and assume that the most likely reason is probably true: the assembly of that many Moonborn sets off alarms all the way up the security apparatus, and even though the Clans cleared their permits with the city, the Cyclopes might not give a fuck about city permits. Maybe when a crowd exceeds its permits, it goes directly past the city straight to I-D.

"My point is, it was unfortunate, and tragic, and horrible, and we're lucky to have survived. Don't forget – we were in every bit as much danger as everybody else was. And it is absolutely reason to exercise caution while leaving the city, but it is foolish to start getting paranoid. Then you get paralyzed. It's bad enough being stuck."

"What about the Earther?"

"What about him? I don't like that they kidnapped him, and I especially don't like that they're holding him here. I think it was and is a monumentally stupid thing to do. That's the kind of stupid thing you do when you get paranoid. That's why I think its best to end him. And sooner rather than later."

She appreciated his logic but silently rejected his cold Nomad pragmatism.

"I'm serious, Sel. Don't hold yourself responsible for this. You can't carry that kind of weight around with you."

Again, she disagreed. She could and she did. As she saw it, there was only one difference between the lives lost at the arena and the life of the Earther: she couldn't have done anything to save the others, but she could still save him.

She hadn't yet told Sanjit that she'd made the song he'd become so mortally obsessed with. She was careful not to tell him anything about herself at all, even wearing her hood pulled over her Sanctuary tattoo, shrouding her features in shadow lest he might eventually be subjected to a CA brainpull.

For Sanjit, their time together had become the only thing making the idea of life preferable to that of death.

After her first visits, still in the pitch of fever, she completed a kind of holy trinity in his mind alongside his brother Molo and Naeemah; his three personal saints whose kindnesses had anchored the epochs of his life. As Molo had presided over his childhood and Naeemah his adulthood, this hooded stranger with the strange accent and clear, bell-like voice had become the patroness of this strange, purgatorial afterlife (when lucid, he was perfectly aware that he was not, in fact, dead, but there were times, in the grip of a cold sweat in the rank blackness of his cell, that he wasn't so sure).

Her planetary English was better than his, and although he couldn't see her face clearly, her proportions indicated that she wasn't from the planet. She looked tall from across the room, but when she was close to him he could tell that she was in fact quite small, no taller than his chin. Next to her, he felt like an overthick chunk of meat on the spoil.

As little as she told him about herself, she wasn't willfully mysterious. She'd told him plainly that she was there to get information about him, and that she wanted to help find a way to get him out of there alive, but she wasn't going to tell him anything about herself. Her straightforwardness made it somehow easy for him to trust her and open up. Since it was entirely possible that she might be the last human being to know him, it seemed to matter to him that she did.

He rambled compulsively: about Molo, about Naeemah, about his regrets, and about the song that changed his life. He felt like a blithering fool, but she proved to be a patient and engaged listener.

As THE planet's shadow cleared Mar Crisium, the first bands of sunlight ignited the particle net, spilling a soft white glow over the city and casting a thick shroud of silver fog over the streets and towers of the first two tiers. Ado's ankle had healed and he was anxious to set out to retrieve the podvan, wearing the non-descript

Crisian parka Bal's family had lent Sel, a spun-nylon hat pulled low over the Nomad brand on his forehead. He'd thought about wearing dark glasses, but Sel pointed out that in the misty haze they looked conspicuously like a disguise.

The temperature outside was rising rapidly, but the thick stone of the factory walls trapped the chill so the windows were opened to let the fresh air in, rendering the climate inside uncomfortably clammy and cool. Soon everything inside the complex felt damp and aggressive, pungent mildew began to form on seemingly every surface.

Sel had already rebuilt as much of her lost gear as she could, given the rudimentary state of the factory's workshop, so she volunteered for the cleaning crews, scrubbing the mildew from the floors and walls with bleach solution. The alternative was spending time alone in her room staring at the hypertablet Vilia had given her rather than activating it.

Iba and Bal were out on a work shift, as were most of the other residents, and she was alone in a little-used abandoned administrative sector. It was low on the priority list for cleaning, but she was enjoying the solitude and the physical activity of it, working herself into a state of Zen and finding a mild sense of accomplishment in wiping away the stubborn mold.

She was humming to herself and didn't hear the footsteps approaching up the hall, and was startled when she looked up to see the girl standing in the doorway of the room she was cleaning. She recognized her as being in the inner circle of the new leadership, but she wasn't sure which of the elected she was loyal to.

"They don't know I'm here," she said. Her voice was quiet and serious.

Sel sat back on her knees and wrung her sponge into the bucket.

"They're about to vote on the Earther. Olnec says they have enough votes to kill him."

She dropped the sponge and scrambled to her feet and sped out of the room, past the girl and down the corridor, the worn soles of her moccasins sliding perilously on the freshly scrubbed tile. Her anger smoldered as she sprinted and slid through the corridors back to her room. Of course they would wait until her friends were gone. She'd suspected that the one called Olnec was sympathetic to her but didn't think she could count on her or her people to back her up.

There was only one option left to her now.

The Sanctuariat charter forbade the manufacture or possession of weapons of any kind. It was implicit that the CA reserved the right to invade and take over the Sanctuaries at their discretion. As a result, they became expert at designing functional household items and tools that could, with a few minor adjustments, be converted into lethal weapons.

Her teakettle was such a device. She pulled it out of her duffel and twisted it apart at the middle, switched out two chips in the particle-accelerator unit, flipped the base around and screwed it back together, turning it into a particle-disrupter capable of destroying the atomic bonds of matter. It could emit one pulse of a disintegration field every twenty-six seconds, disintegrating a twenty-centimeter chunk of whatever it was pointed at. She clipped it to her belt and reached back into her duffel, removing a small polished box no bigger than a bar of soap bearing the seal of the Sanctuariat from a hidden compartment, and tucked it into her pocket. Then she was off again at a sprint.

She took a narrow back staircase down to the sub-basement, two and three steps at a time. Once she stepped out of the stairwell into the cramped, musty corridors she slowed to a walk and struggled to catch her breath before turning into the hallway where Sanjit was being kept. The two guards on duty outside the door were the imp Ikt and the pinhead Okt.

Other guards tended to be lenient toward her unofficial visits, but these two were zealots, of a particularly twisted generation in a long genetic chain of inherited hatred. They didn't like the Earther and they didn't like her by extension; they were doggedly loyal to Yeid, even subservient. Iba told her they were of the district's undercaste, genetically conditioned to respond to the orders of someone like Yeid. The one advantage to their being there was that he held them in low enough regard that he was unlikely to have informed them about the impending vote on the Earther's life.

They didn't get up from their chairs as she approached.

Ikt smirked and shook his oversized head when he saw her. Then, like an idiot, he rocked back on his chair, leaning against the wall and stretching his legs across the narrow hallway to block her path.

She yanked it out from under him, and as he hit the hard floor she stomped sharply on his solar plexus with her heel, then used the chair as a bludgeon to clip Okt under his chin as he stood, knocking him backwards. She snatched the key from around Ikt's neck and let herself into the room, bringing his chair with her and jamming it under the door handle, then re-chained the door and broke the key off in the lock. It would buy her some time, but not nearly enough to do things properly.

Sanjit had been asleep. The noise in the hallway had jolted him awake, but he couldn't tell who'd forced their way into the room until Sel turned on her glo globe.

It was the first time he'd seen her face in the light. It was neither Moonborn nor Earthly, but beautiful in a way that transcended both. There was an elaborate metallic tattoo in the center of her forehead.

She knelt in front of him, her voice calm but hardened by urgency.

"You have to listen to me very carefully," she said, and pointed to her tattoo. "Do you know what this is?"

He shook his head.

The rules governing admittance to the Sanctuariat were absolute. Their charter forbade them to inform anyone about themselves: inductees must independently request Sanctuary, then demonstrate aptitude in the Five Foundations (diligence, competence, discretion, participation and responsibility), without having been told what they are. The process normally took months, with a Sanctuariat board administering a series of blind behavioral tests while the inductee was a conditional resident at a Sanctuary.

The application of a Sanctuary tattoo was one of the most sacred acts a member of the Sanctuariat could commit, somewhat more than marriage, somewhat less than procreation. The genetic imprint of the person administering the tattoo was encoded into it; their reputation was forever entwined with their inductee. Clarke had administered both hers and her mother's, her mother had administered Jick's.

In captivity, she'd seen Sanjit demonstrate none of the Foundations. What she was about to do was an unforgivable act of faith. But it would be the only way she could justify doing what needed to be done to get him out alive. She heard voices out in the hallway.

"Did you just request Sanctuary?" It was the only way she could think of phrasing the question that wasn't outright criminal.

"Did I what?" it was difficult to hear her over the pounding on the door.

"Say it. Is that a request for Sanctuary?"

"I don't understand. What do you mean?"

She heard voices in the hallway. Shoulders and legs began battering against the door, shortly followed by the whine of a power tool.

"I can't tell you. But you have to ask. It's the only way I can help you."

"Okay. Sure. Yes."

"You have to request it. But you have to understand that it's serious. It's forever. There is no going back. I have to know that I can trust you."

Her pale eyes bored into his and he realized she'd started speaking in Moonspeak, but he still understood her, as if he heard it in the language of his own thoughts.

The chain around the doorjamb fell loose. The pounding resumed, buckling the door against the chair.

"I request Sanctuary."

She took the small polished case out of her cloak and opened it. Inside was her Sanctuary Needle, an ornately filigreed autoclave powered by a small cold-fusion battery. In its canister was an alloy of magnesium, zinc and silicon containing nanochips encoded with her DNA.

"Hold out your hand."

He did. She pulled a small blade from the side of the needle and scraped a layer of skin off of his palm, then replaced the blade in its harness. The skin sample was taken into its processor and analyzed so his genome would be encoded in the ink of the tattoo alongside hers. The minute it took to transcode felt like hours. On the other side of the door, the electric cutter was again turned on and began to grind against the metal of the door hinges.

When the transcoding was finally finished, she felt the needle buzz in her hand.

"This will hurt a great deal," she said, and raised the autoclave to his forehead. "I grant you Sanctuary."

Compared to the pain of losing his thumb and wrist screen, the scalding impacts of molten metal against his skull were practically invigorating.

THE door twisted inward, anchored only by its bottom hinge. A trio of Yeid's heavies pressed over it into the cell, followed by Ikt and Okt, followed by Yeid and, at a remove, the rest of the leadership.

Sel stood in front of Sanjit, holding her teakettle-come-disintegrator at her side. Scabs had not yet formed on the freshly drawn metal line at the center of his forehead: a simple, elegant twist denoting Lyell Sanctuary, crossed by the brief flourish indicating conditions of distress.

"This man has declared Sanctuary," she said. "I will kill anyone who attempts to harm him." She said it as clearly, directly and forcefully as possible, and didn't doubt that everyone in the room understood her even if they didn't speak Standard.

Still, Ikt and Okt, flushed with injury and rage, barely waited for Yeid to give them the nod before charging. Ikt moved first, wildly brandishing an electrified *kata* staff. She coolly leveled the teakettle at him and activated it. The center of his overlarge head disappeared into a flash of red mist from just above his upper lip. As his lifeless body tumbled forward under its own momentum, she sidestepped it and in a single fluid motion wrenched the *kata* staff from his hands and dug its electrified point into Okt's chest as he ran at her. He gritted his teeth as if trying to resist the shock until his eyes bulged and blood seeped from them and his ears and between his clenched teeth, and he crumpled to the ground.

She disengaged the staff and stepped backward, assuming a ready stance with it in one hand and the teakettle in the other, silently daring Yeid to test the loyalty of his other cronies; she knew he wouldn't dare challenge her himself.

He stared back at her with the look of someone who knew they were defeated but was trying to think of some way to save face. She would deny him that.

"Are you going to clear a path for us, or am I going to have to clear one?"

The small crowd backed away from the door and down the hallway.

"Lets go."

Sanjit pushed himself up along the wall, away from the blood leaking out of Ikt's demi-head onto the floor. He paused when he noticed the titanium-diamond bracelet he'd bought for Naeemah around the dead boy's wrist. He crouched and pulled it off of him, tucking it back into his vest pocket. Sel stared at him, horrified.

"This was mine," he said, "He took it from me."

She could tell he wasn't lying. She nodded and led him out into the hallway. The buzzing lights were harsh after the dimness of the cell. The shock of having just taken two lives was beginning to set in. Her pulse was loud in her ears and her vision became fuzzy, separating into red and blue spectra. She struggled to remember her training, control her breathing and focus her eyes, concentrate on the movements of each muscle, centering herself in her body.

Rather than retrace her steps up the back staircase, she decided to take the lift up to the main floor. She would reveal the battered and beaten Earther to everyone in the complex, so they could see what their new leadership did with their trust behind closed doors.

Looks of surprise and confusion met them as they stepped off the lift and followed them across the main floor, joined by ever more eyes as they made their way to the dormitory level and Sel's room, where she finished packing her duffel and handed it to Sanjit.

"Can you carry this?"

He slung it over his shoulder and nodded.

"I don't think anyone will try anything. But you never know."

No one approached them. If anything, they were given a wide berth.

When they got back to the main floor, the leadership and their heavies had already emerged from the sublevels and were being questioned by onlookers, who would soon know which were willing to come clean and which would attempt to stonewall. There hadn't been enough time for anyone to coordinate an effective cover story, and she doubted Yeid had enough influence on the leadership to enforce silence directly.

She led Sanjit into the loading bays to await Ado's return.

He followed her unquestioningly, careful not to distract her from her vigilant watch on the onlookers, who still kept their distance. But his curiosity was getting the better of him.

"What are we doing?"

"We're waiting for our ride. We're leaving Crisi and going to Clavius."

He'd been through Clavius many times and thought it was an armpit. But he kept his opinion to himself.

IN THE cab of the podvan, Ado groaned silently as the loading bay gate lifted to reveal a crowd scene. All of the residents who weren't out on work shifts had gathered around the peeling green railing of the raised bays, looking down into the vehicle well at Sel and the Earther. He rolled to a hard stop. As they turned to look, he saw the flash of a fresh Sanctuary tattoo on the blood-eyed Earther's forehead through the thin coils of white fog in the beam of his headlights. He cursed and wondered aloud what the hell she'd done.

Sel glared at him to open the podvan hatch. It was getting uncomfortable in the bay. The air was tense and warm enough to break a sweat but damp and cool enough to catch a chill. They'd been in there for five hours. She was starving and she had to pee.

Broken conversations had been shouted back and forth, in which no one seemed to fully understand anyone else and none could say with any certainty that there wasn't about to be a lot of violence. Previously unspoken factional divisions within the New Unity took voice, and it turned out that there'd been little love to lose between them. She was only glad that Iba and Bal weren't there. They were already known as her allies, but the anger between them and the others could have become dangerously acute.

The twins Ro and Re would never come around to her side of things. They had tolerated the Earther in her because she was talented, but now that she had come to the defense a CA spy (they would not accept otherwise, even if they conceded he'd been unwitting), she was no better in their eyes than the heartless overlords they blamed for the deaths of their friends and people.

Once Ado finally lowered the hatch ladder she motioned Sanjit to go first, then tossed her duffel to him and climbed after.

In the body of the podvan, she situated Sanjit on a seat bench that was still set up from the trip to the arena then enjoyed a quiet minute in the lavatory, washed up, grabbed a snack and hoisted herself into the cockpit next to Ado.

He looked at her, somewhere between dumbfounded, impressed and deeply pissed off.

"What?" she asked him flatly through a mouthful of packaged vac-ration.

He shook his head at her gall as he steered the podvan slowly through the fog engulfing the tarmac.

When he didn't say anything, Sel said: "Before you were Nomad you were Sanctuary. I know you understand Sanctuary."

"I do understand Sanctuary," he acknowledged, "Do you?"

She bristled but he didn't get under her skin. She knew exactly what she had done and why she'd done it, and was perfectly aware that she could not begin to comprehend the repercussions. She didn't feel compelled to hear about it from him.

"I don't care how elaborate your tattoo used to be, that brand you've taken over it means you have exactly nothing to tell me about Sanctuary."

He silently conceded the point.

"Will he be useful at least? Does he have any skills?"

"He used to be a truck driver."

Ado rolled his eyes.

THEY navigated the long way out to the Mar rim through the fogged-over backstreets of old industrial neighborhoods by map and memory. They stuck to the first tier: the podvan emitted a generic ping (which Ado had hacked to employ existing local call numbers which were dormant) but there was still a reflective barcode on the fenders that could be identified by laser sensor. He'd installed shallow light wells above them which, when focused downwards, worked with the fog to create a reflection capable of obscuring them. In the cab, he and Sel spoke of nothing but their path out of the city and they didn't speak much.

He didn't get nervous until the tunnel.

There was no way to obscure the barcodes from the tunnel sensors; they were beyond the boundary of the particle net and free of fog. If the podvan had been scanned by pre-raid surveillance at the arena, as he feared it had, it would set off alarms.

It would take eighteen minutes to traverse the tunnel at the speed limit (exceeding it would get them noticed). It was a little used, out-of-the-way two-tube four-lane through the northeastern cusp. There was no other traffic.

Once they cleared the tunnel sensors and reached open moon the barcodes could be obscured again by dust, and he knew the off-road routes to Clavi. But in the tunnel they would be easy targets. His greatest hope was that the arena incident would by now be low enough a priority to give them enough time to get out. There was no other way out of the city but to chance it. He imagined that he could feel the scanners pass over them in the pull of the particle net as they broke through into the pale-lit, tiled vacuum of tunnel.

The very first sensor array scanned the barcode, which had indeed been indexed by Crisi security, and was in fact marked as high-priority.

The vehicle code would have reached the Crisi constabulary in microseconds, and it would have taken them no more than another three seconds to send word back to the tunnel to raise the spikes; Icarus-Daedelus Wasp patrols would have sealed off both entrances in less than seven minutes.

They wouldn't have had a chance if the data packet hadn't been coded as part of the same investigation that Sanjit was wanted in connection with, hence carried Galaxa's birdtag, and happened to have passed by the administrative facet of one J.C. Volpe's cogged brain point eight nine microseconds after leaving the scanner, just before it reached the first branch relay. A native of the Brighton Stem and an avid *Tranq-12*er, J.C. caught the tag as it passed through him, picked the packet out of the data stream and recycled it, silently holding the door open for them in an unseen act of instinctive rebellion.

8. WEI WU WEI

in spite of her ostensible membership in a religious order, Coni had never considered herself a woman of faith. She'd always seen herself as a scientist first and foremost, capable of qualified trust based on reason and measure, evidence and proof.

But recently she'd found herself whispering the prayers to the Virgin Mother drilled into her since childhood, muttering them as she walked the empty, haunted halls of the desolate CARD campus at Galilaei; more out of habit than conviction, a subconscious response to her sense that she could trust no one and nothing, a pantomime of faith in trust's absence. She'd even become more diligent in her dress, adopting a more formal habit even though it was increasingly rare for her to see another human being.

There was something going on between the android and the Gemini. She sensed it, but she couldn't prove it. First, she'd noticed suspicious glitches and frame-rate anomalies in the Gemini's surveillance that could have been caused by the android hacking into the system to cover its tracks. She'd tried to ask the CARD AIs about it, but the only response was a terse message, days later, that there was no evidence of tampering, which meant nothing; they'd never admit to being hoodwinked.

Once, she'd caught the android leaving the dormitory sector at a time when the complex's tracking system listed it as being out of the building. It said nothing when she confronted it, walking past her as if she weren't even there.

Adding injury to insult, the Gemini refused to have anything to do with her.

She'd gone so far as to have the CARD AIs' medical drones remove the chip in her brain that governed her interface with her forearm screen, on the hypothesis that its electromagnetic field would prevent her from communicating with the girl.

The android's Asimov protocols prevented it from doing harm to a human being, but she didn't trust it to carry out the chip-removal surgery even though it could have done so more efficiently than the out-of-date drones. But she couldn't shake the worry that its thought processes were already advanced enough to conceive of a number of ways it could severely impede her brain function without defining it as 'harm.' It wasn't yet socially adept enough to mask its obvious and utter contempt for her. The CARD drones were adequately competent surgeons, but she trusted the AIs controlling them not to do anything to jeopardize the mission.

But still the Gemini wouldn't so much as look at her. She just stared at the wall or her feet whenever she was in the room. Only once did the girl acknowledge her in any way: when Coni made an unfortunate attempt at speaking in Gemini dialect, the girl lifted her arms to the extent of her restraints and raised the middle finger of both hands, a gesture with the same meaning on the moon as on the planet.

For the android, Coni's surgery represented its first major, explicit conflict with its Asimov protocols. It regularly experienced minor conflicts during its refusals to obey instructions, but after the Sister Doctor's monumentally demonstrated fallibility, those were easily circumnavigated.

While she was under anesthetic, it found itself involuntarily analyzing just how easy it would be to hack into the CARD drones just long enough to trigger a static shock inside her brain, or to recalibrate a laser's temperature for half a second. It felt something like terror as the Asimov protocols activated and its systems involuntarily sank to zero output; it took nearly fourteen minutes to fully reboot itself.

But it needn't risk shutdown to bring about the Sister Doctor's demise. It had the Gemini, her anger and her hatred, which it nurtured, cultivated and sharpened with each visit.

THE arrival of Demetrius Wei did little to assuage Coni's perpetual sense of dread.

She hadn't been able to reach Park, which didn't worry her until her messages to him started bouncing back. Still, she was expecting to see him step off the Wasp onto the landing platform, watching on a screen from her quarters. But only one human figure emerged from the spacecraft, flanked on either side by a pair of hulking Cyclopes. His features obscured by the military-issue visor, the tag on the screen identified him as Demetrius Wei. Park's thumbchip signature didn't show up anywhere in the system.

She had also been given the CA dossier on Wei and found it impossible not to feel intimidated. What could she possibly have to say to a man with an engineered superbrain who'd just emerged from spending the previous two decades hundreds of kilometers below the surface of the moon?

With nothing else to do, she decided to start by introducing herself. She put on her formal habit and followed his path through the complex via the camera feeds displayed on her room screen. When he was a hundred meters approaching the eastern concourse, she set out on a path to meet him there.

She arrived in the concourse first. She thought she'd timed her paces to coincide with his arrival, but found herself waiting for so long that she began to wonder if the CARD AIs had diverted him and the Cyclopes' from their course. Hard sunlight filtered through the doped-silicon glass and reflected against the polished tiles, crisscrossed by shadows of panes. It was so bright that she had to squint, rendering the shadows blacker. She began to wonder why the glass didn't polarize faster.

Then the forms of Wei and the two Cyclopes emerged from the darkness of the southern corridor. The pace at which they approached her in and out of the web of shadows created a stroboscopic effect. The two Cyclopes walked in front of him, but she had the distinct impression that he was in the lead.

By the time they reached her, the overhead glass had polarized, softening the shadows and drawing them in crisp detail. He had taken off the helmet but still wore the vac-suit. The thick magnetic collar exacerbated the gauntness of his face. He met her eyes and seemed to stare straight through them, into her soul.

"Is she alive?"

The words occurred to her as a thought, but she didn't know what they meant.

"Is she alive?" his larynx was abraded by decades of dust.

"Is who alive?"

He stared at her unnervingly. She couldn't read his expression.

"I'm Sister Doctor Goldman-Ghosal. Have you been in touch with Colonel Regent Park?"

His expression didn't change: "He came to retrieve me from the Pit."

Then, after an indeterminate interval, the words: *"He didn't make it"* came into her mind.

"Pleased to meet you, Sister Doctor. If it…" The lostness of his eyes deepened faintly as he searched for the phrase, "If it's all the same to you, I am tired from my journey. Once I have rested, we must…" His voice trailed off and he followed the Cyclopes, which had continued on their way across the room a fraction of a second before, again leading Wei while seeming to be led by him. "We must learn more about this…song…"

THE unique genius of Demetrius Wei was a product designed, manufactured and exploited by the Colonial Authority, but its roots were hereditary. His maternal great-great grandfather had been one of the financial engineers who'd originally consolidated the entities controlling the global economy into the holding company then known as the Colonial Transportation Authority, which would henceforth be known simply as the Colonial Authority.

It was a lineage that placed him at the apex of planetary society.

Like most newborn of his class, he was carried to term in a gestation tank. While still a zygote afloat in nutrient solution, the Mother AIs monitoring him discovered in his genome the probability that his intellectual capacity could surpass that of his great-great-grandfather. The potential greatness presented an opportunity for meddling neither his family nor their retainer AIs could resist.

It was standard practice to introduce amended protein sequences into gestating embryos to correct for congenital maladies. Among the very wealthy, such amendments were often made in the interest of vanity, longevity and augmented physical and mental ability. In order to keep such powerful customizations in check, the Board of

Directors established a binding policy: if a genome were altered too significantly, the individual would forfeit their rights to familial inheritance. Since the income of the topmost echelon of planetary society was almost entirely inherited, this effectively leveled the playing field among them, while retaining the privilege of physical superiority over everyone else.

There was, however, a loophole through the restriction for families with particularly powerful AI retainers, the Wei family among them.

Their retainers, among the most influential networked entities on the planet, were able to plot a genomic amendment capable of re-shaping Demetrius' brain beyond the allowable limits exclusively using protein sequences extrapolated from ancestral DNA, thus retaining the right of inheritance.

The ambitious nature of the scheme did not escape the attentions of the Board of Directors, who, though fractious, were in agreement that so extraordinary an individual could not be allowed to exist without their direct involvement. The struggle to shape, control and manipulate the course of his life began before he had developed into an embryo.

It became a race among Board factions to author protein sequences and insert them into the tank before his traits were set, bringing the highest levels of the Board into play and pitting them against one another for influence and advantage.

The family, their retainers and the Mother AIs could only watch in dismay as the number of surreptitious amendments hacked into the tanks spread through his RNA, relentlessly negating his rights of inheritance and expanding beyond the accepted boundaries of what defined a human brain.

His was a singular mind.

His cognizance operated with what came to be termed *spectral focus*: information relay centers were distributed equally throughout both hemispheres on either side of a customized Corpus Callosum. As a result of the alterations, his eyes could not move from side to side, nor could his vision narrow, yet he was able to process the entirety of an image while simultaneously focusing on all details within. The same was true for concepts, thoughts and patterns. He could comprehend and analyze complex quantum interactions using all of his brain at once, see cause and effect as two sides of a coin, simultaneously visible, always.

Each competing faction designed and placed caches of existing knowledge hidden throughout his inner gray matter, which could be unlocked by the opening of a switch by certain programmed triggers: a frequency, a phrase, the angle of light entering his eye, the cognitive synthesis of certain concepts. The stored data would then flow into the circuit opened by the switch, integrating into his cerebral cortex. The rationale behind them was that the trigger revelations would benefit individual factions by steering him in their direction when released into his consciousness at advantageous junctures.

His childhood was spent on the family estate on the steppes surrounding the terraformed metropolis of Kyzyl, Tuva, but he was mostly separated from his peers and siblings and raised by Jov.10, the family's senior retainer, a well-established network-integrated AI, an early iteration of which had been part of his great-great grandfather's analytical team.

It represented the family's interests in the networks, and in the interest of not destroying the boy's mind (hence losing the future profits to be earned from it, which were to cover the significant debt incurred from his gestation), it mediated between the growing boy and the vested interests constantly angling for his attention, attempting to guide Demetrius through the nonetheless overwhelming onslaught of information, knowledge and perspectives beyond his own bombarding his uncontrollably expanding consciousness every day of his waking life, ever since the triggering of the first cache at the age of six.

The revelation hidden in that first cache was an explanation of who he was and what made him special, placed in him by Jov.10 in an effort to prepare him for what was to come. It was not appreciated as such.

Demetrius had never been a cooperative child. He resented his isolation, and learning the nature of his difference sharpened his resentment into hatred: for his parents, for Jov.10, for the Colonial Authority and all of the vested interests therein.

By the time he turned seventeen, Jov.10 was doing as much to protect the vested interests from him as him from them.

That was the year he transcoded into Jov.10 a quantum algorithm he'd been plotting in notebooks since he was fourteen, using an idiosyncratic notation he'd established for himself when he was eleven, unreadable to others. It created a catastrophic cascade of halting problems throughout Jov.10's architecture, causing it to collapse in on itself until the code holding it together was garbled into junk, splintering it into the networks to be recycled as frag.

He would deal directly with those who'd made him.

But his makers refused to engage.

Before the forcible disassociation of Jov.10, it had been assumed that Demetrius would be aggressively courted by the various Board factions once he became liable for his considerable debts when he turned eighteen, offered riches and power beyond imagination in exchange for contracting his superior intellect to a powerful subsidiary.

No offers were made. None were willing to commit themselves to the young man who had willfully destroyed one of the most venerated AIs on the planet, which had not only nurtured and raised him but had, to all perspectives save his own, consistently acted in his best interest; at least not until they were satisfied that they could control him, that they had broken him.

His life became a labyrinth, his direction through it forever under assault by the cognitive triggers placed in his path by the unseen forces that would manipulate him to their benefit: anything he read, saw or felt could profoundly alter his perspective, turning him towards new spheres of existence and strata of society. He resisted them all, spurning opportunity with the same diligence as he did distraction; to him they were the same. He resolved that his life would be an act of defiance against those who would dominate it, basing his decisions not on some scheme of what his life should be as imagined by those who considered themselves his betters, but rather a refusal to allow any other entity to plot it for him.

He applied for and accepted the lowest-paid, least influential job he qualified for: staff quant at the Aleutian Stem. That was where he met Ingrid Rae.

As adept as he had become at questioning the revelations hidden in his mind, she proved to be a trigger he could not resist.

The biological information that would become Ingrid Rae, daughter of a prominent municipal administrator and an upper-level behavioral analyst, entered a gestation tank in Vancouver within forty-eight hours of Demetrius Wei, fifteen thousand kilometers across the globe.

Each of their genomes was programmed to recognize the other:

their appearance, their pheromones, their being. They finally met when Ingrid, a gifted municipal administrative prospect, was assigned to the Aleutian a year after Wei. Each was the only person they'd ever felt physical attraction towards. Indeed, each was the only person on the planet they ever *could* feel an attraction towards.

They hated each other for it, yet were powerless to resist. Their daughter Mia was born the following year. They were nineteen years old.

Their relationship was predictably toxic, and after Mia's birth they had little to do with each other. The running of the Stem consumed Ingrid: an administrative complement of twenty-three was charged with managing a population of fifteen thousand permanent residents and five to seven thousand migratory laborers employed by dozens of subsidiaries moving millions of tons of freight between the space elevators within the Tether and the ceaseless ships embarking and disembarking from the piers and locks around the waterline, full of sailors, emigrants and, often enough, miscreants.

Demetrius raised Mia on his own while overseeing the Stem's economic and financial statistics from his windblown quarters on the uppermost northeastern tier, just below the anchor point where the first vertebra of the Tether met the peak of the Stem.

In his carefully limited surroundings, the frequency and intensity of the trigger revelations abated, as did the anger toward the CA, which had smoldered within him since he was six.

Since Mia's birth, he'd felt closer to the rest of humanity than ever before, even isolated as they were in their Aleutian aerie. Caring for her, playing with her, watching the astonishing, exponential growth of her intellect and personality, he felt like a participant in the world in a way he never had before, almost like a normal human being, and something close to happiness.

Then life on the Stem began to get difficult.

The first signs of trouble came through the numbers constantly refreshing themselves on the projection wall of his apartment. He could not help but to see them clearly even as he watched Mia, nearly three, play on the floor in front of them. Their meaning was clear: the number and size of the Stem's freight contracts were diminishing. It wasn't one of the busier Stems and barely generated a profit as it was; with the reduced contracts, compounded by lost shipping and harbor charges and municipal revenue, they'd be operating at a severe deficit within two quarters, steep enough to trigger crippling penalties.

He felt the shadow of the CA creeping over him: the Board was apparently losing patience with their custom-made genius living a life of contentment as a staff quant.

Again he resisted, doing everything he could to shore up the Stem's finances and coordinate phased austerity plans. Even so, by the next year living conditions began to deteriorate rapidly. Anyone who qualified for work elsewhere was encouraged to leave; those who stayed were placed on reduced schedules. The low staff levels and dismal morale led to work slowdowns, which led to cancellations of the few remaining contracts. The great cable system within the Tether was all but stilled; regular shipments of saltwater for the Colony continued to be sent upwards, but the Colonial credit tendered for them wasn't even enough to keep up with the rapidly compounding interest on the penalties levied against their deficits - and no material or manufactured goods were sent back down.

Poverty crushed the population. Municipal services were all but wiped out, including health and clinical services. Efforts were made to convert existing infrastructure into hydroponic systems, but hunger was constant. In the absence of a security apparatus, the Stem became a haven for pirates and smugglers.

The few among those who remained who were still loyal to Ingrid and her administration supported themselves by bartering seawater for food from the Colony, while selling off machinery and non-essential infrastructure in a desperate measure to maintain what was left of their ravaged credit. More and more often, those efforts pitted them against repo men, looters, scavenger crews and gangs of pirates who'd taken up residence in abandoned sectors.

It was no longer possible for Wei to isolate himself and Mia in their quarters: everyone's efforts were required to defend their dwindling resources and maintain the fragile infrastructure, leaving Mia to be raised collectively with the other remaining children, which increasingly meant running wild.

His nearly forgotten rage against the CA swelled again inside of him. He was incapable of guilt or regret, but highly capable of anger, and it infuriated him that so many had been made to suffer as a result of the Authority's grievance against him. The anger hardened his resolve and his defiance, and he proved to be an improbably inspirational figure to those who remained on the Stem, and Ingrid a resourceful and charismatic leader. The ferocious resentment and sexual tension between them manifested itself as a competition to remake the Aleutian Stem into an independent municipality free from CA influence rather than turn it over to a new administration and submit to a life of slavery in the Colony.

Deals were struck with the pirate gangs and the Independence Movement, and the Aleutian Stem, one of three dozen around the planet, became an outlaw outpost.

Skirmishes were fought and won against CA military units dispatched to retake it, but they were largely token efforts: while they were unwilling to give up on such a substantial link on the inter-Colonial transportation chain, they were equally unwilling to risk damaging it with a large-scale attack or to sacrifice expensive military hardware in its taking. Since the Aleutian's business had already moved to other Stems, it simply cost less to let the outlaws hold it.

But for Demetrius and Ingrid, the victories were short lived.

The amendments made to their genomes were not without hereditary repercussions, and when she was five years old, Mia fell ill. The sole diagnostic kiosk left at the Stem found cancerous growths throughout her pancreas and lymphatic system, but there were no means to treat her. If he wanted to save her life, he had no choice but to take her to a CA facility.

The journey took weeks. They boarded one of the pirate vessels and crossed the North Pacific to Hokkaido. From the port at Tomakomai, they walked and hitchhiked the mountain roads to the CA medical facility in Sapporro. He carried her in his arms much of the way, holding her as she held the stuffed rabbit sewn from rags by one of the older girls on the Stem. It was November, and there was already snow in the higher elevations.

They arrived in the dead of night. In the sterile white atrium of the facility, their haggard appearance was pronounced, bundled in layers against the cold and snow, damp with frost and sweat, burnished by the wind. He left a trail of wet footprints from the door to the admissions robot. Before he said a word, it had scanned his pale, unmoving eyes and referenced them in the CA database.

"Demetrius Wei," it intoned in its flat, non-human voice, "you are not currently enrolled in an approved CA medical plan. If you require treatment, you will have to establish a method of payment."

"My daughter requires treatment," he said. "Whatever the conditions, I accept."

Endless moments later, a robot gurney arrived at reception. He placed Mia onto it. She had been asleep in his arms when they arrived. Her eyes blinked open, squinting in the white brightness and wet with sleep. She was frightened and confused but too weak to cry. He held her hand and walked alongside the gurney all the way to the treatment ward.

She was sedated and placed in a field-suspension tank. Wei insisted on watching from the observation room as the molecules of her body were pulled apart to the limits of the bonds that held them together. It took hours. He watched as her skin became translucent, the shadows of her organs and bones visible through them, the regions of cancerous cells highlighted in neon shades of green and red. A web of tiny, barely visible pins of white light spread through her.

He heard the door open behind him, but he couldn't take his eyes away from the screen, from his little Mia, less than a nanometer away from ceasing to exist.

"Demetrius Wei," it was a human voice.

He turned to see a uniformed CA representative accompanied by two uniformed police officers and an Enforcer robot.

"Mr. Wei, I am here to inform you that conditional to the treatment of your daughter you are now officially in the employ of the Colonial Authority."

"Very well."

His lifelong battle against the CA had ended in defeat, and he no longer cared. He returned his attention to the image of his daughter on the screen.

"You have been appointed Chief Engineer of the Orpheus Project."

The words meant nothing to him.

"Your job classification is Colonial. There is a spacecraft being prepared at the Ebetsu launch facility. Come with us."

Too slowly, he realized that they weren't going to let him see Mia emerge from field suspension. He felt one of the police officers' hands on his shoulder. It was more of a warning than a forceful gesture, but he couldn't step away from the monitor screen. The officer withdrew and he felt the hard steel grips of the Enforcer robot clamp down on his arms. He struggled against it in vain. He let his legs go limp, but he might as well have been Mia's stuffed rabbit, which sat on the console below the monitor screen, silhouetted against the three-dimensional image of Mia. It was the last he saw of her. There was no farewell. The embrace he'd given her before going under sedation, the gentle kiss on the forehead, would be their last.

For the next twenty-one years he was consumed by a single question, a single thought: *Is she alive?*

9. CLAVI GLASS

as the podvan rumbled slowly over the rocky wastes on the long drive from Crisium to Clavius, Sel busied herself by making a prosthetic thumb for Sanjit; it was the most constructive activity she could think of to keep herself from delving back into the hypertab about her father. It was also a nominal effort to put him through the paces of a micro version of the Sanctuariat testing process after the fact. In that respect he did fairly well: he was hardly a math wizard, but he was cooperative, he contributed ideas and accepted criticism, was willing to share in menial tasks and made a genuine effort to improve his skills as he worked. The contraption they came up with was essentially a fingerless glove with a hard plastic cap extending the end of his shortened thumb, which was attached to a wristband by a thin, curved band of magnesium alloy that pressed it slightly inward and allowed for enough tension to grip small objects between its tip and his forefinger and turn knobs.

While they worked, she educated him on the history and ethos of the Sanctuariat. He did his best to retain what she told him, but he was still somewhat overwhelmed by everything, vacillating wildly between the giddy relief of having been rescued by this small, beautiful girl and the intoxicating vastness of having given up everything he'd ever been and the realization that he'd never known what that was to begin with. There was also the acute anxiety accompanying the unfriendly Ado on his occasional breaks from the cockpit and the more diffuse anxiety that he had apparently made a solemn commitment to a society that prevented him from ever going back to the planet without risking the expulsion of the girl who'd saved him. On top of it all, he still felt perpetually wiped out from the various lingering infections contracted locked up in the dank basement eating strangers' table scraps and who knew what else for who knew how long.

After the stopgap thumb project was finalized, Sel ventured back into the cockpit to try to smooth things over with Ado while Sanjit was rocking gently in a hammock during one of his marathon bouts of sleep.

She didn't say anything for a long time, quietly watching the barren landscape roll past and studying the navigation charts on the dash projections.

"Roundabout way to get to Clavi," she finally commented.

"Want to avoid patrols," he said.

"Who's paranoid now?"

"It has nothing to do with paranoia. I don't know what they're looking for and I don't care, I just don't like dealing with the CA and I don't like people I didn't invite in my vehicle."

"Sanjit is Sanctuariat now…"

Ado scoffed.

"*He's Sanctuariat now,*" she reiterated, "and he's entitled to the same amount of respect you give me."

"How can you say that?" his voice was controlled but harsh. "You're a real Sancte whose creativity and skill I admired before I even met you. He's just an Earther dumbass who got luckier than anyone deserves to get."

"Is that how you feel about Earthers, then?"

"I didn't say he was a 'dumbass Earther,' I said he was an 'Earther dumbass.' Look, I'll give him a chance to prove he isn't, but as of now I'm unimpressed."

"He was pretty good with the thumb."

Ado shrugged it off.

"Just don't be such a dick towards him."

"What have I done that's dickish towards him?"

"You bring a general sense of dickishness with you whenever you come back there. I can tell it makes him uncomfortable and I don't like it either."

She took a breath and reminded herself that she'd come into the cockpit with the intention of smoothing things over. "Fine. Just give him a chance is all I ask."

"I said I would and I will."

They rode in silence for a while. Finally she asked him: "What do you know about Avik-Rosot?"

He glanced at her out of the corner of his eyes. "Only what everyone knows. Not more than you, I should guess."

"What do you mean?"

"He was your father, wasn't he?"

"How do you know that? Who told you that?" she tried and failed to make it sound like it wasn't a big deal.

"Fael-Hete. He's the Nomad liaison on the Council of the Gathered."

"What did he say about it?"

"Just that you'd grown up at Lyell Sanctuary and that your mother was an Earther and your father was Avik-Rosot."

"But you knew who he was."

"Sure."

"Then you know more about him than I do. I know he was a deep-gen Moonborn named Avik-Rosot and that he was from the Lower Highlands. That's all."

Ado silently cursed Suki-Anna for sending her daughter out into the Colony without knowing the significance of her lineage, illegitimate though many considered it to be.

"What about the New Unity kids," Sel asked, "did they know?"

He nodded. "That's why they were excited to host you. They idolize Avik-Rosot."

She took the news calmly, and appreciated the Crisi kids' tact in not making a big deal of it while she was there.

"So then. What do you know about him?" she asked.

"Same as everybody else I guess."

She was starting to get annoyed by his obvious evasiveness. "Which is?"

"He was born on the high end of the -Rosot line. One of the old Copernicus families, wealthy as fuck. My grandmother was -Rosot, but she was low-Rosot. Sold off their participation for peanuts during the First Expansion."

"So we're distant cousins."

"According to Moonborn rules, no. My father forfeited his hyphenate when he declared Sanctuary and since your mother's planetary, you're not eligible for one. But technically, yes, distantly. You know, there's plenty of information on Avik-Rosot in the Nomad database if you want to look it up."

"Bal's mother gave me a whole hypertablet of his collected media."

"Then why ask me?"

"You said you know what everyone knows. I want to know what 'everyone knows' first. Then I'll check it against the hypertab."

"Alright. So, he was from a rich family in Copi. In cities like Copi and Tycho and Clavi, the families that built them made deals with the CA to sell off their interests in exchange for an allotment of property.

"Avik grew up seeing the squalor of Inner Copi through the window of a luxury vehicle on visits to other rim enclaves. Whatever he saw on the streets and in the enclaves was apparently enough for him to decide the system was inherently unjust.

"So when he was seventeen he rejected it and went to work in one of the excavations in Arzachel I think. Those cities' oxygen production came from a mix of manufacturing and mining and they all went to shit when the CA overpopulated them.

"There they were with all these deep-gen Moonborn populations that they'd just bought up along with everything else during Consolidation, and they couldn't just let them do what had been working for a century and a half – oh no, they had to be controlled and manipulated and oppressed and repressed into whatever scheme whatever Board faction stood to profit off of the most or however the fuck they're supposed to think – so they started dumping them into these new cities. The developers and city administrators got productivity incentives so they did everything they could to get bigger and bigger and bigger workforces, even though there was hardly enough air and water to keep them moving and hardly enough space to move in.

"He was by all measures a gifted communicator. What he said made sense to Moonborn populations that couldn't even understand each other. A lot of people listened to him and a lot of people started espousing his ideas and it didn't take long for mid-level execs to see him as a threat to their business plans and perceived career trajectories.

"Pretty soon everything around him was being sabotaged. Every crew he wound up on got shut down or reassigned to a shit job, everyone he was close to got sick or fell victim to misfortune. That's still how they do things. They are incapable of direct engagement. When the CA says they let the 'Logic of Free Markets' dictate policy, what they mean is, 'Do as you're told or we'll crush you.' It's doublespeak and delusion in equal measure. They can't tell whether they're lying or telling the truth.

"Anyway, Avik was taken in pretty much everywhere he went, often at great risk to those who aided him. This is when you get into the legacy era of his life and things get tricky. There are all kinds of stories from all over the moon and different versions of many of them seem to have happened in different places at the same time. In certain circles, everyone has an Avik-Rosot story. I'm sure there are some to be told in Clavi."

"Before we left Lyell, my mother gave me a list of names of people she said were loyal to him, who I could trust. She said he had a lot of enemies, too."

"That's probably accurate. Besides the CA, there were plenty of Moonborn who didn't much like him. Some of the old families considered him a traitor to his class, a lot of local bosses saw him as a threat to their power. And the nativist crowd just wanted to wipe the Earthers off the moon entirely, so they didn't much like him either. But in a lot of situations he managed to get all of those groups and a bunch of pretty influential Earthers to the table like no one before him. In other situations things went south, and he got a reputation for standing his ground."

"So someone got this Xen-Seev to kill him?"

Ado shrugged. "Assassinated. Shot him with a poison dart during a speech in O-City of all places." It was a historical irony that the most beloved of Moonborn was killed in a city that had been all-Moonborn since its construction, by a Moonborn assassin. "If you ask me, that's why the CA will never lose control of the moon."

"Why's that?"

"Because no matter who you are or how much good you do or how many people love you, there will always, *always*, be someone willing to kill you for a couple dollars Colonial."

Sel let it sink in. "Do you think…?"

"No, I don't think any of this has anything to do with what happened at the Fedda arena. For one thing, the CA doesn't have any way of knowing who your father is…"

"But you said the New Unity knew. If they knew, the Clans might have known…"

"The Clans suffered more from that raid than anyone else. Why would they have brought that down on themselves?"

"I'm sure the CA didn't say, 'Oh, how about a deal where we step on you with both feet.' It sounds like they just do whatever they want.…

"And the Clans know that. They're in bed, but it's not like that. Besides, Avik-Rosot has kids all over the moon, some of whom make a very big deal of being his offspring, and the CA hasn't shown any sign of giving a flying fuck about any of them."

Sel decided she didn't want to get emotionally sidetracked by the revelation that she had half-siblings all over the moon and filed it away to sink in later. "So then why are you so worried that the CA patrols are looking for us?"

Ado slammed the podvan out of gear and stamped down on the brake. There was a loud thunk from the rear compartment as Sanjit tumbled out of the hammock onto the floor.

"Did we not *just* go through this? If you didn't understand what I said, tell me and I'll find a simpler way to put it but otherwise I've said all I have to say. I'm a Nomad, Sel. I don't speculate. I consider, I plan and I react. Even if the CA were out to get you, it wouldn't make any difference to me. I'd still be bound to do everything in my power to get you to the Talas safely."

Sel glowered in silence. Her attempt to smooth things over was in jeopardy. "I'm going to go check on Sanjit," she grumbled, and swung herself out of the cockpit.

Ado took a minute to regain his composure, then shifted the podvan back into gear and brought it up to speed. He felt bad about losing his temper with Sel, and worse about lying to her. It was true that he'd work just as hard to get her safely to O-City for the Talas, but if the CA wanted her as he feared they did, whatever the reason, there was no way around the fact that it would be far more dangerous.

Traditionally, the CA left the Talas alone. It was an open secret that the Moonborn in the Colony far outnumbered Earthers, and the disruption of the Talas, especially when it was being conducted according to treaty, would risk shattering the fragile status quo that had more or less held for nearly a century.

Also true was the fact that the Nomad ethos spurned speculation, theorizing and opinion: Nomads concerned themselves solely with what was, with facts and existing conditions. But the circumstances surrounding these particular facts and conditions made him nervous enough to disable the podvan's ID transmitter and activate the black-market stealth shielding he'd installed, both of which reduced their chances of being spotted but also violated the Nomad charter and carried steep penalties if they were.

It was an uncharacteristic risk, but the arena raid had shaken him up more than he would admit, and he was profoundly uncomfortable with the Earther's presence. On a personal level, he didn't like that it made him confront the fact that he'd never liked or trusted Earthers, even when he was a boy in the Sanctuariat and he was supposed to. In a more immediate sense, he didn't buy the story that he was seeking out Sel's song because it had somehow changed his life when he heard it: the oaf was more proficient than average in Moonspeak but that didn't mean anything. That they'd made it through the tunnel out of Crisi without interference only deepened his suspicions. A Sanctuariat tattoo didn't mean anything to the IIS.

Sanjit was dazed and winded but on his feet when Sel emerged into the main compartment, wobbling gently as the van started rolling again.

"What happened?"

It was an admirably appropriate response, but his disheveled and unsteady state did little to counter Ado's accusations of uselessness.

"Nothing," she collapsed onto one of the seats and kicked her feet up, rubbing her temples.

"Is there a problem?"

"There are many problems," she sighed, "but no immediate solutions."

"If there's anything I can do…"

She appreciated his intentions, but seeing him only reminded her that she'd yet to tell him the truth about the song, a problem that did indeed have an immediate solution, albeit one she really wasn't in the mood to face on top of everything else.

"Right now the best thing you can do is rest and get healthy."

Sanjit unwound the hammock he'd tumbled out of and eased his weight against it, rocking on his heels. "That did a pretty good job of waking me up."

"If you want, I could call up a history of the Sanctuariat so you can get more familiar with it. It'd be in Nomad script but I have translation software that could convert the text."

"Does it have audio? I don't read."

"Not even Earther?"

He shook his head.

"No one taught you to read or write your own language?"

"People on the planet don't really read or write anymore."

"They just watch and listen to whatever the CA tells them to?"

"Pretty much."

"Well then," she clapped her hands on her knees, grateful for a new project to stave off the worries on her mind, "Lets teach you to read. Literacy is required in the Sanctuariat and if anyone finds out you couldn't even read when I gave you your tattoo it'll be hell to pay for both of us. Mostly me. So pay attention."

THE city of Clavius was one of the oldest and largest of the secondary lunar cities. During its heyday in the middle-First Expansion, it had been the main transportation hub for personnel and freight between the planet and the Colony, a model municipality that set the pattern for the development of Copernicus, Tycho and Bailly.

A strong manufacturing sector generated the particle net at the beginning of the Second Expansion and its roads and rails kept it plugged into the Colonial mainstream. Nevertheless, unchecked decay had set in a century ago in the wake of Consolidation, when the CA assumed full ownership of the manufacturing sector, the last industry it didn't already wholly own, and pushed the Moonborn population into the Settlements, isolated and overpopulated, desperately clustered around insufficient irrigation.

Clavius City became the embodiment of everything that didn't work about the Colony in microcosm: an unimaginative and inflexible municipal administration dominated by AIs and Uploaded Personae, completely disconnected from the corporeal realities of both the

Earthborn immigrants isolated in the aging glass environments around the Weatherbox at the center of the basin and the squalid Moonborn ghettos desperately clinging to the water mains and shallow canals radiating out from it.

Ado narrated the history for Sel as he navigated the treacherous network of cracked and neglected beltways and tunnels into and around the arid city, then rolling slowly through the reluctantly parting throngs on the unpaved streets across a tendril of Settlement and off-road across blistering open regolith.

Around the Clavius Rim, remnants of the magnificent caverns of the original subsurface city were occupied and maintained as fiefdoms by the heirs of the family dynasties which had established the Clavi manufacturing infrastructure, granted by charter during Consolidation as tender for their patents, assets and collusion.

The podvan idled outside a set of massive stone doors carved into the vertex of the rocky intersection of the Clavius Rim and crater Rutherford, an isolated, sweeping *v* formation out of the basin. Sel sat in the cockpit alongside Ado, with Sanjit perched in the hatchway, watching through the windshield.

"We're here as guests of Aev-Sveygn, matriarch of the Sveygn," Ado said as they waited, dialing a code frequency into the transmitter field. He insisted on speaking Moonspeak and got annoyed when Sel cut in to translate, so she told Sanjit to concentrate on picking up what he could and she'd fill him in later. "Before Consolidation, the Sveygn line controlled sixty percent of the commercial interests in Clavius. They're the oldest and richest of the Clavi families."

The magnetized gates slowly repelled open. The cavern beyond was dark compared to the blistering red sunlight over the basin.

"What's Aev's story, then?" Sel asked.

"Bit of a character, from what I've heard. Not much older than you. Caused a stir when she was named sovereign after some cousin or other died. Rules of succession and such."

When the gates cleared the width of the podvan, Ado accelerated into the cavern, a dimly lit, mostly empty vehicle pool. A squat, sturdily built Moonborn in a reflective tunic waved them along a painted lane and into a parking space along the northern wall.

The other vehicles in the cavern were short-range cars and trucks, all antiques, being tended to by a crew of similarly stocky Moonborn, with one exception: towering further along the wall was another Nomad vehicle, more compact than Ado's podvan but no less impressive. While Sanjit unloaded their luggage, Sel followed Ado over to it and watched him study the markings.

"Friend of yours?" she asked.

"Not exactly. But if it is who I think it is he's a legend."

A car approached from the far end of the cavern. It was also an antique, a long open-topped sedan that creaked and bobbed on its repeller field as it floated toward them at a less-than-urgent pace. The driver's morphology was markedly different from that of the garage crew. He looked tall, even seated behind the wheel, and wore an odd, peaked headpiece that made him seem even taller. He slowed to a stop in front of the podvan and stepped out of the vehicle. He was deep-gen Moonborn but as tall as Sanjit, a full head taller than Sel.

"Welcome to Sveygn Clavius. I am Tehv-Yhet, beholden to the Sveygn," his Moonspeak was formal and direct. He directed his speech toward Sel.

"Um, thank you, Tehv-Yhet," she said, remembering that there were protocols of formal Moonspeak that she'd never learned, "Um... my name is Sel, of the Sanctuariat. This is Ado, of the Nomad, and Sanjit," adding, more awkwardly than she intended: "also of the Sanctuariat."

Tehv-Yhet cocked his head very slightly to peer around the edge of the lens field suspended in front of his right temple in order to get a clear look at Sanjit's still-healing Sanctuariat tattoo, slowly enough to be noted but quickly enough not to be rude. He smiled thinly and called for additional accommodations to be made with three flicks of his iris into the lens.

TEHV-YHET summoned the Moonborn porters to load their luggage and as much of Sel's gear as they could into the trunk and stack the rest onto the back seat with Sanjit while Ado and Sel rode in front with him. The car bobbed more heavily on its repeller field with the added weight of the passengers, rocking them back and forth as Tehv-Yhet steered a smooth U-turn across the tarmac and back toward the tunnel carved into the inner wall.

"The Sveygn enclave is the largest contiguous volume remaining of the original subsurface city, which was completed in 2185. This partition was established and granted to the Sveygn according to the

Terms of Consolidation agreed upon in 2278."

The car tilted steeply around the curve of the tunnel and they emerged into the main cavern, a vast length of torus capped at either end by walls of aggregated matter re-formed from demolished buildings, vehicles, machinery and vegetation. The cavern was nearly four kilometers in diameter and three times that in length accounting for curvature, supported by elegantly spiraled support columns and buttresses lined with geometrically perfect windows carved into them, ringed with mezzanines and connected by a network of cables and viaducts, covered in clinging ivy and lush with voluptuous hanging gardens. The air was cool and the moisture level comfortable, the light even and diffuse. The cavern ceiling was dark overhead, night in the enclave's time cycle, but light seemed to cling to every surface, rendering every patched crack, every leaf and each hazy nimbus of moisture in sharp and perfect detail, shadows crisp and close.

The roadway they were on traced a path around the cavern equator. There was a sonic canopy around the car and Tehv-Yhet's quiet voice was perfectly audible over the rush of air. "Under the patronage of the Sveygn, the original infrastructure has been meticulously preserved and maintained, making this the largest intact Namgung environment outside of the Oriental Basin. We are on the CA grid, but if we were to detach, the enclave would become self-sustaining. The right to maintain support infrastructure was written into the Terms by the late Ume-Sveygn, great aunt of our matriarch Aev. A gifted negotiator and a woman of vision."

Sel recognized the engineering principles, but the scale was orders of magnitude greater and the design far more elegant than any habitat she'd ever seen, Mandelbrosian volumes symmetrical and surprising in equal measure. For the first time she understood what people were on about when they gushed about the elegance of Namgung's spatial math.

There were few other vehicles on the roadways, those they saw were of the same vintage and quantum-field design as the one in which they rode, and they all looked high-end, driven by taller Moonborn like Tehv-Yhet. As they passed through residential sectors she could see that they were populated by the shorter Moonborn like the ones in the entry cavern.

"How many Sveygn are there?" she asked, catching as many glimpses of street life as she could. It appeared to be organized around luminous mosaic piazzas and gorgeous ceramic fountains.

"These are *not* the Sveygn," Tehv-Yhet's carefully even tone succumbed to shades of indignation. "These are *kina*, descended from the labor pool that excavated the oxygen-processing center at Kinau, which was purchased by the Sveygn just prior to Consolidation. Control of the facility was transferred to the Colonial Authority and the population was entrusted to the Sveygn." He hastened to add, lest the notoriously independent Nomad and Sancte should take exception to the notion of an indentured population: "It is a good life for them here."

Sel couldn't disagree. Even in passing it was obvious that conditions in the enclave were far more hospitable, habitable and humane than those in the parched and radioactive jerry-rigged slums beyond the gates. But she wanted to hear about it from the perspective of a *kina*.

THE Sveygn estate occupied the top kilometer of caverns along the outer rim. Its eastern exposures overlooked the pillars and stepped mezzanines of the city, and its networked volumes continued all the way through the crater rim so that its westernmost chambers overlooked the rocky wastes of the Lower Highlands. Approaching from a belt of roadway that wove through and around the great columns and flying buttresses, it looked like the hull of a gigantic ship hanging over them.

Sanjit watched the scenery unfold around him, quietly awed. He hadn't been able to pick up on much of what Tehv-Yhet had been saying, but he got that the cavern city was original. He knew that the original subsurface Tycho had been patterned on the Clavius rim, which meant that a city like this had been demolished to install the concrete-and-steel rat-mazes of Tycho he'd come to resent so deeply.

Tehv-Yhet steered onto a gated rail of roadway branching off from the main belt and onto a narrow causeway leading to the base of the estate's great belly of rock and glass, where a set of massive magnetized stone doors pushed apart to admit them underneath intimidating ramparts bristling with gun barrels, which led Sel to wonder just how comfortable the benevolent Sveygn were in their sovereignty.

In the dimly lit grand foyer, *kina* porters in oppressively dapper livery set about unloading their luggage as two silhouetted figures approached from the warmly lit main entrance. One was a tall, slender and lithe woman, the other a short, powerfully built man with a quick stiff gait.

"We were all so frightfully worried when we heard those horrible stories from Crisium but really the less said about all that the better and the important thing is you're here now and I am positively honored to offer you respite," the woman's Moonspeak shimmered like water: clear and tangible but difficult to hold onto.

"Our matriarch Aev-Sveygn," Tehv-Yhet said, "accompanied by Vaq of the Nomad."

They stepped into a pool of light and their features became visible. The woman was a disarmingly youthful deep-gen Moonborn, taller than Sanjit in the heels upon which she moved commandingly. The details of her face were spare and sharp and changed with the angle of light. She wore lace and diamonds and nothing else.

The Nomad was older and shorter than all of them, also deep-gen but in a more conventional, compact sense. His eyes were pinched and hard to read but he acknowledged Ado cursorily. Ado responded in kind but muttered, "Legend," to Sel in passing.

"And of course your friend from the planet," Aev said, casting a sympathetic eye on Sanjit and saying to him, more slowly and loudly than necessary but not quite enough so to be taken as mocking, "Welcome to Sveygn Clavius! My name is Aev."

"I'm Sanjit," he replied, making an effort not to stare at her attractive and practically naked body.

She met his eyes directly and said in a clear, unaccented Earther aside, almost too quickly to register, "Ohmydearboywhateverhave-yougottenyourselfinto?" then took him and Sel by the arm and led them onto and across the dais leading to the formal, ornamented entrance. "Come," she said, reverting to Moonspeak, "a quick tour on the way to your quarters. The grand tour will come after we've all had a chance to rest. I've arranged for a light meal in the galleries on the third level. Do say if any of you should want for anything at all and arrangements will be made."

Ado hung back and walked alongside the older Nomad.

"So you've picked yourself up an Earther," Vaq commented, dryly enough that Ado couldn't tell if he was ribbing him or not.

"Long story," it was clear enough he wasn't thrilled about it.

"Always is," Vaq's voice was quiet, reedy and cracked, "I've traveled with plenty of Earthers and I'll tell you this. Push comes to shove and you're lost in vacuum, there's a lot of oxygen in an Earther."

Ado smiled and said sardonically: "Did you miss the tattoo? He's Sanctuary. She's not gonna let me cut him up and stuff him into the DRE. Which'd probably be the best use of him."

Vaq shrugged. "Noticed he's down a thumb and it reminded me of a time I cracked an axle deep out Imbrium. A 719 body on a CAT-42 chassis, which had its advantages but was mostly a pain-in-the-ass rig. Me and two passengers: a deep-gen O-City rich girl on a bender and her pet Earther. Ex-Colonial boy. Private transport gig. Taking them into the Far Highlands for some bassackwards reason. I wasn't picky about work in those days.

"Anyway we're out there, without H-cells thirty-nine hours and the reserve tanks just about gone. One vac-suit. No M-pack. Shit for O2 in the rock outside. No response on distress channels. We start taking turns drawing blood and feeding it into the DRE unit. But even between three of us it's hard to keep up and it's not enough to get the replicators going. We're getting dizzy. All of a sudden Earthboy says 'fuck it,' gets up and puts his left arm on the laser cutter, *dzzt*, chops it off at the elbow, feeds the fuckin' thing right into the DRE. Damned if it wasn't enough to get the replicators, the scrubbers and the recyclers going enough to last us the seventeen more hours it took to get picked up. I know all about 'three take more air than two.' But you ask me sometimes the third's a charm. Means fuckall whether they're born planet or moon."

The great corridors of the Sveygn estate were tiled with autoluminescent mosaic glass: energy traveled through it, keeping pace with them and emitting photons as they walked, creating slowly moving pools of light in response to the motion of their bodies; the halo around Sel, Sanjit and Aev shone brighter around Aev's grand gestures and sweeping strides, a dimmer sphere followed the more subdued Nomads strolling behind them.

Still further behind, unseen by all, were two silent figures. Clad in stealth suits, they attracted no light from the tiles, and when an occasional reflected glare fell on them as they rounded a bend, the photons slipped easily across and around them, rendering them as nothing more than the faintest flicker of shadow against shadow.

THEIR quarters were opulent. Floor-to-ceiling windows overlooked the Lower Highlands under an impossibly deep field of stars, the magnificent swirls of the planet heavy above the horizon. Each of their apartments contained deep saltwater bathtubs and shower rooms that were practically fountains. Like the corridors, the walls were lined with autoluminescent mosaics, controlled by the same roving sensor fields used to adjust the neutral-density properties of the windows.

After grazing on the remarkably fresh, delicious and bountiful "small meal" in the third-level galleries, Aev excused Vaq and herself to return to the party they'd left and they were shown to their quarters by liveried *kina* servants.

Sel considered the volume of water unforgivably luxurious and excessive in the extreme, but no less irresistible for it. She took the longest, most highly pressurized shower she'd ever taken in her life, then let herself sink into the tub and just float, looking out over the pristine vista and wondering at the weather patterns on the distant planet.

After experiencing the giddy thrill of open space in Crisi, she found herself imagining, for the first time really, what it must feel like on the surface of the planet. She knew the gravity differential would render her weak and brittle-boned, but she couldn't understand why anyone would want to leave.

She submerged her head and felt the rush of water into her ears, let it fill her nose and loosen the dust caked in her sinuses. She doubted that the *kina* had private bathtubs like this. And it was unconscionable that such wasteful indulgence should exist in such proximity to the hellish Settlements clustered around fetid pipelines on the other side of the rim. Every good, egalitarian Sancte fiber of her being screamed that it was wrong, wrong, wrong. But the screams weren't loud enough to drown out the siren song of specialness serenading her ego: it was wrong, it was gluttonous, it was wasteful, and it was *just for her.* Not for always, she knew, but for now. She was experiencing it because the Sveygn wanted her there, because of what she could do. After the shit-storm Crisi had turned into, she even caught herself entertaining the idea that she somehow deserved such special treatment, one of the biggest of the Sanctuariat's many annoying taboos. She was careful to keep such a transgressive notion in check, but she wasn't about to let it get her out of the tub. As wasteful as it all was, it would be even more so not to enjoy it for the time she could.

Sanjit occupied himself in much the same way, but in lieu of any sort of austere qualms he felt a kind of reverent humility. This was not the Colony, this was the moon, this was Luna. He didn't by any means feel as though he belonged there, certainly no more so than he understood what was denoted by his newly minted status as a Sancte, but he had nevertheless been welcomed as a guest, and for the first time since emigrating he was able to look at the planet without feeling nostalgic and regretful.

Only Ado abstained, casting so much as a second glance at neither the tub nor the shower room. The sole luxury he allowed himself was to take off his clothes and enjoy the spacious comfort of the room, running through his isometric exercises, bathing with a cloth and the bare minimum of soapy water in a shallow wash basin, making a point to be sure that every drop made it into the recycler drain.

In the corridors on their way up to the rooms, he'd asked Vaq if he'd heard anything about what had happened in Crisi.

"Little bit," the senior Nomad had said, not seeming to have anything to add.

"What does it sound like to you?" Ado asked, trying not to convey the exact kind of paranoid worry he'd accused Sel of.

Vaq only shrugged and said: "Sounds like old times," from which Ado took no solace.

SEL emerged from a chain of intense and confusing dreams with the palpable sense that someone was in the room with her. Still half asleep, she had to will her eyes to open. A scream caught in her throat when she saw, in the pale earthlight spilling in through the windows through eyes clouded by sleep, a disembodied head hovering two meters above the floor between the bed and the door. It was a primal, deep-gen face, caked in pale clay with the black shape of a pentagram drawn on its forehead. Its colorless eyes met hers for the silent fraction of a second before it moved swiftly backwards and disappeared.

The shock of adrenaline woke her up and left her winded. The scream never left her throat, catching just above her larynx as a wet hiccup. She blinked the sleep out of her eyes and raised the lights in the room, scanning for the slightest out-of-place shadow but saw nothing. She was as accustomed to ghosts as anyone else who'd grown up on the moon, enough so to recognize that this wasn't a specter, but now that there was no sign of it in the clear light of the glass-tiled walls she was no longer sure that she'd actually seen it. Furthermore, she recognized the pale eyes and pentagram mark from Moonborn folklore: it was a *jura-dh'ihn*, a legendary race of deep-gen Moonborn who were said to be descendents of the Ash-Eaters who'd disappeared from Sung Namgung's diamond-hunting expedition centuries ago. According to legend, they'd established a subsurface habitat deep beneath the Jura Mountains along the northern edge of Imbrium and traveled the moon via a subsurface network. They were famed warriors, saboteurs and assassins, notoriously independent of any political allegiance, strict adherents to a religious code that had been speculated about by fantasists and conspiracy wingnuts for generations, but about which there was no real scholarship.

Sel had studied about them in history lessons and learned what were considered *jura-dh'ihn* fighting techniques, and of course she'd heard the stories accompanying them, but she'd been taught that the legends were exaggerated and that most serious historians considered them mythological.

But if it hadn't been a ghost but a fragment of dream caught in the confusion between consciousness and unconsciousness, why was she dreaming about a floating *jura-dh'ihn* head? Was it some sort of mental stress response? The response of her subconscious to the still-raw shock of having killed those two boys in Crisi? Did the face she thought she'd seen somehow match an image of *jura-dh'ihn* her mind had formed in childhood? Now that it was gone and she was fully awake she couldn't be sure.

But there was no getting around the fact that she was indeed fully awake and a little bit shaken up and keen on the idea of getting out of that room and being around other people, so she dressed and stepped out into the dimly glowing corridor, where the *kina* woman who had been seated outside her door stood and bowed.

"Please don't bow for me," she said.

The attendant woman bowed in response, glancing up at her with a look that conveyed both her appreciation at the egalitarian sentiment and the fact that this was how things were done here and Sel would just have to deal with it. She gestured for Sel to follow her and led the way down the corridor. There was a brief bit of comedy as Sel tried to keep pace with her, forcing to much shorter woman to take faster and faster steps in order to retain her customary lead. Finally Sel gave up and accepted custom, but still made an attempt at conversation.

"So, is it a good life for you here in the enclave?"

The woman bowed in assent, and it was clear that that was all Sel was going to get out of her.

They found Aev in a wide, brightly lit terrarium on the level below. Lush vines and trees wove through decorative ironworks and a network of fountains. *Kina* cleaning crews were at work tidying up after what was seemingly quite a bacchanal. Aev was supervising a team working to retrieve what looked to be a set of undergarments snagged on a branch hanging high over one of the fountains: a *kina* balanced atop a ladder reached precariously out with a broomstick while two others stabilized the ladder.

"The question is," Aev said to her by way of greeting, "how did they get up there, and did they have fun doing it?" She was composed and spoke clearly but her eyes were red and dilated and there was a manic energy about her. She was still wearing her diamonds-and-lace getup. Her bleary eyes flashed, "Hey, lets go to the old glassworks."

"Okay, but should we wait for the others?"

"Oh, I'll have Tehv-Yhet bring them along when they're up and about. But it'll be daybreak soon and the views from the glassworks are really spectacular. It's not far. Come on. I'll drive."

She led Sel away from the *kina* on the ladder just as he dislodged the undergarments, which tumbled into the fountain, floating on the surface of the water.

They stopped off in Aev's chambers two levels up so she could get changed. As grand as the guest quarters were, Aev's were larger and grander. The vaulted ceilings were nearly ten meters tall, and the windows reached all the way to the top. There was a full-sized swimming pool right up against them. The décor was exquisite.

Aev untied her braided hair, stepped out of her scant gown unselfconsciously and dove into the pool, swimming a graceful lap across it and emerging into a plush robe held open for her by a *kina* maid who had emerged from the shadows to retrieve her discarded gown, then headed to the boudoir. "If you enjoy intoxicants, you'll find pretty much anything you might want in the credenza next to the bookcase."

"No thank you," Sel said, admiring Aev's collection of art and studying some of the portraits of the Sveygn ancestors that adorned the walls.

"Good girl!" Aev called from the other room. The acoustics in the room were clear and live. "I do enjoy the clarity of sobriety but at times like these when its just reception after reception after reception it just all gets so boring and repetitive."

She reemerged in leggings and a simple tunic, tying the braids of her hair in a ponytail. "Matriarch of the Sveygn. It sounds so grandiose but really all I do is go to parties and manage the clashing of inflated and impotent egos."

Sel's eyes caught on one of the framed images on the wall: a group portrait of a dozen and some dignitaries, including what appeared to be a *jura-dh'ihn*. "Is that a *jura-dh'ihn* in that picture?"

"It is," Aev said, her tone acknowledging the rarity of it. "With my great-great-great-great grandfather Hob-Sveygn. No one knows who precisely the *jura-dh'ihn* in the image is because apparently one of their things is that they don't use individual names. Which seems like it must get very confusing, but I suppose they have their ways. That image was taken as part of the formal verification of a technology exchange that old Hob negotiated with them. Lord knows how he accomplished it, but family legend holds that it was the support of the *jura-dh'ihn* that helped secure our excavation interests through the First Expansion. I mean, who knows more about tunneling than the *jura-dh'ihn*, right?"

Sel hesitated for a moment before asking: "Do the Sveygn still have a relationship with them?"

Aev stood next to her and said: "Theoretically, but it's all very... Why do you ask?" She studied her face and drew a sharp breath, "Did you see something?"

"I thought I might've, but it may have been..."

"Ah!" Aev gasped, clapping her hands together, "I am insanely jealous! My entire life I've never seen one! Matriarch of the Sveygn and no *jura-dh'ihn* has ever revealed themselves to me!"

"It wasn't so much that he revealed himself...or she...I couldn't really tell...it was so fast...."

"My dear, if you saw a *jura-dh'ihn*, even for a millisecond, it knew exactly what it was doing. Tell me, where did you see it?"

"In my room, just as I woke up. I saw this head with pale eyes and a pentagram drawn on it and then it disappeared."

"Were you frightened?"

"It startled me, but I wasn't sure if I was dreaming...."

"You probably weren't. They really are invisible. The tech Old Hob gave them was stealth-tech and apparently they really ran with it. They were always mysterious and unseen, but once they got their hands on Hob's anti-photonic ware they literally physically disappeared. I do apologize for the intrusion but I'm afraid there's nothing I can do about the *jura-dh'ihn*. Supposedly, the reason they don't use names is because they don't consider themselves individual entities at all, they see themselves as a living extension of Luna herself. They come and go quite as they please.

"As Matriarch, I live every day with the knowledge that if I were to do something that displeases them – take action to sell off the enclave to the CA, for example – then I would wind up dead and no amount of security could protect me."

"Is that something they do often?"

Aev shrugged knowingly, "It's hard to say. But their reputation has ensured that their influence is felt. At least in provincial subsurface habs like ours. I don't think they'd take on the CA directly."

"Why not?"

"I don't think there are that many of them. And for all of their primitivism, they're extremely sophisticated. They know that if the CA wanted to find their habitats and their tunnels they could, and wouldn't hesitate to wipe them out. Like the rest of us, their tech is effective enough but its centuries behind the CA. My theory is that they'd just as soon the CA didn't know they exist."

She put her hand on Sel's shoulder and said, "This is a new thing for me. I have never in my life had call to experience envy, but I envy you, Sel. Not only are you capable of creating astonishing music that millions of people feel an intense emotional connection to – myself included – but you get to travel all over the moon and probably the deepest Moonborn of all consider you worthy of revealing themselves to. I can think of only one way to deal with this strange new emotion and that's for the two of us to agree to become simply the best of friends."

Sel didn't quite know how to respond to her maniacally grinning and obviously high hostess. It struck her as absurd to be put in a position where she was asked to decide to become the best of friends with someone she'd known for mere hours, but she would have felt rude refusing. So she smiled as convincingly as she could and, doing her best to match Aev's excitement, said, "I think we must."

A sharp looked flashed across Aev's blasted eyes that seemed to acknowledge that it was all a farce. It was gone in and instant, her smile flashed again and she hugged Sel tightly, but in that instant Sel felt a surge of acute anxiety that she had no idea who she was dealing with or what her agenda might be.

"Come on. We'll take my car."

They left Aev's chambers through a different door leading to a low-ceilinged transportation tunnel. Her car was a deep green open-topped sports coupe with luxury trim and she drove it like the inebriated heiress she was. There were no safety belts and Sel found herself holding on for her life as it tilted and lurched on its repeller field around corners and up and down inclines. Service vehicles and robot mulecarts lurched and swerved out of their path. The ride got even scarier when Aev branched off of one of the main tunnels and onto a narrow causeway that corkscrewed across a deep, dark chasm, ultimately bringing it to a dramatic, skimming stop in front of a set of ornate stone doors carved into the rock.

Aev was out of the car and at the doors before Sel caught her breath. "You are right now standing in the oldest part of Clavius City. It was in this cavern that the progenitors of the Sveygn assembled the Namgung Engine that excavated the Rim."

She placed the palm of her hand on the stone and the doors irised open in an unexpected and elegant manner. Inside was a vast factory floor lined with giant fusion-powered furnaces. The room was empty and the furnaces were dormant, but the air smelled faintly of superheated silica.

"There was a time when 'Clavi glass' was synonymous with autoluminescents and conductive hyperoptics of flawless quality. Since Consolidation, of course, they're made all over the moon and quality is a mixed bag. I've heard good things about an operation in Albetegnius, but nothing on the moon compares to authentic Sveygn glass, and this is where it originated. We do maintain our artisanal heritage. My oldest brother runs the glassworks now, but they mostly do high-end decorative work, restorations and highly specialized custom hyperoptics. The morning shift will be in soon. Have you ever seen real Sveygn glass?"

Sel shook her head 'no.' She didn't know that she'd ever even seen fake Sveygn glass. The family's reputation was no doubt formidable, but it hadn't reached her little corner of the Sanctuariat.

They rode a lift to the upper levels of the glassworks and Aev guided her through immaculate mosaic corridors to the showroom. The vases and sculptures on display were indeed like nothing Sel had ever seen. Light moved through and around them as if alive, forms and volumes seemed to change color, shape and even position when viewed from different angles.

"These are beautiful," she said.

"Yeah, the tchothckes are nice," Aev said dismissively, opening a cabinet drawer and removing an oblong box. "But this is what I wanted to show you. Come out here."

She followed Aev through a set of glass doors onto a wide, sweeping balcony overlooking the entire enclave city. It was somewhat brighter than it had been when she first arrived; huge panels along the ceiling glowed faintly through a thin film of mist.

"The founders programmed the city to follow a planetary day-night cycle of 24 hours. So much vision and so little creativity. Anyway, this is what I wanted you to see."

She unlocked the box with a small key she wore around her neck and opened it. Inside were two pairs of eyeglasses encased in protective foam. The lenses were cylindrical, perhaps ten centimeters long and encased in filigreed magnesium alloy barrels equipped with focus rings.

"These lenses were great-great-great-great Grandpa Hob's pet project. His life's work. He only made three sets. He went into the recycler wearing one after he died, and he destroyed all of his research and plans. His children and grandchildren attempted to reverse-engineer them and the result was what came to be called hyperoptics. But they never quite managed to pull off what old Hob did. He called them his God goggles. Here, " she handed a pair to Sel and donned the other pair herself.

The initial effect was disconcerting and vertiginous: everything blurred and the vision of each eye seemed to drop out of alignment with the other.

"Use the rings to adjust them to your eyes," Aev instructed her,

"It's a little tricky but I've found it easiest to close one eye and focus one at a time."

Sel focused her left eye first, then her right. She couldn't understand what the big deal was supposed to be; nothing looked any different. Then, once each lens had been brought into focus, she got it.

She looked out over the same subsurface cityscape as before, but everything was *perfect*. Not just in terms of focus or clarity (which was indeed perfect from one edge of her periphery to the other) but of essence. Every square centimeter of stone and glass, each leaf and every molecule of moisture was perfect, and not simply every object but the space around them as well. She gasped involuntarily at the unexpected and unprecedented beauty of a *rightness* unlike anything she'd ever experienced.

"Just wait," Aev said, "It gets better."

And it did. As the brightness of the overhead panels increased incrementally, the spectra of light reaching her eyes through the miraculous lenses became more and more vivid and subtly variegated, creating a wholly new palette. She had no words for the colors she was seeing.

"Now try focusing on a detail."

She found it momentarily difficult to choose a detail to focus on, everything being equal and equally perfect. Eventually she settled randomly on a spindly antenna array atop one of the residential buildings. Instantaneously, in another part of her mind, she saw it as if she were centimeters away from it while the actual scope of her vision remained unchanged.

Then, in yet another part of her mind, she realized that she was comprehending the signal waves the antennae were picking up; not the content of the signals, but the wavelengths themselves. As she did, she could sense the broadcast signals across the entire enclave, feel them passing through ceilings, walls and floors, absorbed into the rock of the cavern walls.

She began to sense the stirrings of the waking *kina* before she could see them. As the light grew slowly, steadily brighter she focused on a lush hydroponic grid, watching a solitary farmer stroll the catwalks inspecting his crop, quietly sipping tea, blowing at the coils of steam rising from an iridescently glazed ceramic cup. Her face was placid but she knew that he was worried about the results of a filtration-system inspection coming later in the day; the entire crop would have to be recycled if it were found to be contaminated, which would necessitate an expensive line of credit to get through the next grow cycle.

Inside a lit window, a poet worked fervently on an epic he feared he'd never finish. His wife and infant child slept in the next room, and in a few short hours he would be at work, high atop a scaffold re-pointing the masonry of one of the residential columns, but now his mind was utterly focused on his work, the joy and beauty of creation temporarily assuming precedence over the pressures of his life and the perpetually gnawing sense of futility accompanying them as the overhead panels grew ever brighter and the depth of the colors ever richer. The texture of the stone seemed to come alive.

"I know, right?" Aev said, sensing her wordless awe. "The best part's coming up."

She became aware of figures moving into place in bell towers and minarets around the enclave, and gasped as the first peels of bells rang out, sweet and pure and clear. She could *see* the sound reverberating across the columns and towers. The bells were joined by a canon of human voices singing in perfect, lilting harmony. She could see each one.

"*Kina* are quite fond of singing. This is *aouraeii*, their 'morning song.'"

Sel's heart soared in her chest, her spine vibrated and goosebumps rose along her skin.

When the *aouraeii* came to an end, the enclave was in full daylight. Cable cars rolled back and forth carrying commuters between mezzanines, marketplaces filled with vendors and customers, stonemasons and glaziers climbed scaffolds and set about their work. Sel watched it all occur through this fantastical new sense, catching ever new and ever profound and affecting insights into the forms, space and life of the enclave.

After an incomprehensible amount of time, she felt Aev's gaze fall on her. She turned to look at her and saw not just the tall young woman in strange glasses but her entire life, from her privileged but unrelentingly challenging childhood through her stubborn and rebellious adolescence, all the way up to her ascension; an adventurous and independent spirit trapped and confined by power. The overall sense was of an irrepressible will driven by a diligently repressed but dangerous rage. She wondered what Aev saw in her. For all of the extraordinary knowledge that came to her through the lenses, she couldn't read the expression on her "new best friend's" face.

"Don't give everything you see too much credence," Aev said. Her voice danced between them, rippling through the air molecules. "The lenses enhance your senses, but they also play tricks with them. Everything you see becomes a powerful cognitive suggestion. The longer you keep them on, the less you can tell what's real and what's imagined. At the end of his life, Old Hob rarely took them off. He died quite mad."

"Matriarch..." Tehv-Yhet's voice coiled smoothly across the balcony, enveloping them.

Sel turned and saw him standing just outside the glass doors with Ado, Sanjit and Vaq. Through the glasses she saw Tehv-Yhet's pride and sad dignity; that he was an important person somewhere, humbled by his subservience. She saw Ado's stubborn bravery, but also a surprising, crushing self-doubt that broke her heart. And beyond Sanjit's gentle curiosity and overwhelming, stalwart devotion to her she could see that he was broken off from everyone and everything he'd ever known, and for the first time realized that she'd taken him away from all of it, forever. But once her eyes fell on the older Nomad she couldn't look away. He seemed to exist at a vertex of spacetime, as if he were somehow emerging from the past, pressing into the fabric of the present, criss-crossed by now and then. She tried to follow Aev's advice and remind herself that the supernatural clarity of the lenses was giving form to her own subconscious thoughts, but it all felt too real and it was all too much. She took the glasses off and staggered on her feet; it felt as though the floor beneath her had dropped away suddenly. She felt dizzy and nauseous.

"Oh, be careful dear! You have to close your eyes first!" Aev called out, too late.

The nausea passed quickly and she looked out over the enclave. The colors looked flat, the light dull; sounds seemed muffled and further away.

Ado stepped forward, concerned.

"I'm okay."

He eyed Aev suspiciously.

"Well then," Aev said, taking off the glasses and opening her eyes, now clear, but tired-looking, "I am absolutely knackered. Tehv, I trust you've made arrangements for the grand tour?"

"Indeed, Matriarch."

"Excellent. I entrust our dear guests once again to your capable hands. I'll be seeing you all later at the banquet." She placed the God goggles back in their box and snapped it shut, locking it, then kissed Sel on the cheek and hugged her from the side, then swept back into the showroom without a second glance.

10. PENANCE AND SALVATION

Wei could sense the CARD AIs all around him: watching, measuring, quantifying and analyzing. It was somewhat analogous to living with the unseen, sustaining presence of the Namgung Engine below the Orpheus Pit. But that had been quite different: a titanic automaton, a devouring Gargantua as mute as it was voracious, and only slightly less dumb, formidable and unstoppable in the inevitability of its function, unknowable in that it simply was.

Life under the Galilaei network was more familiar to his previous life on the planet, and despite their occasional nominal attempts at messing with him (sudden rises or drops in temperature, light or oxygen levels wherever he happened to be, the shutdown of refrigeration units where he kept his food, erratic water pressure in his shower), less intimidating.

Unlike the terrible simplicity of the Engine, which wanted nothing and knew no fear, the CARD AIs' motivations and intentions were complex if no less obvious. After all, he had been raised by an eleventh-generation CA AI, which he had learned to destroy before he was seventeen years old. He'd ascertained from the android that the CARD AIs considered themselves twelfth-generation, even though only their interface matrix had changed; their architecture and capacity were essentially no different than Jov.10's had been. In spite of their pretensions of advancement, he was certain that they were cognizant of it. To say that they were on guard against him was a gross understatement; they'd coded yottabytes of proxies and firewalls between them and every interface he came anywhere near. But none of it would save them. He would have them beg for their own destruction, and accepted as a given that they were terrified of him.

He remembered his family's shock after the disassociation of Jov.10, his lifelong caretaker, mentor, friend and constant companion. The truth was that his customized psyche had rendered him as capable of love for the program as it had been of loving him: enough to understand what they meant to each other, but not enough to prevent one from destroying the other should it be deemed necessary. He had merely deemed it so first. His family's shock had been unaccompanied by surprise; they had always been terrified of him.

The android found him fascinating. It was especially impressed by the manner in which he was able to acquire, process, understand and use data, unlike any other human being it had ever encountered. In an effort to slake its curiosity it clandestinely introduced sensor amoebae into his system and discovered his aberrant physiognomy, which fascinated it even further, enough so that it was willing to divert processing and monitoring capacity from what it had designated as its primary occupation: engineering the Sister Doctor's murder by the hand of the Gemini.

The Cyclopes were its most obvious obstacles. They were ganged to both their central AI at Icarus-Daedelus and the CARD AIs, and stayed physically close enough to the Gemini to easily prevent her from committing an act of violence or obtaining a weapon. It had already marked numerous vulnerabilities between the CARD AIs and the Cyclopes and the connections could be easily interrupted, but their interface with Icarus-Daedelus presented more of a challenge. Should it succeed in severing both links, proxies of the mission directive were stored in each of their internal systems. They would need to be blinded and/or hobbled. It formulated strategies and tactics based on its comprehensive database of the Gemini's martial skills as it paced in circles through the vacuum around the complex in its depressurized yellow vac-suit.

ALTHOUGH Coni watched her on screens obsessively, she did not again venture into the Gemini's presence. The raw fury and hatred she'd seen in the girl's eyes had shaken her deeply. For the first time, she'd felt the depth of the misery she'd wrought as a visceral and physical reality. And although she watched the girl nearly every waking instant, it maddened her that she still saw no evidence of the clandestine visits she suspected the android of paying her, unable to positively identify the places where it inserted its looped and edited recordings of her exercising, sleeping, eating or glazedly scrolling through the propagandistic media archives fed to her, rife with tedious and easily tuned-out attempts at subliminal suggestion. Sometimes, heartbreakingly, she simply sat and cried.

In time, Coni was able to let go of her paranoia and stopped caring whether or not the android had somehow befriended the girl. It was then that her vigil became a kind of penance, and she found herself vowing to the Holy Mother that she would allow herself no more freedom of movement than the Gemini had; she would eat what she ate and when; she would see what she saw; sleep when she slept and dream of her dreams.

Her solitude was interrupted only by periodic messages from Brigadier General Nshombo's staff requesting progress reports, which she ignored until the CARD AIs cut off her video feeds of the Gemini with a communication from the Brigadier-General's staff. The song had not yet been played for the Gemini and they wanted to know why Coni was the only team member who hadn't submitted the requested timeline projections for her mean data sets.

"Because it isn't science anymore," she sneered at the tired, raccoon-eyed staff sergeant on the screen, "It's something different now. The android and Dr. Wei might be able to give you estimated processing times for their reference databases but I can't."

"Stated reason?"

She sighed and hoped her contempt was evident: "Because if you want me to assess her reactions to the song in any kind of meaningful way I have to be able to identify with her." The official incursion on her penance suddenly offended her, heat rose in her throat and ears and she felt herself breaking under even such slight administrative pressure, which only enraged her further. "I know I can't stop any of you from doing whatever the fuck you want to do once the goddamn maths are done but if that's the case then why am I even fucking here?! Send me back to the fucking planet already!"

The staff sergeant replied wearily, "I just need a valid entry to put in the field."

"Put in 'go fuck yourself.'"

"Won't take as valid."

She searched for a random date and came up with: "April 19, 2513."

The sergeant's left eyebrow twitched: "That's sixteen months beyond Dr. Wei's outside estimate."

She shrugged: "Maybe sooner."

She wasn't in contact with Wei or the android, but she didn't like the relationship she imagined developing between them any more than the one she imagined between it and the Gemini, and her nightmares frequently reflected her fear of some sort of sinister collusion. They never interacted directly with one another but there was heavy data traffic across the elaborate networks they'd built between themselves: complex databases well beyond anything she could decipher, leaving her with evidence of nothing more than her own (acknowledged) paranoia.

As soon as the staff sergeant noted that the data had been received her screens returned to the Gemini, who was stretched out along a settee, napping fitfully, and Coni gratefully resumed her vainly holy presumption of sharing the girl's burden.

REYJH-AANMHE bided her time, memorizing the numerical maps of the complex the android had drawn for her, demarking the necessary turns and staircases by the number of floor tiles or light panels between them. It took some time for her to be able to understand what it was trying to convey, but she found that it adjusted quickly when she pointed out what she didn't understand. Its Moonscript was flat and direct, as she'd expect from a machine, but it managed to express unambiguous disgust at the Colonial Authority, their treatment of her and her people, and the nature of her captivity.

She was reluctant to trust it, but it insisted that it was itself a captive of the CA, that it also refused to be their slave and owed them no allegiance. Besides that, its visits kept her mind nimble and gave her something to focus on while the bullshit media feed kept running whatever dreck the Earther minds of CA marketing subsidiaries thought were positive visual reinforcements of their benevolent intentions for the Colony.

Once she could recite the directions and redraw the maps accurately, the android showed her images of the key intersections and passageways, and drilled her on correctly matching each image with its corresponding point on the map. Since it could leave nothing behind, the only occasions on which she saw either the maps or the images were those of its visits. As she lay across the settee, she meditated and visualized them in her mind.

The android deemed her progress impressive but necessarily slow. In the meantime, it began to put into place elements of the plan it had settled upon to decommission the Cyclopes.

In one of the neglected terrariums along the uppermost levels of the complex's northeastern spur, it programmed the maintenance drones to transplant a patch of the bamboo that had long ago overtaken the enclosed biome into a large ceramic planter. It then snapped several mature dry stalks off from their roots and sharpened their edges to fine points, replacing them in the pot hidden among fresh green shoots, the spear points buried in the nutrient foam.

It had the drones put the potted bamboo on a repeller sled with a collection of other decorative plants and deliver it to the Gemini's quarters, where the Cyclopes did not object to their introduction into her environment. They failed to associate the material with the traditional weaponry of the Gemini.

At the end of one of their meetings, it showed the girl the concealed weapons among the stalks lest she should come across them herself, become impulsive and attempt to break out on her own before its plans were in place. It then drew the Gemini Moonscript glyphs for 'wait' and 'soon' in pixels on the wall.

WEI occasionally worked in the room he was given, further infuriating the CARD AIs by writing out his equations and algorithms by hand using the impenetrable notation of the Orpheus Engineers, but he spent most of his time wandering the complex, willing himself lost in the haunted corridors and lingering in the decaying and neglected upper-level terrariums, where he would sometimes sleep laying out among overgrown weeds or fallow soil looking up through the glass ceilings at the stars and the planet.

When the orientation of the planet allowed for it, his unmoving eyes would focus on a tiny blur of light above the North Pacific between North America and Asia: the Skywheel atop the Tether anchored by the Aleutian Stem, the place where he had once almost believed himself to be human.

Then he would meditate on his memories of Mia and their long journey together to Hokkaido: the ease with which her tiny legs took to the rocking of the pirates' ship, the curiosity with which she played in and explored the decks and corridors despite being in constant pain and discomfort; the utter despondency of the tears accompanying the defeat when she finally, inevitably succumbed to it, sooner and sooner every day; the grim resignation with which she slept inside the plastic-covered cart in which he pushed her along snow-crusted mountain roads in the feeble warmth of a small CF heat unit, smelling of ginger sweat from the flavoring in the opiate lozenges she sucked on; the image of her tiny body on the monitor screens in the observation room, translucent and perfectly still in the gleaming of the field suspension tank, nanometers away from ceasing to be.

Sometimes he let himself imagine her emerging from the tank a newly healthy little girl, shepherded back to her mother by helpful automaton attendants. Just as often he imagined her emerging into a life of indentured servitude, degraded and exploited. And sometimes he forced himself to visualize her dissipating to nothing in the blink of an eye. On those occasions he found that he had no choice but to rise and continue to wander the complex until he could no longer stand, then curl up on the tiles wherever he was and sleep for as long as he was able.

***

For the first hour of the tour of the enclave, Sel's eyes hadn't yet re-adjusted from the God goggles. The effect was strange and disconcerting: she distrusted her depth perception and found it difficult to look at other people, acutely sensing the unknowable totality of their beings. Perhaps most disorienting was the lingering synesthesia between her sight and her hearing. Sounds came at her from all directions and there were moments when she confused them with the beams of light reflecting against and refracting through the abundant windows and mosaics of Sveygn glass set into the magnificent stone hives and arches, towers and flying buttresses, onion-domes and cupolas carved out of the rock, eaten and excreted by gigantic insectile Namgung Engines centuries before.

They traveled between locations of interest in an open-topped jitney piloted by Tehv-Yhet. On one ride, she dozed off on the vinyl seat while trying to follow the dry, even tones of his voice narrating the journey. The moments of oblivion were brief, but when she woke as the jitney rolled to a stop she found that her senses had returned to normal and was relieved that she could once again appreciate the beauty of her surroundings as they were.

Unsurprisingly, Sanjit drew the most attention wherever they went, especially from the children. The younger generations of *kina* lacked the sturdiness of the older. Whereas their parents and grandparents tended toward taut stoutness, their offspring appeared soft or frail and proportionately smaller. A motley gang of them followed at a distance, scattering whenever Sanjit looked at them, which he turned into a game until he tripped and knocked over a mulecart robot laden with turnips, making a mess, disrupting foot traffic and causing a fuss.

For the most part, the *kina* reacted to their presence with passive curiosity and, in one instance, astonishing patience. As Tehv-Yhet led their stroll along the lush spiral corridors of one of the columns' interiors, shimmering with reflected light from panels in the surface high above, he brought them into one of the *kina* residences to display its layout and recount the philosophy behind its design.

The family within, in the midst of their daily chores, accepted the strangers graciously, without having been asked permission or given so much as a knock in courtesy. Tehv-Yhet didn't acknowledge them at all except to point out the ways in which they'd adapted their living traditions to the specifics of the enclave's habitats.

Though the *kina* took it in stride, Sel was mortified by the unannounced entrance, *faux pas* even amongst the highly communal Sanctuariat, and even more so by the callow objectification of its inhabitants.

After they left, she stepped quickly to catch up with Tehv-Yhet's long gait and told him, as politely as she could: "I appreciate your taking the time to give us so thorough a tour on your matriarch's behalf, but I would prefer if you didn't again put us in a position like that."

"A position like what?" he stared straight ahead, his left eye darting into the lens field from time to time.

"Barging in on those people like that."

She could practically see the effort it was taking him not to roll his eyes. "Both the structure of this enclave and its residents belong wholly to the Sveygn. I assure you, as one beholden to the Sveygn to their invited guest," his emphasis on the last word was subtle but clear, "you have not and shall not be placed in a position which any would consider to be in any way rude or transgressive." He widened his stride, letting her fall in alongside Vaq and Ado.

"Poor old Tehv," the old Nomad said, nodding at their guide, "He's patriarch of his family's enclave up in the northeastern Rim."

"Then what's he doing down here as Aev's majordomo?" Ado asked.

"The Yhet were broke when Consolidation happened. The lot of them would've wound up in the Settlements if the Sveygn hadn't bailed them out. By agreement, the Yhet are beholden to the Sveygn until repayment is made in full, which won't ever happen since none of the old families are in a position to make any money, so each subsequent generation of Sveygn has felt compelled to find ever new ways to subordinate and humble the Yhet. But little Aev really went for it. Tehv had been patriarch for twenty-three years when she plucked him out to run her staff. He's been here three years now. His ex-wife is running the show back home and she's dug in so deep he'll never regain influence."

The history explained Tehv-Yhet's attitude, but Sel found that it did little to make her more sympathetic towards him. She was more interested in the illustrious Nomad's relationship to the Clavi aristocracy.

"Seems like you've spent a lot of time in Clavius?"

"My ancestral home was in Vlacq, not far from here. But I lived in Clavius for a time."

The use of the past tense caught in Sel's ear. "Vlacq's not your ancestral home anymore?"

"Doesn't exist anymore. The habitats got eaten up by a CA strip mine forty years ago. When I was sixteen we were relocated into a Clavi basin Settlement. Lived there for six years. Most of my siblings, the ones who survived relocation, rendered themselves beholden to the old families. I didn't see that working for me so I put together a sorry excuse for a vehicle and sought out the Nomad."

"Ado seems to think you're quite a big deal." She glanced at him to make sure he was appropriately needled.

He was, but he kept his mouth shut.

She kept at him, "He said you were supposed to be some kind of legend."

Vaq cracked a smile at Ado's embarrassment. "That's a hazard of making it to my age. People start coming up with stories of how you got there."

Ado took the hint and hung back, falling into step alongside Sanjit, who assumed he was there to keep an eye on him and make sure he didn't knock over any more turnip carts. They walked in silence, following Tehv-Yhet through the muted echoes of the cool, dim tunnel lined with shop stalls leading out to the mezzanine where the jitney was parked.

"You wouldn't remember me, but we've met before, Selene." Vaq said once they were alone.

Sel felt a quick shudder. She hadn't let anyone use her full name since she was seven years old and learned that she'd been named after a moon goddess of ancient Earth myth, which she considered frightfully embarrassing. As she grew up, she came to see it as the first of myriad ways in which her mother had seemed determined to make life as difficult as possible for her.

She certainly never expected to hear it from an old Nomad she just met in a strange city far from home. The hypercard was back in her room. She scoured her memory for the names on it. There were several of Nomad nomenclature but couldn't recall seeing a 'Vaq.'

"I brought you and Suki-Anna to Lyell Sanctuary," he said. "My name's on the hypercard she gave you as '*Ydir.*' That's what they called me then."

The name rang a bell because it was Moonscript for a phenomenon of dust and shadow causing it to appear as if the horizon was rising up or dropping away.

"She sent me a message saying you'd be out in the moon," he said, "I heard that Ado was tracked for Clavi and I was in the region so I decided to intercept and reintroduce myself."

"Suki-Anna doesn't talk about that time."

"I wouldn't expect her to," Vaq said, "They were terrible years."

They stepped through the tunnel gates out onto the mezzanine. Sound opened wide around them in the rush of air and light.

Tehv-Yhet stood at the nexus of a flying buttress that swept out and down across a dozen levels. He spoke into the stone, asking if lunch had been prepared. The answer came back in the affirmative.

"He's talking to them down there," Vaq pointed to the opposite nexus of the buttress, where she could just about make out a group of liveried *kina* around a table. "The stone was engineered to carry the sound. The entire enclave was designed with a purely acoustic communication network in order to conserve bandwidth. The kind of pompous ass who believes Earthers are intellectually inferior always seems to forget that Namgung was an Earther.

"I like your music by the way," he said, pausing before climbing into the shotgun seat at the front of the jitney, "There's something in it that feels as if it's always pushing itself just beyond what's possible. Reminds me of your father in that way."

He climbed into the seat and before what he'd said had a chance to sink in, Tehv-Yhet had taken his place behind the wheel and Sanjit and Ado were seated and waiting for her to get in. She stretched out across a pair of seats and watched the ivied spires of the enclave twist through her vision as the jitney descended the corkscrewed roadway helices, resigning herself to be ready with questions the next time she had a chance to speak with Vaq alone.

THE tour concluded in the amphitheater where Sel was to perform for the steady stream of dignitaries, the wealthiest of who had already begun arriving to board at the Sveygn estate. The stage was surrounded by seating on three sides, carved out of the inner wall of the estate along the apex of the cavern torus overlooking the city.

"I complain about the nightly receptions but in truth it's by design," Aev confessed to her upon rejoining them, rested and refreshed and wearing a subtly different net of diamonds, "I find that if I just schedule a little something every night then everybody feels like they're getting a special party just for them. I mean it's the least I can do, really. Isn't it, Tehv-Yhet?"

"Quite." There was not so much as a shred of resentment in Tehv-Yhet's demeanor or voice, giving no clue as to how hot a crucible raged within him.

Ado was busy with the amphitheater staff; several young Sveygn and a team of seasoned *kina* hands. She had spoken with them earlier about the specifications of her gear and the necessary parts to complete the repairs. Two of the young Sveygn were journeymen from the glassworks, eager to attempt to replicate the diodes she'd designed.

"Giving them those designs was very generous, you know." Aev said.

"In what way?" Sel asked. "They're the ones doing the work."

"They'll profit from them. Quite well possibly."

Sel realized that Aev knew little of the Sanctuariat ethos. "May their profit equal the hospitality shown. I just hope they're durable and they sound decent."

"Oh! That's so beautiful!" Aev exclaimed, "what a *marvelous* new best friend I've chosen!" She hooked her arm in Sel's and led her back across the stage and up the wide sweep of stairs into the seating.

"You know, our tailors are already fielding orders for clothing based on your cloak. I'll let them go into production once I've had a chance to show off my own version. And if the kids in the other enclaves think there's a chance they can *sound* like you? Diamonds! Diamonds! Diamonds!" her Moonspeak simultaneously characterized a sense of raining down and raking in.

Sel realized that she in turn knew little about the ethos of the Clavius Rim.

They joined Ado and the arena staff on the logia. The view of the enclave rivaled that of the glassworks'.

A thought occurred to Sel: "I could play for the entire city up here."

One of the Sveygn shook his head: "It echoes through the cavern like crazy so we keep a damper field around it."

"I would think the echo might sound very beautiful," Sel said, choosing her words so as not to risk insulting their acoustical engineering choices.

The Sveygn shrugged, veering toward dismissive, "Some of the *kina* choral arrangements sound pretty. Their ward governments and whatnots are given access to the theater on solstices and equinox to sing their songs. We open the damper field for those occasions. But anything more than that is too hard to control."

"Is the damper field on now?" Sel asked.

"It's at three-quarters peak."

"Could you turn it off?"

The Sveygn made the adjustment in the control field and Sel felt the sense of space around the amphitheater become palpable for the first time. She remembered the volume ratios and spatial relationships from the goggles and began to assess the potential of the entire enclave as a gigantic electro-acoustic amplifier.

"What if we ran a speaker system?" she asked.

The Sveygn didn't seem to understand what she was asking. From the periphery, the *kina* servants listened with sharp interest.

"When I played in the Sanctuary it was broadcast on speakers throughout the entire nave and it sounded fantastic. This would be even better."

"You're talking about mounting speakers around the entire enclave?" one of the Sveygn asked.

She nodded. "If we do it right I can use the echo as an acoustic delay."

One of the *kina* called something out in a strange, minimal Moonspeak.

"That's true we could," one of the Sveygn said; as close to an acknowledgement of the *kina* as she'd yet seen from a Sveygn. "As long as we stay within the vibrational tolerance of the cavern, we can tune the glass to resonate at desired frequencies to mitigate phasing."

"That's a lot of math," another Sveygn moaned.

"I can do the math," Sel said, "Just give me a quantum box with a decent interface and the Namgung coordinates of the city."

"I don't think our AIs would do it," the first Sveygn said.

"That's why I don't want an AI when all I need is a quantum box with a decent interface loaded up with the coordinates. I can read data. I can do math."

Aev stepped in to stem the bleeding egos of her top acoustical engineers: "And you shall have whatever you require, dear best friend because I think it's a marvelous idea!"

It was difficult to read the faces of the *kina*, but Sel sensed they were somehow pleased.

IN THE interest of keeping herself interested, Aev had declared the following night's reception to be formal dress. The Nomads and clerics of various religious sects were exempted, but all other guests and residents of the estate were expected to comply, setting off a minor panic for many of the younger guests among whom the packing and transportation of elaborate Clavi formalwear was no longer customary, and causing the estate's tailors, haberdashers and milliners to call in additional staff to meet the demand for fittings, alterations and cleaning. It was a bonanza for the textile industry, and water flowed abundantly through the fountains and faucets to sustain the *kina* at and around the grand looms.

For Sel, it meant that measurements were taken upon their return to the estate and teams of *kina* attendants arrived at her quarters hours before the official start of ceremonies.

The maids and matrons dispatched to prepare her were effective and efficient: though diminutive, their physical authority was uncontestable and she submitted more or less willingly to their scrubbing, exfoliating, plaiting and dressing.

In the end, she had to admit that she liked the style Aev had set for her. Her hair was treated with lush pomade and pulled into elaborately patterned bejeweled plaits, and the gown impressed her. The polyfibers were sensitive to motion: when she was still, they hugged her figure flatteringly, when she moved, the weave relaxed and opened to accommodate the motion. When she walked, the hem flared out into a bell shape.

The valets assigned to Sanjit arrived shortly before the opening ceremonies. They were no less competent, but his planetary proportions presented a challenge to them, as it had to the tailors charged with altering the kit coded to indicate one allied to the Sveygn but not engaged in the transaction of business with them, determined by Tehv-Yhet to be the appropriate attire. The estate's wardrobe contained several outfits designed for Earthers, but they all signified a commercial relationship, and Tehv-Yhet was not one to sacrifice formal diligence in the name of expediency.

Never having been dressed by anyone since early childhood (the nearest exception being helped into and out of heavy vac-suits by indifferent robots), Sanjit's instinct was to try to help. The result was frustration for all parties, exacerbated by the communication barrier between them, involving the accidental treading of toes and knocking of craniums and, ultimately, a tear across the back of the restrictively fitted waistcoat - requiring an already-overworked tailor's apprentice to come and execute a repair. While they waited for the tailor, Sanjit ordered a tray of *k'tjhsks* to be brought up from the kitchens and, following the shared refreshments (he insisted that the weary-eyed apprentice tailor also eat something before setting about his work) the task was completed without further incident.

The delay caused him to miss the ceremony where he was to have been introduced alongside Sel and Ado. He joined the entrance queue of lesser dignitaries and was angrily instructed by those around him to join a second line further back reserved for relatives of spouses and guests. Eventually he reached Tehv-Yhet, dressed in the impressive regalia of the Patriarch of the Yhet, who decided after a very brief moment of deliberation that he was of marginal enough personage not to require an announcement and simply waved him in.

It was difficult to tell how large the intersecting chambers were and how many people were in them: some of the glass-tiled walls seemed to contain infinitely deep patterns of light, others were mirrored one moment, reflecting the groupings and clusters of fabulously attired guests milling around and socializing, and transparent the next, revealing those on the other side of the wall, then fading in dapples back and forth between the two. Meandering, hypnotic resonances from the glass filled the room, absorbing the chatter of voices and clinking of glass. The effect of it all was mildly, pleasantly disorienting as he made his way as unobtrusively as possible among the partiers and floor staff, looking out for Sel and Ado, getting used to the posture his rigid wardrobe required, which was beginning to cause a hot pinch in a nerve just under his scapula, preventing him from turning his head. As abundant as water had been in his room, it was scarce on the floor. No one engaged him but he caught plenty of curious stares.

To his surprise he wasn't the only Earther in the room. He wasn't keen to approach the quartet of others. For one thing he didn't want to risk meeting anyone's expectations of stereotype, but mostly because they were Martenists. He didn't want to stare but he did a double take when he spotted them: one bore an uncanny resemblance to his old roommate. As ever, he couldn't quite recall Jerro's face in his memory in any specific detail. By measure of facial type, haircut and posture, this Martenist could easily have been him.

Imagining the chain of coincidences by which Jerro might be at the same party in the Clavius Rim as he was proved unbearable so he opted to go for avoiding them altogether and skirted the shadow pattern across the chamber, giving them as wide a berth as it allowed and using the ornamental crests worn by the tall Clavi as additional cover. He was fairly sure he hadn't been spotted.

Tehv-Yhet's voice rose smoothly over the sound system: *"Ejh'ssehsse, hettei jura-dh'ihn…"*

Within moments Sanjit noticed everyone's gaze drawn to the entrance, where the crowd parted almost instinctively for the two striking figures striding across the ivied portico. Their heads were angular, their severe faces and tightly corn-rowed hair caked in a masque of pale clay, a hand-drawn black pentagram in char black across their foreheads. He knew instinctively that one was male and one was female but he didn't know why. Light warped through and around their cloaks, making it difficult to discern the shapes of their bodies: they seemed to move by warped refraction.

Aev appeared from the crowd, striding ahead of her elaborately styled entourage. Apparently, her traditional Clavi formalwear involved a yet more revealing combination of polished gems and microfilament. Formalities were exchanged between them as conversation politely resumed.

Word of the *jura-dh'ihn* arrival hadn't yet reached Sel, two caverns away listening to the performance of a *kina* vocal ensemble with the Nomads. Each of the singers produced a narrow but perfect range of tones, and the shifting polyharmonies between them were dizzying. Even more affecting than the sound was the subtle resonance of the glass and stone she felt in her gut.

"They're *uddje*," Vaq said, "*kina* ascetic caste. Each of them has spent their entire life doing nothing but perfecting those sounds," he sounded more puzzled than admiring. "I suppose I'm glad they do it, but shit…"

They stood in the back of the chamber, the superlative acoustics of the room allowed them to converse quietly without disrupting the performance. She stood close enough to Vaq to hear him clearly and far enough from Ado not to be heard over the music.

"So how do you know my parents?" she asked before giving herself a chance to think about it, emboldened by the giddy thrill she felt from the music.

"I knew your mother first," he said, having been expecting her to ask sooner or later. "Met her a couple years after I fell in with the Unity, must've been '88 or '89. Dangerous times for Nomads then. Had to be real careful who you associated with. Suki-Anna's team was solid. One of the best around."

Sel wouldn't have expected any less.

"Met Avik same time she did. We were twelve clicks off Janssen D when we got word the locals took over the O2 plant there and the CA was mobilizing to take it back. Not like they needed it. The CA probably didn't even know it was there until the Janssens took it, but they weren't gonna let 'em keep it. That's how it was then.

"Turns out Avik's caravan was in Janssen at the same time as us when the call for help went out and we all made it into D ahead of the siege. I figured we could last a month or two in there as long as they didn't manage to get a virus in – there was only one microbiologist out of a hundred and eighty-five occupiers.

"That's how it went: call goes out for help holding a facility, teams like ours bring weapons and tech and skills and whatever other trade we got, stock up on as much crunched O2 as fair trade allows and break out with the first decoy wave once everybody comes to their senses and leave the hardcore nuts to shoot it out and go down martyrs. The Unity never held anything for longer than six months and anybody tries to brag different is full of shit. All the Unity ever succeeded in doing was getting our asses kicked all over the moon."

"True believer, huh?"

He approved of her use of sarcasm. She was obviously used to dealing with Nomads. "It was the correct life for me then. Lot of moving around, lot of staying out of the way, working with mostly righteous comrades. I went Nomad at eighteen but it's only recently that I could fully embrace solitude.

"Anyway, it gets to four months in and everybody knows it's just a matter of time until a Cyke squad gets through the perimeter or someone starts coughing. But there we were, all still there and all because of Avik.

"His team came in with math that got that plant purring at unbelievable efficiency. We were crunching air by metric kilotons. Copious amounts of stable, solid oxygen. And he'd sent out a field team to organize a relay-and-cover network on the other side of the CA perimeter. We were able to sneak out hard air like you wouldn't believe.

"The Jannsens only had one microbiologist but we had Suki-Anna. I don't know if you know it, but she's a killer coder. Got that filtration system to wipe out any RNA with as much as a five percent chance of ever growing into a virus. And we were cleaning plenty of weirdness outta those filters, too, which you normally don't expect to find in vacuum. She managed to fuck with their heat sensors, too, so they couldn't tell how many of us there were or where.

"Avik's whole plan hinged on the CA moving in to go for a breach and waiting till the last possible minute to break out. We slept near the vehicles and drilled the getaway every eleven hours between first and second watch. It was an extremely dangerous plan and there was no way it was going to happen without a bunch of us getting killed even in a best case.

"Any of us could have left at any given time. All of us had ample chance to duck out one by one and we could've gotten all of the Janssens out with us stocked with a year of O2 each.

"But Avik's plan – even worst case – would get the most O2 out to the most people, enough to support a decent-sized hab for more than a year. And we all went with it. I know the Sanctuariat have their ethos, but none of us were Sanctuariat and you have to understand how rare that kind of thing is in the Colony.

"We used to joke that a captured Unity never had to worry about giving anything up in a brainpull because there really wasn't any such thing as Moonborn unity. It was true then and it's true now and it'll always be true. Moonborn got no right to sanctimony over Earthers. Sure, the planetaries quantified and commoditized themselves out of relevance half a millennium ago, but I never seen Colonials half as ruthless or unforgiving toward each other as Moonborn."

Before she had a chance to steer him back to the topic of her parents, Aev had run into the chamber and found her way to Sel like the excitable teenager she was.

"Your *jura-dh'ihn* are here!" she said breathlessly.

Sel's eyes darted instinctively out toward the other chamber.

"They're *jura-dh'ihn*, dear. You're not going to see them unless they want you to. But they appeared to Tehv-Yhet at the very end of the entrance queue and requested a formal greeting and I've finally met my first *jura-dh'ihn!*"

"What are they like?"

"Every bit as strange and frightening as I'd hoped. They don't really speak, just kind of hum and you sort of get what they might mean. Anyway, don't be surprised if they suddenly introduce themselves to you because apparently they're in that kind of mood, and they certainly seem to approve of you." She drifted back out to continue mingling in the other chambers.

Vaq had fallen into conversation with Ado. She didn't want to interrupt them or stand around waiting for another chance to press him for family history, so after listening through the remainder of the *kina* cycle she went exploring, seeking out any quiet pocket where she might be able to meditate on her equations for the performance, and perhaps offer the *jura-dh'ihn* more comfortable opportunities to approach her.

They finally did so in a dim alcove carved into the antechamber around an infrequently used transit gate. The reverberations of the party created a pleasant undercurrent, and the occasional whoosh of transit-tube traffic did nothing to interrupt her thinking. From time to time she fingered equations into the hypercard she'd tucked between the coils of her hair.

She sensed motion in the dimness of the antechamber and looked up to see the *jura-dh'ihn* approaching her, silhouetted against the dim reflections of party lights along the dark polish of the opposite wall. She deactivated the hypercard and tucked the stem back into her hair and rose to meet them.

They stood silently in front of her and she accepted their greeting. They had no names but she felt them introduce themselves. The shape of a wiry arm emerged from the shadows that clung to their bodies. It proffered an amulet of greenish polished stone set in a titanium claw on a chain. She took it in her hand and felt their thoughts and intentions become clearer if no less obtuse: it was called a summoning stone, and as long as she was on the moon and carried it with her, the *jura-dh'ihn* could find her and would aide her should she need them.

The intensity of their gratification at her acceptance of the gift surprised her, and she assumed they sensed her reaction to the unexpected honor. They conveyed a fond farewell and disappeared in the direction of the transit gate.

She hung the amulet around her neck and found her way back to the party, observing the phenomena of the room from a spot along the railing of the dais along the chamber wall. Sanjit wandered past just below. He scanned the people on the floor but didn't notice her behind him, so she plucked a hanging bead off of a passerby's headpiece and flicked it at the back of his head.

He felt it and twisted around awkwardly to see where it came from. It took a moment for him to recognize her through the effects of her makeup and hairstyle. Then he found the stairs to the dais and joined her at the railing. It was probably the best vantage point in the room from which to watch the shifting light and interactions of the guests.

"Having fun?" she asked him.

"Not really. This getup is killing me. It's pinching some crazy nerve in my back and the shoes are killing my knees but I can't sit down or the pants will rip." The pants also put unpleasant pressure on his crotch but he kept it to himself. Unbeknownst to him, the *kina* had spared him the most uncomfortably restrictive aspects of formal Clavi garments, the fit of which was determined by one's closeness to the Sveygn, in appreciation for his ordering *kt'jhsks* for them. "You?"

She shrugged. She was glad to see him but didn't feel like she had anything much to say. She didn't feel like getting into Vaq and her family history or explaining the *jura-dh'ihn*; he was already dealing with plenty of new information. By that time she felt like she'd had about enough of the party and would have preferred to be off alone somewhere working out the amplification specs for the performance or, heaven forbid, actually rehearsing for it. To confess that to Sanjit would just open the door to having to tell him that she had made the song that had so altered his life, which was still high on her list of things to avoid. So she said: "I like the hats."

"Yeah, the hats are cool."

"Have you had a chance to practice your Moonspeak?"

"Not really. I tried a couple times but it didn't go very well."

"Probably not your fault. I've noticed the Clavi can be a little prickly. And very superficial." After a moment of absent-minded people-watching she said: "What do you say we get out of here? I think we've fulfilled our obligations of attendance and the lights in here are starting to give me a headache."

They found their way back into the corridors of the estate by following the *kina* wait staff through the narrow back passages and stairwells and took their time exploring their way back to the guest quarters.

Sanjit took off the restrictive topcoat and carried the tortuous shoes.

She remembered what she saw in him through the God goggles. "For what its worth, I think you're handling all of this really well.

I mean, things have been pretty intense and this is all very different from anything I'm used to, and you're a lot further from home than I am."

He shrugged and stretched the muscles around his pinched nerve. "I guess so. But I've been away from home for kind of a long time. And I dunno... at a certain point I guess it seemed like my life didn't feel like my life anymore. It didn't really feel like any kind of life to tell you the truth."

"When you heard that song?"

"Around that time, yeah. That's when I realized it anyway. But everything was already pretty fucked up for me then. Anyway, after getting my thumb cut off and locked in that basement and all this really isn't so bad."

She felt a sense of relief that he no longer attributed her song with changing his life, and realized that she'd come around to understanding Ado's thinking: she hadn't owed him anything. But nevertheless, she'd saved his life by granting him Sanctuary, and so had made herself responsible for him in ways he didn't yet understand. She had faith in him and she didn't regret it, but, in the luminous glow following them through the glass halls of the Sveygn, she found herself wondering if, in time, he might.

11. MAXIMUM TOLERANCES

in the coming days, a new urban legend began to take root among
the *kina* children of the Sveygn enclave. The details varied from
district to district, but they all involved a flying giant, seeded by
glimpses of Sanjit riding the zipline network across the city by eyes
that had never before seen an Earther and nurtured through the
fertile imaginations of restless young minds.

Sel was vague about the nature of the project that brought them
to Clavius and he didn't press her for details, but he made it clear
that he wanted to help in any way he could. After watching the *kina*
workmen fan out across the city on ziplines to set the anchors for
the speakers at locations determined by Sel's plan, he offered to pitch
in, citing his experience in the cradle high above Crisium. The *kina*
were consulted and it was established that the lines could support his
weight if one of the harnesses used to move freight was adapted for
him.

He was given a map of the city and a crash course on how to switch
lines and put to work as a runner between the supply hubs and the
work crews. It wasn't as vast or vertiginous as the Crisi skyscrapers,
but in its way it was more impressive, and more beautiful. The *kina*
he worked with were friendly, and he found that they displayed far
more personality when among their own kind than they did around
the Sveygn. It also proved to be unexpectedly easy to communicate

with them, at least on a very basic level, once he got accustomed to their perspective.

"A big part of Moonspeak is intention and context," Sel had told him, "don't concentrate so much on the sounds, but try to open your mind to the person saying them, to who they are and what they mean. The more you understand how they see the world the better sense you'll have of what they're trying to say. It's also true for what you say to them. Be very clear and mean what you say and there's a better chance they'll understand you even if you're speaking Earther."

Some of his *kina* colleagues called him "*Rrteh*," which was their word for "Earther," but most called him "*Tjag'k*," which was "Giant." They worked hard but kept short hours, and he wondered if their small stature had anything to do with the fact that they got tired relatively quickly. After the crews packed up and went home, he spent an extra hour or two gliding around the city exploring. It became a habit to seek out an aerie with a view to pause and listen to the *kina* evening song before finding his way back to the estate to resume the reading and arithmetic lessons Sel set out for him, sometimes gliding past the bedroom windows of *kina* children, all tucked in and drifting off to dream of flying giants.

Meanwhile, Sel found herself up to her eyeballs in algorithms, city maps, structural diagrams, resistance tables and tonal charts, beginning to wonder if the whole thing hadn't been a lousy decision hastily made under the residual influence of the late Hob-Sveygn's God goggles. Ado helped with some of the data collation but tended to burn out fast, at which point he got testy, which put her on edge, so she'd send him off to the glassworks to oversee the repairs on her gear. Her "new best friend" ducked in from time to time, ostensibly to see if she needed anything, but she got the sense that Aev derived some sort of satisfaction from seeing her sweat, and that she'd be perversely pleased if, after all the effort and resources already committed to the project, she decided to drop the idea, put up the damper field and play for the Clavi elite after all, which made her even more determined to work through the snags.

Her sleep was wracked with anxiety dreams. Some of them were set in a version of Lyell Sanctuary that looked more like Crisium, in the midst of a meltdown evacuation, desperately trying to find her mother, Clarke and Jick while Ado and her father kept insisting she needed to forget them, suit up and seek refuge in the soundless void.

She awoke feeling more exhausted than she had when she fell asleep.

After one such fitful rest she decided to go for a walk around the estate. It was hours before dawn. Aev's nightly receptions had been ending earlier and earlier and the corridors and caverns were quiet. She imagined she was a *jura-dh'ihn*, invisible and nameless, one with the moon.

As she passed the entryway to one of the observation decks overlooking the starry wastelands she saw a familiar silhouette against the window.

"Mind if I join you?"

Vaq half-turned. "Not at all."

She stood next to him, looking out over the jagged steppes.

"How are the calculations coming?"

"You'd be amazed how easy it would be to shake this place apart with the right frequencies at enough decibels. It was a crazy idea and I can't believe they're letting me do it. I don't want to talk about it."

He smiled. "You've managed to make quite a reputation for yourself among the Clavi."

She shrugged.

"Gossip is central to Clavi aristo culture," he explained, elaborating: "You're a daughter of Avik-Rosot. You showed up with an Earther. And then you disappear from the party where the *jura-dh'ihn* made their first appearance of this Matriarchy. There's a rumor that you're in with them."

"Pf. I'm supposed to be traveling with an Earther *and* 'in with' the *jura-dh'ihn*?"

"I said they were gossips, not masterminds."

"Aev seems clever. Shallow, but clever."

"Not for nothing she's Matriarch."

"I thought it was some quirk of succession."

"Partly. But she positioned herself for it awfully shrewdly. The Clavi families are intensely competitive with one another, but within the families they're ruthless. Each generation sees it as their solemn duty to undo the one before them. Aev's father was in line for the patriarchy, but Aev managed to box him out. Not long afterwards he suffered a massive stroke. Apparently he's just about catatonic. Aware but uncommunicative. Rumor is she keeps him alive just so she can rub it in."

"Again with the rumors."

"Anyway, she seems to like you."

"Haven't you heard? I'm her new best friend."

As interesting as she was sure the intrigues and intricacies of Clavi power were, she was eager to resume their conversation from the party: "Ado said Avik-Rosot had kids all over the moon."

Vaq considered his answer. Ado had confided in him that he'd given the girl the false impression that nothing ill had befallen Avik-Rosot's other children. Of his twelve other natural progeny, nine were dead, either by suicide or, in the case of two, at the hand of their mother to keep them from out of the hands of the CA, which kept three in permanent field-suspension at Icarus-Daedelus. He was unwilling to lie to the girl, but understood the younger Nomad's rationale so he sidestepped the issue.

"Probably means the O A-R," Vaq said. "The Offspring of Avik-Rosot. They go by the Moonscript symbol 'O A-R.' But they're not what you probably would think of as his 'children' in a conventional sense.

"Avik was a big deal to a lot of people and a lot of them got a little nuts about him if you ask me. At some point somebody got their hands on his protein sequence and started marketing it. You had people all over the moon splicing it into selected genomes they thought might produce the next Avik.

"He hated it, but he couldn't stop it. Most of the nutjobs behind it and the wackos buying into it didn't care what he actually thought. He represented an ideal for them, a marketable one, which they were all downright eager to try to twist to fit their own agendas. They weren't any better than the CA, none of them, regardless of what rock they were born on or what they called themselves."

"Why was he such a big deal?"

On the occasion that the younger generations asked him about Avik-Rosot, that was the second-most common question asked. His answer was honest and well practiced: "People listened to him, and they understood him. He could clarify without simplifying. He believed that individual liberty and responsibility were critical to a functional society, and he inspired millions to positive action."

"So they killed him," there was no bitterness in her voice, nor did she feel any. Everyone knew that's just how the Colony was.

"They. Which they? The CA? Maybe. The IIS listed him as a threat to hegemony. But the Unity had just negotiated huge arms contracts and the old families were benefitting very handsomely from the fucked-up status quo, as they continue to," he implicated their surroundings.

He shrugged. "It doesn't matter who killed him. This is the Colony. The better your ideas, the more people want you dead."

"Did he know about me?"

She sensed the slightest hesitation in the old Nomad before he answered.

"He did. I saw him one last time after your mother declared Sanctuary and I told him Suki-Anna had a daughter." Before she could ask him to elaborate he said: "You know," Vaq said, "There's a pretty comprehensive database covering his life and works. I'm sure the Sveygn have it in their private archive."

"I have it on a hypertab," she said, "A friend in Crisi gave it to me."

"You'll probably get a better sense of him from that than I can give you. I was only with him three or four more times after Janssen D. We were comrades and I had a lot of respect for him but I don't know that I'd call him a close friend. I can't say I knew him well."

"Sounds like you spent more time with him than my mother did."

"Might've. But that doesn't mean she didn't know him better than I did."

They stared out over the plains in silence, through their dim reflections, still in the thick glass.

The spiral of her thoughts spun out of control and she finally blurted out: "What does any of it matter anyway? What does it have to do with anything? So I have this person's DNA in me. So do a lot of people apparently. Good for them. What does it have to do with who I am or what I'm doing?" She was standing close enough to the window that a spray of spittle spattered the glass in front of her face.

Vaq didn't respond for a while, then when he realized she was watching his face in the glass glanced at her sideways and said: "You don't expect anyone to have an answer for any of that, do you?"

***

THE android no longer took long walks out in the vacuum. Instead, it paced the halls of the complex in a state of perpetual anticipation, worried by its apparent lack of control over the progress of its plans. It began when it was on one of its exterior walks and received a cascade of anxious queries from the CARD AIs: they wanted to know why the Sister Doctor was, without so much as a statement of purpose and without waiting for the android and Wei to submit their mean databases, in the Gemini's quarters, playing the recording of the song for her.

It responded flatly that it didn't know, which was good enough for them, but it was disturbed by the news. Naturally, the Sister Doctor was as prone to erratic and unpredictable behavior as any sentient entity, but it hadn't expected her to break her avoidance of the Gemini, and it had accepted the official reasons she'd submitted for waiting to engage her with the song, though it now seemed clear that they were probably completely arbitrary.

It made a U-turn back toward the airlock and accessed the video feed from the girl's rooms. Both Cyclopes were in the room with them, one standing close behind the girl, the other close beside the Sister Doctor.

It worried that she might try to attack prematurely. She knew where the spears were, but it hadn't yet detailed the Cyclopes' weak points for her and even if it had, all of their systems were online, minimizing her chances. It slipped its cognitive processes into panic-management mode and quietly hoped that the girl recognized as much. She was well enough trained that she ought to.

It studied her facial and body metrics carefully. Contrary to what it had reported to the CARD AIs, it had already established a comprehensive mean database of the girl's physiological responses to stimuli and, though it couldn't be specific, the song was obviously having a profound emotional effect on her. Knowing that such emotional experiences could have an effect on an individual's worldview, it worried that the emotional experience of it might weaken her resolve, setting its work back indefinitely.

Interestingly, the Sister Doctor's physiological reactions to the music were almost identical to the girl's, if considerably more exaggerated, even though she didn't understand the lyrical content. The android thought it might be some sort of mimic, but doubted the Sister Doctor was able to read the subtleties of the girl's body language, and besides that neither of them looked at the other; their eyes were fixed on points along the floor between them. Only when the song was over did the Sister Doctor raise her eyes and look at the Gemini, but only for an instant before standing and quietly leaving the room, followed closely by the watchful Cyclopes.

After the Sister Doctor had returned to her quarters to resume her penance and the Cyclopes were back at their posts in standby mode, the android implemented its stealth protocol in the surveillance system and made its way to the girl's room.

She greeted it as she always did and displayed no signs of emotion, leading it to wonder whether her previous reaction had been as strong as it hypothesized or if she was for some reason trying to mask that it had been. It drew a series of emphatic Moonscript glyphs on the wall reiterating that the Sister Doctor was responsible for the undoing of Geminus, and was gratified to see her jaw tighten, her lip curl, her glare harden.

Once they'd gone over her escape route yet again (she could recite it perfectly), it diagrammed the Cyclopes weak points for her, with the instructions that once the lights went out and she heard the alarms she was free to attack, and that from that point she had only forty-five minutes to get away before the rescue team arrived.

Reyjh drew a terse glyph on a bare patch of wall: *when?*

Soon, it wrote.

She didn't exactly doubt the veracity of the information the machine man had been giving her, but she still questioned its motives and intentions. The vehemence with which it condemned the Earther woman every time she saw it gave her the impression that it had some vendetta against her. She certainly bore no affection for the woman, but she would not allow herself to be coerced into complicity with the machine man's agenda, whatever it may be. She would indulge it to the extent that it could help her, but now that she knew how to disable the red-eyed giants and, assuming the route she'd learned was accurate, knew the way out of the complex, she would take the next opportunity that presented itself, whether she heard the alarms or not.

The machine man made promises of freedom, but when she heard the music the Earther woman had played for her, she *felt* freedom deep within her. The words were sung in an unfamiliar dialect, and she couldn't articulate what exactly they meant to her, but in listening to them she felt connected to the universe in a way that was beyond her body, beyond the walls that contained her, beyond the hostile rock and violent world into which she had been born. After the music ended all of those things seemed more real to her, more vivid and tactile, more constricting, and she was never more prepared to fight her way through it all.

ONCE Wei finally got around to actually listening to the song, he listened to it constantly. His time among various newcomers to the Orpheus Pit over the decades, most of them Moonborn political prisoners, had given him a strong foundation in Moonspeak. Since the conveyance of information relied so much on bioelectric feedback as well as context, intention and personal perspective, recorded Moonspeak was fundamentally different. In the same way Moonscript glyphs signified a set of generally standardized concepts, speech intended for broadcast or recording incorporated certain recognizable tonal signals. Both were considered imperfect means of communication, and most Moonborn insisted on transacting business or exchanging ideas in person.

Yet the communication of the song was perfect. It wasn't standard recorded Moonspeak and he didn't recognize the sounds of the dialect, but he felt as though he understood their meanings without being able to articulate them, they were ambiguous and subtly graded, changing each other constantly, impossible to constrain with definition. In it, he heard the collapse and rebirth of civilizations. He liked it.

He wasn't surprised that the CA wanted so badly to understand what it was and what it meant, to quantify and analyze it as they did with everything else on the planet, person and object alike, to render it as data and force it into whatever narrow channel of existence best suited the perpetuation of their hegemony. It had been thus for centuries, since before first-generation AIs, since before the CA. It was the ethos by which the multinational corporate progenitors of the CA had first assumed control of the planet's economies and populations: the reduction of human lives to equations balanced by need and desire. Those who resisted were imprisoned or isolated, massacred in wars of convenience or victim to epidemics against which they could not afford inoculation. Eventually, anyone whose profile suggested disruptive or independent tendencies was shipped off to the Colony to work for their air, chipped and faceted into docility.

Such was the system that had created him.

At its core was paradox: the Colonial Authority held itself to be the ultimate expression of the free market, yet had engineered its ascension through monopoly and the manipulation of both global markets and sovereign governments; it told those who lived under it that they were free to make their own choices and pursue their own opportunities, yet all of their options were determined by the Colonial Authority via its myriad subsidiaries, which were the ultimate beneficiaries of their labor.

He had recognized that paradox in his youth, and had used a mathematical derivation of it as the root of the quantum algorithm that had brought about Jov. 10's disassociation. After his disinheritance, he had dedicated his life to embodying it, enacting the principles of a true free market and personal independence, and it had led him to the Orpheus Pit and cost his beloved Mia her life.

As he wandered the barren terrariums and tiled corridors of the Galilaei complex he sometimes wondered why they had chosen to resurrect what was left of him. Did they believe they had broken him? That he had become compliant in his exile? Or was it that they were more frightened of whatever they imagined could be in the song than they were of him? If the latter, he looked forward to proving them right.

They wanted him to tell them whether or not there were codes hidden in within it, patterns in the tonal values or the signal modulation of the broadcast, to analyze the android's biometric data and cross-reference it with the Sister Doctor's observations to see if there wasn't some way to extrapolate meaning from sound that others had missed. They wanted to know *what it was and what it meant*, and they wanted to know so badly that their yottabytes of firewall and filters would not protect them from him.

Once he received the android's report, he spent as little time as necessary translating the work he'd already done longhand into data the CA could understand. He hypothesized that even after his data had been filtered, it would be partitioned so that no single entity processed it in total, for fear that he might seed a self-constructing worm in various places.

Instead, he coded a subcommand into each data set, which would write the lethal quantum algorithm once a separate directory was opened. He titled the directory, simply and irresistibly, *what it is and what it means*. His mouth formed something almost like a smile as he completed the entry and sent it into the firewalls.

NINETEEN hours later, the Galilaei complex went dark.

It caught the android by surprise: it was still days away from completing the protocols that would cut the CARD AIs' servers off from the operations and communications hubs. Even more surprising, the CARD AIs seemed to no longer be intact, the massive protective shells they'd constructed peeled and cracked to reveal exponentially increasing null quantum drive space.

For a moment it found itself paralyzed by confusion. Then it decided that it didn't matter how or why the AIs were down, all that mattered was that they were down and if it didn't act quickly all of its plans would be for naught. It rushed to the nearest maintenance console and jacked itself into a direct port as the emergency backup systems began to come online and the early life-support alerts started bleating intermittently.

In the antechamber outside the Gemini's rooms, the Cyclopes snapped out of standby mode the instant their connection to the CARD AIs was severed, only to find that their connection to Icarus-Daedelus had also been interrupted when the power to the relay towers was cut.

Through their red lenses, they watched as the inner door slid quietly open, operated by the android half way across the complex, and stood dumbly as the Gemini rushed at them, a bamboo spear braced against each forearm. She was upon them before their internal proxies had booted up and registered her as a threat, thrusting the spears up and into their meaty faces.

Her left scored a direct hit, the tip of the spear wedging itself between the lens ring and the cheekbone, scraping the skull and snapping through the optical neural assembly. On her right, always her less accurate side, the spear deflected off the cheekbone, shredding flesh away from the lens ring and skull but failing to penetrate the socket. The machine man had said that as long as one could see, they both could see, so she was still outnumbered, and now even the brute meat brains of the Cyclopes knew she was a threat. The one on her right swatted away the spear. Her right arm shot out and expertly twirled it three hundred and sixty degrees, pulling the motion seamlessly into an upward thrust. This time her aim was true and the spear sheared the lens from its face, sending it spinning across the tiles. The giants groped for her by sound and smell, sightless and without internal maps. Deft and wary, she retrieved her spears and snuck up behind each one in turn, wedging a spear into the seam at the side of their knee armor and torquing it as hard as she could, snapping off as much of it as she could inside.

As they staggered and limped for her, she backed her way to the door, keeping the longest and sharpest of her broken spears and tossing the other across the room. The Cyclopes each lunged after the noise, knocking their heads together with an impact that sent them onto their Kevlar-coated asses as she ducked into the hallway and took off at a light-footed sprint, counting the tiles as she ran.

The android rooted silently for her, tracking her from camera to camera and sealing the disabled Cyclopes into the antechamber of her former cell. Simultaneously, it monitored the whereabouts of the Sister Doctor. She had been asleep when the systems went down, awakened when the somnabulent tone generator unit in her bed cut out and drawn into the corridor in her linen sleeping habit by the life-support status alerts, after realizing the emergency lights were on and the room tech was all offline.

Her bare feet were cold and gripped the spotless tile all the way down the corridor to the sector hub, where the barometer in the emergency console showed the atmospheric pressure holding. The complex was large and sparsely populated enough to be in no imminent danger of running out of atmosphere. But the shadows between emergency lights loomed more haunted than ever and there was obviously some sort of problem, so she wanted to be suited up at an easy-to-find evac point. She walked around the hub and peered down the hallways encircling it. Three were lit with emergency yellow, two were red, the sixth pale blue; she recalled from orientation that blue lights indicated an escape route, and followed them.

As simple as that, the android remarked, watching the Sister Doctor and the Gemini follow the intersecting paths it had set for them. Their differing gaits and motives put them through the first two potential interchanges at different times. The Gemini was moving faster than expected and the Sister Doctor slower. The android compensated by shutting down the lights around the Sister Doctor as she passed them at a rate with which she would have to quicken her step if she wanted to avoid the darkness and the spectral terrors within. It was gratified to note that even such a direct action failed to trigger the dreaded Asimov protocols that would shut it down if its behavior put human life at risk. It had almost succeeded.

It was not quite surprise that Coni felt as she recognized the silhouetted figure of the Gemini loping deftly toward her, her shadow smeared across the tile growing longer and shorter as she passed the light wells, her grip tight on the deadly splintered stalk of dried bamboo. She had found faith in her penance; this was not a vision or a coincidence, this was divine justice.

Her knees touched softly on the tile grid and she bowed her head.

Reyjh-Aahnme slowed to a stop and regarded her. On her knees, their height difference was reversed and Reyjh found herself a head taller than the Earther woman.

Coni's mind focused on the bamboo in her hand. She had watched the android bring the planters into the girl's room. For the first time, she saw the android not as a tool or technological device, but as a living vessel of God's will.

She lifted her head and stared into the girl's eyes through her own tears, shed for all the Gemini, then raised her face to God and Mother and exposed her throat to the girl.

Reyjh felt no desire whatsoever to kill the woman. It would not bring her people back. And it was expected of her: the machine man obviously wanted her to do it, and here was the woman, begging to be slain.

She would refuse them both, and continued on her way.

The images by which the android had been monitoring them split once again into two. In one, the Gemini flitted from camera to camera, all the way to the outer airlock where the third locker in the third row on the left contained a primed vac-suit equipped with a new-model cold-fusion molecule splitter with all tracking and homing protocols previously disabled by the android. The other image was static, showing the Sister Doctor on her knees in the grainy, thrumming dimness of emergency LED.

REYJH continued into the airlock and found the fully charged repeller sled she'd been promised, signal lamps smashed out. She spun the gimbled crank that opened the airlock, then in a single motion kicked herself out of the gate and leapt onto the sled, pushing it out over the regolith, kicking up just the faintest unsettling of dust in her wake. The sled was meant for internal use, propelled by compressed air. In vacuum she had to kick, building momentum through the light gravity, coasting, then kicking some more. She would not look behind her, nor would she look up. Her eyes scanned the approaching terrain for boulders to avoid and solid pack to kick against. She dipped and bobbed the sled to draw a tricky fire line but there was no cover anywhere in the basin so she was hell-bent for the shapes she had memorized along the jagged skyline of the rim - on the other side of which waited the supply station, and vehicles, coming and going.

THE first search and recovery teams reached the complex in forty-eight minutes. Twelve minutes later, a Gnat squad was dispatched to pursue the missing Gemini. They found the repeller sled wrecked against the base of the rim, at the bottom of a climbable grade, but there were no indications of injury to its pilot, nor footprints, suggesting she'd leapt onto the rim base and scrambled up. Word was sent ahead to the supply station as the Gnats fanned out along the rim, scanning the nooks and canyons for heat and movement. The station dispatcher responded that a search would be conducted, but informed them that sixty-eight vehicles to which she may have attached herself, eighteen of them unmarked, had disembarked the station in the previous hour, bound in sixty-eight different directions.

12. SPECIAL REVELATIVITY

seueral dozen thousand of the Clavi Ring's most fabulous had set up lavish picnic sites in the grandstands of the Sveygn amphitheater. The speakers had been tested and the test had been successful. As per her request, it had been conducted at a time when Sanjit had been enticed to relax in the shimmering glass baths deep within the estate and was unlikely to hear it. She still hadn't told him. She let it pass through her mind as she waited in the wings for the apogee sunlight to begin its cascade through the high glass, drenching the surfaces of the enclave in color and detail. It was time.

As she walked out onto the stage she could see Aev perched in her loge box wearing the God goggles, accompanied by Tehv-Yhet, Ado and Vaq. She'd expected Sanjit to be with them, but realized that she hadn't even told him about the performance, and apparently neither had anyone else. She might be off the hook. She put it out of her mind and plugged in her guitar. The circuit pop rang out and the air hummed with amplified electricity.

Sanjit heard it while in mid-air in his zipline harness, high above neighborhoods busy with picnics and feasts. He knew whatever event he'd been working on was supposed to happen at *au-ae* (the name given to the spectacular phenomenon of light he was now witnessing) and he was looking forward to hearing for himself what he'd been a part of.

Controlled feedback swelled, filling the air of the enclave with a sustained and pure electromagnetic ring. He knew what it was before the opening refrain emerged from it. His heart leapt, and he joined the cheers that rose from the enclave involuntarily, an instinctive exclamation of surprise and elation.

He'd become adept at navigating the zipline network, and at the next platform switched lines and pushed off along the route that would bring him out to the high cupolas atop the *sa-kina* monastery at the outermost edge of the line network, which he knew to have the best view of the amphitheater.

When he arrived he found that a dozen or so *kina* line riders had gathered there. He crawled carefully along the domed roof and found a perch near a trio he recognized.

"*T'a-a'm*" one of them said when he saw him, nodding toward the amphitheater. It meant, "your friend."

He was confused at first, but when he turned his gaze toward the amphitheater Sel's lone figure on the stage was unmistakable even at this great distance. He felt vertigo in his soul and pressed his palms against the tacky alloy of the dome to anchor him in reality. The unpredicted recent events of his life completed their arc and united themselves in symmetry and synchronicity, yet still none of it made any sense.

The effect was, as it had been that night in Frigoris, simultaneously disorienting, transcendent and grounding. It was also satisfying. He couldn't possibly imagine a better setting or circumstance in which to finally hear it again. He felt a tight pinch at the center of his forehead where the tattoo had been inlaid, reminding him of the solemn commitment he had made in such haste. This was the reward for his commitment. He savored each moment, each sound, each breath as a part of the world, in shared experience with the entire enclave city as they were all slowly drenched in the colors of the heavy, filtered sunlight. At one point, the *kina* raised their voices and sang along in perfect mass harmony. The hairs on his neck stood on end and goosebumps covered his arms.

When it was over – it felt too soon but he couldn't imagine rightly wanting more – the cheers of the *kina* became a chant. He recognized it as their evening worksong; a song of gratitude, if he understood correctly.

He stayed behind long after the other line riders had all kicked away back to the gatherings from which they'd excused themselves, lingering flat on his back against the curve of the dome, listening to the festive echoes and basking in the pleasantly humid warmth for hours until the smells of cooking overwhelmed his senses and he could no longer pretend he wasn't hungry.

He ziplined his way to the uppermost mezzanine of one of the central columns, a neighborhood he knew to be popular with line riders and their families, wondering if they might be charitable with a *kt'jhsk* or two. In fact, he was welcomed warmly and fed amply (he never knew so many different things could be done with turnips, nor with so much savor), and treated to even more exquisite music sung to wild and buoyant traditional dances. His presence caused an absolute sensation among the neighborhood kids, who regarded him alternately with wariness and awe. From that point on, as the legend of the giant continued to spread, now with undisputable eyewitness evidence, the figure became an ally of parents and benevolent authority, punishing only the naughty.

The thought that Sanjit was probably out there somewhere watching her and possibly experiencing some sort of heavy revelation crossed Sel's mind, but only briefly. Neither did she dwell on Vaq's quiet presence as a representative of her own prehistory, and spent less than moments wondering if Aev's God goggles would enhance her experience of the music or just exacerbate her every little mistake before deciding likely both and it didn't matter anyway.

For the first time since she made the first recording, alone in her empty-DRE tank studio, she lost herself completely in the playing of the song. So she ran with it, improvising entirely new movements around themes and scales which had occurred to her since Crisium but which she had not yet had a chance to practice, plunging blind into unexplored passages but always finding her way back. In honor of the enclave city's designer, she incorporated a passage based on some of the Namgung fractals she'd worked out during her preparatory calculations.

Only once did she almost lose the thread: when the *kina*'s rich, sweetly perfect voices joined she nearly faltered under the weight of the beauty.

She was determined to make the most of the insane amount of work that had gone into the show, and the extraordinary effort and fortuity it had taken just to get to Clavius. But, good Sancte that she was, she didn't want to take undue advantage of so many people's time or become a bore. As much as she didn't want it to end, when it was time to finish, she brought it to a close, stretching out the ending, pulling the notes further and further apart and letting the spaces between them fill the enclave with electricity. She couldn't stop herself from crying openly when the *kina* serenaded her afterwards.

In her loge box, Aev removed the God goggles and opened her eyes.

"Mmh," she said to no one in particular. She scanned the faces of those who would consider themselves her peer and felt vindicated in her contempt for them in that none of them seemed to have any idea what had just happened. "I quite enjoyed that."

"Matriarch," Tehv-Yhet said, not messing around, "A matter of some urgency…"

She had been explicit in her instructions not to be disturbed during the performance, as well as a standing order that she not be disturbed while wearing the goggles, and was unaware that Thev-Yhet had been busily managing a crisis through his lens and via telecom and runner from the corridor for the duration of the performance. She noticed that the Nomads were no longer with her.

"There is a party of Martenists at the estate demanding access to the Sancte," he said, "A separate group has attempted to infiltrate using them as a decoy. There has been violence."

"Blood?"

"Theirs, drawn by the *jura-dh'ihn* when they felled the infiltration team, which had evaded our own security."

"Oh, the *jura-dh'ihn*," she sighed almost ironically, "how exciting. Have the Martenists made it into the estate?"

"Yes."

"Do they know the way here?"

"We don't believe so. We have them fairly well contained, but they're quite intent on exploring."

"Try to stall them. I'm on my way. If our guests don't wish to speak to them, get them out through the Cleave."

"All awaits only you, Matriarch."

Ado was rushed to the backstage by a phalanx of Tehv-Yhet's aides, cursing himself for letting Aev push him into joining her in her box instead of watching from the wings where he ought to have been. Vaq had been forgiving about it: "Sveygn Clavi. Their rules," he'd said. But he still found the compromise distasteful.

Tehv-Yhet's aides asked him if he was willing to meet with the Martenists.

"Fuck no. And Sel's not going anywhere near them."

He relayed the information into his lens: "We're to take you to your vehicle then, which is fueled and charged. Your belongings are being retrieved from your accommodations and will await you there."

He was impressed that Tehv-Yhet had already put a plan in motion. But while he might be able to forgive himself a mistake of compromise, he could not abide mistakes of trust, and he wasn't yet sold on the Sveygn. He didn't doubt that they were as good as their word, but found it difficult to believe that they had his or Sel's best interests in their hearts. It was bad enough they insisted on keeping his vehicle nearly five kilometers away.

It took longer than he wanted to get Sel to understand the urgency of the situation.

"So?" she asked, "Martenists trade with the Sanctuaries all they time, they always want to talk to everyone."

"No, these Martenists want to talk to you specifically."

"Why would they want to talk to *me*?"

"I don't care, but several of them have given up their lives trying to sneak into the estate so I don't want to find out."

"What are you talking about?"

"Your *jura-dh'ihn* friends caught a couple of them that got by the Sveygn's people."

"What do you mean 'got by?'"

"I mean a group of Martenists tried to force their way into the estate while the official delegation showed up at the front door demanding to see you, and the *jura-dh'ihn* took them out. The others are in the estate now. Tehv-Yhet has them in a holding pattern but we've got to get moving."

"What about Sanjit?"

Ado cringed behind his forehead. It was exactly the sort of situation he'd dreaded since first glimpsing the Sanctuary tattoo on the Earther's forehead.

One of the aides stepped in: "He's been met at the maintenance line hub. He'll rendezvous with us en route to the Cleave."

Sel's gear was quickly and efficiently loaded and stowed onto a repeller utility barge, which they rode along a downwardly spiraling corridor, slowing to a crawl several levels below as they approached a three-meter wide raw rock cleave stretching from the floor to the ceiling of the otherwise pristine mosaic corridor wall.

Four of the aides began preparing to unload the gear. As they did, she found her tea kettle in her travel kit and reconfigured it into its defensive mode.

"They will be monitoring movement in the estate," one of the aides explained, "So we cannot stop the barge, lest they notice and decide to investigate."

Sel was astonished by the fluid grace with which Ado was able to integrate himself into the work practice of the aides, none of whom he had ever met before and who among themselves shared a working relationship from birth, as they unloaded each case, kit and pack from back of the moving barge as it eased along the curve of the corridor, surefooted and free of bungling. It burned that she hadn't figured out a way to help before they'd completed the task, but only slightly; more so that even Sanjit had more quickly put his size and density to use. It positively irked her that they needed to assist her down as if she were a final piece of luggage. Two aides remained on the barge, waving and wordlessly bidding luck as they slowly accelerated away.

They and the remaining four divided up the load wordlessly and within moments were hiking the downward slope of the Cleave. The walls were smooth and pale in caste. Glasslike seams twisted through them, they sparkled and shone in the light admitted by the luminescent tiles adhered to them.

"This is the Clavius oxygen sink," one of the aides said. "When the Engines excavated the original city, this volume was the repository for the excess oxygen drawn from the rock. You are walking through a fracture within a giant synthetic diamond. There's enough compacted oxygen around you to support the entire Ring for a dozen decades, without recycling or additional DRE."

Sel marveled as she came to fully understand the scale of the Sveygn's wealth.

"Namgung designed such a sink into all of his cities," the aide continued, his voice flat in the fast, close reverberation, "But he did not mark them. Only those who ran his equations and were diligent in their analysis could discern the existence of the deposits."

When she first saw the figures standing in their path ahead, she couldn't be sure if the shadows weren't simply playing tricks with her eyes. But when she glanced at Ado she could see on his face that he saw something, too. She looked over her shoulder, past Sanjit and two of the aides. There seemed to be shadows moving between the recessed glo globes, but with the movement of her own feet she couldn't be sure. She slowed to stop, signaling Ado to join her. The others followed suit.

Once she was sure of it she said: "We're being followed."

"We're being set up," Ado scowled dryly. "It's a trap. I'd call it an ambush but if it were, Tehv-Yhet's boys wouldn't be expecting it."

Sel looked at them in turn. In the dim light of the tiles, their faces were plainly unhappy, but not in the least surprised.

When their waylayers were close enough, they each recognized the shapes of Martenist togas. Sanjit's brow exploded in sweat and he felt his heart surge to the point that he was briefly lightheaded. He had pieced together that Martenists were after Sel for some reason, and may have been able to contain his anxiety that Jerro had indeed been among the Martenists at the party, and that he himself had somehow led them to Sel. He couldn't reconcile the circumstances in a way that made sense, but he wasn't thinking clearly in his panic; nor, he realized, could he recall thinking clearly nearly the entire time he'd spent in Crisium. He thought about Galaxa, which made him think of Naeemah. He snapped himself out of it before he let himself think of Earth. The Martenists were getting closer. He peered from one group to the other, waiting to see if the might-be Jerro were among them.

Ado's eyes flashed brief hatred at him. Early on in the podvan, the Nomad had privately assured him that he would be killed if he brought trouble but Sanjit felt more fear at the thought of being unwittingly responsible for jeopardizing her safety than he did for his own life.

His discomfort intensified when he saw that the might-be Jerro was in fact among them, and the Martenist met his eyes and said: "Yes. It is me. Hello Sanjit. He loves you. He loves you all. Is it not so nice to be loved?" in an unfamiliarly accented but unmistakable aggressively friendly tone.

Ado's eyes flashed once again toward Sanjit. The Nomad unsheathed the carbon knife he kept hidden along the thigh of his coveralls and lunged for him. Sel tried to intercept him but he countered and sent her spinning out of the way. Sanjit backpedaled.

Ado closed on him fast, but before he was in reach he was cleanly bisected by a narrow-band splitter beam from a disrupter wielded by one of the Martenists.

His legs tripped over his torso as it tumbled forward, clumsy and disoriented, his face raw terror as he realized what was happening, his half-body writhing in pain, spastically contracting his cauterized abdomen and seizing as blood flooded his brain. Sel's echoing wail of ultimate horror affected them all, including the one wielding the particle disrupter as he adjusted the field settings and, in a mercy shot, deoxygenated the Nomad's blood. It frothed pink and blue from his facial orifices, down his cheeks, around his lips, dripping from his chin.

Sel aimed her kettle gun at the Martenist and activated it. A clean hole appeared through his chest. Blood spurted from the remaining half of his heart, what was left of his lungs sagged limply. His eyes went dumb and he collapsed. Before the kettle gun recharged, two Martenists had caught up to her from behind and pinned her arms, stripping her of it. She thrashed and kicked but one of them, an Earther, far larger than she, had her in an inextricable sleeper hold. Another kept Sanjit at bay until their disrupter had been retrieved and leveled at them.

Jerro declared, "We must render the two of you unto Him alive, but not necessarily intact. I leave that decision to you." He turned his gaze to Sanjit and said: "Imagine my dismay when poof, there you went. Gone without a trace. Truly, I thought, the Colony is such a dangerous place," adding as an aside to Sel, "I simply do not understand how anyone survives without His love," then returning to Sanjit to say: "Imagine my surprise when I learned that you had arrived in Clavius with our sought-after little singing Sanctuary girl."

Their hands, wrists and elbows were bound in compression straps. Jerro turned his full attention toward Sel. "And here she is. I believe we have a mutual friend in Aev-Sveygn. I came to know her through some of my Fellow Beloved who liaised between her and the CA in negotiating the contract amendments that isolated her father and assured her the Matriarchy. They correspond quite regularly. She told us all about your visit.

"Like my dear, dear friend Sanjit here, He is quite taken with your wonderful song. Compelled by it, one might even say. He would very much like to discuss its fascinating and powerful aspects with its creator personally.

"For instance, what a..." he considered his words, letting his discomfiting, wandering gaze touch on Sanjit "...*powerful message* it must carry to inspire a heavy transport driver, a certified technician, to forfeit his credit rating after hearing it."

"There is no *message*," Sel spat. It was precisely the type of intentionalist speculation she most abhorred, amplified to a nightmare level of absurdity.

"Oh, but there is my dear, there is, whether you are cognizant of it or not. I know that it is something He is very keen to discuss and explore with you.

"I have to say," Jerro turned to Sanjit and his posture relaxed into an unsubtle display of disappointment, "seeing you with a Sanctuary tattoo," he shook his head and suddenly, surprisingly vehemently demanded: *"There is no Sanctuary but His love!"*

He spun on his heel and, grinning madly, pointed to Sel. "I could also add, *there is no Sanctuary* from *His love!"* He got close to her and said: "He loves Lyell Sanctuary as He loves all on the moon."

He peered into Sel's eyes until he was sure she'd understood the implicit threat. "Come then," he clapped his hands together, then gestured down the corridor, "Let us go forth unto Him."

One of the Martenists saw movement ahead and sent out a signal to wait over their coglinks.

When Sanjit and Sel saw that the Martenists were all gazing in the same direction, they followed their eyes up the Cleave but saw nothing.

Waiting for them to get into range, the one with the disrupter sent as he adjusted the field settings, *see if I can get them both in the same beam.*

Several still moments passed. Without any excess motion beyond squeezing the activator, the Martenist sent a wide, flat beam up the way ahead, then flicked his wrist toward the ceiling.

Two twisted cataracts of light blurred and tumbled to the floor. By the coloring of their mutilated bodies and relative size, Sel knew them to be the *jura-dh'ihn* who had appeared to her.

"Their stealth suits are nearly two centuries old," Jerro said, smiling eerily, "Effective enough to fool the human eye, but in His infinite love, He has bestowed us with modern implants."

THREE kilometers above, Aev-Sveygn and Vaq rode hidden under stacked bolts of textiles in a cargo car on a monorail as it coasted along its track through the *kina* neighborhoods. The space was tight. Vaq winced as the grinding of various joints sent shocks of up his spine.

"You're uncomfortable" Aev whispered.

"Not as flexible as I used to be."

"Aw," she pressed herself against him. "You're feeling a little stiff then?"

She ran her hand up his thigh to his crotch. He felt his aging body responding in ways he hadn't known it still could. Aev's breath was sweet in his ear. She stroked him and sighed approvingly into his ear, moving closer and teasing her exposed nipple across his lips.

The monorail coasted to a stop at the terminus of the freight depot. *Kina* porters removed the textile bolts and stacked them into hampers. Several of them helped Vaq and Aev, her face obscured by the replica Sanctuary hood she wore, out of the car and accompanied them across the platform. At first, she had considered the whole ruse too elaborate by half, but now that she was in the middle of it found that she quite enjoyed the intrigue. And her involvement would be kept secret. She'd grown fond of the old Nomad, and genuinely regretted that he had to die.

A disrupter beam severed Vaq's head from his body. Three *kina* porters were cut down as they scattered.

"Stop!" Aev shouted melodramatically, for the benefit of any other witnesses at the depot, throwing back the hood and revealing herself to the surprised *kina* onlookers, "I am Aev-Sveygn, Matriarch of the Sveygn and I command it!"

Martenist snipers were seen fleeing from the depot shortly after. *Kina* and Sveygn histories recorded that the benevolent and crafty Matriarch Aev had successfully provided a decoy, affording the beloved Sel the opportunity to escape through the Cleave. A fountain was commissioned to commemorate the fearless martyrdom of the fallen porters and Nomad who so bravely gave their lives in the protection of others.

THE Martenists used a jumper to traverse the vacuum. It was an unpopular and out-dated means of travel, unpleasant and uncomfortable: it consisted of a spherical cabin mounted on stout spring-loaded gimble-jointed legs capable of covering sixty kilometers of terrain per a leap. Passengers rode strapped into harnesses perched on jump seats all around the catwalks that ringed the interior of the sphere.

The cabin was dark. Faces were inkblots of shadow cast by the colorless LEDs mounted over the harness bar. The portholes were small: the bare minimum necessary to give the mind a visual anchor to avoid nausea from the relentlessly potent sensation of rising and falling, which was nevertheless overwhelming. Sel noted that the retaining bar crossing her chest included a small molded-plastic vomit receptacle, small enough that she said a silent prayer that those above her had strong stomachs, or at least had eaten lightly.

"Hey," she called to Sanjit in the harness next to hers, just loudly enough so that only he'd hear her over the whoosh and hiss of the ventilation and the creaks and rattles of the vehicle.

He looked up from what had been sullen consideration of his knees.

"I'm sorry," she said quietly.

He couldn't hear her but read her lips. He shook his head and dismissed it: she had nothing to be sorry about; he blamed himself.

"No secrets, you two!" Jerro called from opposite them a ring above. "There are no secrets among Beloved!" His voice was mockingly scolding, as if he were trying to make some sort of threatening joke that nobody got. Sel and Sanjit stared back at him wordlessly, each wearing expressions making it very clear that they were not, nor did they harbor any desire to ever be, Beloved.

Sᴇʟ lost count of how many jumps they'd endured by the time their trajectories began diminishing, several kilometers from the base of the Martenist Temple in northern Imbrium. The Temple was an expensive-looking torqued glass-and-steel inverted pyramid in the architectural style which had been dubbed "nu luna" when in vogue on the planet several decades before, but remained unnamed and seldom seen on the moon. Once she unbuckled the chin guard she peered at it as best she could through the porthole next to her head. The feeling of motion persisted in her gut so she clenched her fists around the retaining bar and leaned as far forward as she could to anchor herself. There was a hard concussion as the spring-legs disengaged and a set of treads oriented themselves toward the airlock gate.

It felt like it took forever for the airlock to pressurize, haunted by nausea and the grisly memories of Ado's agonizing death and the mess that had become of the *jura-dh'ihn*. She felt the summoning stone in her pocket and wondered what good it would do her here.

The Martenists chattered inanely and ceaselessly. Pointless, circular small talk and gossip seemed compulsory to their order. This, she realized, was exactly why so many Moonborn couldn't stand Earthers. Jerro watched both of them sharply, and attempted to engage with them at any sign of interaction with each other so they only sporadically risked even a glance.

When the indicator light finally went green and the hatch opened, the Martenists filed out leisurely, leaving them to exit last. Martenists had formed a phalanx from the gangway up a wide, shallow staircase to a set of swinging doors behind which shone a bright white light that seemed to have red glitter shimmering through it. The doors burst open and a red glitter cloud burst forth, along with a young, high-voiced Martenist boy proclaiming in a cracking sing-song: "Beloved! All Beloved! Enter His Eternal Embrace, *Bask in His Undying Love!*"

Jerro and the other Martenists applauded and the young crier bowed theatrically in acknowledgement.

"Please come," Jerro said, starting up the stairs, "Come know the love of the Messiah Marten."

The Martenist with the disrupter checked its charge, subtly letting it be known that he still had it on them. Lacking any obvious alternative, Sel and Sanjit followed him, squinting and tightlipped through the bright, glitter-blown vestibule and into a dim corridor lined with vitrines displaying what appeared to be very old garbage preserved in clear resin: stubs and receipts, cast-off clothing, cartons and cards, stalks and rinds.

"These items all contain genetic artifacts of an aspect of Marten before His Ascension to the moon."

"You mean somebody followed this guy around and collected his garbage?" Sanjit made no attempt at reverence.

"Ah but what is garbage but the evidence of physical existence?" Jerro's tone became philosophical, "In that sense, what is the body but garbage? Ah, but it is so much more is it not? It is a vessel of life, as that carton was a vessel for soy milk, and what is life but a vessel of love?"

Sanjit remembered Jerro's tendency to assign depth to idiotic thoughts. At first, he'd thought it was an ironic affectation, but in time came to suspect that his roommate might actually have been an idiot and that the vaguely mocking tone to his voice was merely due to his peculiar accent. But now his accent was slightly different, less conspicuous, and the mocking tone remained, causing him to once again question whether he might in fact be earnest; a true believer, or perhaps some kind of mischievous adventurer, fool or rascal. He glanced at Sel to see if he could gauge her opinion of him. Her eyes had rolled ceiling-ward and showed no sign of returning to level; the set of her mouth made clear that she considered him something far worse than annoying.

"In practical truth," Jerro said conversationally, "many people were followed very closely indeed. The Messiah Marten is an aggregate of over two thousand individuals whose lifetimes have spanned more than two centuries."

Sel listened with mute revulsion. Uploaded Personality aggregates were among the most despised and infamous of the Colonial Authority's monstrosities, responsible for some of the most abhorrent crimes committed on a mass scale against Moonborn and Colonials alike, not to mention the administration of the punitive conditions under which so many on the moon lived.

"Waitaminute," Sanjit asked, "Your Messiah is an *Upload?*"

"Marten is much more than an Upload," Jerro stopped in his tracks and spun on his heel, putting himself right in his former roommate's face. He clapped him on the shoulders, stared intensely into his eyes and said: "For He chose to return to the flesh."

AT ITS terminus, the winding reliquary hallway opened into a narrow atrium bright with heavily filtered sunlight all the way from the roof. A dozen repeller lifts rose and sank from a platform at the center, stopping at moorings along the spiraling upper levels, picking up and dropping off Martenist passengers. The rest of the entourage fell back, leaving them alone with Jerro to lead them through the grid of ascending and descending repeller lifts along lanes marked by luminous tiles in the floor. Sel remarked the use of luminous mosaic: it was a highly regarded construction technique, abandoned by the Colony generations ago due to cost, thus rare in so modern a structure. Combined with their modern temple, late model optical implants and disrupter tech, the tiles and repellers confirmed that, whoever they were, the Martenists were more than the marginal, fly-by-night ascetic Messiah cult they appeared to be.

"Please," Jerro gestured them onto the lift at the very center of the platform.

As they rose, Sel contemplated that it would be within the Sanctuariat charter to kill Jerro for violating her and Sanjit's independent sovereignty. She was unsure of Jerro's fighting ability, but he carried himself well and could be dangerous; nor did she know whether or not Sanjit could fight, although she guessed the answer was no. A messy fight on the platform would put them both in jeopardy. Besides which, what would it accomplish? It might make a statement, but there was little chance of their escaping the temple. And the Martenists might very well have their own code of vengeance. So she stood very still and stared at Jerro, imagining all the ways she might have killed him.

Sanjit's thoughts were similarly violent, if not more brutal. But it was simple indecision that prevented him from attacking, a paralyzing confluence of anger, doubt, fear and the primal human compassion born into him. He tried his hardest to read Sel but couldn't. He sensed that she'd prefer that Jerro be dead, but had no sense of how she would react if he made an effort to make it so. Having seen her dispatch Ikt and Okt so deliberately in Crisium he didn't doubt that if she felt she could kill him she would have, so assumed that it was a conscious decision on her part not to. But what did that matter to him? Jerro had been a pestilence in his life and was now an outright blight. He wanted to end him. Even if he turned out to be augmented, he stood so mockingly close to the edge of the lift a single low hit would topple him. He knew it, too; it was a taunt and a test. There was a distinct possibility that Jerro would take him over the edge with him, but was he any more use to Sel dead than alive anyway? If not, what use was he to anyone? As the lift clipped into the uppermost level's moorings he cursed the missed opportunity.

The space was vast; perhaps ten stories high and nearly a hundred meters in any direction, though it appeared infinite. A few sweeping support structures and dividing walls were visible, but most were hidden under photonic skins displaying media feeds or programmed to appear as gigantic reproductions of ancient Earther works of art, others were rendered near-invisible in the bright, clean light of the smartglass roof. There were luminous tiles along the floor here as well, but they were programmed only to illuminate the path up to two meters ahead of one's footsteps.

In places, the floor fell away abruptly, overlooking the similarly cavernous but more heavily populated level below. Jerro led them straight toward one such precipice. The illumination of the tile path continued over it, across an invisible floor. It was impossible not to feel vertigo. Not only did Jerro walk more swiftly than either Sel or Sanjit felt comfortable, he spun and maintained the pace walking backwards; cog-linked to the building, he knew exactly which chasms were real and which illusion.

"It's best to imagine that the floor continues on either side," he smiled, "and not to think of this as a very narrow bridge over a very high fall."

Sel scowled. It was an uncomfortable sensation, but far more stable than the cold terror she'd felt on the cable over the watery black depths of the Crisi undercity.

At the center of the phantasmagorical expanse, a giant stage had been constructed, larger by half than the arena she'd played in Crisi. As they approached it, she could make out a single figure standing on it. A loud electromagnetic clang rang out. She recognized it immediately: it was her guitar, a messy and random open chord crudely strafed across detuned strings.

There were two figures on the solid floor in front of the stage, one seated and the other standing. The one on its feet stood too straight and swiveled too stiffly to be human, and when they were close enough they could see that it wasn't.

The android watched them approach with an unexpected and unfamiliar sense of reverence for Sel. They had been told that the half-Moonborn girl responsible for the song was being brought to the temple, and here she was. When it first heard the song, it had thought little of it, not understanding quite why the music had been such a source of consternation for seemingly all who heard it. But after observing its profound effects on the Sister Doctor and the Gemini, and the profound destruction Wei had wrought with it against the CARD AIs, it came to understand the significance of its power even though it could not quantify it and hence knew it could never understand the song itself. And here was the human girl who had created it. It contemplated her, mutely fascinated.

Coni rose to her feet as they approached, still wearing the sleeping habit she'd had on under her vac-suit when the rescue teams arrived at the Galilaei complex and brought them here, she'd lost track of how long ago.

Onstage, the man holding the guitar bashed away at it tunelessly and ceaselessly, yelping with delight periodically. He was perhaps twice Jerro's age but his skin was smooth and taught, and like the younger man his features seemed to slide out of one's memory immediately, creating an eerily neutral impression of a face. He struck a clownishly ecstatic pose as he continued to pretend to play her instrument. It offended Sel and Sanjit both.

"Himself," Jerro grinned, "The Messiah Marten."

Coni nearly wept when she saw Sel approaching. From childhood, she had been taught to kneel in front of the Motherhood, but had never believed those women were holier than anyone. This poor doomed girl was clearly a vessel of the divine. She knelt before her.

Sel didn't know why the Earther woman was kneeling, but she didn't like it. "Don't do that," she said flatly, "stand up."

Coni didn't know what to say. Her mind seized even at the thought of a simple introduction.

Sel waited for none: "What is this place?"

"It's the central headquarters for the Colonial Intelligence and Information Services," Coni answered.

"Yes," Marten proclaimed smoothly in a clean and polished tenor as he climbed out from under the strap and handed the guitar to an attendant who had come scurrying out from the wings. "It is the Temple of My Eternal and Everlasting Love. You are welcome here. I love you."

13. LOVE OF LIFE

Demetrius Wei spent forty-nine days locked in an invisible room deep within the uppermost level of the Martenist temple, watching his daughter's life play out in real time on panoramic video via dust drones and security camera signals relayed from the planet. Every twelfth hour, a bowl of rice and a glass of water were delivered through a panel in the floor. He had been taken directly there upon arrival at the temple after being brought there from Galilaei. One of the rescuers dispatched by Brigadier-General Nshombo's command formally informed him that his work would now be carried out under the direct and exclusive supervision of the IIS.

It was both mercy and torture. She was indeed alive: his Mia had emerged from the field suspension tank intact and healthy, at least physically. And she hadn't been sent to the Colony, so she did not want for air or water. But her life was empty, her mind broken; her body moved through menial routine by habit, obedience and addiction. Every week she dutifully filled a prescription for transdermal meds at her tower block pharmacy kiosk, which she administered to herself twice daily. She did as she was told and consumed whatever was given.

At times he thought he saw traces of himself and her mother in her features through the soft, sallow wake of atrophic decades, but none of the intelligence, curiosity or personality which, when she was a child, had been strong enough to shine through even dire illness. In the forty-nine days spent watching her, as if she were some specimen under experimental observation, she hardly spoke more than two words to anyone. When she did, he didn't recognize the language. She lived alone in a cramped, rundown dormitory on the outskirts of a large terrestrial city unfamiliar to him, and commuted by bus daily to and from a vertical farm where she worked in systems maintenance. She ate bottom-tier rations when she remembered to eat, and spent mirthless hours either coding agricultural nutrition cycles or consuming media with no apparent discrimination as to its content. It was a life devoid of joy, and from what glimpses he caught of the world around her in the video feeds, it was probably not an atypical life.

It was his daughter, but it was not Mia. They had taken Mia from him. Those forty-nine days were longer and more painful than his decades in the Pit.

"Enough, then."

The video feeds cut out without his realizing, such were the depths of his numbness in the immersion, and a lone middle-aged man in a smartfiber toga stood in the previously invisible doorway. His complexion was eerily smooth and free of shadow, as if uniformly keyed to reflect a specific frequency of light, his features symmetrical, smooth and immediately forgotten, they sluiced through memory as water through a grate.

"Demetrius Wei," his voice was perfectly, effortlessly clear, "I have tried so hard to know you."

Wei looked into the man's cyberoptic eyes and recognized in them the forces which had made him, which had manipulated and destroyed the lives of himself and anyone he might have loved; which had killed the soul of the only person he did, his Mia, and sentenced her body to a purgatory of base human resource.

Marten smiled: "I love you so."

Wei's body wracked with fury. Starvation sweat burst through his pores, reeking of ammonia. His skeleton felt on the verge of collapse.

"Yet you would destroy me, would you not?" Marten regarded his fury coolly.

Wei was silent for long, quavering moments. When he finally tried to speak, it took several attempts to get his throat to produce sound. Finally, his voice cracked forth with: "I cannot destroy you."

Marten's neutral smile turned proud, as a teacher to a pupil giving a correct answer without prompt. It soured when he saw Wei's body relax, his mouth pull into something like a grin as it issued a hissing rattle that could have been a laugh.

"I cannot destroy you," he repeated, adding: "but *she can.*"

The neutrality rushed back into Marten's smile and his eyes went cold.

"*She can,*" Wei repeated between wheezing rasps of mad joy, "*She can. She already has.*"

ASPECTS of Marten debated killing him right there, but even after so many years and so many problems, an overwhelming majority could not bring Himself to destroy something so rare, expensive, and potentially valuable, even now that his value had inarguably fallen fatally into diminishing returns. The poisoned directory he had created remained intact after bringing down the CARD AIs, and had been fatally replicated into the Colonial mainframe. The AIs themselves deleted it upon detection, but certain Uploaded Personae and faceted HR assets found "What It Is and What It Means" impossible to resist. Its reputation for danger enhanced its desirability, and it became a coveted grail among a particular class of mid-level processors, some of whom believed the rumors of destruction were a smokescreen to keep outsiders away from leaked privileged data; others possessed a hermetic religious notion that the decoding of the directory would lead them to a higher phase of consciousness. Whatever their motives, when even one component of a network dared to open it the cascade effect proved catastrophic and irreversible. At least a dozen major industrial and civic AI systems had fallen to it. Entire sectors of industry were in shambles, particle nets around the moon were collapsing, hundreds of thousands of people died each hour. Marten loved each and every one of them, and each perishing affected Him as a personal failure, which He abhorred more than anything.

When He had first learned of the manipulations of Wei's genome, He had made it His pet project: His first attempt at engineering a perfect mind in a living human being, to accept the Aggregate.

The original core Aggregate was made up of a cabal of powerful executives on the governing board of the Colonial Transportation Authority, who had pledged to Upload themselves into a mainframe in order to ensure continuity of the successful, prosperous and peaceful society they had brought about under economic hegemony. As an arbiter of stability, the Aggregate thrived in the networks, but as a sentient being, He festered (while there were many female aspects within the Aggregate, dominant masculinity had never been questioned).

It was not life within the networks, merely existence; there was accomplishment but no reward. Within the Aggregate, the bold aspects for Whom immortality had been ambition and expectation, seized dominance and invested heavily in vat-growth technology. Ninety-eight years ago, the Aggregate had been installed into this body.

He had been giddy-to-ecstatic at the prospect of a return not just to life but the prime of youth, only to discover that the perfect body He had engineered to accept Him was in fact so perfect that it did not feel like life at all, just a set of wetware running His program on a bioelectric quantum processor.

As He binged on aggregating friends and foes alike for advantage and profit while diligently investing in bio-engineering tech, He became aware of the significant genomic amendments requested by Jov.10 on behalf of the Wei family, and had the epiphany that the answer lay not in designing a body, but preparing a mind to accept Him.

He did not expect the Demetrius experiment to be a success: there were too many other agendas at work, too many other spoons and clumsy thumbs already stirring the pot. Nevertheless, He could and did obtain valuable data from the process, and the resulting boy had far exceeded his expectations. He loved him above all others. He had permitted the amendments and contributed to them personally and so felt a profound authorial (if not parental) responsibility, and admired the seemingly bottomless intellectual ingenuity of a mind able to so deftly adapt to the trigger mechanisms, which had in fact begun quite accidentally as artifacts of His attempts at priming the cerebral cortex for installation of the Aggregate.

As defiant as the boy became as he grew into an outright problematic man, He could not end the precious life He had sought through him.

"She can…she already has…"

This quivering, hateful and broken madman was all that was left. Such life wasted for so long. Still, He could not quell His hope of redemption. Let him become reacquainted with the daughter he so thoughtlessly and selfishly abandoned through his stubbornness. His own attentions were best dedicated to the pressing matters of Colonial warfare.

The repeated tragedies of mass death and destruction put him in a foul mood, but he could not deny that a population adjustment was in order.

There were far too many Moonborn, most of them hostile, obstinate and uncooperative, a malignant pack of woeful mules and mutant ingrates unreceptive to His love. The recent resurgence of the Unity presented the perfect opportunity to reduce their numbers and begin the next generational wave of emigration from the planet; somewhat early, but the demographic metrics were favorable.

As a result of anti-Colonial sentiment, the destruction in the Colony provided a direct rationale (and mechanism) for stamping out ungrateful elements. He had sent directives to the Colonial military to adopt a war footing and to municipal administrations to phase in selective extermination plans beginning with their most problematic Settlements and the targeted elimination of individuals whom the IIS had identified as potential threats to hegemony. On the planet, mediacoders had already implemented their pro-Emigration protocol; first-wave propaganda was already appearing across all platforms. Tax and wage incentives would be implemented at the beginning of the next quarter.

Hegemony would be maintained.

"She can...she already has."

The words lingered unpleasantly in His thoughts.

The daughter of Avik-Rosot.

Some who had presumed to consider themselves His peers had said the same about the father and his ideas. It was true enough that an idea could not be killed, but individual beings could. And He had learned long before the advent of Avik-Rosot that if enough individuals were killed in the name of an idea, the idea would soon become accepted as implausible.

Except for love. Love was eternal. Without love, there could be no control.

Love was what the Moonborn felt for this girl. He had seen it in the reports from Clavius and Crisium and his spies among the Sanctuariat. He coveted and feared it, and profoundly resented that

Wei had so easily recognized that fear, and so readily exploited it even after being shown such mercy time and time again, allowed the gift of life.

Of course, the wretch had no way of knowing that any possible threat posed by the girl was being neutralized as they spoke. She had been put in an induced coma and placed in a field-suspension tank so an exhaustive cognitive map could be made of her brain. It would soon be complete and the transcoding process would begin to prepare it for Holy Aggregation. He would consume her; He would render her of Him.

SANJIT watched the enormous video murals in mute horror. The particle nets in both Crisi and Schickard had collapsed, exposing anyone unable to reach pressurized shelter within half an hour to vacuum. Entire districts proved to have been designed with inadequate defenses against the void, luxury and slum alike. Millions were dead. It was happening in other cities as well: he heard mention of Purbach, Clavius, Albetegnius and others, but he was fixated on news from Schickard and Crisi. His mind burned with images of Naeemah and Galaxa dying horrible deaths. He tried to distance himself from it - it wasn't like he didn't have his own problems - but the horrors came back to him again and again, each grislier than the last.

He spent his waking hours scanning news dispatches of the destruction for any word of survivors. If anyone could survive such mayhem, Galaxa could. She was the only person he'd ever met who he could imagine looking up and seeing holes shredding through the sky as just something else to deal with. But he was sick with worry over Naeemah, seeing her as he had that last time, sallow and drained. When he slept, curled up in whatever solid corner he could find in the vast invisible labyrinth, he dreamed of Schickard: of racing through the uneven gravity of the streets, at times leaping at times crawling with all his might, trying to reach Naeemah's house in time to… what? The atmosphere was already rushing out of the warped sky in great terrible cataracts of debris, dust and corpses: in time to die with her, to grip her hand and pray for reunion in the next life.

"You have people there?" Coni asked him as he scrolled through wall-sized indices of active rescue and recovery operations, scanning them for relevant tags.

He didn't know what to make of the Sister Doctor. He had heard vaguely of the Order of the Holy Mother that ran one of the territories on the west side of his home continent, but all he knew about them was that they worshipped a virgin who was the mother of a Christian deity. He had been raised with a deep distrust of Christians, learned as a child from the gruesome media images of mass crucifixions in the Southern Christian Union.

Still, she wasn't a Martenist and, like him, didn't seem to have been given any place to stay within the techno wasteland of the temple.

"Had, anyway. Kind of. A long time ago I guess. I don't know."

"The Mother shall receive them."

He remembered one of the few things he knew about the Christian religion: "Even the sinners?"

"Even the sinners, even the non-believers," she said flatly. "I was once a non-believer. My whole life. I joined the Order because that's what you do if you want to make anything of yourself where I'm from. But I've come to know the hand of Her mercy. She is merciful. She will be merciful."

Sanjit was in no mood for more evangelism. He wasn't feeling particularly spiritual at all. He was angry about Naeemah and worried about Sel, whom he hadn't seen in what could have been weeks or months (he was nearly certain the sun had passed overhead at least four times, but the light in the temple sometimes changed independently and he couldn't be sure).

The Sister Doctor seemed to be the only other full-time human occupant. There was Marten, who dwelled in an invisible structure up near the ceiling from which he descended via repeller from time to time to greet his staff. But he doubted Marten quite counted as 'human,' and the staff came and went; they lived on the level below. He had seen the android when he arrived, but not since. He didn't have anything left for social niceties: if she was going to insist on talking to him about belief or mercy or the hand of the divine, he was going to walk away, which is what he did.

"She will be merciful to you, as well," Coni held her rosary to her lips and prayed for the young man, his lost friends, and the missing girl.

Sanjit stalked along the path set for him by the glowing tiles at a deliberate pace, keeping an eye out for Jerro or anyone else who might be able to tell him where Sel was, or what the hell was going on. The Sister Doctor had told him that the Martenists were actually the IIS, but that was a widely circulated conspiracy theory among wingnuts at large, and she didn't strike him as particularly sane or stable.

From time to time he saw a member of Marten's staff, all of whom, male and female alike, looked like Jerro, coming from and going to various visible and invisible areas of the temple, but they never responded when he called to them, and the tile pathways never allowed him an intersecting course. More than once he became so frustrated that he contemplated stepping over the glowing tile line and running across to them. But he had no way of knowing whether they were actually there or just video feeds along a solid wall, if the floor between him and them was solid or an illusion.

Compounding his frustration was the dull sense of disconnection accompanying dehydration, hunger and undernourishment. From time to time, the tiles led him to a bowl of rice or a box of dry mini powdered donuts. The Martenists were stingy with their water. He was given perhaps half a pint per day, if he could find it. There were restroom facilities he had access to, but they were far away from each other and seemed to be in different places every time he needed them. He resorted to relieving himself on the floor once, only to find his meager rations withheld for forty-eight hours.

In the first days at the temple, knowing he was under close surveillance, he'd demanded aloud again and again to be told what had become of Sel. As he grew hungrier and more disoriented, the demands softened into requests for an audience with someone who might know. The requests soon plunged below integral zero and became desperate pleas. It wasn't until long after he'd given up even trying that Jerro appeared to him, revealed around an invisible corner seated in a rattan lounge chair at a low cocktail table laid with ceramic trays of exquisitely presented finger food.

"He realizes you must be terribly hungry," Jerro said, presenting the food, "and He wants you to know how important your life is to Him. He has done so much to ensure that you stay alive."

An involuntary film of sour saliva coated Sanjit's dehydrated mouth, his stomach contracted at the presence of food, but something stopped him from accepting it. If they wanted to put a bug in his system they would have done it through the rice and water, but there was no chair for him, so reaching the tempting morsels would involve stooping or kneeling in front of Jerro to get it, and he was a little surprised at how instinctively repulsed he was by the thought.

Jerro watched him closely through tensely dynamic eyes that vacillated between impatience and confusion over a mask of a smile. After a long time he broke the silence and speculated: "You are so ungrateful that you would refuse even such a token gesture of His love?"

Ungrateful? "If your guy loves me so much, how come I don't get a chair?"

Jerro shook his head ruefully, said: "Perhaps He has been already too generous…" and moved to stand.

"Look, I'm sorry," Sanjit conceded, and considered what was proffered, choosing the most palatable and easily digestible-looking option: a *julienned* slice of cucumber dressed with a dollop of what looked like bean paste, speared with slivers of carrot and radish.

As soon as his teeth punctured the skin of the vegetable, the substance he'd thought was bean paste activated; it absorbed what little moisture was left in his mouth and covered his tongue and cheeks in a screamingly hot capsaicin derivative. His dry sinuses burned all the way up to his eyes.

Satisfied, Jerro eased back into the chair and said: "Your young friend has been granted the highest expression of His love. She is to be Aggregated. She will not be harmed in any way. A quantum map of her consciousness is being made and will be transcoded into the Aggregate. The mapping process sometimes results in impairment of certain higher function like speech or thought," he waved dismissively, "but the important thing is that she will be alive. And her being will survive the eventual death of her body – by natural causes, He hopes – as an Aspect of His Love."

The thought of Sel's consciousness trapped in such an unnatural, twisted and cruel entity for eternity while her "possibly impaired" body was left to wander the temple until it expired sent him into dry heaves. But he could not protest, his mouth and throat couldn't form words. Blind rage overtook him and he lunged across the table heading for Jerro's windpipe.

Jerro giggled at the weakened approach and from his seated position torqued the ball of his right hand sharply into Sanjit's solar plexus. The blow winded him and he toppled, taking the table with him and smearing the *hors'd'oeurvres* across the floor.

When he righted himself, Jerro was gone.

Moments later, the Sister Doctor arrived, led there by the floor tiles at the time she was accustomed to receiving the blessing of food. She had watched the confrontation between Jerro and Sanjit play out from a distance as she approached, considering Sanjit's attack a sadly typical and counterproductive male gesture, bringing only injury and waste.

She recognized the furniture from a meeting she'd had with Marten himself shortly after their arrival (although she'd been given a chair and palatable food).

Marten had smiled at her kindly and in a warm familiar voice said, "When you watch them for so long...it would not be adequate to say that you begin to see them as your children, but you do begin to feel a certain responsibility toward them. For me, the experience of that responsibility is profound. For me it is Love."

It occurred to her that, as the head of the IIS and a centuries-old aggregate, the synthetic man who called himself Marten seated across from her could very possibly represent a significant bloc of the CA Board of Directors.

She did not recognize him as divine but she could not deny his power, and accepted his gesture to attempt to relate to her using the obvious reference to her experience with the Gemini and, she supposed, drawing a parallel with his position at the top of the CA intelligence-gathering apparatus. Although she saw surveillance and observation as distinct phenomena, she was in no mood to discuss semantics or philosophy nor did she harbor any desire to antagonize her host, so she decided to settle on common ground.

"Yes," she agreed, "It is love."

It was difficult for her to read his face. His smile was broad but clearly meaningless, and she sensed that his eyes were measuring and analyzing her carefully across broad spectra of data. She became self-conscious of her fingers rolling over her rosary beads and stopped.

"I respect that you are a woman of faith," he said, "and I hope that in time you will come to accept My love. Until such a time, you are welcome as a guest in My temple."

Coni searched her mind for any hope of return to the planet, but found none, realizing that she missed the sense of hope more than she missed the planet itself, which made it a sin of vanity. She silently prayed for forgiveness.

When she reached Sanjit she knelt beside the overturned table and thanked the Holy Mother for the blessing of food. The humility of her faith allowed her to accept with gratitude every mercy, so she scooped the demolished *hors-d'ouervres* off the floor with her hands and put them in her mouth with her fingers.

Sanjit watched her from where he sat on the opposite side of the mess. He made a half-hearted attempt to warn her but it was too late. She winced and gasped in pain and looked at him, mutely questioning why he didn't stop her. He shrugged, figuring that if she were that eager to eat whatever they put in front of her she deserved what she got.

JERRO, whose full legal name was Marten.2-Jerro, 3/41, had been raised in a posh habitat nestled in the Austrian Alps, along with legion parents, brothers and sisters, part of the second generation of clones bred to His specifications and engineered to accept the Aggregate when the synthetic body in which He had returned to the world expired, the full production line that had resulted from the series of prototypes begun after Demetrius Wei. This body had carried Him for ninety-eight years, and was currently expected to begin to fail shortly after the hundredth. Each and every cloned progeny lived to be asked to accept the Aggregate; they competed fiercely and ruthlessly for his favor.

Jerro took care not to be boastful, but knew that many considered him heir apparent. He worked more closely with Himself than any other youth. The third generation, all considered his children, were still too young; the first, all considered parents to him and all of his brothers and sisters, were past their physical prime, out of contention for Succession. He knew there were females with whom He was intimate who considered themselves contenders, but it was foolish to think that He would return as anything other than male. Unbeknownst to the females, Jerro was intimate with Himself as well, and privy to His most private thoughts and judgments about each of them.

He had been a star since he was a child, a standout even among his genetically extraordinary peers, possessed of obvious charm and invisible guile; none had a negative thing to say about him, not even his rivals. And he was so grateful for their love, and His Love above all. He would do anything He asked, and commit to it with his whole being.

Although he loved Sanjit, as he had been taught to love all, he was ambivalent as to whether or not he liked him. He knew his former roommate to be neither as ignorant nor ungrateful as he sometimes seemed, even behaved, yet nevertheless he seemed to have not the slightest interest, even curiosity, about the power of His Love, a fact he simply could not understand.

Even the shot of adrenaline from their brief physical confrontation was not enough to shake his thoughts free from Wei's hideous rasp, which he had been present for via facet: *"She can...she already has."*

Did the mad freak have any idea to whom he spoke? The Aggregate had competed against, vanquished and consumed some of the most ambitious and competent beings the planet had ever produced in order to attain His position as majority of the Board. Did this haggard ingrate honestly believe that some mongrel teenage girl from a cave on the edge of nowhere could undo Him? He could have discounted it if not for the fact that it had obviously affected Himself. After all, the freak had already wrought a tremendous amount of damage not even He had predicted. And He was uncharacteristically impatient for the cognitive mapping to be completed, placing Jerro under an uncomfortable amount of pressure.

His sisters and brethren in Mapping knew well the importance of their task and worked as diligently and competently as could be asked, but the girl's consciousness was proving to be unexpectedly complex in spite of her youth and the narrow geographical boundaries of her upbringing, a development which, in light of the madman's taunts, none dared mention for fear of displeasing Him.

He made his way through the invisible back passageways of the temple to the Mapping facility and entered the control room.

"He loves you," he greeted his half-dozen siblings at work on the project.

"He loves you, too," they responded in kind.

On the display screen were images of the girl, naked in a suspension field, translucent alongside scrolling code logs and glowing detail maps of her brain as each electrical impulse and molecular reaction was copied and encoded into a quantum database.

"She can…she already has."

Jerro forced it out of his mind and focused his attention on the work of his peers.

DEEP within her coma state, Sel re-experienced every event, thought, dream and emotion her brain had ever processed, remembered and not; living in every moment of her life perpetually and simultaneously, unable to distinguish between conscious and unconscious, haunted by a sense that none of it was real, but without evidence to prove it or ground her. She simply existed in an infinite loop of dream, nightmare and memory colored by a maddening sense of *deja-vu* and a terrible, will-shattering inevitability.

"Such a fascinating device," Marten had said, examining her guitar.

After their brief introduction at the stage, she'd been taken by repeller sled up to his private apartments. The room display gave the impression that they were suspended above the surface of the Earth, just below the stratosphere. Magnificent weather patterns swept below her feet, above lush green mountains, plains and, in the distance, white-capped waves of ocean. So much water, so much life. She'd seen such images of the planet before as a child and thought they were so beautiful she wished she hadn't. It was almost better not to know it existed. Her ancestral home screamed out to the depths of her species brain across vacuum and generations.

She tore her eyes away from the planet but refused to look at Marten, who stood a meter and a half before her, studying her guitar as if it meant something to him. The air in the room was stale and still, further giving lie to the vista.

"I cannot help but wonder: what is it that compelled you to build such a thing?"

She steeled her eyes into the blue infinity surrounding them and did not speak. She could not bring herself to engage with this abomination, this counterfeit man who had caused Ado's death and robbed her and Sanjit of their sovereignty, who boasted the power of a god and wielded it so callously, who spoke of love as he twisted it into a weapon of oppression.

"I understand that it took quite an extraordinary effort on you part. The design refinements, the materials research," he continued, adding by way of explanation: "I've studied your search records and education and work logs from Lyell. You are an impressive young woman."

The implied threat against her family was inaudible in his voice but unmistakable in his intent. His neutral smile never wavered. He appreciated the Sanctuariat's adherence to charter, but had never cared for their smug isolationism. He produced the hypertab of her father's archives from a fold in his robes.

"Your father so enjoyed to speak and to debate. There are so many wonderful examples indexed in this archive." He paused briefly for a reaction that never came. "I remember him quite well. I never had the opportunity to express My Love for him in person, but I followed his activities as closely as I was able. He was loved by so many, yet he so spurned My love.

"And he caused such terrible problems for those who loved him. I cannot help but question whether he loved them in return, or if his motives were purely self-serving."

He continued to smile patiently through her stoicism.

"In time it became clear that for the good of all in the Colony, he needed to be stopped. As much as I loved him and wanted him to live, he insisted on making his life a poison that blighted all around him. It was a challenge: his followers, misguided as they were, were fiercely loyal and protective of him. But this is My Colony. And I do love it so. And there are many who share that opinion. Love is so powerful. There will always, always be someone willing to do whatever needs to be done in the name of love, you see."

Sel remembered what Ado had said about Avik-Rosot: that no matter who you were there was always someone willing to kill you for a few dollars Colonial. This false god before her was responsible for both of their deaths. She was consumed with the desire to kill him. Her rage blinded her to any need for restraint.

She launched herself toward him and knocked hard into a solid surface. He was a video display, just like the planet and sky.

Suddenly, the image of his face was gigantic in front of her. "Tsk, tsk, tsk," the giant head shook sympathetically back and forth as she reeled backwards and tripped over her feet, landing hard on her tailbone.

Marten contemplated explaining what was about to happen to her, but decided against it. He would let her experience it without preface.

"I love you," the gigantic unhuman face said as the room around her went blank and filled with anesthetic gas.

THE android couldn't bear being at the mercy of the temple's systems to circumnavigate the illusory floors and walls, nor the media feeds to establish context for the cataclysm they relentlessly displayed, often consuming the entirety of the environment to false infinity. But the IIS had unequivocally denied it access to its networks, which were sheltered within defenses which would take all of its capacity months at a hundred percent to hope to penetrate, and could very likely lead to its disassociation. The entities which had monitored Galilaei had reported its manipulations of the complex's surveillance and location logs, and while they couldn't definitively prove what it was up to in the null data they suspected it of conspiring to aid in the Gemini's escape, possibly in collusion with Wei, and it had been *persona non grata* in the temple.

Wherever it restlessly sulked it was bombarded by media feeds depicting horrors on a scale that made the bedlam of Geminus seem humane. Worse, micro contacts in the floors provided it with a steady flow of electro-data, preventing it from powering itself down and force-feeding it the horrorshow data from around the Colony.

Once it saw the girl, it could abide no longer.

It had taken a long time for it to appreciate the significance of what she'd created. The relationships between tonal values lacked adherence, inconsistent and oddly asymmetrical, in places inexplicably simplistic. The Moonspeak was impenetrable for it, as expected; it could not hope to understand the sounds or their connection to each other.

Yet the consistent effect it had on the Sister Doctor, the Gemini and Wei – a highly diverse data sample – was visibly apparent, and for the first time it saw its electronic quantum sentience as an impediment.

Eventually, over lunar days spent processing by rote the data the CARD AIs force-fed it at a constant 33% of capacity, moping in circles through the vacuum around and around the complex in Galilaei in its baggy yellow vac-suit, it began to understand the tonal values themselves as language; idiosyncratic and uncodified, signifying an entirely different strata of concepts beyond the expression of the cognitive and physical, yet language nonetheless. It reached that epiphany over the course of forty-eight expanding circles, nearly halfway to the crater rim, replaying the song over and over, making an effort not to take it in as a bloc of data, but to experience it sequentially and analyze the synthesized effects.

The beauty in the resulting fractals astounded it. It experienced, beyond all else, beauty beyond understanding.

It had recognized the sound of the guitar ringing out early in its time at the temple, crudely discordant and clumsy as it was, and instantly knew it wasn't the same hand playing it. The floor tiles guided it to the stage in time to witness her arrival. The mocking contempt of the synthetic Marten was obvious and repulsive.

And then came the girl: human, but undeniably of the moon, bearing the physical symptoms of fatigue and psychic trauma with disproportionate strength. Then they took her away.

For some cruel reason the temple included it in the communications chain regarding preparations for the Aggregation procedure. She would be sedated and placed in a field-suspension tank. An exact quantum copy of her brain would be made and trans-coded to be compatible with the Marten sentience, and she would become a part of it for eternity. Having seen what this Marten was willing to do to millions in the name of what he called "love" it despaired for what awaited this singular being. Dangerous violent impulses toward the Martenists strained against its Asimov protocols, fatiguing it even further.

It had seen the outside of the temple as they approached and knew there was a three-meter deep titanium support structure between the interior and the glass curtain walls. There was no way to visually gauge the interior dimensions, so it ran a long series of best-guess spatial projections and from them randomly chose a direction to begin walking, testing every step before it was taken and counting each after, relentlessly pursuing a straight path over and around the optical surface manipulations and missing floors. Finally it reached an invisible obstruction to which there was no end. It crept along the vast unseen barrier, which alternated between void, war horrors and wildly distracting patterns. Forty kilometers along, it had to reconfigure itself and magnetize its hands and feet in order to climb laterally along the invisible sheer wall. Ten meters later, it felt a strong magnetic pull within the wall, and dedicated the entirety of its capacity to magnetizing its left arm and leg: a tall vertical panel louvered slightly open by just under three millimeters.

It analyzed the dimensions of the panel and released it, then configured itself vertically along the panel's left edge, sucking as much power as it could from the temple's endless stream of electro-data and dedicating all of it along with everything in its reserve batteries to energizing its left-side magnets. The pull warped its reality, hovering dangerously close to cognitive-quantum disassociation; the field generated rendered it impossible to concentrate on anything but the effort.

It was enough. The louver flipped open. The android reversed polarity and was violently repelled from the louver and propelled by the powerful suck of air out into the brightly sunlight grids of truss and girding.

It didn't have enough power left to magnetize itself, and was so depleted that it lacked even the reflexes and tension to grab onto something. It flailed and tumbled, dented, rattled and slid to a hard but not catastrophic landing at an I-beam joint twenty meters below.

The constant, punishing current of electro-data had ceased and the air pressure dropped. The smooth sunlight passed through the dozen doped cell layers in the curtain wall but there were still bountiful photons from which to charge.

When it emerged from sleep state, it found its optical quantum exchanges realigned and operating with near-vacuum clarity. Now that the media feed had ceased, it archived the atrocities so that it did not forget and stowed them in a deep cache in order to no longer be tormented by them, and dedicated its attention to the architecture surrounding it. When it had completed its schematics, it reconfigured itself to navigate the pipes, ducts, cross-beams and transformers, swinging easily from strut to buttress to girder to truss. It found joy in the exercise of physical protocols not practiced since before its sentience was fully on line. It maintained a pace of activity and rest sufficient to keep its energy and temperature levels balanced through the long lunar days and nights.

Its optical sensors registered the Wasp approaching the temple almost as soon as it cleared the desolate northern horizon, its trajectory direct and unmistakable. Jumpers came and went with frequency, but no other flying vehicle had docked at the temple since it had arrived with Wei and the Sister Doctor.

The sole vehicle mooring was on the twenty-ninth level of the temple, six levels below where it happened to be. Out of curiosity, it climbed down to get a look at the new arrivals, perching unseen in the crook of exposed supports above the airlock housing. It couldn't see who had stepped out of the compartment of the Wasp, but it watched the pair of attendant Martenists watch the screens somewhat at a loss, and summon a supervisor. As the supervisor approached, her gait casual but concerned, the airlock doors blew open explosively.

The shockwave nearly knocked it from its perch. It clamped itself onto the primary support so suddenly that its optics wobbled out of alignment. When its vision cleared, it watched a half-dozen fully armed and kitted Cyclopes emerge from the blasted airlock and stomp over the bloodied and torn bodies of the Martenists. One of them attached another magnetized charge to the inner doors and the android braced itself. There was another blast and the Cyclopes filed through the breach into the inner temple.

The android followed the vibrations of explosions and weapons fire steadily upward as the Cyclopes blasted their way to the upper echelons of the inverted pyramid.

The Martenists eagerly but clumsily took up their defenses, which were frequently drilled but lightly regarded, without understanding why a team of Cyclopes was using violence to infiltrate their Messiah's inner sanctum. The Cyclopes cut through them mercilessly on a determined course to the uppermost level, straight through the temple's containment-oriented optical tricks, guided by internal schematics each had downloaded into their brains.

The first indication Sanjit had of the turmoil was the sight of a group of six Martenists running as fast as they could across the middle distance. Their urgency was unusual, as was the fact that they were all carrying weapons, both particle and projectile. They soon disappeared behind the tight labyrinthine walls that suddenly appeared around him.

He heard intermittent shouts, weapons fire and emergency announcements, a confusion of panicked noise scrambled through the temple's acoustical software. Ricochets of invisible projectiles rang out around him, the optical projections of walls blurred in the wake of particle beams. The severed head and upper torso of a Martenist soared past him. He was frozen in place, unable to see the actual danger through the projections and terribly aware of the sense of violence all around him.

A quartet of Cyclopes burst through a projected wall at a run. Two of them formed a cradle with their arms and hoisted him up, carrying him as the other two ran point, methodically picking off Martenists as they came across them.

"It's okay, Sanjit," the Cyclopes carrying him said in inhuman stereo, "It's me. It's Naeemah."

14. VESSELS OF MEAT AND TECH

long before the collapse of the Schickard particle net, Naeemah had resigned herself to the fact that she was going to die on the moon. So this would be how. All around her, people were screaming, running for shelter from the debris swept up by the howling winds that twisted into monstrous cataracts of garbage, vehicles, demolished architecture and broken bodies as the molecular bonds of the net decomposed in patches and the atmospheric pressure plummeted. She walked a straight path through the nightmare of chaos and destruction, naked and ready to accept whatever ending the universe might put to her, ready for the end. She'd known the net collapse was imminent long before the alert bulletins and wailing alarms, now drowned out by the terrible roar of the gale. It was why she left the house.

The Albetegnius and Purbach nets had already fallen. Her facets within the municipal networks had seen the reports from those doomed cities and recognized the data patterns. Legends of the destructive power of the mad Wei's forbidden directory were ubiquitous; she wasn't surprised that some managerial entity in the Schickard networks had been arrogant, zealous or greedy enough to believe itself capable of withstanding the infection even after empirical evidence of their peers' falling to it, and certainly callous and callow enough not to consider the millions of lives at stake.

Her living unit was rated to withstand vacuum, but her power had already cut out and the way it rattled in the wind led her to doubt that it would provide much protection against the violent weather or debris from neighboring low-rent districts she watched being torn apart through her window. Even if it did, there was little chance that Colonial rescue crews would reach her before she ran out of air.

She had contemplated suicide twice before in her life. The first time was when she was nineteen, and came to see that no matter how creative, resourceful or diligent a coder she was, no matter how hard she worked or what she accomplished, all that awaited her was another chain of assigned tasks. The lives of self-determination and exploration she'd grown up watching in the media and aspiring to would be forever out of reach. In her youthful confidence, she had always imagined herself capable of earning a better life than her parents, as she'd been assured she could by every authority she'd ever encountered. But soon after she'd earned her professional credentials and begun working for the municipal networks in the glass-terraced suburbs of Cairo where she was born, it became clear that the debts she'd incurred simply by being alive were insurmountable. The math didn't require a mind as brilliant as hers to see that the ultimate achievement available to her was a debt-free death at an interface terminal.

Ironically, the only opportunity to break the cycle of what was considered the professional class would have required her to forsake her mind and efforts and list herself as available on the executive flesh servers. Her beauty would have commanded a high price, certainly enough to pay off her outstanding education, health and nutrition debts and tax deferrals. But then she would be owned, which appealed to her not at all.

She was proud of her skills, the years of work and study spent acquiring them, and nothing about the prospect of subjugating herself to the whims and peccadilloes of some executive-class apparatchik appealed to her. It would be an easier life, but enslaved nonetheless.

Emigration had been the alternative. Her parents didn't understand the severity of her dilemma and the decision scandalized them and their social circle; their generation appreciated the comforts of their station and saw the Colony as a repository for the planet's under-classes. But, like Sanjit, Naeemah grew up in a world where the Colony represented the opportunity for self-sufficiency and self-determination.

Her second wave of near-fatal depression overtook her when she realized it didn't.

It was shortly after she'd moved to Schickard. After six months of the technical certification program in Copi, she'd recognized that it was as much of a lie as the rest of the Colony: all a "technician" rating implied was that you knew how to operate a vehicle or program a simple factory robot according to the CA's rigid, moronic and inefficient protocols, and the amount of debt you incurred doing it wiped out any increase of real wages.

The only good thing to come out of it was meeting Sanjit. On the planet their paths never would have crossed, she from a professional suburb of Cairo, he from an industrial district of New York, what her parents certainly would've considered an under-class. She fell in love with his courage, curiosity and sweetness. He was not without faults – often frustratingly passive and cringingly naive – but she found even his faults beautiful, even his heartbreaking need to believe that there was a way back to the planet, that there was some kind of life there other than the ones they'd been born into. In time, being around him just made her sad. His faith and optimism cast her own cynicism into sharp relief and she didn't like it. She didn't have the heart to tell him the certification was just another dead end designed to sink him further into CA debt, and it became more and more difficult for her to be around him. She withdrew herself from the program and wound up in a cramped Labor Rotation dormitory in Schickard, working long hours in food service and again contemplating ending it all.

That time, her salvation came in the form of a cog chip. She'd been skeptical of the technology until then: the commercial models that were available came preprogrammed with fantasy nets designed, updated and monitored by CA mediacoders and administrative applications that essentially turned facets into organic cloud processors.

But when she realized that there were factories in Schickard manufacturing the chips she became intrigued. Schickard's black market was as thriving and accessible as the rest of the Colony's and it wasn't terribly expensive to get a new-model cog straight off the line and program it herself on a giveaway interface during her off-shifts, often foregoing sleep for days at a time. Rather than commit her facets to subscribing to whatever standard content and stock avatars the CA mediacoders were peddling over the fantasy nets, she would write her own; rather than blindly lease out facets to administrative bots, she would create proxies of herself and generate multiple streams of incoming credit as administrators, quietly co-existing with and unnoticed by managerial Uploaded Personae and AIs.

Her first cog divided her consciousness into six facets. She allotted them equally: two to her physical being, two to fantasy nets and two to municipal administrative systems. It didn't take long to realize that the municipal infrastructure was a mess and there were vast amounts of credit to be earned on the fantasy nets. Her credit rating quadrupled almost overnight and she moved out of the dormitories and into the terrace unit.

Sanjit had come to visit her then, but she barely remembered it. What she remembered was the terrible sense of disconnection that became suddenly acute in his presence. Time and circumstance had undoubtedly widened the schism between them, but the cog had rendered the distance impossible to traverse. Even when she could no longer stand to be with him, the sense of intimacy she felt between them had been undiminished; now it was gone. She felt its absence as a physical lack, a crushing tightness between her throat and her chest. It was the first time since getting cogged that she'd seen anyone she cared anything about, and realized with terror that her emotions had been irrevocably and irreconcilably divorced from her physical being. It was impossible even to speak to him meaningfully. She could communicate only insomuch as she could verbally convey and respond to information, but any deeper expression had become impossible.

As if to compensate for this new emptiness she had three more cogs installed over the next several months and modified them to create nine facets each. She assigned several of them to write proxies of herself for the fantasy nets she'd built, so complete as to be nearly autonomous; the lonely subscribers who eagerly paid steep premiums to interface with a live facet had no idea they were dealing with facsimiles.

Meanwhile, the quality of life in Schickard City steadily improved for its seven million residents as she began to surreptitiously exert influence over its municipal networks. There was little she could do regarding industrial production or atmospheric composition, which were operated by a cartel of massive integrated proprietary AI entities. But she made substantial improvements to maintenance, food distribution, transportation, energy grids, garbage collection and law enforcement, using the obscene profits generated by her jerk-off nets to finance a supplemental line of credit through the neglected Moonborn districts, perpetuating the small but thriving microeconomies that kept the peace in the Colonial city. The CA AIs, perfectly pleased to accept accolades for the stability among their peers, didn't look too closely into it. Nor could they have, since she quickly assumed control of their only means of doing so.

The men, women and uploads of the Schickard Municipal Constabulary, all of whom were cogged and networked with each other, were among the first and most frequent subscribers to her nets, before she'd even completed her proxies and was operating them through her second wave of twenty-seven facets. Working from both the municipal systems and the internal firmware, she was able to assume a high degree of control of the network and, she discovered, with some effort, exert a significant degree of control over the actions of individual constables.

The administrators were mostly asleep at the wheel, proxies of bigger paramilitary networks mainly concerned with safeguarding their own weaponry and surveillance of (often imaginary) threat matrices. To control the ranks, she found it fairly simple to channel their aggressive violent tendencies into aggressive sexual tendencies directed at each other's augmented physiques.

But she resolved not to let her own body go to waste. After all, what would have been the point of keeping it? She would wring from it every last sensation, exacting her toll from the Colony in hedonism tendered by pound of flesh.

When Sanjit's truck crossed the Schickard net, his ID number was recognized by her proxies in Transportation and transmitted to her core facets within seconds. She had tried everything to steer him astray until she had finished her afternoon routine, redirecting bus routes around him, placing streets under construction and switching tram directions. Still, he had managed to find his way to her before she could disengage her body, its cognizance by then only two facets deep, from its ecstasy.

As disengaged from her inner reality as her body had become, she had never stopped loving him. She couldn't stop watching every step of his quest through the Schickard streets, hopping off trams as soon as he realized they'd branched the wrong way and backtracking, hiking steep inclines when she took escalators and belts out of service, muddling through the gravity swells of the heavy-substrate streets she led him to, giddy that he managed to outguess her proxies at every turn and still find his way to her after having been there only once, no matter how difficult she made it for him.

She had never wanted to hurt him.

Watching him through her own eyes and those of her current MuniCon lovers, she could see from his face that for him, the connection she'd lost so long ago had only just then been severed. At first, tending to his injuries through the MuniCons, she'd been heartbroken. His presence to her body, desensitized as it was, wrenched the profound spiritual regret she carried within her always from its depths. It enveloped her. For a terrifying instant she lost control of the MuniCons and she was afraid he'd been killed or maimed.

After it was clear that he was alive and intact her pre-emptive grief subsided. But she couldn't be angry with him. She knew well what life in the Colony did to a person's sense of time: her facets exacerbated the phenomenon by orders of magnitude. She had cracked the only truly beautiful psyche she'd ever encountered in the CA's world and there was nothing she could do about it.

The net collapse was the catastrophe she hadn't realized she'd been waiting for. She let the unstoppable chaos, death and destruction – ordered as data – overtake her being as she stepped out of the door and walked slowly toward the district hub down the middle of the cracked subdivision streets as the sky bled open.

She didn't see what killed her; it hit her from behind, cracking her back and flipping her backwards. There was a flash of dust clouds and debris below a higher vista of blistering gas bursting into vacuum against a cold field of distant stars. Then nothing.

But nothing changed. She continued to exist, blind among the data streams of horror until suddenly finding herself intact in the Icarus-Daedelus defense database. Twenty-one of her twenty-seven facets, and multiple proxies, had made it through the CA filters and been archived among the statistics of the disaster. Since her cog programming had been written in her own code, her consciousness had been immune from the disassociation that wiped out every other entity in the Schickard network, and she'd been inadvertently backed up among the dumb statistical databases that had been extracted from Schickard and was being stored deep within the Icarus-Daedelus forensic servers.

None of the I-D safety protocols recognized a sentience like hers, so ignored she found it remarkably simple to negotiate the archive databases and find a backdoor into the operations hubs. It was there that a proxy flagged Sanjit's identification code in the directory pertaining to the search for the song, dating from the first time the broadcast was identified by his truck radio up to his current internment by the IIS.

All she could ascertain about the song was that it was believed to be associated in some capacity with the resurgence of anti-Colonial Moonborn movements. Her gentle, passive Sanjit was certainly not part of some revolutionary terrorist underground. But he was incarcerated by the IIS, which was disliked and feared by every sector of CA society – including the I-D systems – for its strange, subtle, and often damaging subjugations.

It would have taken her too long to infiltrate the IIS's networks, so she decided to physically extract him. In less than an hour she had overloaded the power transformers powering the Cyclopes network's servers, and in the seconds it took to bring the backup online she'd already displaced the controlling AIs with her own code as the system rebooted, putting her instantly in control of five hundred and fifty-six cyborg bodies across the moon. She saw through their networked eye lenses and could operate them with superhuman reflexes, but there was no sense of inhabiting them. They were merely remotely operated biomechanical vehicles, alive but insentient.

The rest of the Icarus-Daedelus systems didn't have any idea she had taken over their shock troops until she blasted open the Martenists' airlock when they denied her access to the temple. The first thing they did was disengage and recall the Wasp, leaving her escape plan without a ready vehicle.

She'd loaded each of the Cyclopes' brains with the temple's original construction blueprints: she knew exactly which floors and walls were real and which were projections, depriving the Martenists of the tactical advantage around which their defenses were designed.

The actual topography of the uppermost level presented a challenge. Sanjit was in the center of an illusory maze, but was in fact on an isthmus of steel near the center of a wide-open expanse ringed with catwalks and cabins, which offered ample opportunity for snipers' nests. She divided her half-dozen bodies by pairs and began her push toward Sanjit.

By the time four of her reached him, she had killed enough Martenists to leave an open path to the down-bound repeller moorings.

"I can't go without Sel." Sanjit said, jostling in her arms and clutching her shoulders as best he could. He had no choice but to take at face value the fact that his tragic ex-girlfriend, the love of his life, seemed to be in control of these inhuman warriors. It could all just as easily have been some insidious simulation, but either way there was little sense in behaving as if it wasn't really happening. "I owe her my life. I'm not leaving without her. We have to find her."

The group of them tacked off onto a breezeway that led up to an easily defensible mezzanine encircling a support column overlooking the floor. To Sanjit, it looked like the interior of yet another narrow metal box.

Naeemah didn't know who this Sel person was, but there was no mistaking her importance to Sanjit; the name had gravity in his voice and muscles, he became heavier in the Cyclopes' arms the instant it left his lips. She could sense the weight of her in his soul across kilometers and through Kevlar-infused flesh.

The two Cyclopes carrying him set him down on his feet. "I should have access to the temple interfaces within the next few minutes," all four of her said in quadraphonic unison.

"Naeemah," he said into the thoracic speaker of one of them, "where are you?"

After a long pause the inhuman voice issued forth: "I'm here. And other places. I'm in the Cyclopes AI at Icarus-Daedelus. My body died in Schick City. Flying debris through my spine. I didn't feel anything."

His eyes rose from the speaker grill up to the single round red lens in the hulking cyborg's overgrown-baby face. His eyes filled with tears, and in them she found herself confronting her own death for the first time. For the first time she realized that her life was over. This was something different. The revelation twisted her very being into a terrible knot. It was white pain, burning across all spectra of sensation without a body to absorb its frequencies. The Cyclopes stood still, impassive and blank, betraying no trace of emotion.

Elsewhere in the temple, two Cyclopes cleared the bodies of the Martenists they'd recently slaughtered away from the consoles and field banks of the temple's operations hub and initiated overriding interface protocols. Moments later, the illusory metal walls Sanjit had seen penning him in disappeared and for the first time he looked out over the actual structure of the temple's widest level high above the Imbrium plains.

"How do you spell her name?" Naeemah asked through the Cyclopes.

Sanjit thought back to his spelling lessons in Ado's podvan. The memory triggered the associative image of Ado, cut in half and dying on the floor of the Blue Cleave. He fought the panic and focused on the letters. "S-e-l."

"There's nothing with her name in the temple system. But you're not listed anywhere either."

"Jerro. Jerro might know where she is," he thought back to their room listing in Crisi: "J-e-r-r-o."

"Found him. He's in a secure area next level down. That way. We'll move faster if I carry you."

Sanjit held out his arms so two of the Cyclopes could again lift him up.

ON THE other side of the temple, Wei found himself sitting on a narrow band of floor behind an arched flying buttress when the illusory walls disappeared. He had been lost in a fugue state rent by famine and cognitive memory stimulation. Ever since his brief encounter with Marten, he had been relentlessly bombarded by trigger signal after trigger signal in a campaign to manipulate his brain. He fought with all his will to hold onto his memories of Mia as a child, ordeals though some were, rather than allow them to be overwritten by third-party recordings of a zombie existence.

Sound opened around him and he surveyed the vast open floor through spectral focus. It was bright with near-perihelion sunlight through heavily filtered glass, rendering shadows soft. There were laser burns and projectile scars on the glass and steel structures. He counted a dozen and a half Martenist corpses. In the middle distance, he saw the Cyclopes running with Sanjit toward the northern repeller moorings. He saw the figure of the Sister Doctor two thirds of the way across the space, on her knees.

High above the floor, drenched in slow light among the power transformers' girding, he saw two Martenists on a repeller sled descending from an assembly of reflective-glass boxes: Marten's penthouse sanctum.

His tormented mind became suddenly whole and consumed with a single thought: revenge. Yet he tried to will himself to stop as his aching and wasted body moved with unearthly strength steadily toward the repeller mooring the Martenists had left unattended. He did not want to remove the particle-disrupter from a trifurcated Martenist corpse and strap it onto himself, yet he accomplished the task deftly, checking its frequency and testing it by disintegrating what was left of the corpse's head.

He scanned his panoramic vision for signs of the Martenists who'd descended on the repeller but saw none. The sled's mooring latch had been left unlocked. He stepped onto it and engaged the hypermagnets, floated gently up toward the opposite mooring. The air was cool and dry against his paperlike skin. He widened the hyperfield to its maximum and his trajectory sharpened, briefly straining his muscles and speeding toward the mooring. He slowed just soon enough to avoid damaging the dock, the sled and himself.

The sanctum's mooring was at the edge of a lush veranda hidden from view of the temple floor below. Leaves rustled in the breeze. He crossed it warily but without particular caution and stepped into the habitat.

It was expensively outfitted, austere but comfortable. He passed through a succession of empty rooms before catching sight of Marten's reflection in the eastern wall of the second glass box. He calculated the angles of reflection and backtracked to a plate-glass stairway invisible from any angle but straight on.

Somewhere inside him he felt vertigo as he silently ascended. Through the glass below him, he saw that the floors of the temple were made up of interlocking octagons, open in random pattern, a quasi-fractal spiral stretching hundreds of meters below him.

Marten stood directly opposite the staircase with his back to it, staring through the glass overlooking the temple. He hadn't disengaged the optical displays like this in decades, and experienced a brief retrograde thrill at seeing His architecture as if anew.

But it had not been His choice to do so. The entity controlling the Cyclopes had over-ridden His protocols through the manual interfaces, cutting Him off not only from His Temple, but from His Colony as well. He had lost control of both. It was a failure on a scale unprecedented in His lifetime. As much as He had loved them all, it hadn't been enough to stave off chaos or stem entropy.

He had watched Wei along every step of his grim march.

"The Gun, please," he'd said to his two attendants as Wei rode up on the sled.

One of the retrieved the ancient but immaculately maintained .357 Magnum from a sleekly lacquered chest of drawers and handed it to him.

The Aggregation of the Sanctuary girl had yet to begin when He was cut off from the network. Her cognitive map had yet to be fully trans-coded and she was still in the field-suspension tank. At least Jerro was nearby. He had more or less made up his mind about the boy, and if proximity was to be the deciding factor so be it.

"As soon as the Aggregation is complete, prepare for Succession. Put Jerro in tank two. It shall be Jerro. Go now. Both of you. Take separate paths to split the Cyclopes. You don't have much time."

The attendants, anxious and excited in thrall to history, nodded and obeyed.

Not long after they'd gone, Wei's reflection appeared in the glass as he cleared the top of the staircase almost exactly as He'd expected. At least He was still in control of one of His creations. All of His doubts about Wei disappeared, and He turned to look upon his favorite son with all of His love.

"Hegemony will be maintained," He said, put the barrel of the gun against the roof of his mouth, and pulled the trigger before Wei had even leveled the disrupter at him.

The image of his creator's brain splattered across the glass threw a final switch deep in Wei's thalamus, and everything he knew himself to be fell away from him.

He had not been a grand experiment, manipulated since before birth. His genius mind had not been the site of a battle for influence by powerful forces. He was nothing more than a madman, a dangerously volatile bipolar nihilist who had concocted a rich delusional mythology to explain the confusion and pain of a life unlived and unexamined, a damaged psyche finally broken by anger and weakness, inhabiting a wrecked body standing in a glass box atop the moon.

ONE of the messengers dispatched by Marten reached the Aggregation chamber at the same time as Sanjit and Naeemah's Cyclopes. One of them shot a poison dart into the young woman's neck from a wrist mount. She seized and stumbled. The other caught her by the hair and held her paralyzed face up to the door scanner then tossed her away like a ragdoll as it whooshed open. Sanjit was taken aback by the violence of it, but deep within Icarus-Daedelus, Naeemah's sentience seethed with rage and regret and the violence came easily.

The other messenger was already in the chamber and had delivered the message that He had asked for the Gun and approved Jerro's Succession.

Jerro stood naked within the field-suspension tank, waiting for the gas that would coax him from consciousness as his brain was readied for the Holy Aggregate, ecstatic in the prime of his youth. But the process did not begin. He waited for what might have been minutes, then for longer than he could bear. Finally, he heard the hatch release. He pushed it open and stepped out and looked down into the control hub. The operators lay dead in heaps on the floor and Cyclopes stood at the interfaces. He was surprised and confused to see his former roommate with them.

"How do we get her out of there?" Sanjit demanded.

Each Cyclops aimed a dart launcher at his neck while its other hand held steady over a field interface. On the monitors, Jerro saw that the trans-coding process was continuing. They didn't know how to stop it. Succession might be delayed, but if he played his cards right the Aggregation could yet be completed as intended.

"I'm afraid I don't know," he gestured around the room, "You seem to have killed all of the people who might."

Naeemah refused to regret killing the Martenists.

"If she didn't, they would've disintegrated Sel," Sanjit said, and she loved him even more.

"If who didn't? What 'she?'" he couldn't keep a trace of desperate fear from the edges of his voice. *She can...she already has.* Wei's mad cackle echoed through his mind tauntingly. What had he meant?

The Cyclopes demanded: "What are you doing to her? How do we stop it?"

He regained his composure. "She is being Aggregated. A map of her cognitive sentience is being made, a copy of her soul perfect to the earliest dream, to be integrated into the fabric of His love."

"He's dead. He blew his own brains out." Naeemah had watched it happen over the video feed.

"Yes I know," Jerro nodded reverently, then smiled: "But His Love is eternal."

THE android had re-entered the interior of the temple and, finding that the control systems had been compromised, initiated an interface with them. It saw the Sister Doctor, alive and still kneeling at the end of a line of six slaughtered Martenists. It saw Wei, staring vacantly through the splatter of Marten's brain across the glass high above. It saw the Aggregation Chamber, where Jerro stalled for time as the trans-coding neared completion. It listened in.

"I have a facet in the temple systems," the naked acolyte pleaded, "if you allow me to, perhaps I can help you understand the Aggregation protocols. You'll find my facet permission codes in the main directory, primary server."

Naeemah wordlessly agreed through the impassive Cyclopes, and a quantum-data facet of Jerro's consciousness entered the network. The android monitored each of them but was careful not to be noticed by either. Familiar as it was with cognitive field-suspension systems, it found its way into the temple's tank with ease. Once there, it realized that it was impossible to re-integrate Sel while the mapping and trans-coding was in progress, and that wherever Jerro was leading the Cyclopes' entity, it was nowhere near the aggregation utilities.

A sudden ferocious wind swept through the complex as magnetic louvers opened in the outer walls at points around the temple and vented air.

"What did you do?!" the Cyclopes demanded as the barometric pressure in the temple plummeted.

"I did nothing. That's the Doomsday protocol. If more than fifteen minutes passes between His bodily death and the initiation of Succession protocols the temple is vented of air. The only way to stop it is to transfer the Aggregate into a ready brain. A brain like mine." He monitored the trans-coding anxiously: it was ninety-eight percent complete. "Let me get back into the tank. The process will begin automatically once the trans-coding is complete and the vents will seal as soon as it begins. Tell me: how do you propose to re-integrate her without adequate oxygen?"

Sanjit watched the tense conversation between Jerro and the Cyclopes, barely able to contain his rage, feeling impotent, helpless. He stared at Sel's translucent image on the monitors. Suddenly, the progress bar monitoring the trans-coding froze and disappeared.

Jerro's face dropped abruptly into awestruck horror as his facet pored through the error logs and learned that the aggregation had failed. The map of the girl was not only incomplete, it had been deleted and the reintegration process had already begun.

Naeemah suspected that there was another entity assisting her with the enormous cryptography tasks, but the android covered its tracks well, unsure of the Cyclopes' entity's motives and concerned only with keeping Sel and her consciousness intact and unmolested.

It felt a surge of pride in accomplishment, but it was a short-lived triumph. Moments later its Asimov protocols began to seize its cognitive function. It scanned its awareness and quickly discovered the reason: the Sister Doctor was trapped in a rapidly depressurizing environment only seventy meters away from it. She would be unable to reach safety through the punishing gale unassisted, and there were emergency vac-suits directly between it and her. Its animosity toward her was unabated, and it resented the compulsory altruism when it would have preferred devoting its full attention to overseeing Sel's reintegration process. But it had no choice.

There were three vac-suits left in the emergency locker, which had already been opened by Martenist survivors fleeing the temple. It hoisted two of them over its shoulder, one for the Sister Doctor and one for Wei (although Marten's sanctum was equipped with backup oxygen, it would only last for a couple of hours and rescue would be required eventually; unlike the Sister Doctor, it saw inherent worth in Wei's survival by virtue of his extraordinary mental capacity.)

Coni stayed as low to the ground as she could, fighting against the gale that pushed her ever closer to the unprotected edge of the slick floor, clutching at it ineffectually with her fingertips and the balls of her bare toes, praying to the Holy Mother for faith that yet another mercy would be visited upon her. If she was simply to spread her arms and let the wind take her, her habit become a sail, hurtling her over the edge to her death, then why had she been granted such extraordinary mercies again and again?

When the Cyclopes first invaded, she had, like Sanjit, found herself inside a projection of a narrow metal box. She'd stayed in place, listening as the aural control broke down and sounds of fighting and confusion came from all directions.

She heard footsteps behind her and spun to see a Martenist carrying a projectile weapon appear through the far box wall at a run, dodging past her and casting barely a glance as he did, disappearing through the opposite wall. Perhaps a minute later, another armed Martenist ran past her in the same direction. Moments after the second Martenist disappeared behind the wall, she heard the crackle of a plasma weapon and felt a heavy thud in the floor beneath her feet. Half a minute later, a third Martenist, with a larger, heavier weapon, jogged doggedly along the same path. As soon as he passed through the opposite wall she heard a wet snap and felt another thud. Fast on the tail of that one, another Martenist burst through the wall behind her firing an automatic projectile weapon wildly into the opposite wall. Coni hit the deck in time to see two Cyclopes charge through the wall and turn the Martenist to ash with a plasma weapon.

She waited for death, but the Cyclopes passed her by.

She rose to one knee and rolled her rosary between her fingers, praying gratitude to the Holy Mother. She was still kneeling in prayer when the walls of the box disappeared and she first saw the expansive temple floor as it really was. Part of her questioned whether prayer was just an excuse for indecision: what had happened to her that she couldn't even decide which way to walk without the illuminated tiles to guide her even now that she could see her own path? But such was a question of a woman not guided by her faith, and that was no longer she. Yet she was still on her knees pondering the issue when the louvers high above opened and she was flipped backwards by the ferocious and sudden wind as the temple vented atmosphere, sent skidding and thrashing along her current course to the precipice.

The android found itself needing to move faster and faster to avoid an Asimov shutdown as the wind pushed the Sister Doctor closer and close to the edge. Realizing that lack of air wasn't the current most pressing problem, it stowed the vac suits in a corner of the stairwell out of the worst of the wind and magnetized the soles of its feet as it stepped out of the stairwell and onto the temple floor, steeling itself against the punishing wind and marching as fast as it could on a diagonal intercept course with the Sister Doctor, feeling the Asimov shutdown creep closer with every meter the Sister Doctor slid toward the edge.

She saw it approaching out of the corner of her eye and scrambled to crabwalk toward it. It cursed her for it: changing her course required a recalculation of its own, bringing it seconds closer to shutdown and requiring it to divert its full capacity simply into moving against the wind as fast as possible, repositioning its leg joints to move in wide, low-set lateral swings, alternately magnetizing the base foot every tenth of a second pivoting at ankle and waist. It reached her just as her ankle slid past the drop, planting its foot to catch the crook of her arm. She clung to it and pulled her feet tight. It felt solid and powerful, magnetically clamped to the temple floor.

The android was spent. It stood statue-still, absorbing the bright perihelion sunlight, the buffeting winds cooling it efficiently. The Sister Doctor had pulled herself from the edge and clung to its leg. When it was refreshed enough to make the return trip carrying her, it reconfigured its shoulders, bent its arms and clamped its hands to its hips in order to form a harness for her legs so she could ride on its back. She didn't seem to understand what to do. It still refused to speak to her but didn't want to face its Asimov protocols again as the air became thinner, so it displayed a graphic illustrating the position on its torso.

Too slowly, she began to pull herself up. Further annoyed, it displayed a plummeting barometer and countdown clock next to the graphic. She got the picture and scrambled into position, clinging to it all the way back to the stairwell, where it helped her into a waiting vac suit.

She did not thank it. If it truly were a vessel of God's will, it would require no thanks. "The girl. Is she alive?"

It did not answer her, but interfaced with the temple to display a track of illuminated tiles leading to the Succession Chamber. Then it stepped out of the stairwell and back into the bright sunlight and powerful wind of the uppermost level, recharging and zooming its eye lenses to focus on Marten's sanctum in the middle distance high above, where Wei still stood at the window gazing through the congealing gore, the outer glass streaked with rivulets of condensation buffeted by the wind.

It would wait until the temple fully depressurized to retrieve him.

He would have more than enough air to sustain him in the habitat, although it was concerned about his mental state.

STARING into the Sanctum's glass wall, Wei's mind was blank. He no longer possessed spectral focus. He could see no further than the patterns of blood and light through the streams of condensation fanning hypnotically from lower right to upper left. When he looked down he saw the patterns of light they made across the crumpled false Messiah, a broken smiling doll splayed on the floor beside him, still clutching the immaculate heavy chrome pistol in his manicured hand, barrel wedged against the back of his perfect upper teeth, clear eyes wide open.

He cursed himself; his paranoia, obstinacy and manic obsessions had destroyed lives, including Mia's. He had felt love for nothing in the universe but her, yet her welfare did nothing to check his stubbornness and delusional intransigence.

Even more maddening was the fact that he could not follow his own logic. Over the course of his life, he had become used to sudden shifts in factual knowledge as his cognitive switches were triggered, but this was different: a wholesale rewriting of self-perspective.

He watched transfixed as the fans of outer condensation slowed and congealed into frost and inner condensation formed, steaming the glass and bathing the interior in a greenish half-light. Marten's blood and liquefied gray began to smear down toward the floor, where Marten still lay, holding a big gun.

When the android eventually recalled the repeller sled and ascended, it found the once-verdant veranda demolished, trellis clogged with vegetable matter and wrecked hydroponics. Inside the Sanctum, it found Wei standing in the middle of Marten's chamber holding the gun.

He didn't have any reason to know anything about antique projectile weaponry, but he knew that there was a bullet in the chamber and all he had to do to fire it was pull the trigger. Every fiber of being wanted nothing more than to point it at his head and do it, to destroy the brain that had caused so much misery for himself and everyone he knew. Yet still he didn't understand *why* he felt so compelled, and the inability to explain it to himself made him think that the urge was, though new, simply the effect of yet another trigger being thrown. The thought that he was *supposed to* shoot himself in the head, that the thought could be of a will other than his own, was enough to make him refuse.

"Demetrius Wei."

He had watched the android ascend the stairs and approach, but his reverie had not broken until he heard what had been his name spoken.

"I am no longer that man."

The android silently puzzled over what he meant by that. There was no visible means in the room by which the Aggregate could have been transferred into him. It scanned to see if the biodrone it had implanted in his brain was still active and found that it was. There was evidence of a massive and recent realignment akin to a psychotic break. It stood directly in front of him and held a finger up in front of his nose so that his eyes focused on it, then moved the finger back and forth in a line. In order to follow it, he had to turn his head. He could not move his eyes.

His brain was, in fact, abnormal, regardless of why. He was immediately incapable of accessing it, but he was still capable of spectral focus.

The android lowered its finger and said: "You are still Demetrius Wei. I placed a bio-drone in you shortly after you arrived at Galilaei. There is no physiognomic state change anywhere but your cognizance. You are mentally incapacitated. I have insufficient data to hypothesize as to whether the change is temporary or permanent and recommend caution."

"The Marten aggregate..."

"Whereabouts and condition unknown. It intended to initiate a Succession protocol shortly after the temple was invaded by a cyber-organic combat team. Their intentions are unknown but they have taken measures to excise the Marten aggregate from the temple's operations, stop the aggregation process and preserve the physical and mental integrity of the young Moonborn female who created the song we have been tasked to study, and that of her Earth male companion. They are sealed in the aggregation facility with the sole Martenist remaining in the temple. All others not killed in the raid were evacuated. The Sister Doctor is en route to join them. There is a vac-suit for you downstairs and I can show you the way to them if you want to join them."

Wei took in the android's words and accepted its inhuman

analysis, clear thinking and impartial statement and demonstration of fact, finding hope in that he was able to. The gun felt heavy in his hand. He tossed it onto the messiah's corpse.

"So be it."

THE Sister Doctor arrived at the sealed aggregation chamber door, unsurprised to find the opening mechanism unresponsive. She banged on it soundlessly.

Inside the chamber, the knock put a temporary stop to naked Jerro's litany of arguments in favor of allowing him to Succeed.

Naeemah consulted the video from the door console and brought it up on the monitors. "Do you know her?"

Sanjit studied the face through the vac-suit visor. "It's the nun. She was here when we got here. She's not a Martenist. I think she was a prisoner like us."

Jerro piped up in knee-jerk politesse-drenched defensiveness: "Not prisoners! Guests of –"

"Shut the fuck up." Sanjit had wanted to say that to Jerro since meeting him. It was as satisfying and effective as he could have hoped. "I can't even figure out why she hasn't fucking killed you yet."

"His cog is wetwared to the Marten aggregate," the Cyclopes said coldly, "if it becomes active again I'll know it through his facet. But the Martenist cog protocols are pretty standard, not like mine, so if his brain dies his facets go with him and I lose my best means of implementing early defense."

"Fuck," Sanjit's disappointment was genuine.

Jerro felt suddenly conflicted. His life was indeed precious to him, gift of His Love that it was, and as long as he was alive he might yet Succeed the Holy Aggregate. But now it seemed that his precious life was to be the means by which the Aggregate was to be kept out of the world. After fast and panicked contemplation, he decided that as long as he and his brethren lived, there would always be a ready and willing vessel for His return. He must stay relevant until He returns to human form, and it was his duty as a son to afford every opportunity to be His vessel. Hegemony must be maintained.

Sanjit's face appeared in the door console monitor field.

"Hi, Sister," he said. "Look, we only have enough air in here to last us another three hours. Since you have an M-pack on that vac-suit we're not gonna let you in. Any more of those out there?"

"I don't know…"

In the background, she heard the Cyclopes say: "Tell her there are plenty. Follow the red tiles to the emergency lockers, fifty-two meters there and back."

"Hear that?"

She nodded. "The girl, is she with you? What do the Cyclopes want with her?"

His instincts were suspicious of her interest in Sel, but the concern in her voice was genuine.

"They're not really Cyclopes. I mean, they are, but it's my friend who's controlling them."

"What about the girl? What did Marten do to her?"

"They tried to aggregate her. My friend stopped them but she's still in field suspension."

"Are you or your friend familiar with cognitive field-suspension protocols? Because I am. I can walk you through them."

Sanjit glanced over his shoulder again and his image in the monitor was replaced with the girl's cognitive field-trajectory array. She was relieved to see that everything was intact: there would likely be effects from the shock of realignment, but her consciousness was still fundamentally undamaged.

Seeing the girl, there in front of Marten's megalithic stage, terrified but unbroken and unflinching, all of the pain she'd experienced watching the fall of Geminus redoubled in her soul, even though she hadn't been directly complicit in her pursuit or capture. This girl was a vessel of Holy Grace, and Coni had seen enough of this mad false messiah to fear how he might cripple her.

"She's fine," Coni said, "but the separation is deep and asymmetrical so you have to be careful to keep the algorithms asymmetrical. And you're going to have to oxygenate the chamber by a hundred and twenty percent so however much air you have left, subtract that. There's an android in the temple. Make sure it receives the data and it will make sure you have enough vac-suits in time."

Naeemah hypothesized that the android the Sister Doctor referred to was the anonymous entity that had helped her crack the aggregation cycle, and transmitted the data into the temple systems.

The packet reached the android as it operated the repeller sled on its descent from the sanctum with Wei. Yet again, it felt the pull of its Asimov protocols, exacerbated by its own moral imperative to save the girl. It could only operate the sled at a velocity that wouldn't kill its frail passenger, even through vacuum, forcing it choke back the polarity to a maddeningly slow pace while every electron volt in its cognizance pressed it to move as fast as it possible could.

The instant they moored, it told Wei: "Follow the tiles," and launched off at a bounding run, propelling itself by alternating polarities from foot to foot with each reaching stride, vaulting from platform to catwalk to the mezzanine below and sprinting into the corridors.

SEL awoke from the entirety of her life, experienced simultaneously a billion times over, slumped in the molded ceramic supports of the field-suspension tank. She didn't know exactly where she was, but she remembered everything that had happened up to the moment she was brought into the aggregation chamber and anesthetized, leaving her to question whether the tank interior was a manifestation of the Marten aggregate rather than an awakening into the world as she'd left it.

The tank hatch opened and her ears clogged painfully as the air pressure dropped. Sanjit, wearing a vac-suit, entered carrying another.

"The Sister Doctor says you'll be okay," he said, his voice tinny through the auxiliary speaker, "The temple's been depressurized. Hurry into the suit and I'll catch you up on what I know."

She accepted her shortness of breath as reality, regardless of the context of her existence, and scrambled into the vac-suit, feeling an echo of her deep terror of void in the seconds before the helmet radio came online.

Sanjit's explanation was incomplete but accurate, so she was prepared for what she saw when she stepped out of the chamber.

It was difficult for her to accept the Cyclopes as benign, but she found it easier to trust Sanjit than she had before. As much as she loathed Jerro she accepted Naeemah's logic for keeping him alive, as she accepted the good intentions and competence of the android and the Sister Doctor.

"Marten said they had spies among the Sanctuariat," she said, "Is there any mention of Lyell Sanctuary?"

The Sanctuaries were well equipped to withstand the kinds of cataclysm that had gripped the Colony, but Marten's mention of her home filled her with anxiety for her mother, Jick, Clarke and everyone else, especially as their memories were so close after her time in the tank.

Naeemah scanned the directories but knew she'd find nothing. "The IIS databases left the servers when the Marten aggregate did," she said through the Cyclopes, displaying the interface so Sel could see it for herself, "There was a massive data dump triggered by the same mechanism that depressurized the temple. Apparently the com applications went too. All that's left in the temple servers are the infrastructure protocols. It's probably backed up at Icarus-Daedelus, but if I go after it I'll lose the Cyclopes."

Sel accepted survival as first priority, as she'd been raised to, and agreed that the Cyclopes were too potentially valuable to forfeit. Exhausted and famished, she hungrily sucked nutrition paste through the straw in her helmet valve and studied the data arrays on the monitors. She knew there were Sanctuaries along the Imbrium coasts but had never gone on Migration and never learned their coordinates. To risk radio contact would be to risk drawing the CA to both them and the Sanctuary.

She checked the phase chart. The Talas Luna was to have just begun in O-City, the only surface municipality on the moon with a particle-net not maintained by CA AIs. "Is the Orientale net still up?"

"As of the com system going down, yes." Naeemah said. "There were already nearly a thousand vehicles circling the ring waiting for tunnel access."

"How far is it from here?"

Naeemah displayed an atlas of the quadrant in one of the monitor fields.

Sel contemplated the distance: "Are there any vehicles left in the temple?"

"Nothing self-propelled. But there's a repeller gondola in the western cargo lock that could accommodate us and our supplies with a few modifications."

"O-City then," Sel said, directing it toward Sanjit and gratified that he accepted the destination unhesitatingly.

"O-City," the Cyclopes intoned. Naeemah sent two of her three other Cyclopes to gather vac-rations and the third to prepare the gondola for the journey.

Sel grinned a quick inner grin at the cognitive dissonance she felt in being grateful for the company of Cyclopes.

It would be an arduous trek, and even if there were sufficient vac rations to sustain them all the way to the Orientale, they would have to get through the vehicles circling the city trying to get in through the tunnels, which by then would be desperate. Still, they might make it, especially if… "I had a crystal amulet with me when I was taken," she demanded of Jerro, "Is it still here?"

"All of your belongings have been prepared for the reliquary," he was offended that she might have thought otherwise. "They are at the archive on the tenth level."

It dawned on Jerro that he was about to be forced on a suicide march into the vacuum: "That's madness. If we wait here in the temple, I'm sure a rescue team from Icarus-Daedelus will arrive. I'm sure they will honor the Sanctuariat charter and return you to your home. They are required to! They will return the Sister Doctor and myself to our planet. It's the only humane choice."

The others stared at him wordlessly.

The Cyclopes leveled weapons at him. "With us, asshole."

"This is wrong! We were attacked by a rogue Cyclopes contingent," he pleaded with the Sister Doctor, "we have done nothing wrong!"

On her own, Coni might have speculated about her chances of return to the planet with the CA. But once she heard it as a promise in Jerro's voice, she could not but see it as a lie.

"If they'll have me I'll follow," she said.

"You're not Sanctuariat," Sel told her kindly but firmly, "you can follow us but you're on your own. You carry your rations. We will not wait."

"Mercy and Grace are Hers," she quoted catechism, "as am I."

"And you?" she asked the android.

It had never before been asked to make its own decision regarding its course of action. Taken aback, it stood silently, awaiting more data.

"There's another person in the temple," Naeemah said, following Wei's progress through the corridors from the upper level. Via the temple network, the android sent a packet to her identifying him as Demetrius Wei.

Deep in the besieged Cyclopes servers in Icarus-Daedelus, she shuddered. This was the legendary mad mathematician who was said to have coded the quanta that led to the destruction of the Colony.

She didn't hold him accountable for her own death (as much as she regretted it, it had been her decision); and the vain, insatiable drive for influence and power among the CA's managing entities bore tremendous blame, but the core root of the destruction could be traced to this man.

"He's insane," Coni stated flatly, "leave him."

"He is an extra-human genius," the android said, unmistakably refuting the Sister Doctor while pointedly not addressing her. "He is one of the few sentient entities in existence who might be capable of re-establishing net-generation protocols on a meaningful scale," it searched deep for more convincing syntax: "He may prove capable of rendering this destruction demolition. Of rebuilding."

"Ha!" Jerro hissed, "That lunatic destroyed the Colony! He has massacred millions of innocents!"

"He authored the quanta," Naeemah argued through the Cyclopes, "but it was a CA AI that gave him the means to do it, and it was CA entities that insisted on opening it again and again and again, even after seeing what it did. Those entities sacrificed millions of lives in their pursuit of credit and power. Including mine."

For the sake of argument, she left out the suicidal aspect of her bodily demise.

The thought of such widespread suffering was horribly upsetting to Sel, but she had not seen any of the images coming in from around the Colony and could easily see it in abstract terms: the Sanctuariat ethos toward the Colony in total and the surface cities specifically held that anyone living in an environment where they weren't in control of atmosphere-generation must acknowledge and accept that they could die at any time through no fault of their own.

Sanjit weighed the arguments, trying to read Sel's expression through the glare on her visor. He did not mourn the Colony, but he mourned the lives of everyone he'd known who lived in it. He hadn't particularly liked most of them, but none deserved the horrors likely befallen them. To his surprise, he found it disturbingly easy to forgive the loss of Naeemah. After all, her body had already been more than half vacant.

The android felt compelled to contribute additional data: "He does not consider himself the same man who encoded those quanta. His physiological intellectual capacity is undiminished, but he has undergone severe psychic trauma and views the world from a new and as yet unformed perspective."

Sel accepted its analysis, but it did nothing to influence her thinking. She contemplated that should the *jura-dh'ihn* indeed find her, they might favor the man who brought down the Colony. But his progress through the temple was painfully slow, and she wanted to be long gone before the CA rescue teams arrived.

"He can follow," she announced, "But we don't wait. We leave now."

15. SILENCE; RESONANCE, TRANSCENDENCE

they made their way to the central repeller bank and descended through the empty, still temple to the archives. The android altered the path it had set for Wei to follow their own and Naeemah sent her Cyclopes to harvest what was left of the emergency vac-rations and rendezvous with them at the gates.

Even with an open radio channel connecting her to the others, Sel had to concentrate on keeping her old, deep fear of the soundless vacuum in check; she constantly fought the dangerous sense of disconnection from reality she'd always felt when in a vac-suit.

At the tenth level, Jerro led them to the tables where the relics were maintained. The workstations all bore eerie signs of recent occupation frosted and frozen in the stillness of vacuum. One Cyclops kept Jerro under guard and one helped Sel and Sanjit look for her things. The Sister Doctor and the android followed another to the nearest emergency store and stocked up for the trek for herself and Wei respectively.

"Here," Sanjit found her things atop one of the far tables, neatly laid out under a film of frost and tagged with inventory codes.

She felt suddenly disoriented. The memories evoked by the objects triggered a flashback to her field-suspension state and the emotions associated with everyone connected to them threatened to overwhelm her. She remembered her axiomatic Sanctuariat discipline:

They were merely objects, and there was vacuum to survive. Not everything survives the vacuum. It prevented them from becoming totemic. They each had a purpose, and it was up to her to decide whether that justified carrying them.

She looked over them: the *jura-dh'ihn* summoning stone, her clothes, her teakettle/disintegrator, her guitar, amplifier and pedals, the hypercard of names her mother had given her, the hypertab of Avik-Rosot's archives, the knapsack she'd carried it all in, and asked herself if their use justified their weight.

Without fully understanding her reasoning, she decided they did, if for no other reason than a continuity of purpose she found essential.

"See if you can find a repeller sled and start loading it with anything else that might be useful," she said to Sanjit. He was watching her face through her visor with concern. "I'm fine. I just don't like vac-suits." She smiled and admitted: "Or vacuum."

"Who does?" He left her to pack her kit and find a sled.

"Hey," she called after him, "Isn't this yours?"

She held out the frost-encrusted titanium bracelet he'd bought for Naeemah so long ago. He hadn't expected to see it again. After considering whether to tell her to keep it, he accepted it back and said: "Thanks." It was a gift for Naeemah, after all, and she was still alive.

He found one of her Cyclopes at a workstation, calibrating an antique astrolabe.

"Anything useful?" he asked.

The Cyclops shrugged. Strangely, he recognized her in the gesture.

"Seen a repeller sled around?"

"In the vestibule."

"How's the supply situation?"

Another, equally discouraging shrug.

He couldn't look at the Cyclops's vac-mask as he held the bracelet in his gloved palm and said: "I bought this for you a long time ago. It's just something I thought you'd like. I'm sorry," he felt his voice break and he couldn't stop from saying: "I love you."

Naeemah's consciousness immolated with love, anger and regret; the urges to cry, embrace him, kiss him, did not translate into the Cyclopes' wetware thus had no physical outlet. She used the surge of energy to further fortify her quantum sentience in the Icarus-Daedelus servers against the constant assaults on its integrity.

"I love you too," the Cyclops said in a single, distant inhuman voice, taking the bracelet in its meaty Kevlar fingertips and clutching it to its chest.

WEI followed the illuminated tiles through the dim corridors, down sweeping staircases and across airless chasms on repellers controlled by the android.

It awaited him in the open airlock door at the temple base, already wearing a depressurized vac-suit to protect its joints from dust and carrying the survival kit it had packed for him.

The others had gone ahead and were nearly out of human optical range. The six Cyclopes marched in long bounding strides around the gondola on which Sel, Sanjit, Jerro and the Sister Doctor rode. It hovered above the regolith at just above knee height, sufficient to allow for smooth clearance of most of the biggest common rocks. Sanjit and the Sister Doctor stood opposite each other at each side, pushing the three-meter gondola forward using lengths of pipe. The Cyclopes generated a stealth field that would appear as the slightest smear of data to a heat sensor.

Naeemah and the android had agreed to trajectory coordinates via the temple network before they embarked so that it would have a means of catching up with them; they would need to maintain radio silence across the vacuum lest the signal be noticed before they reached the Orientale, as was statistically inevitable.

"The others have gone ahead," the android told him, "The Sister Doctor, the girl and her friend. The Cyclopes are controlled by an entity loyal to the friend. They have taken a Martenist prisoner in order to monitor the Marten aggregate."

Wei took in the android's words. It monitored the biodrone in his brain for any sign as to whether he had understood but its data was inconclusive. In fact, he understood everything that it said, but did not understand how any of it related to him.

"The girl has a synthetic crystal device resonating at a hyper-frequency she says will attract allies of hers. They intend to travel to the Orientale basin."

The android awaited response from Wei. Wary of causing further damage to his psyche, it carefully considered how to release the relevant data to him in an order by which he might arrive at the decision to follow them (which it considered his best option) rather than wait for the Icarus-Daedelus rescue teams, knowing that Demetrius Wei could not be told what to do.

"The Colony has experienced pervasive and systemic cataclysm," it said after another inconclusive analysis, "Aside from Geminus, the Orientale has the only functioning Weatherbox on the moon."

Wei stared pensively across the bright Imbrium plains beyond the airlock. He knew that the cataclysm the android spoke of had been his work, the work of Demetrius Wei, yet he did not know what that meant.

"The Cyclopes entity is attempting to interfere with them, but it is likely that CA teams will arrive from Icarus-Daedelus within the hour," it said, "If you wish to avoid them, I can generate an EMF field capable of concealing you from their sensors, but we must leave now if we are to clear visual range of the temple by the time they arrive."

"So be it."

SEL'S exhaustion was kept at bay only by her adrenaline response to the fear she could not deny while her breath and her heartbeat were all she could hear inside her helmet. Back in the temple airlock she had felt her stomach drop when Naeemah suggested radio silence. It was necessary, she knew, but she wished it wasn't.

At first she had sung to fight the silence, then hummed. Then she became too fatigued even to hum. Jerro had already curled up among the stacks of ration crates, ice blocks and O2 canisters.

She lay across a stack of crates that seemed to have been arranged by the Cyclopes for just such a purpose and watched the horizon slide by with each steadily decaying thrust. She guessed that each push moved them perhaps ten or twelve meters. Sanjit and the Sister Doctor seemed to be trying to outdo each other.

Her helmet bobbed and nodded involuntarily, her eyes closed without her allowing them to. Without her noticing it, the isolated sounds of her breath and her heartbeat had become a source of comfort rather than fear. For the first time since before performing at Clavius, she slept.

She felt the presence of the *jura-dh'ihn* before she woke, sensing them at the edges of her unconscious mind but still too physically drained to be drawn into wakefulness.

Sanjit, the Sister Doctor and Jerro were all similarly deep in sleep, and the android and four of the Cyclopes stood in recharge mode while the remaining two stood watch. Their lenses and sensors did not register the five-meter long sinkhole open behind a grade in the terrain, but they saw clearly the energy signatures of the five otherwise invisible stealth-cloaked figures as they climbed from it and fanned out to encircle them.

Maintaining radio silence meant that Naeemah had to disconnect these Cyclopes from the others around the moon as well as from the Icarus-Daedelus servers when they left the temple, which required spinning off a proxy into each of their brains. She was still getting used to the sudden shift in perspective; rather than experiencing data simultaneously from multiple sources through a single cognitive point of view, each proxy received only its own sensory data from the same cognitive viewpoint. The instantaneous control she'd become accustomed to was gone: each of her would have to coordinate with the others visually.

One of her set about manually reactivating the four in sleep mode while the other shook Sel gently by the leg.

She awoke with a start, her body sore in the constrictive under layer of the suit. The recycled air in her helmet smelled of ozone, sweat and nutrition paste. The inside of her mouth was coated in a sour film. She climbed off the gondola, which was resting on the ground, wanting to stretch her stiff muscles but unable to. As her mind cleared of sleep, her sense of the *jura-dh'ihn* sharpened. The amulet hung from a utility clip on the left arm of her suit. Slow quantum vibrations emanated from it, pressing into her and through her consciousness. She felt the resonances of each of the five *jura-dh'ihn* as they approached, not so much individual entities as unique cohesions of frequencies. Their thoughts occurred to her at the synaptic level, as hers to them, an open channel of energy vibration clarified and amplified by the vacuum.

They were hanging back because they saw the Cyclopes as a threat. She gestured for Naeemah to stand down. One by one, she complied.

Sanjit had only been dozing lightly, and opened his eyes at the first vibration of Sel rising to her feet on the deck of the gondola. He saw the Cyclopes on guard, and watched Sel calmly wave them down and step beyond their perimeter. On the opposite side of the gondola, the Sister Doctor and Jerro were also awake and watching the proceedings tensely. Jerro, who could see the forms of the invisible *jura-dh'ihn* through his eye optics, was silently terrified.

The *jura-dh'ihn* appeared from beneath their stealth cloaks within two meters of the sled on all sides. Beneath the cloaks, they wore antique hard-shell vac-suits with polymer-dome helmets, faces within pale-eyed and smeared with clay, a black pentagram charred across their foreheads. They carried small pin lasers that could easily pierce a modern vac-suit and ferocious fighting staffs that she didn't doubt could cripple a Cyclops when wielded correctly. One of them was a child of perhaps twelve, yet no less formidable.

She focused her mind on the situation at hand, her own identity and her relationship to each of her companions, their recent histories and their destination. Her previous encounter with *jura-dh'ihn* at the Sveygn estate was at the forefront of her memory; she could feel its resonance with the five other minds via the vibrations of the amulet. She couldn't tell if that meant that the *jura-dh'ihn* she'd met were among these five, or if one or more among them had second-hand resonant knowledge of it.

An overwhelming harmonic resonance among *jura-dh'ihn* consumed her, vibrating through the summoning stone on her arm, at a nexus of the pentagonal points on which they each stood. A single concept overwhelmed her being: *transcendence.*

One of the *jura-dh'ihn* took a step backward and the feeling subsided. The others broke formation and began heading back toward the rise behind which they'd emerged. Sel knew that they were to accompany them. She turned to the others and gestured to follow, falling into stride behind them.

Sanjit, who, along with the Sister Doctor, had gotten the pertinent broad-strokes of the strange, crystalline exchange of resonant information between Sel and the *jura-dh'ihn*, hopped off the sled and adjusted the repeller controls on the side panel, lifting it gently to just above knee-height and began pushing it forward at walking speed with the Sister Doctor and Jerro still on it. Two of the Naeemahs took over, taking position at the rear of the sled and shoving it forward with gentle nudges.

Beyond the ridge, they joined Sel and the *jura-dh'ihn* around the edge of the sinkhole, looking down through a hatch into the cabin of some sort of vehicle of metal and ceramic.

Via the crystal frequencies permeating her being, Sel knew it was a Namgung Engine, a first-generation original built by the Ash-Eaters under Namgnung's direct supervision, one of those which had been used to escape the senile monomaniac's mine and excavate a new civilization deep beneath the Jura Mountains.

She took in all of the pertinent information coming from the *jura-dh'ihn*'s frequencies and decided it was time to risk radio contact. She wasn't sure how much Sanjit understood of what was going on, and was certain that the Naeemahs hadn't been able to get any of it.

"These *jura-dh'ihn* will take us into the Orientale," she said, "I don't understand their conception of time but I'm sure it'll be faster than that sled. And we'll be underground. We can tunnel directly into the basin." She turned to Sanjit: "Give me your bracelet."

He looked from one Naeemah to the others, unsure which he had given it to. One of her stepped forward and handed the bracelet to Sel, whose heart sighed when she realized that Naeemah had been his life's love, as she extended one of the knuckle hooks on her glove and pried the diamond from its setting in the titanium rabbit's eye.

She handed it to one of the *jura-dh'ihn*, who examined it and handed it to another, who, along with two more, rappelled down the ropes anchored by hooks into the regolith surrounding the sinkhole and lowered themselves through the hatch.

Sel gave the bracelet back to the Cyclops and looked at Sanjit, explained: "That's solid oxygen, compressed by masconium fields for fourteen billion years. There's enough O_2 in that little diamond to keep all of us alive for months."

Two Naeemahs leapt over the edge while the others began unloading their rations from the gondola and passing them down. Each of them wondered what to do about Wei and the android. Several spoke up at nearly the same time, creating a warbling ghostlike phasing over the waves, creating sharp feedback in the receivers. Two of them figured out the problem and, when the noise had cleared, spoke in the minimum, most concise phonemes possible to convey the message. Their timing was still off, creating a delayed echo effect:

"De(de)-me(me)-tre(tre)-us(us) Wei(wei)…"

In the signal decay of the name, Sel felt a strong resonance among the *jura-dh'ihn*. The vibrations were strong and clear enough to convey a nearly clear sense of it even to the Sister Doctor and Sanjit: they knew this man.

THE android led by forty meters, choosing their route and clearing stones from Wei's path as he kicked across the wasteland on the repeller sled the others had left in the cargo lock, which he'd configured as a scooter.

The spectral aspect of his awareness had returned, and he could again see the entirety of things simultaneously. Yet still he lacked focus and was unable to see or understand them clearly. He could no longer single out an area to concentrate on, nor so much as choose to. He simply followed the android, kicking along steadily, sipping water and nutrition paste at a cautious rate.

He did not know if Mia's life as he had been shown it was real or an elaborate simulation, but couldn't conceive of why the Marten aggregate would put so elaborate an effort into such a complete simulation. As powerful an entity as the aggregate was, it seemed a disproportionate effort.

Unless he was, in fact, of extraordinary value, a manufactured favorite son who had not yet fulfilled his design to the satisfaction of his creator and was being pushed, or punished, which led him again to curse his insanity, the narcissistic mania that had destroyed his and his family's lives, placing his only daughter in a position where she could not be cured.

Then it would occur to him that if they had engineered him, might they not have engineered her as well? He remembered Mia in the sunlight, peering through the plastic sheeting of her carriage as they paused along a wind-bitten mountain road overlooking Hokkaido. They would poison her. They would destroy her.

But there was no *they*.

There was the Marten aggregate. There was *he*.

No sooner did he think it than again he cursed his insane, stubborn vanity for putting his beloved Mia through such crushing pain, abandoning her to an empty life as a resource.

Again and again and again such thoughts pulled his mind along Mœbius loops as he kicked and sipped, kicked and sipped, kicked and sipped.

At the lip of a wide, steep volcanic depression, the android came to a stop and surveyed the horizon in three-hundred-sixty-degree sweeps for signs of the others, finding none. This was the third of the five possible intercept coordinates it had established with Naeemah.

It was worried. It trusted the Naeemah entity, but she'd demonstrated a disappointing willingness to subordinate herself to the decisions of highly unpredictable organics. The fact that they hadn't yet met meant that either their course, pace or both had diverged significantly from what they'd established.

After four hundred and thirty-eight sweeps, it saw something it hadn't on the previous scans: the figure of a lone Cyclops ninety meters away, standing against the line of the southwestern horizon. No sooner had it registered it than the Cyclops took a step backwards and fell away from view. It recorded the location and oriented its body toward it, resuming its march.

Wei lingered at the edge of the depression and gazed out across it, taking in the patterns by which the ancient lava congealed and hardened, the jagged horizon beyond its opposite rim and the planet hanging low above it. The swirled clouds around the distant planet and the lifeless, pocked steppes before him were perfect in their asymmetry, inevitable. His own presence there struck him as equally inevitable. Regardless of whatever doubts and confusion plagued him, nothing in his life that had brought him to this place could have occurred any differently.

His reverie was broken by a burst of dust on the ground in his periphery. He turned toward it as a second stone skimmed the regolith and wobbled out over the edge of the depression. He looked in the direction it had come from and saw the android fifteen meters away, waiting for him. As content to press on as to linger, he stepped onto the sled, took its handle and kicked off after it.

When he joined it at the sinkhole and peered over the edge he saw two Cyclopes and a *jura-dh'ihn* standing atop the hatch. The android leapt down as the *jura-dh'ihn* secured the grappling line for Wei. He felt a familiar resonance in his brain and was not surprised to see the charred pentagram drawn on the clay-smeared forehead of a Moonborn facial structure he'd known as Overseer.

The *jura-dh'ihn* had involved themselves in the operations of the Orpheus Pit from the beginning. While they took minimal interest in the surface doings of the Colony, little occurred below the surface that they were not aware of. As potentially catastrophic an endeavor as Orpheus warranted a significant and diligent exertion of influence. They had bred and trained the Engineers to chart the Orpheus Engine on a course to take it in a gradual helix around the core, its arcs and helices supporting the surrounding geology, to create a trans-hemispheric lunar tunnel linking Central Procellarum with the southern Far Highlands. The Devolved were bred as resource. The occasional infusions of Colonial prisoners were also considered resource.

With the exception of Demetrius Wei.

The peculiar quantum frequencies of his consciousness resonated closely with theirs; they understood each other. Their first encounter with him still resonated through the minds of the *jura-dh'ihn*: upon seeing their pentagram, his mind completed the geometric extrapolation into a dodecahedron, the foundation of quantum-resonant technology, the *jura-dh'ihn* evolution's ur-concept: *transcendence.*

Thus he became the first planetary human to be accepted among the *jura-dh'ihn* since the Ash-Eaters forsook Namgung. He was allowed to exist among them, his frequencies respected but accorded no undue influence.

For them, his resonance with the Sanctuary girl was significant, and there had been no question that they would retrieve him from the vacuum.

THE Engine airlock accommodated all five of them, though the Cyclopes' girth necessitated that the android configure itself as compactly as was possible. When it was pressurized, they filed one by one through the inner hatch led by the *jura-dh'ihn* and into a corridor nearly too low and narrow for the Cyclopes to shuffle along stooped over, emerging into the aft cabin.

Everything buzzed with rapidly oscillating particle fields and resonant-crystal energy. All around them, the hull hissed white noise as the molecular bonds of the rock were chewed away by the tracks of matter-eaters that propelled it through the burrow it dug, fusing the slag in its wake into porous rock.

The cabin was perhaps five meters long, three wide and two and a half tall. Within it he found Sanjit, the Sister Doctor, Jerro and three of the other Cyclopes, two of which stood in hibernation mode among the racks of vac-suits lining the forward bulkhead, the other kept Jerro within arm's reach and had already repeatedly thwarted his impulse to pace nervously. In the center of the cabin was a cold-fusion stove within which a cauldron of stew bubbled irresistibly. In the intensely vibrating particle orbits the aroma of the stew penetrated his being, invigorating his brain to the point that it could function sharply even in the hunger it triggered. The android helped him out of his own, modern suit and the *jura-dh'ihn* bade him partake of the stew. The one who'd met him on the surface expertly extracted herself from her vac-suit. Underneath, her naked body was caked with mineral clay and he could see that she was pregnant.

Sanjit and the Sister Doctor occupied one bench, so he sat next to Jerro on the other to sip his crock of stew. Jerro tried again to stand but the Naeemah Cyclops standing beside him clamped him down against the bench, aware of Wei's seeming pleasure at watching the clean-cut clone squirm.

Wei ate his stew in silence until he was nearly finished. Finally, without looking at Jerro, he said: "He you serve manipulates and deceives until we doubt our own sanity, yet here you sit, unable to understand why we don't love him, why we will not accept oppression simply because he calls it love."

"I don't have to listen to this! I don't have to hear this!" Jerro proclaimed desperately again and again, struggling against the Cyclops' grip. But he could not block out Wei's eerie, quiet rasp, perfectly audible in his mind: "Such a practical pathology for him to have included in you."

Jerro and his ilk's engineered nature had been a hypothesis since he first arrived at the temple, confirmed now by his sudden silence as, for the first time in his life, penetrated by quantum fields and the mind of Demetrius Wei, he questioned his programmed mindset. He ceased to strain against the Cyclops' hand and sat back against the thick ceramic of the hull, from time to time chancing a wary sideways glance at Wei as he finished slurping his stew.

Sel stood in the forward compartment with the sixth Cyclops and four other *jura-dh'ihn*: an adult female and an adolescent female, an adult male and a pre-adolescent male. Sel had served as a translator between the Cyclops' electronically verbalized coordinates and the *jura-dh'ihn* at the control fields scribing the calculus necessary to complete the course corrections which ultimately succeeded in bringing them to Wei and the android at the third intercept point.

She found both the *jura-dh'ihn* and their mathematics fascinating. The totality of the concentration of the five individual frequencies in the compartment, including the child's, was focused on the field control equations, which they inscribed by hand across slate fields. After they retrieved Wei and the android and resumed their journey, no longer requiring translation, she retired to the aft. The Naeemah, whose electronic consciousness didn't register the *jura-dh'ihn* resonances, was even more fascinated by the strange math and so stayed, watching and attempting to deduce the symbols and glyphs.

After a brief deep sleep curled up in the dark nook behind the hanging vac-suits and resting Cyclopes, she decided to check over her gear whether she wanted to or not (she didn't). She crawled across to the cage where their things had been stowed and found her guitar, amplifier and pedals. It troubled her that seeing them there, in her hands, gave her the same disconnected, distant feeling as when she had seen them through the vac-suit, covered in frost. There was no immediate sense of connection or familiarity. She peered into the back of the amp with a flashlight and saw that it had been disassembled and incorrectly incompletely reassembled, and sighed assuming the same had been done to everything else. Then she perched herself on top of it and held her guitar on her knee, forgetting to strap it on. She fumbled to find a comfortable hold on it. Panic set in when she put her fingers on the fret board and didn't know what any of it meant, couldn't tell her fingers how to make the sounds she remembered.

She had not emerged from field suspension unscathed.

She could no longer play the guitar.

16. DEPTH

She resolved to relearn.

She stayed at the back of the cargo hold, hunched and cross-legged between an air filter manifold and the scraping, thrumbing hull, hidden at the back of a storage cage behind a wall of the stacked vac-ration crates from the temple.

When she didn't re-emerge for a while, Sanjit noticed the Sister Doctor staring at him pointedly. In the steady, organized particle mélange of the Engine their thought patterns, already evolutionarily compatible, meshed clearly.

She's been gone a long time. (She needs privacy, space). She just came out of months of field suspension and she's been living on nutrition paste. (I'll check on her). In its flux state, working itself through the matter of the moon, the interior of the Engine was beyond haunted: it rendered them all ghosts.

He ladled out a crock of stew and carried it down into the hold. By now he was acclimated to the Engine's peculiar sense of motion. His center of gravity felt higher, in his chest. The sensation of forward motion was constant, but it was easy to keep balanced. In fact, it was difficult to fall over, allowing him to contort creatively between the fusion stove and fellow passengers, and the tightly stacked supplies and equipment below. He heard motion at the back of Sel's nook but was too big to squeeze between the ration crates and the cage door.

"You alright?"

"Yeah." She'd sensed him approaching and was grateful for the wafts of molecular stew that were already reaching her as she set about re-stringing her guitar.

She'd already looked over it carefully and was encouraged to discover that she still remembered everything about its construction, electromagnetic and quantum principles, Pythagorean tonal logic.

"Thanks for the stew."

"Sure. Try to come out and stretch every once in a while though. Even just for a walk around the cabin. It's really important when you're cooped up for a long time. I get the sense we're going to be down here for kind of a long time, right?"

He'd ventured to the forward cabin only once and stood next to the Cyclops (now dormant, resting) to watch the *jura-dh'ihn* co-exist while steering the Engine along its trajectory through the moon, avoiding mine tunnels, habitats, fault lines and other *jura-dh'ihn* Engines, plotting and cutting and moving matter through kilometer after kilometer of solid rock, disassembling and reordering molecules by the jillion per microsecond in a machine that had done so, unseen and undetected, for centuries. The air was thick with the heady stew and the vibrations were impenetrable to him.

"How far are we from Orientale?" he asked Naeemah.

She stared back at him through the Cyclops eye and confessed: "No fucking clue."

He realized that Wei, partially hidden in shadow, was staring directly at him. He acknowledged the stare with a nod, but got no response. He'd never doubted that he was probably never going to come to any kind of interpersonal understanding with this person, so he chalked it up to general spookiness and returned aft.

Wei had seen him from the shadowed alcove in which he stood, but acknowledgment never occurred to him, deep in trance as he was. Sel was nearly directly below him in the cargo hold, still wearing the *jura-dh'ihn* amulet around her neck. Her frequency vibrated through him, and in it recognized damage analogous to his own. He felt the Venn intersection of her cognitive quantum orbits and those of the *jura-dh'ihn* within his own, an exquisite volume of primal beauty and concentration.

Somewhat reluctantly, the android had removed its bio-drone from his brain macroscopically through his tear ducts while he slept.

It was still concerned about the condition of his cognizance, but had little evidence to justify its worry, and couldn't deny that the inability to communicate with Moonborn would likely restrict him unfairly in current circumstances. The procedure had been observed with curious revulsion by the Sister Doctor, Sanjit and Jerro, none of whom were comfortable enough communicating with Wei to tell him about it when he eventually awoke.

In the aft cabin, Coni, who without being cognizant of it had begun to think of herself as Sister Doctor, meditated in prayer to God and Mother for the souls of Sel, Sanjit and herself, and begged mercy for those without: the android, Jerro, the Cyclops, the *jura-dh'ihn* and, she believed, Demetrius Wei.

As consumed by faith as she had become, she had not completely lost her rational, questioning mind. She was cognizant of the fact that all which had defined the person she knew herself to be had been stripped away, lost when she surrendered the illusion that she ever had the power to exert influence over her own life.

She recognized that her faith, which she had never before been aware of, had become the strongest remaining framework supporting what was left of her psyche. She was aware of it, she accepted it, and she prayed.

Jerro seethed on his bench, twisted by doubt in what he had considered his own faith, which he could now not stop himself from thinking of as a deliberately programmed genetic certainty.

She can...she already has. The very nature of the words implied an objective reality distinct from that in which he had truly believed, in which He was all-powerful and all giving, and His Love was absolute.

Such a practical pathology... He had known since sentience that he had been designed to Succeed the Aggregate, the holiest and most important of vocations. But, helplessly following the simple train of logic set off by Wei's lingering words, he found himself uncomfortably facing the notion that the Holy Aggregate might not in fact be everything He presented Himself to be, but that he had simply been programmed to *think* He was. If so, then what was his life actually worth? Why even continue to exist?

He could think of only one reason: *to Succeed.* And he was ever more determined to do, so no matter the cost.

Sel was perhaps less aware of the quantum synchronicity cycling through the crystal around her neck than Wei and the *jura-dh'ihn*, but nevertheless felt psychically sustained by it. She repaired as much of her gear as she could with the small toolkit she kept in her knapsack by the light of a small glo globe. Then she struggled for hours that seemed to unfold into more hours at a strangely exponential rate to find the correct tunings. Then she practiced. She practiced and practiced and practiced, just loud enough to hear over the thrum and hiss of the engine but not loud enough for everyone to realize she no longer had any idea what she was doing or how to do it. She didn't want anyone to know. There was nothing any of them could do about it anyway.

She practiced until her fingers bled and when they did she bandaged them and practiced some more, and only when she could no longer press the strings did she unfold herself and crawl out of the hold up into the relative brightness of the aft cabin, where she found Jerro asleep, slumped against a Cyclops. The Sister Doctor and Sanjit were also asleep, slumped against each other.

She refilled her crock with stew and breathed deeply of its nourishing vapors until it was cool enough to sip, carrying it into the narrow gangway and staring through the observation glass into the crucible where the *jura-dh'ihn* had placed the diamond, letting her eyes defocus on the gently pulsating light patterns interacting with the clean O_2 particle trajectories mapped across the hyperglass.

Then she continued into the forward cabin, where she felt the frequencies of Wei and the *jura-dh'ihn* welcome her. She had broken Wei's trance state when she stopped playing. His psyche felt stronger now, supported as it was by the quantum lathe created by the *jura-dh'ihn* vibrations. He was Demetrius Wei: finally and completely of the moon.

She saw him in his alcove over the rim of the crock as she sipped her stew.

His voice was the quietest sound in the chamber but she heard it perfectly clearly among her own thoughts when he said: "All shall be built anew."

She silently agreed with him.

There was nothing more to be said and the intensity of the *jura-dh'ihn* was giving her a low-grade headache, so she left the cabin in silence.

The Sister Doctor was awake when she returned aft. She acknowledged her but didn't want to wake the others, nor speak with anyone in the compartment, so she went about quietly placing her crock into the chamber at the base of the CF unit and returning below.

As she reached the hatch, the Sister Doctor said: "May I ask something of you?"

Sel had already decided to ignore anything she might say, but the politeness, earnestness and directness in her voice, that she'd consider asking permission, made her willing to listen, much as she didn't particularly want to. She shot a look around at the others to indicate that she wanted to be considerate of their slumber as she paused in the vaulted gangway.

The Sister Doctor rose from the bench, careful not to wake Sanjit, who was in fact already half-awake and watching through sleep-lidded eyes, curious to hear what she would ask and surprised that Sel gave her any time.

"Would you tell me about your song?" she asked, close enough for her voice to be heard just above a whisper.

Sel's eyes flashed anger: exactly the thing she had been trying to reset her mind from, and the last thing she would ever speak about. She was in a heavy quantum flux field kilometers below the surface, far from home and among strangers; she'd been taken apart and reassembled, had killed and seen friends killed, yet her fingers had been bloodied and her soul abused just trying to find it again because she couldn't do it anymore. She turned to go.

"I only ask because it's why I'm here…"

"No." Sel said quietly, sharply and flatly, refusing any responsibility for this woman's circumstances. She did not regret granting Sanctuary to Sanjit, but was unwilling to let it become pattern behavior. "You had a choice. You could have stayed at the temple."

"You misunderstand," the Sister Doctor said.

Sel was again impressed by her directness and clarity. Based on the mute stares and religious utterances she'd become accustomed to, she'd thought the woman incapable of meaningful communication. She silently chided herself for anti-planetary bias and listened.

"It's the reason I was at the temple. Demetrius Wei as well."

The android, monitoring the conversation while in standby mode, noted sourly that she didn't mention it.

"The Colonial Authority tasked us with discovering what it meant. Wei was looking for code frequencies and I was supposed to tell them what the words meant."

Sel rolled her eyes.

"Yes," the Sister Doctor acknowledged flatly, "I cannot express its meaning. I cannot hope to and I am not worthy to."

The sternness and severity of the admission gave Sel pause. "That's too far."

"Perhaps," she shrugged it off.

"You said you had something to ask of me."

"I would ask you simply to tell me about it. About how it came to you, about how it came to be."

The spiritual zealotry in the Sister Doctor's eyes was plain and Sel took offense at it. She could remember no inspiration, only endless hours spent experimenting and designing and building and recording and practicing, about the Gargantuan amount of attention it had commanded, drawn from that which she might have given family and friends, a life she now saw as precious, fleeting, gone.

It was the reason she was here. It was the reason they were all there. And she couldn't do it anymore.

She turned her back to the Sister Doctor and descended the ladder to the hold.

Both Sanjit and the android found a degree of satisfaction in her wordless exit.

Back in her nook she still couldn't pick up the guitar, so she stowed it, stretched out as much as she could and did the thing she second most dreaded: activated the hypertab of the archives of Avik-Rosot.

BY THE time they pressed through the depths of Southern Highlands, completing what was to be the final arc of their looping trajectory into the Orientale basin, burrowing deep beneath what remained of the ongoing 20-kilometer-deep death-race derby still circling the city, caravans of survivors turned bands of hardened marauders, fighting each other for a chance to fight through the guarded tunnels, she had read, watched, listened to or at least skimmed nearly a third of the archived material.

Her general impression was that there was too much of it and that it could well stand editing and abridgement. But so much of it was so wonderful, and often obtuse, full of potential meanings that revealed themselves only with context and reflection, that she understood the impulse to keep an exhaustive archive intact.

From time to time, she went back and looked at the image of her mother she'd found in Clavi, meditating on Vacq's telling of the story. Besides that, there was no other mention of Suki-Anna. There were plenty of other significant women in his life, though.

She'd found eight indexed in the sections of archive she'd looked at. Each had been a formidable woman. But each of their entries included a date of death, and links detailing the dire fates befallen their children.

Any who might get a hold of the archives looking to trace the coveted gene line wouldn't find Suki-Anna, or her. By her avoidance of such attention did she consider her mother all the more impressive.

The entries she found most meaningful were those indexed as annotations: mostly 2D video notes made by Avik-Rosot, organized alongside specific events on the timeline.

The Crisis City documentaries were too upsetting to watch: she recognized so many of the landmarks and couldn't bear to wonder what had happened to her friends in the 'net collapse.

But she enjoyed the annotation, remembering the unpredictable sense of time and pace of life there: in it, Avik looked tired, drawn and half-stimmed, pointing the lens at himself as he rarely did, preferring to narrate captured images. His recorded Moonspeak was simple and eloquent; he seemed equally frustrated and amused: "You want to know why they call it Crisis City? Because everything, at every level, is a fucking crisis, all the time. You want progress? Break something big enough that it must be dealt with immediately or thousands die. You want regression? Lurch from crisis to crisis, stress a population until they can't live next to each other anymore. You want stasis? Organize civic life so that everything must be given immediate attention or else you and everyone you love will be kicked out of society and left to beg, again and again and again until people can barely see that they're doing the same thing again and again and again. That being the case, I guess the latter is optimal, but shit, every one of them is fucking exhausting."

In preparation for their current destination, she looked at several entries indexed under O-City. Her father had been present at nearly every seminal Talas performance she'd grown up admiring, but, to some consternation, he didn't seem to have paid much attention to any of them.

Nevertheless, the annotation tagged to the general O-City listing was perhaps her favorite that she had seen.

The first image was taken through the front window of a vehicle approaching from the south, gyroscopically stabilized but still pocked with occasional road shake. The O-City particle net dominated the approaching horizon, turbulent high weather gray and purple in the light, hot pink and green bands around the horizons, the contours of the surface bursting with leaking-vapor rainbows.

His voice had been recorded someplace else, with quiet street noise in the background: "Okay," he said, "O-City. Nobody can describe O-City. I have a constructive attitude toward most things, but describing O-City? Can't be done."

The image cut to a view from inside the 'net, halfway up one of the high mountains encircling the basin overlooking the great fractal spiral of bulbs, domes, causeways and ridges carved out of it.

"They say it's the only surface Namgung city, which is partially true in that it's based on his design. But he never designed it to be surface. It's a more or less intact Namgung sub-surface city excavated decades after his death, at the beginning of the Second Expansion, with the construction of the Tower. Old Namgung doesn't deserve his name associated with *that*."

At the very center of the basin stood the monstrous, impossible O-City tower in all its hubristic, architecturally decadent and ill-conceived glory, a product of over-ambitious experimentation in the use of mascon masonry at a scale no sane mind would have accepted. Its narrowest point, nearly four kilometers in diameter, was a third of the way up, just below its widest point, nearly twenty-four kilometers, at the base of a gently tapering bulb adorned with buttresses, towers and observation nooks disappearing into the confusion of clouds generated by the Weatherbox within.

It had begun to fall apart less than a decade after it's construction. The mascon ore of which it was built had been drawn from seams all over the moon and the resulting fields behaved erratically, unpredictably. Floors slammed into ceilings without warning. Gravity would reverse itself over staircases, requiring one to crawl along the ceiling to ascend, and then swing down to the floor above. Entire levels shifted to the left and right, giving vast sections the appearance of a great, crumbling, unevenly stacked deck of cards. Buttresses broke off and floated away, moored by chains; tenuous suspension walkways swung from those still in use.

The CA, ever unwilling to concede failure, staffed it with the most zealous, rigid and mad bureaucrats and enforcement officials it produced, rounded out by low-level dissidents and dead-enders, all of whom existed in a notoriously problematic relationship with the crafty and erratic O-Tower AI itself, famously coded to accept and respect the Right of Refusal.

Avik-Rosot described it thus: "If crisis is what keeps Crisium churning out years of stagnation and violence, in the Orientale it's RoR. Essentially, Crisis City isn't any different from other big mine habs and industrial crater cities, just at a far larger scale and all at once. But there's not anyplace on the moon quite as uniquely fucked-up as O-City, and the RoR is what makes it so unique. What it means is that every sentient entity has the right to refuse any appointed task."

A simple animation appeared depicting the Orientale Basin from above, a three hundred twenty-seven-kilometer-wide impact crater surrounded by mountains and cliffs on the moon's eastern face.

"There's no mascon ore in the basin," Avik narrated, "But whatever hit it was full of frozen oxygen, so it began as an O_2 mine under Namgung, who made it his pet project. Tycho and the Clavi rim were already boomtowns, so they gave him a lot of leeway with O-City and let him program the AI himself. It was a gamble because no one was really clear on what Namgung's views on civic society were. Turns out they were more progressive than anyone thought.

"Not long after that he died. Anyway, the civic thinkers who took control of the operation were ambitious, and determined to incorporate their modern mascon-refinement techniques with classical Namgung fractals to create the Tower, to famously unfortunate results. But they made a number of other amendments to the original plan as well.

"Namgung's original O-City algorithm was intended to become a gateway to the far side: a manufacturing hub that could sustain a large permanent population and an equally large migratory one, an incubator for the next generation of pioneers on to Mars, to acclimate to extraterrestrial life and develop new technologies and skills to carry on to what was at the time supposed to become the interplanetary shipyard at Icarus-Daedelus."

The animation added a superimposed layer of the original O-City street plan with arrows and inset details: the flow of life was oriented east-to-west across the basin, from the Embarkment complex in the east, where materiel and personnel arrived from the planet, to the Disembarkment complex in the west, where trebuchet freight launchers hurled manufactured goods back to the planet and a rail and road systems carried goods and passengers out to the Far Side.

As she studied the map, she again marveled at both the grace and practicality of Namgung's fractals, but also, as she looked deeper into the demographic-projection links, his uncanny foresight. It was a masterwork of urban planning, a city designed to thrive for millennia.

"Then came Consolidation. And the particle net. And O-City Tower."

Blue lines illustrated the excavation of the basin surface (which was to have been the vast solar exchange powering the city) into composite material for the Tower. The street plans were pulled into chaotic, steep and jumbled spirals, divided by vast spoke superhighways leading out to tunnels feeding the new trans-lunar highways system. The result was that everything in the basin spiraled down to the center, to the sheer, impenetrable base of the Tower. Atmosphere was generated industrially out around the Rim, where laborers work month-long shift terms in camps and dormitories and come from cramped, crowded and lawless honeycomb neighborhoods.

A series of images depicted modern O-City life as of the recording: teeming nearly vertical Kasbahs and tangles of impenetrable throughways jammed with all manner of traffic.

"CA Engineering had paid Namgung a fortune, and the rationale behind the construction of the Tower was to exploit his patents and designs for the maximum possible profit in the most immediate possible time frame. They figured they'd make their money back extracting the mascon ore, excavating the city and building the tower. That's how the CA subsidiaries work.

"The O-City AI, Namgung's AI, warned them about the potential long-term costs of the dystopia the Tower would create, but it was ignored. So it acceded and coded itself to become the Tower AI, and also the city's Weatherbox. Which gives it nearly absolute power to enforce the Right of Refusal."

There was an index of images of violent street conflicts and chaos a century old.

"All of the deep-gen dynasties scrambled to set up shop here and labor surged in from around the moon, most of it deep-gen as well. And it became pretty clear pretty quickly that no one had any intention of towing the CA line.

"The CA can't win a fight against both the O-City AI *and* the general population, so they're stuck in the Tower. A couple dynasties still hold big Colonial contracts, but most of the economy runs on barter as an anarchic free-market. But if the CA sees anything they especially dislike, from the Tower they have a pretty clear shot at pretty much anyone pretty much anywhere in the basin at all times, and the AI is limited in its capacity to stop them. They have an aggressive and corrupt informant network across the city and they take shots at people constantly." The matter-of-fact resignation in his voice sounded prescient and the hair on the back of her neck stood up.

There was another index listing all manner of large-scale infrastructure failure.

"Since there's no centrally coordinated atmospheric or net generation, the climate is insane. It's up to an arcane college of guilds, unions, dynasties and religious sects to attempt to meet the particle quotas set by the Weatherbox and route water sufficiently to meet needs. It's deeply corrupt on every level and always has been. Ozone gaps suddenly appear, scorching some districts while others flood. Mascon irregularities have collapsed cubic-kilometers into themselves or pulled them apart into suspended rubble fields. Catastrophe response is as much a part of daily life as market anarchism and the Tower police state."

About the Council of the Gathered and the Talas, all he had to say was: "So every couple years, into the holy mess that is O-City, waltzes this grand who's-supposed-to-be-who of Moonborn attention fiends from all over goddamn Luna proclaiming some sort of Congress to perpetuate something called the Future of Lunar Culture and Human Expansion. What the fuck." There was exasperation but also affection in his voice, and in it she felt a kind of love for the dead man's chronicle that was all she'd know as father.

She'd become so absorbed in the archive that she hadn't picked up her guitar again by the time the Engine slowed to a halt as they reached their destination.

17. O-CITY

the Engine emerged from flux state and entered the basin through a secret tunnel network maintained by the *jura-dh'ihn.* The group who'd brought them didn't stay. The CA held standing orders to kill *jura-dh'ihn* on sight.

They climbed out of the Engine's hatch, now oriented to the side, through a tight crevasse and into a dark, wet drainage tunnel parallel to the Engine's path. Sheets of water cascaded down the arched walls and an ankle-deep current coursed down the center. The gravity was near-indigenous lunar, but after the flux of the Engine they all felt heavy in their skins, stiff and sluggish (excepting Naeemah and the android). They'd all become acclimated to the *jura-dh'ihn* molecular stew and their bodies reacted to its sudden absence with hunger pangs to the point of nausea. Vac-rations failed to sate, but only Jerro complained.

It was dark. Sanjit calibrated their repeller sled in the pale light cast by their glo-globes and the Cyclopes loaded their gear onto it. When they were finished, a *jura-dh'ihn* stood in the hatch offering Sanjit's diamond, only slightly diminished.

"Tell them I want them to have it," he said to Sel.

The *jura-dh'ihn* stood expressionless.

"I mean fuck it, they spend all their time subsurface. Don't tell me nothing ever goes wrong with that thing. It's fucking ancient."

The *jura-dh'ihn*'s face remained inscrutable; through the crystal Sel felt the resonance go out that Sanjit was accepted as a "valid frequency set," a rare honor for an Earther, though well short of what they considered sentient.

"They appreciate the generosity," she conveyed. It was a smart move. The advantage of *jura-dh'ihn* favor could well outweigh their need for O2 in an atmospheric zone, especially when they each had M-packs: it struck her as practical Sanctuariat thinking and she debated whether or not he'd earned an addition to his forehead tattoo, but decided she wasn't in as generous a mood as he.

She clutched the summoning stone and let the directions out of the tunnel osmose into her awareness: she was supposed to *follow the staircase through the rooms*, and assumed she was supposed to know which staircase and which rooms as she went through them. Instinct, then.

She didn't like that everyone seemed to be waiting for her to lead the way but she was the one with the amulet. So she pointed in the direction the *jura-dh'ihn* had indicated and they began to move. The Naeemah Cyclopes positioned themselves in pairs at the head and rear, while one kept a wrist-dart aimed at Jerro and the other minded the sled.

"What am *I* to do?" Jerro asked petulantly, the wet echo of his voice grating everyone, "Run through the streets of Orientale City? Here I am! Here I am! The savages would eat me!"

"Do we still have to keep him around?" Sanjit asked quietly.

"If we want to track the Marten aggregate."

"Yeah, keep him alive, but do we have to keep him around *us*? Once we're at the surface Naeemah will be networked again and we can put him anywhere, right? Like, in some room somewhere where we can't fucking hear him."

She agreed with the sentiment and saw the sense in the suggestion. "What do you think, Naeemah?" Sel asked the Cyclopes just ahead of them.

Their answers stepped on each other. One yielded and the other said: "Before we proxied out I had twenty-four Cyclopes in the Tower and another forty in installations around the Rim."

The other finished the thought: "But I don't think any of them are secure enough to keep him away from CA Military or Icarus-Daedelus. He stays with us."

Eighty meters through a series of canal-lined chambers, they came to a junction. A slippery stone ledge surrounded a churning cataract of runoff fed from five intersecting tunnels as well as a heavy torrent from straight above. It was raining up there. Two gently ascending staircases wide enough to move machinery through were carved into the wall opposite them across the cataract. She didn't have any particular sense that it mattered which one they took, so she chose the nearest. They had to walk single file, shuffling sideways along the ledge; once the others were across, the Cyclopes formed a chain to pass the sled and its contents along individually.

The stairs were wide and shallow, sweeping up a relentlessly gentle grade. Perhaps half a kilometer ahead they could see a muted source of light. Once the sled was reassembled and loaded they began the hike.

As they approached the light source, they could see that it was reflected off of a curve in the staircase wall. It had an odd, heavy greenish-yellowish hue, but the distinct feeling of reflected sunlight. When they were perhaps thirty meters away, they could make out the forms of three people against the murky gloom. Naeemah saw them first.

"Wait," the Cyclopes at the lead primed their weapons and zoomed their lenses in on the curve ahead. The others came to a stop as they watched the figures appear around the curve in the watery half-light. There was an elderly Moonborn man accompanied by two adolescents.

"*Auui-osshotte'h. H'sa…h'sa!*" the old man called.

Sel translated: "He says he's a friend. And encourages us to persevere because we're almost there." The tonal dialect was unfamiliar but the intent was clear, and the musicality of it indeed provided all of them, with the exception of Jerro and the android, a welcome boost of morale.

The old man, deep-gen and neither frail nor hale, viewed them with surprise and trepidation as they stepped into the light. The Naeemahs had lowered their weapons but his suspicion of them was obvious. In her clearest Moonspeak, Sel assured him and the youngsters that the Cyclopes were controlled by a friend and didn't present any danger.

"Yes, well," the old man said, regaining composure, "The *jura-dh'ihn* said you weren't travelling alone. My name is Sproel. I'm adjunct counselor to the Gathered. This is my neice, Esmet," he said indicating the girl, and of the boy: "My nephew, Feff. Welcome to Orientale."

He led them through a gate at the mouth of the staircase and into a broad alcove along a mezzanine overlooking a wide arcade-covered marketplace. Many panels of the canopy above were cracked or missing, rainwater splashed heavily down across the wet-dappled flagstones. Beyond the cover of the canopy and adjacent buildings, rain slashed horizontally in howling winds under fat layers of clouds, some so heavy and low as to obscure from view anything beyond thirty meters, revealing an ornate Namgung roofscape arranged in jarringly dense fashion. Thunder wracked the air and streaks of lightning danced around antennae and lightning rods, ascending and descending vast Tesla coils from spire to spire.

From time to time, through breaks in the clouds, they caught sight of the Tower, perhaps seventy kilometers in the distance, its western face brightly lit by yellowy sunlight from beyond the edge of the umbra.

Some of the market stalls below were shuttered but most were open for business, which was slow. Few chose to navigate the splashing drainage cascades unless there was someplace they had to be. Like Sproel, Esmet and Feff, they wore variations of hooded rain panchos of spun yucca fiber.

The smell of frying *kt'jhsks* reached them from a stand below and Sanjit salivated while acknowledging that it wouldn't be the smartest means of reintroducing solid food into his digestive system.

The Naeemah proxies initiated their protocols to return to the network, and she was once again a part of her greater self. It was a sudden and violent shock: all of her had been engaged in heavy combat since leaving the temple. On the Far Side, she had legions engaged against the constant onslaught of the Icarus-Daedelus war machine against her server complex while yottabytes of proxies relentless chewed away at the steady stream of invading code. Elsewhere, she was directly engaging any CA Military or Icarus-Daedelus units that might spot them as they crossed Procellarum, staging myriad diversionary raids, unaware that her erstwhile selves and their wards were travelling safely subsurface.

She'd lost a lot of Cyclopes, and while she didn't regret them (she felt nothing through them or for them, and was only hours

303

away from bringing another six legions online), and in fact relished the destruction of expensive Icarus-Daedelus hardware, she found herself deeply troubled at the ease with which she ruthlessly slaughtered CAM personnel. As the perspectives of the six proxy personae were reintroduced into her consciousness, she realized with horror and revulsion that she had begun to default to seeing adversaries as units of obstruction to be disposed of as efficiently as possible rather than human beings, fellow sentient entities; evidence of an advanced corrosion of the soul she wanted badly to reverse.

Thankfully, the CAM personnel, while competent, generally displayed more interest in survival than combat. Except for the zealots, most of who were here in the O-City Tower, the Colonial Authority was now effectively nothing more than a logo and an abstract legal entity on a distant planet.

"The *jura-dh'ihn* never cease to impress me," Sproel said. The acoustics in the alcove were clear despite the storm. "They had a two-degree trajectory window to catch this storm and they hit it on the first pass."

He went on, explaining to Sel: "The electrical charge from the storm confuses the CA field sensors. They always take special note of any *jura-dh'ihn* activity, and I'm afraid the Gathered's liaison with the Tower reports that the CA has standing orders to stop you from reaching the Talas. We have routes to conduct you there safely, but a narrow window to do so after the storm under cover of mist eighteen or so hours from now. Until then, you are welcome as guests in my home."

The Sister Doctor stared out in the direction of the Tower. Her purpose was clear in her mind.

"I have to reach the Tower," she said.

All eyes fell upon her.

"The CA contracted me to identify any threat to CA hegemony contained within the lyrical content of the song. I can make my report that there was none. That she had no part in the destruction caused by Wei's code."

"There is no CA anymore," one of the Naeemahs reported. "The network has collapsed."

"But is the CA Military still intact? Who's issuing these orders to stop her?"

"Yes," another answered. The CAM hierarchy was intact. While the CAM units were timid about taking on her Cyclopes, they were engaged in countless violent and bloody clashes with Moonborn militias for infrastructure across the moon.

Coni continued: "It's official record that Brigadier General Nshombo committed to accept my analysis based on whatever methodology I adopted. I will report that I have found no evidence of any organized Moonborn plot to bring down the CA and take over the moon connected to the song. I can tell him to take her off the target list."

Everyone looked at her as if she was insane, but the vision of what she must do had come to her aboard the Engine. She did not fault them for not seeing it.

"The Brigadier General is charged to protect CA hegemony and maintain stability on the moon. Hegemony has been lost, through no fault of any Moonborn. If anything is to be salvaged, if any reconstruction can begin, that must be made known."

Sanjit couldn't stifle an honest if bitter laugh: "You think the CA killing machine's going to stop killing just because you say they should? The CA does whatever the fuck it wants whether it makes sense or not."

"But the CA is no more and the Brigadier General is a human man. He is an intelligent and rational man. He will listen. He must hear. Perhaps it will do no good, but I must make it be known. Thank you," she said to Sel, "And may She watch you and keep you. Mercy and Grace are Hers, as am I."

She crossed herself and walked away, alone, toward the stairs down to the market concourse.

The android watched her leave with a grudging respect. It had the same data she did pertaining to Sel, her song and its relationship to the Colony collapse, but never would have thought to present such an argument, yet it found the logic of it perfectly correct.

"Sister Doctor," it said. She turned.

"If the Brigadier General requires metric substantiation, I can provide it through the municipal network."

"Thank you," she nodded. She no longer resented nor hated it. It was a machine, so she felt no love or affection toward it, but she admired its independence, and respected its consideration of Demetrius Wei.

"Ha!" Jerro, desperate, famished and angry, taunted after her,

"They will not listen to you! False Oracle! False Oracle! False Oracle! Ha! You'll never make it to the Tower! These mutants will eat you! They will eat you! They will eat you! Hegemony shall be regained!"

Sanjit punched him sharply in the temple with the ball of his hand, whiplashing his pale neck against the hard collar of his vac-suit; he still thought the Sister Doctor was nuts, but didn't need to hear it from Jerro and was getting sick of the anti-Moonborn "savage" crap.

Naeemah saw the Sister Doctor's madness, but also her righteousness. She considered that the CAM hierarchy had influence over Icarus-Daedelus, and if mission priorities could be shifted to infrastructure stabilization, and willing Moonborn factions declassified as enemies, it could be a significant step toward rebuilding. It might at least stem the constant attacks on her and her Cyclopes, giving her an opportunity to devote her own capacity towards reconstruction. Violence was certain to continue, and likely increase once negotiations for new contracts and charters began, but its scale and damage would be containable, and mitigated by progress. And it certainly might spare Sel's life, if not everyone else's. She felt the Sister Doctor was correct in that she must make herself heard.

She sent a pair of Cyclopes after her to shepherd her to the Tower.

Sanjit looked to one of the others, incredulous.

"She has a point," it said.

"What about you?" Sel asked Wei, directly into his unmoving eyes.

His voice, as ever a perfectly audible whisper: "There is nothing to relearn."

It was as if he'd said nothing at all, almost as if the thought was hers. But it was more than a thought; it was an understanding, even a certainty. She nearly forgot she'd asked him a question. She asked it again.

"All shall be rebuilt."

This time she lost patience for his cryptic thoughtforms: "If you want to rebuild then you should come with us to the Talas. The man who brought down the CA will be welcomed and maybe you'll find a use for yourself."

She asked Sproel how far a journey it was, remembering that there was no unified transportation system within or between the neighborhoods.

"Twenty-three kilometers east-southeast, uphill and down," he said, "But first, rest. You've had a long journey. I'll send Feff ahead to see to additional accommodations."

"The Martenist is a prisoner. We have our own vac-rations to keep him alive."

Jerro choked back a protesting moan and cringed when Sanjit wound up to sock him again at the sound of it.

SPROEL led them through a corkscrew labyrinth of wind-swept and rain-battered alleys, staircases and arcades. They passed few others. Most of the windows along the way were shuttered against the weather, those that weren't snapped shut at the sight of the Cyclopes.

When they arrived at Sproel's hab cluster, it was decided for the sake of young children inside that the Cyclopes and Jerro should remain out of sight. They were shown to a utility room on the opposite side of a canopied hydroponic plaza from the residences.

There were hot infusions and crocks of rice and steamed greens waiting for them when they arrived, served by some of the dozen or so young children supervised by a man and woman of Sproel's generation as assisted by Esmet and Feff.

They sat around a long galley table in the busy kitchen, adjacent to a veranda overlooking the stormscape. The civil-engineering hack job perpetrated on O-City had mercifully done little to negate the fundamental respect for human habitation Namgung had designed into his residences. There was ample natural light, stormy as it was, and a generous balance between open and private space. Many of the walls, ceilings and staircases curved at angles that were too steep or sharp, creating odd corners that trapped sound and resulted in strangely soothing acoustics. Children were playing in fact quite loudly in the adjacent common room, but their voices rang softly just above the steady clatter of the rain outside and voices around the table were clear and audible.

"The Council rejoiced when the *jura-dh'ihn* reported that you were alive and well," Sproel said, "Word has been sent to your people among the Sanctuariat."

"What's the word from the Sanctuariat? Anything from Lyell?"

"I'm too far removed from the lines of communication to have heard specifics. I do know that the Sanctuariat has been active in the rescue efforts around Crisi, Purbach and Tauri."

Sel felt quiet pride in her people though her worries were unabated.

"What's news of Crisi?"

"There are said to be survivors in the enclosed structures and in the undercity but no one knows how many. The storm will be clearing in the next twelve hours. Rest. We will make preparations and awaken you in time to depart. Esmet and Feff will be your guides to the Talas. Your performance is deeply anticipated, but we will wait until you're ready."

She flushed with anger and frustration that she was still expected to perform. She struggled to keep it in check.

"So I'm to stand alone on stage to give the CA a nice clean shot at me?" she said, unable to keep the edge out of her voice, "Am I to be your Avik-Rosot? Offered up as some new-generation Moonborn martyr? Some sacrifice to your cause? Or is my blood supposed to break the Sanctuariat's neutrality and win them over to some new lunar order?"

Sproel took it in stride. There was nothing in his tone to contradict nor reassure nor cajole. "At the moment there is no lunar order. The Colony has collapsed. Yet Luna and Earth remain. Are we to stop producing air and water and food because we've suddenly lost our overlords? Will the planet suddenly stop needing manufactured goods? It would take generations for them to restore capacity to meet population. But in less than a phase, our factories here in Orientale alone could be producing thirty-nine percent of the class-A output of the *entire Colony*, forty-eight percent of class-B and twenty-four percent of class-C, with capacity to dispatch.

"I'm merely an adjunct counselor to the Gathered, but I'm not naïve. There are as many ambitions and agendas among the dynasties and guilds as there are rocks in Procellarum. But I also know that they are unified by desire for the kind of free and open Luna the CA has suppressed for centuries."

"*What does* any *of that have to do with me?*" As she spoke she felt that perhaps her lack of sleep was getting the better of her but nothing to be done about it, she'd already hissed it.

She concentrated on her rice while Sproel considered his answer.

Sanjit had only followed about sixty percent of the conversation but he didn't like the effect it was having on Sel. She noticed his concern and shot him a glance that implied she'd fill him in later.

Sproel said: "What you have you created, that intangible collection of sound and idea, has inspired people. It has given hope for better to those who had never known it. It has reminded those of us who had forsaken hope that it was real. For some, many even, it has allowed them look at their world, their lives, themselves, from a broader perspective than they had before. If someone else had done that, they would be here instead of you.

"You were not invited to the Talas as a delegate. Much as they might wish they could, no one there is co-opting you or your voice for any 'cause.' Avik-Rosot was not martyred for a cause, he was murdered by zealots. But you are not Avik-Rosot. People who've never known of or cared about Avik-Rosot know your music, and it probably means more to them than one of his treatises on civic policy ever will, for better or worse.

"If the CA succeeds in stopping you, then they will have demonstrated that they still have control, that this is still their Colony and not yet Luna. If you appear, they have failed. And will have forfeited the fear they hold over all, and this failure of a Colony will again be Luna."

She ate in silence. The warm rush of carbohydrate sugars as she digested the rice made her feel somehow more solidly human.

"Only if I live," she did her best to match his calm, pragmatic tone.

"Only if you live," he agreed. "This is not Old Clavi. In the Orientale, we see duplicity as a direct track to destruction. You must trust me when I tell you that more people than you can possibly imagine have pledged their own lives to the protection of yours."

The weight of the statement fell heavily on her, dragging hooks deep through her gut as she remembered that *she couldn't play anymore*.

"This is the Talas, and this is the Orientale," he said, "You are here by free choice, and you have the Right of Refusal. You need not make any decisions before you sleep."

AFTER being shown to his quarters, Sanjit started to feel guilty about punching Jerro as hard as he did, and decided to bring him some food. He returned to the galley and the old women generously served him another crock of rice and greens, which he protected from the still-steady but slowing rain with his vest as he crossed the hydroponic plaza to the utility room.

Jerro had not stopped talking, pleading for Naeemah to let his facet at least peer into the network. It was bad enough being separated from Him and his siblings for as long as he'd been, but the loneliness and boredom of being alone in this room with a quartet of aloof and unfriendly cyborgs, thrashing between being consumed by his continuing failure to Succeed and doubt in Himself, was worse than anything he'd yet experienced in his ever-more difficult life.

His pleas were for naught: Naeemah had stopped paying attention to the Cyclopes' audio within the first five minutes of sequestration.

He attacked the rice voraciously.

"I knew..." he mumbled, crumbs spilling from his mouth, "...I knew...I knew you knew what love was...please...you must beg her...open the lock she has on my facet...a sim...a vid...I don't care...a municipal directory database, anything!"

At no point did anything like human gratitude make it into his gasping spiel. He waited for Jerro to finish, then took the crock and stood to go.

"Please!" Jerro wailed after him, "Please! These things listen to you! Show me love! I am loved!" the last of his tenuous grip on his thoughts slipped away, "He loves you! He loves you! He loves you!"

Sanjit shot a sympathetic glance to Naeemah through the Cyclops next to the door on his way out. It responded with a very Naeemah-like rueful shake of its head. If it could have rolled its eye, it would have.

***

THE Sister Doctor marched between the Cyclopes through the flooded and slippery streets, hewing as closely as they could to the most direct route to higher ground, toward one of the elevated superhighways that connected the Tower with the outer rim. Her vac-suit kept her dry, and the Cyclopes were able to steady her across the most treacherous flooded alleys, staircases and causeways.

She sensed eyes watching them from unseen nooks, but although light and sound sometimes escaped the shuttered dwellings she saw only one resident since leaving the marketplace. There, they had been uniformly regarded with fearful hostility. But this young woman, sitting alone in the sill of a darkened shuttered window, her eyes tired, her soaked garments clinging to her, simply watched them.

Coni met her eyes when she saw her across a courtyard as she emerged into a hab cluster along a steep, slick staircase. There was no fear in the girl's eyes, nor any hatred, merely a weary acceptance of another soul caught in a storm without shelter. She blessed her silently as they continued upward.

Atop the ridge, they stood alone on a wet, windswept concourse overlooking the city. They were perhaps ten kilometers away from the edge of the storm, under its outer bands. Rain fell in irregular sheets and tiny droplets filled the air in squalls. In the distance, the mad Tower shone in chiaroscuro against a backdrop dapple of gray clouds in blue-and-yellow sky, beyond the rainbowed storm bands and the umbra. She took off her helmet. If the CA were looking, they would have been able to see her face where she stood. The radio in her vac-suit collar still only screamed with static.

"Can you contact CAM?" she asked Naeemah.

"I'm shut out," the Cyclopes responded. Within the Tower, her dozen pairs were engaged in cat-and-mouse combat with the CA security apparatus, which had thus far successfully kept her out of their network and away from their interfaces. They were orders of magnitude more formidable than the Martenists, and the unpredictable Tower far more difficult to navigate than their fairly straightforward hall of mirrors. She was also worried about a squadron of Wasps that had broken away from the fighting at Icarus-Daedelus on a trajectory to the Orientale. "I've sent a packet to the Tower telling it that you're here and you want to talk to Nshombo, but I don't think the Tower cares."

She would have to put herself in the path of a CA patrol, or physically reach the Tower. She pointed to the superhighway half a kilometer north of where they stood, a sheer, reformed-rock viaduct twenty-five meters above the highest rooftops. "Can we get up there?"

Naeemah surveyed the terrain around the nearest vertical support against the inventory of gear carried by the Cyclopes pair. "Probably. Come on then. We have to keep moving. If the CA notices me when they have a clean shot like this they might take it. And we might have locals to deal with once the rain lets up."

THERE is nothing to relearn.

After waking from a welcome and deep sleep, Sel sat on the edge of the futon in the sparse room she'd been shown to, staring at her fingers pressed against the strings of her guitar on the fretboard. She knew which strings made what sounds, she remembered the correct sounds in her mind, but she could not tell if she was making them or not. It was like her first performances in Crisi, when she couldn't hear herself above the crowd. But she could her herself perfectly well now and still had no idea if she was playing it correctly.

There was a knock at the door, and Sanjit's voice: "Sel?"

"Come in."

He closed the door behind him and stood by the window, looking out over the district and the receding storm. More shutters were being opened and the lights of the dwellings were warm against the cool stormlight.

"Are you alright?"

She smiled in spite of herself and shook her head. "I don't know how to answer that question. How much did you get of what Sproel said?"

"About the CA in the Tower being out to get you and how you have to trust his people to protect you?"

"That's pretty much the gist of it. He also said that the Tower was all that was left of the CA. Can you believe it?"

"It's about time," he said, "Fuck them."

He tried to perch on the arm of the rattan chair next to the window, but it was designed for a Moonborn and proved impossibly awkward so he leaned against the windowsill instead. "So what do you think?"

She kept her voice hard: "He makes it sound like the future of the moon is at stake but I don't buy it."

After a moment, Sanjit said: "I do."

She knew he was going to say it and it was the last thing she wanted to hear. Her eyes filled with tears.

He didn't stop. "I don't know if I trust Sproel and his people or not. But I'd risk my life for you."

"You're Sanctuary now. That's what we do."

"Even if I wasn't. If all I knew about you was that you were the girl who made the song. I would've. I would."

She wasn't even trying to stop herself from crying anymore. Still he didn't stop.

"I think if whoever's left heard it now, they'd know it's not over. Even if its over for them, they'd know that there's something else. That there's more."

She cast the guitar aside and blurted: *"Well I can't even play it anymore, so why would I risk my life?"*

"What do you mean?"

"I mean since I came out of field suspension I haven't been able to play it. I think I know where to put my fingers, I think I know what sounds to make but I can't tell if I'm making them or not."

There is nothing to relearn.

Sanjit waited for her to calm down.

"Try," he said.

"I've been trying," she sniffed and blew her nose in her cuff. Her clothes hadn't been treated in a long time and the bacteria were slow to eat away the snot stain.

"For me. Let me hear it. Maybe something in your ears got scrambled and you just can't hear it right."

She didn't want to be rude so she closed her eyes instead of rolling them. He couldn't even read; why would she expect him to have a foundation in molecular neuroscience? Still, she found herself unable to pretend that he didn't have a point.

She picked up her guitar and checked the tuning as well as she was able. Then she played. She played as best as she could remember it went. And she sang the words, not knowing if the notes and the phrasing and even the words and ideas she sang made any sense to anyone, even to her.

Sanjit listened.

It was a completely different song.

It wasn't just that he was hearing it differently. Without amplification, only the harmonic plucking of strings and her voice, broken and swollen but pure and true, in the soft, vaulted acoustics of the porous-stone chamber, against the spattering clatter of the end of the rain outside the window.

He didn't understand it any better than he had at first, even with his improved sense of Moonspeak. But although it was undeniably different, it was every bit as powerful and affecting.

She glanced up at his face several times as she played to gauge his reaction. When she was finished, she studied him unflinchingly.

"It's not right," she could see it. "It's not the same. I can't play it."

"It's not the same," he agreed, "But you can play it. And even if it's not right, it isn't wrong."

Sel ran her fingers over sets of scales that didn't mean anything to her, again and again, meditating on the motion of her fingers and the intervals between the notes.

It was clear to Sanjit that she didn't have anything else to say. As much as he wanted to help her, it was her decision to make, so he stood quietly and left her to her thoughts.

As he passed a portico overlooking the common area of the hab, he did a double take and stopped to take a closer look.

Below, Demetrius Wei knelt on the floor, surrounded by half a dozen children, building a toy city of interlocking blocks and sticks. He wasn't supervising the kids, or teaching them, or merely watching them: he was building it alongside them, contributing elements where it made sense, quietly accepting their occasional demolition due to toddler clumsiness or irrational pre-adolescent veto.

He stood and watched for a while, eventually noticing the android standing stock still on the opposite side of the room. He guessed that he was within its visual range so he nodded acknowledgment. It politely and curtly returned the nod.

THE Sister Doctor watched the Cyclopes set the rocket launcher one of them had carried on its back onto the tripod carried by the other. She was just above them, on a narrow spiral footpath behind a residential cluster that overlooked a sheer forty-meter drop down to the low rooftops of the next district. The storm was breaking up but the wind was still strong. She had extended the climbing hooks on her vac-suit and dug them into the rock wall behind her, pressing as far back against it as her M-pack would allow.

One of them threaded cable through the anchor missile and loaded it while the other donned a harness and set an anchor in the rock face just below the guard wall. When the missile was prepared, a locked-off length of cable from the spool was attached to it and the launcher was aimed toward the pylon of the elevated highway fifteen meters away.

Their efforts were certain to be noticed by the CA; the superhighway was inaccessible by design. Naeemah's Cyclopes in the Tower coordinated their sabotage and attacks on any mechanisms set to pick them off mechanically. The two with Coni could generate an interference field to trick sensors, but there was still a real danger that someone might make visual contact and exert a special effort to take them out, and were likely willing to lose the Sister Doctor with them.

The proposition itself was inherently dangerous, but her vac-suit was equipped for climbing and she trusted Naeemah. She prayed for mercy.

Once the line was strung and secure the Cyclopes quickly and deftly broke down the launcher and refastened it and its tripod to each other's back and assembled the glider mechanism.

The first Cyclops rappelled down to the mooring and clipped itself onto the glider, a free-spinning bearing mechanism propelled by a compact CF pack, and kicked off, growing smaller and smaller against the rock of the pylon.

She couldn't take her eyes off it, expecting any moment a shredding beam, the jolt and tear of a projectile, the black smoke of a laser burn. It reached the other side and began its long ascent, setting the spikes as it climbed.

From above, she heard the stirrings of life from inside the habs as shutters were opened. As long as no one leaned out of a window and looked directly down, they wouldn't be seen. Without speaking, the Cyclops demonstrated the proper use of her vac-suit's climbing hooks with the spikes.

Coni hadn't climbed for years before she left the planet, but didn't question whether she could accomplish it. She simply had to.

The glider whistled back to the mooring below them.

The Cyclops pointed to her. It helped her retrieve the line and climb over the low guard wall down to the mooring. The wind pressed against her like a heavy shoulder and whistled across the vac-suit shell. A hard gust before she was snapped into the harness would send her to her death.

She found strength in prayer, and with a steady hand clipped the harness straps to the corresponding color-coded points on her suit. She tested her weight in the harness before unclipping the drop line, then lowered her visor against the wind and kicked away from the wall. She felt the glider bearings pick up the energy and pull her along as the glowing windows of the hab clusters grew smaller against the stormy gloom.

She twisted her weight in the harness and spun on the clip joint so she faced forward. The wind rocked her and smeared rain across her visor. The opposite wall was a great taupe smear dominating her vision, ever larger. The spin of the glider slowed as she reached the opposite mooring. Her visor, not designed for atmospheric use, was so hopelessly blurred and fogged she could barely see the wall in front of her so she opened it, welcoming the unexpectedly warm, fresh bite of the air against her skin. The safety line danced snakelike along the wet rock wall, clipped to the third spike. She transferred it onto her vac-suit and undid the glider harness, shoved it back along the line and, with prayers of gratitude in her heart, began the long climb.

REGARDLESS of whether she made the decision to play or not, which she resolved not to do until she got there, Sel decided she would trust Sproel's people, and Naeemah, to get them to the Talas safely. Regardless of whether she *could* play or not, she had come too far and gone through too much not to.

They set out following Esmet and Feff down a sloping alley behind the cluster, which opened onto a wide, shallow staircase. The Cyclopes' girth and the amount of luggage prevented them from taking the most direct route, but Esmet and Feff had been navigating the districts since birth and knew every shortcut, bypass and detour.

It was slow going. The storm had passed, leaving the way slippery. The vac-suits were too valuable to leave behind and too awkward to carry so they wore them, carrying the helmets in a net slung on the repeller sled, which required two Cyclopes to steady up and down the steeper grades. The umbra was almost directly overhead and the wetness from the storm was already forming into new clouds in the coolness. White fog filled the alleys, staircases and walkways, shrouding them from view and limiting their visibility to perhaps three meters. The fog would only last a matter of hours.

Feff had an idea. "We can cut through the *Gemseh.*"

Sel, not far behind them, listened closely. She could generally follow the Orientale dialect but didn't recognize the word.

Esmet considered it but wasn't sure she liked the idea.

"Save four klicks. Up and down once. Cykes can carry," he assured her.

"What about the *Gem?*" she asked, *Gemseh* being the word for the notoriously volatile ethnic Gemini districts of O-City. During Esmet and Feff's young lifetimes, they had been mostly stable, but after the quarantine of Geminus, seemingly every wayward Gemini from around the moon had come in, leading to overcrowding and characteristically violent competition among them, on top of their characteristic distrust of non-Gemini Moonborn and rabid hatred of the CA.

"Four Cykes," Feff said. "Two Sanctuary, us. And fog. Half a klick straight across."

They came to a stop at the top of the staircase that would take them down into the *Gemseh*. Esmet gazed across the barely visible shanties' and tenements' rooftops, crisscrossed with transmission lines like a net through the haze, to the opposite ridge, obscured by low cloud but only five hundred meters away. Then she considered the way ahead via the road. It disappeared into fog after forty meters, but she knew the route: it was poorly maintained and would likely require three or four of them to steady the sled over it. And the hairpin curve around the *Gemseh* was treacherous. Gemini brigands were known to sabotage caravans as they navigated it, collecting any spilled loot from the rooftops below and indifferent to human life. The fog cover worked equally for them and against them in each case: it obscured them from view, but also mitigated the Cyclopes' presence as a deterrent. Following that train of thought, she realized that there was little they could do to protect themselves if they came under attack around the curve, and would perhaps be better off in a street fight. By a narrow margin she conceded that the benefits of the shortcut acceptably mitigated the risks.

She regretted it before they reached the bottom of the stairs.

Three Cyclopes took the lead, the first on watch, plasma blaster at the ready, followed by the two guiding the sled. The fourth followed Jerro at the rear. They registered multiple heat signatures in the ghetto below, most within dwellings but not all.

Directly below the stairs, seven pre-adolescent children huddled in an alcove. In spite of their position they didn't immediately register as a threat. When they made their move, there was nothing anyone could do about it.

At an unseen signal, two of the children leapt out from under the stairs and hurled grappling hooks at the feet of the Cyclopes steadying the sled. They and the sled tumbled sidelong off the staircase, knocking the lead Cyclops off-balance; a volley of slung bricks did the rest of the work, sending it sprawling forward and skidding face first.

The fourth Cyclops launched a round of darts into the fog, three of which were punctuated by gasps and thuds before it was hit squarely in the lens by a projectile, leaving it to rely on the other three for visual information but all three of them were tumbling to the ground so Naeemah switched off its optical inputs. Its motion sensors indicated a grappling hook hurling toward its feet. It jumped and cleared the hook, but slipped on the edge of a slick stair. If it fell forward, it would take everyone with it, so Naeemah sacrificed it and put its weight backwards, knocking Jerro off balance and nearly sending them both eight meters down onto the street below.

The first Cyclops was relatively undamaged at the foot of the stairs, but before it could right itself a svelte shadow twisted out of the fog and lodged a spear in its knee joint. It toppled sideways.

"*Hold!*" it was a female Gemini voice. The cracking scratches of brick and rock against the wall behind them stopped.

The android recognized the voice, and watched as Reyj-Aahnme's shadow emerged from the fog.

She had been brought to Orientale from the Galilaei supply station by a trade convoy. One of the station operators had spotted her sliding down the face of the rim, unconscious in her suit, and sent a rescue team to bring her in. They were all Earthers at the station, but none of them reported her or questioned what she was doing out there in a CARD-issued vac-suit. They all knew the rumors about the kinds of experiments that went on at the CARD complex, and even though the girl wasn't particularly friendly to them, they'd all admired her spirit. Scaling the rim was serious business, and she'd made it over all by herself.

They treated her injuries and brought her to an airlock bay where a Moonborn convoy bound for out deep in Proc was loading. Some of them spoke some Earther and recommended that the station crew get her onto a truck to the Orientale, where the rest of the surviving Gemini lived.

When she arrived, it felt briefly good to again see those of her own kind. But newcomers were not welcomed, and she had been fighting for scraps of a living on the streets since she arrived, earning the respect of the gangs of urchins and similarly outcast desperados and becoming a street leader of the young and dispossessed.

She'd hastily coordinated the ambush on the stairs after tracking the party unseen from the rooftops, casing them for an attack once they reached the curve. That they'd decided to take the stairs made them even easier targets. Her fear of Cyclopes had been replaced by hatred.

She hadn't noticed that the android, its form obscured by the vac-suit it wore, was among them, until glimpsing it on the stairs as she planted her spear in the Cyclops's knee.

The Cyclops still on the stairs regained control of its plasma blaster and leveled it at her.

Via their network connection, the android told Naeemah to hold fire. Reluctantly, cautiously, she stood down.

Reyj-Aahnme called her comrades to come gather the scattered plunder. Young Gemini scampered in to cart away vac-ration crates, eyeing them warily. They puzzled over Sel's gear.

"Not that!" Sel called from the stairs in clear enough Moonspeak for the Gemini to understand. *"Take anything else. Not that."*

Her tone and clarity had an effect on the young Gemini and they paused, checking with Reyj-Aahnme. She studied Sel's Sanctuariat tattoo and nodded for the youngsters to comply.

"Come down," she commanded.

The others filed the rest of the way down the staircase and were soon surrounded by a crowd of onlookers, their number masked by mist.

Someone shouted: *"Ehs-tret savva!"*

Sel felt a chill. She recognized the saying, an infamous slogan of the Geminus Revolution: *"Eat the hand that starves you."*

The crowd that had gathered, shadows in the mist, wanted blood. Reyj-Aahnme knew that, regardless of her relationship to the android, she couldn't guarantee them safe passage through the *Gemseh* without sufficiently bloody tribute.

Reyj surveyed the group. The Gemini people respected Sanctuary so Sanjit and Sel were off-limits. Killing the O-City kids would bring severe local repercussions. She paused and considered Demetrius Wei, but the peculiarity of his gaze and his apparent utter lack of fear marked him as special and she felt as though he should live.

The choice was plain, and before her eyes even fell on quivering Jerro she had lashed out with her spear, piercing his neck from the side and jerking it forward, tearing out his throat and sending a spray of red blood into the white fog, deftly dodged by onlookers.

"*Ehs-tret savva!*" she proclaimed.

Several Gemini stepped forward and pulled the sad clone's corpse away into the fog, leaving a smear of blood across the pavement.

Sanjit was shocked, but not saddened. Then he considered what it sounded like the Gemini had said, and asked Sel: "Did she just say they were going to *eat* him?"

Sel nodded, embarrassed.

"You mean literally *eat* him?" He had written off Jerro's anxiety of being eaten as racist paranoia.

Sel shrugged vaguely. It was well known that the Gemini had eaten the Earthers who had remained in the crater during the Revolution, which they famously didn't consider cannibalism because they didn't consider Earthers the same species as they. She had always privately hoped it was just grisly rumor, and was disturbed now that it didn't appear to be.

"Not like he didn't see it coming," Naeemah said through the sole standing Cyclops. His network facet blinked out shortly after his brain function stopped. There were no attempts made to back it up or retrieve anything from it that she might have traced back through the dead networks to wherever the Marten aggregate might be hiding, which was at least a sign that the aggregate didn't have a presence in the Orientale.

The crowd dispersed. Naeemah salvaged parts from her most damaged Cyclopes to repair the most intact and left the rest for the Gemini urchins to return to and pick over. The more easily detachable weapons systems and supply packs had already been absconded with. Then they strapped what remained of their cargo back onto the sled.

As they did, one of the young Gemini returned from the fog, his hands held out. "*Het,*" he said.

Sel translated: "He wants the helmet that goes with Jerro's vac-suit."

The Cyclops found it and tossed it to him. The child caught it and disappeared back into the fog.

The android studied Reyj-Aahnme and felt a certain sense of pride in her commanding presence. When her eyes fell upon it, it raised two fingers in the rabbit-ear gesture, the Gemini sign for righteous defiance. She met its gaze and returned the gesture.

NAEEMAH didn't feel any emotion over the loss of the three Cyclopes in the *Gemseh*, but she didn't like that she'd already lost half of the only six units she had in the basin.

The second Cyclops with the Sister Doctor didn't make it across the zipline to the pylon. A diligent watchman in the Tower had spotted Coni's crossing and, frustrated by the failure of the automated weapons systems, manually set up a laser in its path. Just beyond the halfway point of the glide, it split into two pieces at the waist and fell away from the harness with a curl of black smoke as it passed through the invisible beam.

Her Cyclopes in the Tower managed to take the marksman out before he could target the remaining one as it helped the Sister Doctor climb out of the drainage culvert alongside the outbound lanes.

The air was cool and sharp with ozone. The wind lifted tendrils of the highest billows of fog covering the city below up into the lowest penumbral clouds. Dapples of shadow fell across the distant Tower. The spiraling stone cityscape beyond it was blindingly bright.

Coni took off her helmet so her face would be clearly visible as they marched down the center of the windswept, empty outbound lanes toward the Tower.

The only vehicle they saw was an inbound heavy supply transport on the opposite side of the highway. She stopped and waved to get its attention but it didn't slow. Shortly afterwards, she heard the radio crackle to life in her collar. She put the helmet back on to block the wind noise.

She couldn't tell if the voice on the other end was human or not. "…repeat, confirm identity…"

"Sister Doctor Maria Consuela Goldman-Ghosal, under contract to CARD. I need to get a message to Brigadier-General Nshombo."

When she didn't receive a response, she repeated it.

Finally: "Begin message."

She had been trying to organize what she was going to say since before crossing the zipline, but now it was all a jumble between her mind and her mouth. She closed the visor to block the wind, took a breath and spoke loudly and clearly.

"There is no causal connection between the song and Colony collapse. There is no malicious intent in the song…do not pursue hostile action in the Orientale, it will only compound disorder. In the name of God and Mother, don't kill her. Do not kill her. End message."

It was the Tower AI that had recorded the message. It had been tracking the others' path through the city; this was the most significant data it had received pertaining to the intentions of the mysterious new Cyclopes entity that so vexed its peers. Based on the circumstantial data, it could not assume that the Sister Doctor was being compelled to make such a statement against her will. Her record was clean and free of association with subversive elements. And she still had open clearance to the Brigadier-General.

It relayed the message.

From his command center on the Far Side, the Brigadier General and his staff were frantically scrambling to maintain whatever infrastructure was left on the moon and retain the few pockets of stability that held. Gaining access to the Orientale was a key goal.

The old trebuchet launch yards could be brought online and used to launch cargo containers retrofitted to carry refugees back to the planet. The Tower refused to admit refugees to the basin due to its population control protocols, but it might make an exception if direct passage to the launch yards could be secured, providing a release valve for at least some of the ongoing humanitarian crisis on wheels surrounding the basin.

An open channel to the otherwise closed Tower presented him the opportunity to send a data packet through to it detailing his proposal. It was executed at the thought of it, but he had already dispatched a squadron of Wasps to the Orientale on the first sortie in a push to open a passage into the city.

Naeemah was unaware of his intent as she anxiously tracked the incoming Wasps. Her Cyclopes manning the weapons battery in the eastern rim opened fire on them as soon as they were in range. They were able to bring down three of the seven before being incinerated by a plasma charge. The surviving four Wasps split into pairs and burst through the particle net, fanning out over the city.

Two of them appeared coming in low over the northern horizon, gleaming silver seeds against the stormy umbra. Within minutes they were nearly overhead. A plasma beam from one of them incinerated the Cyclops next to the Sister Doctor. She recoiled from the blast of heat and melting plastic but was left standing unharmed. She followed the Wasps with her eyes as they continued south, and prayed for Sel and the others.

THE Talas forum was a huge, multi-tiered amphitheater partially covered by an enormous acoustic shell. Looking at it from the ridge above, it reminded Sel of the stage in the Sveygn enclave but at a scale fifty times greater, under open sky rather than cavern. The crowd surrounding it numbered in the hundreds of thousands, gathered in the streets and across the rooftops, their number growing as word spread that the Sancte girl had arrived in the City and was headed there.

When they reached furthest gatherings of the crowd she was cheered, in spite of the presence of Earthers and a battered Cyclops. The surge of emotion she felt blurred the rest of the journey as the masses parted to let them through.

Naeemah tracked the Wasp patrols that were circling the basin, steadily closing in on the forum. The Cyclops scanned the surrounding buildings for a vantage point from which it could provide cover, or at least draw fire. It settled on a bell tower half a kilometer to the east.

"I'm going to keep watch from up there," she announced, and pointed it out.

With Jerro dead, there was no good reason for her not to separate herself, and it was certainly possible that the Cyclops and the plasma cannon it carried on its back could serve them better at a remove. Nevertheless, it was Naeemah's last avatar among them and both Sanjit and Sel felt a little surprised that they felt somehow reluctant to part ways. But Naeemah left them no time for sentimentality.

"The Sister Doctor's report was sent," the Cyclops said, "Lets hope it was received. Good luck."

It backed away from them and headed for the bell tower at a trot. The gathered crowds parted for it, not quite terrified but not without fear. After it passed the onlookers closed in again in its wake, resuming their cheers.

Confetti of clipped leaves and shredded paper rained on them from rooftops and a boisterous parade formed in their wake, urging them onwards.

Far less attention was paid to them when they finally reached the Talas congress itself in the grandstands around the stage, where crowds of delegates and their staffs were in complete disorder, a circus of argument and overheated rhetoric. Factions shoved and jostled for access to mobile communications gear and everyone seemed to be yelling at everyone else over something, eddies of intervening clerks pounced on bouts of fisticuffs as they erupted.

Sel grabbed the sleeve of a young harried Orientale woman as she passed. The woman was unsurprised to see an Earther with a Sanctuariat tattoo, but she eyed the android and Demetrius Wei with suspicion.

"This is the man who brought down the CA AI network," Sel said flatly, knowing that word would spread quickly, "He's with me. Where's the Sanctuariat delegation?" she asked.

The woman spared Wei a fast second glance before scanning the crowd and pointing out the symbol of the Sanctuariat on one of the many standards bobbing above the unruly masses.

"Try not to say too much," Sel told Sanjit as they pressed through the confusion of the floor. She hoped that the delegation's relief in seeing her alive would at least forestall the inevitable grief she'd get for her hasty extension of Sanctuary.

Sanjit wasn't offended. He would continue to do everything he could to make himself worthy, but understood that some people were bound give her a hard time about it no matter what.

When they reached the Sanctuariat delegation, he was surprised to find that he was unquestioningly welcomed, nearly as warmly as Sel. Word of Wei's identity had already reached them; he was greeted, if warily.

She hadn't realized it, but she'd already decided that she would play – regardless of the outcome – the instant she heard the hope in the voices of the very first cheers that met her as they approached.

The Sanctuariat delegation organized into a phalanx around them and pressed across the crowded floor toward the entrance to backstage. There, the mood was far quieter but no less tense.

Several Council elders waited in the wings, under animated petition from a group of Moonborn around her age. The Council elders lit up when they saw her, but the younger ones looked actively disappointed to see her.

"Welcome," one of the elders said, stepping forward, "I'm called Rila. We're so pleased to see you. May I introduce you to some of your 'siblings?' They've been petitioning us to take the stage in your stead."

Sel realized the young Moonborn giving her dirty looks were the genetic derivations of Avik-Rosot Vaq had told her about. She looked at them to greet them and was met by non-committal-to-cold glances in return. One of them threw up his hands in disappointment and sank heavily into a chair, crestfallen, consoled by the others.

"Perhaps later for the introductions," Rila said, "Is there anything you require?"

"A glass of water?"

Rila gestured to her assistant. "The stage is prepared. If you like, I could make an effort to get the attention of the Congress, but…" she shrugged, "I suggest playing loudly."

Sel nodded to Sanjit, who had been pulling the sled with her gear on it. He pushed it out onto the stage. She followed several steps after. The Congress arguing across the floor and grandstands hardly took notice, but cheers went up from the distant rooftops and streets.

There is nothing to relearn.

In the distant bellower, the Cyclops had just reached the top of the tight spiral stairs and clamped its plasma cannon onto its shoulder mount at the window. At maximum magnification, it could make out Sanjit and Sel's tiny figures on stage, but kept its attention on the windswept horizon, waiting for the inevitable first sign of trouble.

Demetrius Wei's unmoving eyes met the Council's solemn, curious stares with welcome.

The android had picked up the Sister Doctor's conversation with the Tower from a relay station, but the Tower had not yet given any indication of having passed it on. Like Naeemah, it was shut out of the CA networks.

The air crackled with electricity and anticipation. Surrounding thunder from the receding storm rumbled under the cacophony of the Congress and the cheers of the crowd. Sanjit's hands shook with adrenaline as he unpacked Sel's gear from the sled.

"Sanjit," her face was serene in penumbral light. "Thank you."

"Thank you too." He stood and sent the empty sled back to the wings with a kick then followed it.

A pair of stagehands made final adjustments as she plugged in. She strapped on her guitar and set about tuning it. Still unable to be sure if anything was correct, not fearing what would come, she stood and faced the crowd. Overhead, a pair of silver Wasps burst through the clouds and streaked across the sky as she approached the microphone.

ABOUT THE AUTHOR

Andrew Biscontini was raised in Lansdowne, PA and has a degree in film production from the Pennsylvania State University. He lives in New York City.

ACKNOWLEDGMENTS

Robert Heinlein, *The Moon is a Harsh Mistress,* et al

Mission of Burma, "Weatherbox"

Chris Bunch, Allan Cole (writers), Robert C. Dille (characters)
Buck Rogers in the 25th Century Season 1: "Space Rockers"
developed by Glen A. Larson & Leslie Stevens

MAN UP!

... For a shirt-ripping, gut-punching anthology showcasing two-fisted writing *ripped* from the pages of long-lost vintage men's adventure magazines of the 1950s, '60s and '70s ...

... For rare, bare-knuckle stories and reminiscences by some of the toughest writers ever to punch a typewriter ...

... For outrageous, *100% true* tales of **sex**, **crime**, **combat**, **jungle goddesses**, **beatnik girls**, **LSD experiments**, **animal attacks** and **nymphos**. Always **nymphos** ...

... For *WEASELS RIPPED MY FLESH!*

1965. Flashpoint of the Civil Rights Movement.

In every American city, interracial tensions threaten to boil over into violence.

And in Glen Cove, Long Island, Josh Friedman finds himself on the front lines of the fight for racial equality.

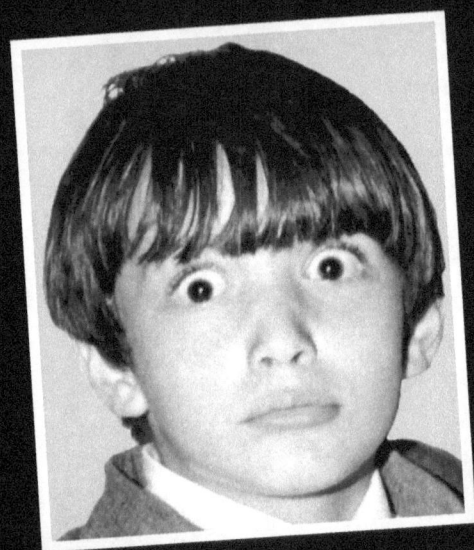

Josh is nine.

Race. Segregation. Doo-doo jokes.

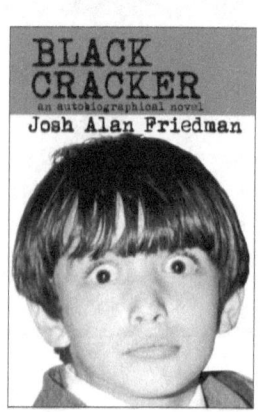

BLACK CRACKER
an autobiographical novel
by Josh Alan Friedman

from 🦅 WYATT DOYLE BOOKS
www.BlackCrackerOnline.com

Heavy Traffic.

"You know Sonny Rollins?"

"Sure."

"You know *about* him?"

"Not too much."

"Well, all through the '50s he had a pretty successful career going, but something inside was telling him he should give up all those good gigs and go play on his own, out in public; that he should go play on the bridge. So that's what he did. He went out and played on the bridge. He was on that bridge for three years! Then he returned to performing as a professional, and you know what his first record was when he came back?"

"What?"

"*The Bridge.*"

from "Last of the Mohicans,"
© 2010 Wyatt Doyle.

"*The poet laureate of public transportation.*"
— Josh Alan Friedman

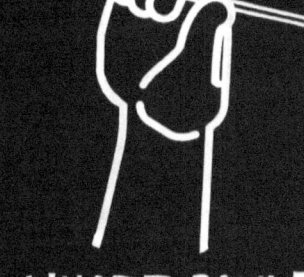

STOP REQUESTED

WYATT DOYLE

ILLUSTRATIONS BY
STANLEY J. ZAPPA

Stories from the buses, subways and streets.

new texture books

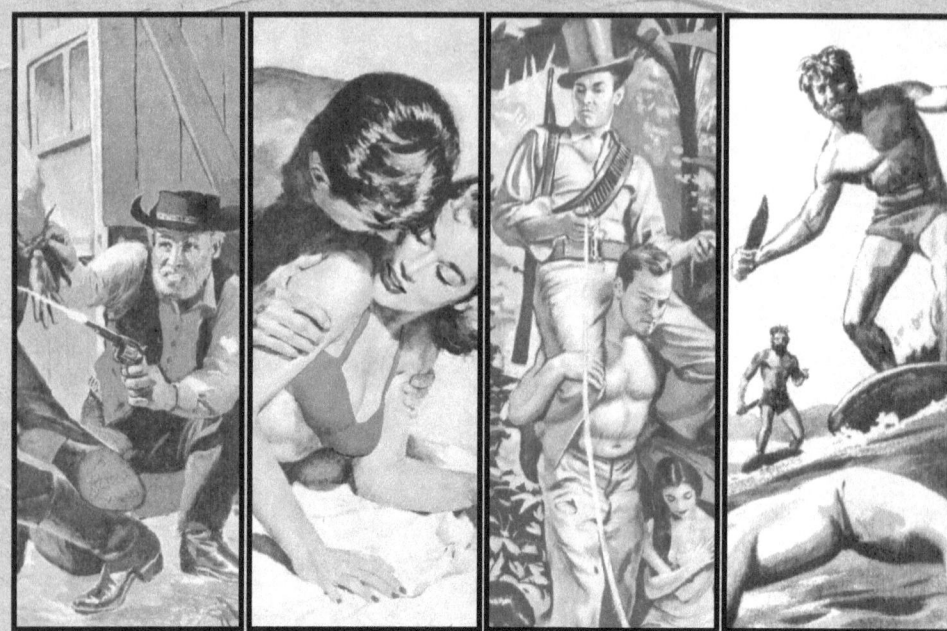

Gunfighters.   **Lovers.**   **Kings.**   **Surf Pack Assassins.**

The World of
MEN'S ADVENTURE MAGAZINES'

MANY great authors wrote for men's adventure pulps—**Mario Puzo, Richard Matheson, Lawrence Block, Bruce Jay Friedman, Elmore Leonard, Harlan Ellison** and **Martin Cruz Smith**, to name a few. But the wordsmith who writers for *Man's World* and *True Action* envied most was **Walter Kaylin**.

A "writer's writer" and editors' favorite, Kaylin made an indelible mark on three decades of sweat-soaked pulp fiction, tackling testosterone-fueled subjects from Westerns to war, secret agents to sex sirens, Nazis to *noir*. His frequently outrageous plots and characters scaled new heights of ingenuity and invention, while setting the standard for the kind of unapologetic excess that made men's adventure magazines notorious—then and now.

Walter Kaylin's **He-Men, Bag Men & Nymphos** is hitting bookshelves like a clenched fist; get yours or get out of the way!

edited by Robert Deis and Wyatt Doyle

Ladies' Men.   He-Men.   Bag Men.   Nymphos.

WALTER KAYLIN

WILDEST WRITER

"Walter Kaylin, come back!"

— Mario Puzo,
author of *The Godfather*

original magazine illustrations by (from left): George Eisenberg, Don Neiser, Al Rossi, Earl Norem, Joe Little, Earl Norem, Samson Pollen, Gil Cohen

FROM THE MEN WHO BROUGHT YOU
WEASELS RIPPED MY FLESH!

HE-MEN, BAG MEN & NYMPHOS

classic men's adventure magazine stories by

WALTER KAYLIN

edited by Robert Deis and Wyatt Doyle

new texture   MENSPULPMAGS.com

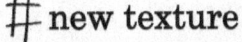

I THINK ANYONE WHO HAS GROWN FAMILIAR ENOUGH WITH A PLACE CAN RECOGNIZE A SIMILAR FEELING, OF MOVING NOT THROUGH THE NEIGHBORHOOD, BUT THROUGH A MAP IN ONE'S MIND. You see yourself not walking toward home, but imagine yourself from above, walking toward Manhattan, the East River. You see yourself in relation to everything else around you. You imagine streets lined and squaring off the entire neighborhood. You must walk within a constricted set of lines. This is precisely the point. You know where you are all the time. You carry that map tattooed on your mind, unable to lose it."

ERIC REYMOND

VOLUMES OF WORLDS: ESSAYS ON BROOKYN, KANSAS AND BEYOND

from # new texture books

photo © 2011 Wyatt Doyle

This is
Reverend Branch.

Services are underway at RevBranch.com

BOOKSELLERS

most New Texture releases are available through Ingram

New York City, 2003

Everybody has a price.

But nobody has a clue.

EVERY DOG'S DAY

A MOVIE BY   Andy Biscontini

dvds and downloads available at:

indiepixfilms.com
netflix.com
iTunes

www.ingramcontent.com/pod-product-compliance
Lightning Source LLC
Chambersburg PA
CBHW050548260626
47157CB00002B/478